With a first class honours degree in Classics from Cambridge, David Dickinson joined the BBC, where he became editor of *Newsnight* and *Panorama* as well as series editor on *Monarchy*. His novel *Death of a Chancellor* was longlisted in 2007 for Theakston's Old Peculiar Crime Novel of the Year.

Praise for the Lord Francis Powerscourt series

'A leisurely period whodunit with Dickinson's customary historical tidbits and patches of local colour, swathed in an appealing Victorian narrative.'

Kirkus Reviews

'A cracking yearn, beguilingly appealing from start to finish.'

Peter Snow

'Fine prose, high society and complex plot recommend this series.'

Library Journal

'Lovers of British mysteries will enjoy Powerscourt's latest adventure.'

Booklist

By David Dickinson

DEATH in a SCARLET COAT

DAVID DICKINSON

ROBINSON

Constable & Robinson Ltd
55–56 Russell Square
London WC1B 4HP
www.constablerobinson.com

First published in the UK by Constable,
an imprint of Constable & Robinson, 2011

Published in this paperback edition by Robinson,
an imprint of Constable & Robinson, 2012

A copy of the British Library Cataloguing in
Publication Data is available from the British Library

ISBN 978-1-78033-158-4

Printed and bound by CPI Group (UK) Ltd, Croydon, CR0 4YY

1 3 5 7 9 10 8 6 4 2

For Leo, who's just arrived.

PART ONE

THE MORNING HUNT

The stately homes of England!
How beautiful they stand,
Amidst their tall ancestral trees,
O'er all the pleasant land.
The deer across their greensward bound
Through shade and sunny gleam,
And the swan glides past them with the sound
Of some rejoicing stream.

Felicia Hemans, 1828

1

It was very cold at nine o'clock on a breezy autumn morning in Lincolnshire. The mounted men and the handful of mounted women of the Candlesby Hunt were ranged round the forecourt of Candlesby Hall. Two outlying pavilions were connected to the wings of the main building by a couple of long walls with large niches left for statues of classical antiquity. As with so much of Candlesby Hall, ambition outran reality. Two hundred years after their creation the niches were still waiting for Cicero and Caesar, Pericles and Plato to drop in from Greece and Rome and grace the front of a gentleman's house in the East of England. They were as empty today as they had been on the day they were created. The pavilions themselves were joined by a tall black railing with a grand opening in the centre.

The wind had abated since last night's gales, but clouds of fallen leaves still swirled and eddied in the forecourt. Inside the square formed by the house and the pavilions was a circle of grass with a path round the edges and a broken fountain in the centre. Even in the gloom the hunters' coats of scarlet and black and dark blue, with their cream and white breeches and stocks, made a brave show. The conversation was animated, men and women speculating about the forthcoming hunting season. One or two claimed to have spotted foxes trotting through the countryside in the weeks before. Latecomers were saying good morning to the hunt officials. The true aficionados were more excited than they would have cared to admit. They could hardly wait for the sheer delight of the hunt, the wind in your face, the rain in your hair, the sensation of speed as your horse raced after the scarlet coats at the front, the alarming moment when it left the ground to clear another hedge or wall, the cry of the huntsman's horn, the shouts of your friends close by, on and on and on across the countryside with the fox smarter than the hunt today and only a handful of riders left in pursuit. It made the blood race, even to think about it.

People more interested in architecture than in hunting might have paused after a careful inspection of the great house behind them. On top of the front was a group of three statues. Only one had all its limbs and features intact. The others were suffering from various ailments – heads fallen off, arms left as stumps, stone staff of office broken at the hilt. The great pillars jutting out at the front of the house were no longer of uniform colour but stained with dark green and a dirty yellow as if they had some terminal disease. On the top floor, where the servants had their quarters, half a dozen windows were broken and remained unrepaired.

The Candlesby butler, old, white-haired and stooping over his tray, was moving through the crowd with his stirrup cup, a mixture of port laced with brandy to fortify the hunters against the cold. The master was not here yet. The master was often late. Cynics whispered that the master was not very good at getting up the morning after the night before. Nobody would have dared say such a thing to his face, for his temper was the most feared in the county, the violence of his language capable of reducing strong men to tears.

Three of his five sons were here today, turned out for the hunting field like everybody else: Richard, Lord Bourne, the name inherited by all Candlesby eldest sons, thirty years old, heir to Candlesby Hall and what remained of its estates, who had inherited so many of his father's characteristics; Henry, the second son, three years younger than Richard, who had inherited most of his father's vices and none of his virtues, if any of those had ever existed; and Edward, the third son, twenty-five years old, who seemed to be having trouble controlling his horse. An earlier Dymoke, the original family name, Sir Francis Dymoke, had been made an Earl by Charles the Second for services to flattery according to the cynics. He had taken the name of Candlesby in Lincolnshire for his earldom and his great house, originally built on lands given him by his King.

Still the master did not appear. The officials and the field master and the whippers-in and the terrier men exchanged anxious glances. Some of the hunting party began peering in at the windows of the house to see if there was any sign of the master in there, checking the buttons on his coat perhaps, shouting at one or more of the servants. He had always been an eccentric master, John Dymoke, Earl of Candlesby, ever ready to change the hunting colours one year, or alter the dates of the opening and closing of the hunting season another. But nobody could remember a day when the master hadn't done his duty to the hunt and led them out across the county in pursuit of the fox wherever the chase would lead, however many broken bones might be acquired along the way. Those with highly strung or nervous horses took them on little sorties around the circle of grass. The hounds were swarming about on the far side of the railings under the watchful eye of the huntsman, barking and yelping as they waited for the chase. The more adventurous spirits took a second or a third helping of the stirrup cup, saying it would help them over field and fence. A number of people were looking at their watches now. Some were thinking of abandoning the hunt and going home. If the master failed to turn up there would probably be a row about who should be the acting master that might go on all morning.

It was the butler with his tray of empty stirrup cups who saw him first, or thought he might be seeing him. From the forecourt of Candlesby Hall a road led out of the gates in the railing, and then straight as straight could be across hundreds and hundreds of Candlesby acres for well over a mile until the ground dipped down and the road was lost from view. Something was moving very slowly along this road, past the scattered branches blown down in the great storm the night before. It might have been just a horse, or it might have been a man walking beside a horse. A hunting bird followed the little procession, like a mourner at a funeral.

The butler whispered something into Richard's ear and continued to peer down the road. Gradually the other members of the hunt began staring at the little procession advancing so slowly towards them. The huntsman appeared to think of blowing a message of some sort on his horn but thought better of it. There was definitely a horse, and the animal seemed to be carrying something fairly heavy. There was definitely a man, walking beside the horse, turning his cap round and round in his hand.

The riders began to back their horses up against the walls, blocking out the niches meant for the heroes of antiquity. Henry Dymoke suddenly noticed that the little parapet at the top of the pavilion to the right of the entrance was broken. He could just make out sections of broken pillar lying across each other. The hunt was growing apprehensive now. There was something uncomfortable in the little procession of horse and human making their way ever so slowly towards the great house. The butler made another round with the last of his stirrup cup. Nobody spoke, all eyes locked on the party coming toward them. There was definitely a package on the back of the horse, completely covered by a couple of blankets. There was, Henry Dymoke with his quick eyes noticed, something familiar about the shape on the horse. He knew, before anybody else, that it was his father's body he was looking at, making its last melancholy progress back to the house where he had been born.

Even the short-sighted could make it out now, a horse with what looked like a body thrown across it, wrapped in blankets, accompanied by a middle-aged man twirling his cap in his free hand, advancing towards the neighing horses of the Candlesby Hunt and their apprehensive riders. The very sharp-sighted thought they could see the corner of a scarlet coat poking out underneath the blanket. The men and women of the hunt were mesmerized by the drama unfolding before them. It was as if they had been rendered incapable of movement. The only noise was the barking and howling of the hounds. When they were a hundred yards or so from the railings, man and horse stopped. The man gestured to Lord Bourne to come forward.

'I'm terribly sorry, my lord, but that is your father wrapped up on that horse.' Jack Hayward was senior groom at Candlesby, the man who held sway over the horses and their kingdom, one of the few people the Master was never rude to, admired as much for his horsemanship as for his common sense. He was speaking very quietly, almost whispering. 'Don't look at him now, for God's sake, not in front of these people. It's a terrible sight. I think you should send them all away, my lord, and then you could look at him in peace. I'll take him over to the stables and then I'll go and fetch the old doctor if he's still with us.'

Richard nodded. How strange it felt, he thought. For so many years he had waited and hoped and dreamt about becoming an Earl, Lord Candlesby, master of Candlesby Hall and all its acres. A month after his thirtieth birthday he had come into his inheritance. Now the moment was here it was nothing like he had ever imagined. 'Today's hunting is cancelled,' he said in a harsh voice when he was back where the hunt could hear him. 'Please return to your homes. You will be informed about the next meet as soon as possible.'

Perhaps, he said to himself, as the hunt trotted off, I should have told them the truth. Then they would have something real to gossip about, rather than the fruits of their imaginations. For the Master of the Candlesby Hunt had come at last, not mounted on his horse, but wrapped across it in blankets like some vagrant found dead by the roadside.

Lord Francis Powerscourt had fallen in love. This was not the aching, all-consuming love of youth, or even the love to the last that parents have for their children. His wife Lady Lucy was a partner in his passion, and his children had to be restrained from showing their feelings when they encountered the object of his affections. For Powerscourt this was a love he had never known before. Some men fall in love with horse racing or hunting or cricket or fly fishing. He had fallen in love with a Ghost.

More precisely a Rolls-Royce Silver Ghost, first produced by Mr Royce the year before and sold to him by Mr Rolls for a king's ransom, a ransom his brother-in-law and chief financial adviser Mr Burke told him he could afford after some successful share dealing in America. The Ghost could seat four or five people comfortably. It had a great shiny silver bonnet and a cream body with red leather upholstery and a hood you could take off in the summer. A mighty horn warned passers-by of your arrival and two powerful headlights illuminated the Ghost's passage in the dark. Its top speed, a fact which so delighted the Powerscourt twins, Christopher and Juliet, that they had to be told the figure every time they climbed into the back seat, was sixty-five miles per hour. Why, the Ghost was as fast as a train! As it happened, Powerscourt's great friend Johnny Fitzgerald had bought the twins a new book the previous Christmas called *The Wind in the Willows*, about a group of animals who live by the side of a river and a toad who develops an unhappy obsession with motor cars. Sometimes, when they were in the back seat, Christopher and Juliet Powerscourt would serenade their father with the toad's battle cry of 'Poop-Poop!' Johnny Fitzgerald never tired of reading them the final chapter, which contained a great battle between the four animals and their enemies the Wild Wooders, marauding bands of stoats and ferrets and weasels.

So here he was, Lucy at his side, bowling happily along the road that led past Candlesby towards the cathedral city of Lincoln. Neither Rat nor Toad nor Badger could have helped Powerscourt at this moment. He was not driving particularly fast, he seldom did, but as the car went over a humpbacked bridge he was not ready for the sharp left-hand turn on the far side and the front of the car sank slowly into the ditch, making a nasty mechanical noise as it went. Lady Lucy, he discovered, was unhurt. They decided to walk to the nearest town or village, which Powerscourt thought couldn't be very far away.

At Candlesby Hall three sons of the dead man, a corner of his bloodied scarlet coat still visible, blankets draped across his face, set about the doctor. The last Earl was still in the stables where his body had been taken. The medical man, Dr Miller, had just arrived. He was well past retirement age and had a frail appearance now, like one of his elderly patients. There were only wisps remaining of what had been a fine head of white hair. His teeth were not what they had once been either, leading him to tell his house-keeper that he was particularly fond of dishes like soup and scrambled eggs. His eyes were the worst affected by the ravages of time, but a pair of thick glasses left him still capable of reading.

The three sons crowded round the doctor. Richard, the eldest, had a great shock of red hair like the hair that could be inspected on the portraits of his ancestors inside the house; Henry, the second son, was extremely tall and thin; Edward was short and tubby. Charles, the fourth son, was believed to be in London and had been summoned home. James, the youngest, was in his rooms, not invited out for this melancholy interview. Richard had refused to allow any of his brothers to take a last glance at their father.

'I'm the head of the family now, I'll have you know, and I forbid you to look at him. I absolutely forbid it.' Richard did not trust Henry or Edward not to let something out in their cups or in the taverns of Spilsby close by.

'Now then, Dr Miller,' he began, 'I should like to remind you of the amount you owe this family. I'm referring, of course, to things more valuable than money, debts of obligation, favours that have to be repaid.'

'Hear, hear,' said his brothers, advancing still closer towards the doctor. They might not see eye to eye with Richard about very much, but on questions of family honour they hunted like a pack of hounds.

'I'm not sure what you mean,' said the doctor, shaking his head sadly. 'What is it you want me to do?'

'That's better,' said Richard grimly, 'that's more like it. I want you to say on the death certificate that my father died of natural causes. It was a heart attack or a stroke that killed him, whichever you think will be the most convincing.'

'But that wouldn't be the truth,' said the doctor in a puzzled tone. 'You, Richard, saw the body and the condition it was in. You're asking me to lie about the death of one of my patients.'

Richard nodded to his brothers. They moved closer to the doctor, Henry bending down a great distance to pick up a pitchfork lying on the ground.

'What about that wrong diagnosis you gave on the butler here a couple of years back? The medicine you prescribed bloody nearly killed him.'

'You're asking me to break the doctor's oath of loyalty to his profession. I've kept the Hippocratic oath for nearly fifty years and I'm not going to break it now.'

'Damn your Hippocratic oath!' Richard was growing angry, his face turning the same colour as his hair. 'You're just a bloody hypocrite. They say in the village that three women down there have died in childbirth in the past two years who should be alive today. All because of your incompetence! What's a death certificate compared with that? My father was dead long before you got to him. This time you weren't personally responsible for someone's death, even if they were only a peasant woman down the road.'

Henry turned his pitchfork the other way up and moved one of the prongs quite close to the doctor's face.

'All you have to do is to fill in the death certificate or whatever it's called.' Richard was speaking very quietly now, a sure sign to his brothers that he was incandescent with rage. 'That doesn't take long. I don't see how it should trouble your conscience that much. And we'll make it worth your while, doctor.'

This, Richard suddenly realized, was where he should have started. Nobody knew how they knew, but all the Dymokes knew the doctor liked money, liked a great deal of it in fact. People said his late wife had very expensive tastes.

'How much?' asked the doctor, sounding like a drunk unable to resist another glass.

'Let's discuss that once you've signed the death certificate. It'll be a goodly sum; you need have no fear about that.'

The doctor was not strong any more. His will had ebbed away in the Lincolnshire breeze. Eventually he did what he was told. He entered 'heart attack' as the cause of death of Arthur George Harold John Nathaniel Dymoke, Earl of Candlesby. There was no need for a post-mortem. The corpse was duly prepared for burial with nobody, apart from his doctor and his eldest son and

11

his head groom, knowing the cause or the manner of his death.

Forty-five minutes after the accident the Powerscourts were sitting in the drawing room of the Candlesby Arms, the principal hotel of the town of the same name. The manager had secured the service of a local farmer with a powerful tractor to remove the Powerscourt car from the ditch the following morning and a skilled mechanic who worked nearby would check the engine and the bodywork. The hotel manager had inspected his visitors closely. Lord Francis Powerscourt was six feet tall with curly brown hair and pale blue eyes. Something told George Drake, the hotel manager, that he had seen service in the military in the past. He was to learn later that Powerscourt was one of the most distinguished private investigators in the country. Lady Lucy, his wife, was half a foot shorter than her husband with curly blonde hair and light brown eyes. She had, Drake thought, an air of great vivacity about her as if adventures were there for the taking and boredom might be the greatest enemy of all.

All was not well in the hotel that afternoon. There was a constant stream of visitors with long faces come to confer with the manager. As afternoon tea was being taken he came to talk to his new guests. They were, he said to himself, his last hope, and a pretty forlorn one at that.

'You seem to have plenty of visitors this afternoon, Mr Drake,' said Lady Lucy cheerfully. 'Is there some big social function on this evening?'

'You could say that, Lady Powerscourt,' said Drake, stirring his cup of tea slowly and sadly.

'Is there anything we could do to help, Mr Drake?' asked Powerscourt. 'You have been more than helpful to us here in our time of trouble.'

George Drake looked at them carefully. It's worth a try, he

said to himself. It's a pound to a penny they won't be able to do a thing, but you never know.

'This is how it is,' he said finally, 'if you have the time to listen to my troubles. The local vicar and I run the choral society here in Candlesby. I do the organizing, book the hall, get the tickets printed and sold around the town and so forth. The Reverend Moorhouse is in charge of the singing, the works to be performed, that sort of thing. He's got a beautiful speaking voice himself, the vicar. They say some ladies come from miles around to hear him take Matins on a Sunday morning. He was a singing scholar or whatever they call them over in Oxford when he was younger. His congregation shrinks whenever they hear his curate, Reverend Flint, is taking the services. This is the problem, my lord, my lady. There's a performance of Handel's *Messiah* scheduled for this evening. The choir have been working on it since July. It's been advertised all round the district for weeks. Vicars far and wide have mentioned it in their parish notices. The local newspaper has run a whole series of articles about the performance as if nobody has ever sung in Candlesby before. The Bishop of Lincoln himself is planning to attend.'

George Drake paused. Powerscourt had a faint suspicion, nothing stronger than that, about what was coming.

'Forgive me if I'm boring you,' said Drake, looking anxiously at his visitors. 'I'm coming to the point, I promise you. Those people at the hotel this afternoon were all here to cry off tonight's performance or to cry off on behalf of their friends or relatives. We've had a terrible dose of the influenza round here this week. Some of the choir can't speak, let alone sing. To cap it all, the old Earl up at the big house was brought home dead on his horse this very morning and God only knows how many people might have to miss the performance because of that. Not', Mr Drake added with feeling, 'that there will be many local mourners for the vicious old bastard.'

'Surely, Mr Drake,' said Lady Lucy in her most emollient tones, 'it doesn't matter if you lose a bass or two. The others can just carry on. I don't know what size your choir is but surely it won't make much difference if you have five basses rather than six, if you see what I mean.'

'I do see what you mean, Lady Powerscourt; I can see it very clearly. That's not our problem, I'm afraid. It's the soloists. Two of them and the two understudies, tenor and soprano, all laid low, every single one of them. The chief tenor has to croak to speak with his wife. The soprano woman has taken to communicating with written messages on slips of paper as if she was back at school. What are they going to sound like in the great high spaces of St Michael and All Angels in Candlesby High Street with the Bishop in the front row in his mitre and all? I don't know what we can do. I'm told the vicar is on his knees even now praying by the High Altar. I'm not sure how that's going to help us, I'm really not.'

'Correct me if I'm wrong, Mr Drake,' said Powerscourt. 'It seems to me that the position is as follows. Your choir has been booked in for this recital for weeks if not months. You can't cancel it now because you can't reach all the people who might be coming. My Lord Bishop', Powerscourt checked his watch, 'may even have set off from his palace by now if he is a cautious traveller anxious to arrive in good time and sprinkle a few benedictions on the locals. Your choir is like a cricket team that has lost its best batsman and its best bowler and has nobody left to be twelfth man.'

While Powerscourt paused briefly, Lady Lucy took up the story.

'Surely, Mr Drake, it's perfectly obvious what you have to do. You just have to make do with what you've got. Explain to the audience at the beginning that you have lost all these people through the influenza. Apologize for the fact that the sound will not be what you hoped. That is the best thing to do, is it not?'

'We've thought of that, Lady Powerscourt,' said Drake, 'and we don't think it will work. You see, it's the tenor and the soprano who have gone. Without them the whole oratorio is going to sound wrong, let alone missing the different solo parts they perform within the *Messiah*. It would be like *Hamlet* without the Prince or *Macbeth* without the witches or *The Tempest* without Caliban. It's not as though they were singing some new work nobody had ever heard before. There's a tradition of singing Handel's *Messiah* in Candelsby church that goes back generations. Some of these people know it virtually off by heart. They come to each new performance like a bunch of wine lovers going to taste the latest Château Lafite.'

'You did say tenor and soprano, didn't you, Mr Drake?' Powerscourt was looking meaningfully at Lady Lucy as he spoke.

'Yes, I did,' said Drake, looking perplexed.

Powerscourt managed to raise an eyebrow in inquisitive mode in Lady Lucy's direction. There was a slight but unmistakable nod in reply.

'Well,' said Powerscourt, 'if you're willing to take a chance, Mr Drake, then we might just be able to help you.'

'What do you mean?' said a confused Drake.

'This and only this. Lady Powerscourt and I have sung the tenor and soprano parts in the *Messiah* before. The tunes are so memorable you never really forget them but I think we would need a quick refresher course in the solo parts at least. What do you say to that, Mr Drake?'

The hotel manager was on his feet, shaking them both by the hand and performing a sort of impromptu jig on his carpet, nearly knocking over the Earl Grey and scones of a couple of elderly spinsters come to the hotel for a peaceful afternoon tea.

'Thank God!' he cried. 'Thank God for the crooked bridge that brought your car low! Thank God you are here in our hour of need! I will bring you straight away to St Michael's and the vicar can run you through your paces. I must just tell Mabel to mind the hotel while I've gone. She's much better at it than I am anyway.'

Two minutes later the three of them were walking briskly up the street towards St Michael and All Angels. Attentive passers-by would have heard a female voice singing, 'I know that my Redeemer liveth and that he shall stand at the latter day upon the Earth.' Lady Lucy's voice soared upwards into the evening sky and was lost before it reached the stars.

2

'At least we'll be able to get our hands on some money now the old bastard's dead.' Edward Dymoke, tubby third son of the late Lord Candlesby, was addressing his elder brother Henry in the saloon of Candlesby Hall, a mangy dog with three legs lounging at his feet. Richard the redhead, the eldest son, the new Earl, was reading a newspaper at the far side of the room, as if he wished to put as much space as possible between himself and his brothers. Most of the space between them was occupied by a disused billiard table with two pockets hanging out and a rug concealing whatever damage the young of Candlesby had managed to inflict on the playing surface over the years.

'Absolutely,' said Henry. 'I'm up for a spot of money too. I'll be able to place some decent bets at the races at last. Do you know, I think I might take a holiday in Monte Carlo and have a flutter at the tables. What are you going to do with yours?'

'I thought I would escape from all this dreary countryside for a start,' said Edward, kicking a decrepit stuffed fox by the side of the hearth. 'I've had enough of fields and grass and wheat and harvests and rain and trees and wet leaves and beefy women who look as if they've done nothing but bake and wash clothes all their lives. It's the city life for me. London? New York? Paris? I've been told there are plenty of gorgeous whores on the Champs-Elysées and the Boulevard Saint-Michel.'

'I wonder how much there is,' said Henry reflectively. 'Money, I mean.'

'God knows,' said Edward, reluctant to return to Candlesby Hall from his trysts with the good-time girls of Paris, 'but if you stand at the highest point near here up by that dreary mausoleum on the hill – it's not what you'd call high but it's the highest thing for miles around – all the land you can see belongs to us. Maybe we should sell some of it.'

There was a cackle that might have been a snarl from the far side of the room. Richard put down his newspaper, revealing a large damp patch on the wall behind him, and advanced towards his brothers.

'You stupid pair!' he began. 'Who in heaven's name do you think you are, to start talking about money and how you're going to spend it? What makes you think you are going to inherit any money?'

Richard had reached the other side of the room and was now in spitting distance of his brothers. He glanced at them both in turn in a gesture of supreme contempt.

'How do you know there is any money, for God's sake? Or are you just assuming there must be some because you'd like to get your hands on as much of it as you can? Well, let me tell you one or two things that might not have occurred to you.'

Richard sat down and continued to address his brothers as if they had just failed the entrance test for England's stupidest regiment.

'Let me remind you for a start of the batting order round here. I am the eldest son. I inherit the title. You don't. I inherit the estate. You don't. I inherit this house. You don't. You don't inherit a thing. Quite soon I shall be called to London to be installed as a member of the House of Lords, where I shall make my views known to my fellow countrymen. I shall do everything in my power to make life difficult for that vulgar little commoner Lloyd George. You two' – he stared balefully at his brothers – 'are younger sons. Younger sons, unless they are very lucky, do not inherit. They do not inherit anything at all. That is why so many occupations like vicars and wine merchants and those people who play with money in the City of London were invented; it's all to give younger sons something to do, something that can stop them being a drain on their families. Monte Carlo? The prostitutes of Paris? I think not, brothers!'

As he made his way to the door Richard turned for a parting shot. 'There's one other thing you should be aware of,' he said. 'You talk as if there was money, as if the estate and everything is solvent. Well, I had a talk with our steward this afternoon. There isn't any money. There are only debts, mortgages, loans that could add up to as much as seventy or eighty thousand pounds, maybe more. We don't know the final figure yet. That's not money we've got. That's money we owe other people. There's absolutely nothing for younger sons!'

An elderly verger was lighting the candles in the church of St Michael and All Angels as Drake and the Powerscourts arrived. An erect old lady with white hair was dusting the pews one last time, paying particular attention to the two front rows, where distinguished visitors could be expected to sit. Specks of dust, after all, might be clearly visible on the Episcopal purple. Kneeling by the rail in front of the altar as if he were a candidate for communion, the vicar, the Reverend Peter Moorhouse, could be heard faintly, praying for deliverance.

When the introductions were made and he realized that here were a new tenor and a new soprano, risen from the ditch by the humpbacked bridge to solve the problems of the Candlesby *Messiah*, he seized them both by the hand.

'Truly,' he said, 'salvation is come to us here. May the Lord bless you and keep you. May the Lord make the light of his countenance shine upon you and be gracious unto

you and give you his peace . . . Heavens, I'm confusing
the prayers for Evensong with my thanks for you; how
silly of me. It is surely as the poet says: more things are
wrought by prayer than this world dreams of. And I had
thought it almost presumptuous of me to ask God to send
us reinforcements. Now then, I'm talking too much. My
dear wife always tells me I talk too much – what were you
saying, George, a little rehearsal, was it?' The vicar still had
the lithe figure of the long distance runner he had been at
university. The Reverend Moorhouse also held the record
for the longest sermon ever delivered from the pulpit at St
Michael and All Angels at one hour twenty-seven minutes.
The more sporting members of his choir and congregation
placed bets on the duration every week.

'I think our guests would find a little rehearsal helpful,
Vicar,' said George Drake. 'Just the solo arias they will have
to sing this evening, not the whole thing.'

'Of course, of course,' said the vicar, virtually running to
the organ and ferreting about among the sheet music.

'Now then, let me give you both a little word of advice,
if I may.' The vicar was turning over the pages as he spoke.
'Most people', he waved a hand upwards in the general
direction of the roof, high above, 'think they have to try
really hard to make their voice carry all over this church,
because it's so high. But for some reason – you wouldn't
have thought late medieval stonemasons would have known
about the reach of the human voice, would you – that's
not so. The acoustics are almost perfect, so you can sing well
within yourself and it'll carry beautifully. Now then, Lord
Powerscourt, I think you open the batting. I'll give you the
cue with my right hand, so.'

The vicar began playing. Powerscourt didn't need the
cue. I was only seventeen years old the last time I sang
this, he said to himself, taking a deep breath and launch-
ing into 'Comfort ye, comfort ye, my people, saith your
God. Speak ye comfortably to Jerusalem . . .' Soon he was

so lost in the beauty of the music and his own memories that he forgot to work out how many years had passed since he sang this aria with the local choir in his parents' church in Ireland, his mother watching proudly from the second row.

'Excellent,' said the vicar as they reached the end. 'That will do splendidly. I don't think we need try out any more in case your voice grows tired. I'm sure Lady Powerscourt will be even better. Which aria would you like to sing, Lady Powerscourt?'

'The shepherds? Would that do?' asked Lady Lucy.

The great organ boomed forth. Lady Lucy sang. The vicar was delighted. George Drake was conferring with the cleaning lady about the Bishop.

'Seven o'clock start,' said the vicar. 'I expect everybody to be here in good time. Thank you so much, Lord and Lady Powerscourt. I cannot tell you how much we owe you.'

The three eldest Dymokes were back in the saloon, bickering among themselves over drinks before dinner. They were about to embark on a fruitless argument about the size of the family debts when the door opened and a pale youth with blond hair and good looks that were almost feminine came in and sat down by the fire.

'Good evening, brothers,' he said to the company.

'My God,' sneered Edward, 'look what the cat's brought in from the madhouse upstairs!'

'Bedlam has closed its doors for the evening,' said Henry. 'Have you left your jailer upstairs? You haven't come down here to eat with us, have you? Heaven forbid! Why don't you just head back up the stairs to your own apartment and lock the door behind you?'

James Dymoke was fifteen years old. He was the youngest of the five sons. His mother had died having him and the elder brothers always maintained that she hadn't had time to finish James off properly before she passed. Bits of him were certainly missing. The doctors thought he was suffering from an incurable form of epilepsy about which they knew very little. On many days he was perfectly normal and showed no signs of illness at all. On others he would have fits, he would be withdrawn and behave briefly like a mad person. He lived in private rooms far from the rest of the family on the top floor with a medical assistant to look after him. Very few people outside Candlesby Hall knew of his existence. He had never been to school.

'I just thought', James said hesitantly, 'that we should be together on the day we lost our father.'

'We should be together,' Henry said, pointing in an arc that included his elder brothers but did not include James, 'but that doesn't include you. You're not proper family. You're not even a proper person. You're just a freak from the upper floor.'

After all his years in Candlesby Hall James knew that he could expect little better from Henry and Edward. Richard would pretend to be above the fray but would never take his side. James suspected the other two had a private contest to see who could make him cry first. His only supporter was the brother who wasn't there.

'He was my father too, you know,' said James defiantly.

'She was our mother, too,' Edward snapped, 'until you killed her being born.'

'That's not true, you know that's not true,' James shouted, tears beginning to form in his eyes. His brothers had known for years that their mother was the weakest spot in James' armour.

The door to the saloon was suddenly flung open. 'B-b-brothers! P-p-please! Could we not have some family harmony on the day of Father's death? Arguing is so p-p-pointless these days!'

Charles Dymoke, twenty-two years old, was the fourth in line to the indebted estate. He had become rather a dandy down in London, sporting on this sad day a light brown hunting jacket with a crisp white shirt and a blue cravat.

'I'd have been here hours earlier, my dears, except some b-b-beastly p-p-porter lost my luggage. So tiresome! Tell me about the arrangements, p-pray. Is Father going to be buried in that divine mausoleum on the hill? I do hope the vicar is going to show up in his finest vestments, lots of p-p-purple rather than that drab grey he seems to wear most of the time. I've always thought it would be worth dying if one could be laid to rest in the mausoleum.'

'Do shut up, Charles.' Richard was rather enjoying the role of paterfamilias. 'We should all go in to dinner. It'll be the first time all five of us have been together for years. Who knows, maybe it'll be the last.'

The St Michael and All Angels choir's performance of Handel's *Messiah* began exactly on time. The vicar was conducting now, and the headmaster of the local school was in charge of the organ. The choir was about sixty strong with a surprising number of young people in the ranks. Powerscourt wondered if the vicar had worked hard at this element of his team so the choir would become known as a promising place to meet members of the opposite sex.

'Every valley shall be exalted and every mountain and hill laid low.'

'And the glory of the Lord shall be revealed and all flesh shall see it together.'

Tenor and bass, soprano and alto, full choir – all took their turn to drive the music on. Powerscourt, after two solos near the beginning, was not needed to sing on his own for some time.

'O thou that tellest good tidings to Zion, get thee up into the high mountain . . .'

The choir was growing in confidence as the evening progressed. When they reached the chorus, 'For unto us a child is born, unto us a son is given, and the government shall be upon his shoulder and his name shall be called Wonderful, Counsellor, the mighty God, the everlasting Father, the Prince of Peace,' it was as if they had forgotten the audience and the organ and the church and the vicar and were communing directly with Georg Friedrich Handel himself.

Then it was Lady Lucy's turn.

'There were shepherds abiding in the field, keeping watch over their flock by night.'

Suddenly Powerscourt remembered where he had heard her sing like this before. It had been the previous year, in France, and they had gone to visit an ancient Cistercian abbey south of Bourges called Abbaye de Noirlac. It was a beautiful summer's day and the site was virtually deserted. The ancient abbey with its enormous nave was completely empty. Lady Lucy, he remembered, had gone to stand where the monks would have stood centuries before. She sang 'I know that my Redeemer liveth', the same aria that she would sing later this evening near the end of the *Messiah*. Her voice had filled the huge church. It came out clean and clear and soared around the space, like liquid gold being poured into a phial, or a goblet of perfect Chassagne Montrachet glittering and winking in its glass in the sunshine. Powerscourt had stood perfectly still, tears running down his face, until some fresh visitors arrived and Lady Lucy's concert came to a sudden end. Her voice had the same clarity tonight.

Powerscourt looked around the church once more. The Lord Lieutenant of the County with his sword was in the front row beside the Bishop in his purple. The local MP was here. People said his wife was very fond of music. The citizens of Candlesby and the surrounding villages were out in force. This church is England, Powerscourt said to himself. England's dead of centuries past are buried here. The buildings have survived the change of rule from a crimson cardinal and a choleric Henry the Eighth to a queen who burnt heretics at the stake and later kings who cared not for religion at all. Candlesby has lived through Civil War and Restoration and the loss of the American colonies. The church bells above me, Powerscourt thought, will have rung for the defeat of the Armada and the victories of Malplaquet and Trafalgar. The latest casualties of Britannia's wars have just had their own memorial built, to those who died in the Boer War. There are other Englands, of course, he said to himself, the daily throng marching across London Bridge to work in the city of London, the workers toiling in some huge factory in Manchester or Bolton, the crowds at one of the great race meetings, the Derby or the Oaks, the sailors on some modern warship of the Royal Navy, patrolling the cold dark waters of the North Sea to keep their country safe. There were so many Englands, he thought. Suddenly he realized that he had lost his place in his score and that he was going to have to sing again quite soon. The vicar sent him a secret smile as if to say it's all right to dream dreams every now and then.

The audience had fallen very still. The Hallelujah Chorus was upon them, an aria as glorious for those who sing it as for those who hear it. 'Hallelujah! for the Lord God omnipotent reigneth.'

It was Easter time when I sang this before in Ireland, Powerscourt remembered, and the daffodils were all out round the edge of the lawns and that soft light of Ireland made everything look magical, as if the dream of that great house between the mountains and the sea would last for ever.

'The Kingdom of this world is become the kingdom of our Lord and of his Christ.'

Some of the audience had closed their eyes. The boys and the men, Powerscourt noticed, had their eyes firmly fixed on a small group of very pretty girls, deployed by the vicar in the front row of the choir. One middle-aged lady, dressed entirely in black, in the fourth row of the congregation was weeping uncontrollably, tears rolling down on to the stone floor. Maybe the last time she had been to the *Messiah* had been with a loved one, a lost husband perhaps, a dead child.

'And he shall reign for ever and ever, King of Kings, Lord of Lords.'

The vicar was a vigorous sort of conductor, not one of those minimal ones who make the smallest possible movement to attract the attention of choir or orchestra. His arms moved in great arcs, as if he were sending semaphore messages to the back row. Way above him a couple of gargoyles, merchants or masons perhaps at the time the church was built, stared down at the proceedings, their mouths wide open for evermore.

'For ever and ever. Hallelujah. Hallelujah. Hall-e-lujah.'

Powerscourt had always wondered why the Hallelujah Chorus wasn't the last aria in the *Messiah*. But it was Lady Lucy's turn now to sing 'I know that my Redeemer liveth', which she did with the same conviction she had brought to it in that French abbey a year before.

Then it was all over and everybody made their way back to Mr Drake's hotel for refreshments. Powerscourt found himself talking to an elderly medical man who told him proudly that he had attended on the death of the Earl of Candlesby that very morning. The doctor was fascinated to hear that Powerscourt was an investigator with a long track record in solving murders and mysteries. He insisted, Dr Miller, on writing down Powerscourt's address very carefully in his little black book.

Up at Candlesby Hall the candles were still lit in the dining room. It was harder to see the cracks in the walls in the dark. It was very late. Only Henry and Edward were left – the others had all retired for the night. One decanter of port stood in front of them; another was waiting in the wings. Their eldest brother Richard had left a bell on the table for them to ring if they became incapable of making their way up the stairs on their own and needed help to get to bed.

'Can you guess what I would like to know more than anything?' There was a pause while Edward hunted the thought down in his brain. 'What killed the old bugger. Can't have been anything normal. Not the way they all carried on. Not gunshot. Not sword or spear. Not blunt object. What the hell was it?'

Henry stared intently at his brother and poured himself another glass of port. They were using extra large glasses this evening.

'Tha's a good question,' he said, slurring his words slightly. 'Very good question.' He too paused until his mind stopped spinning and came to rest on a new theory.

'Not human at all,' Edward managed. 'What killed him, I mean. Wild thing. Animal. Mystery beast. Hiding in the forest since Hereward the Wake or whatever his name was. Lethal bite. Huge claws.'

'That's good. Oh yes, that's good. Couldn't have put it better myself. Picture the scene. Papa on foot. Lincolnshire monster feels peckish. Long time since breakfast. Leans forward to seize Papa.' As Henry leant forward in the manner of the monster he found he couldn't stop. He collapsed face forward into the table. Edward rang the bell.

3

The next day the Silver Ghost was restored to health and the Powerscourts continued on their way. Mr Drake of the Candlesby Arms insisted that they could stay at his hotel for the rest of their lives for nothing. The vicar gave them God's blessing and promised to send advance notice of the next recital. He had, he told them confidentially, already ordered the sheet music for Beethoven's Missa Solemnis. They caught a brief glimpse on their way north of the Candlesby mausoleum, a tall, circular neoclassical building perched on a little hill that looked rather like a lighthouse, illuminating the journeys of the dead on their voyage to another world.

Two days after that, their mission to witness the christening of one of Lady Lucy's relations' newborn baby in Lincoln Cathedral complete, they were heading back to London. Their family in Markham Square had recently received a temporary addition, in the person of the daughter of one of Lady Lucy's sisters from Scotland. Selina Hamilton was twenty years old with bright blue eyes, curly blonde hair and a figure that could have advertised clothes in the women's magazines. She had cut a swathe through the young men of Melrose and Hawick and the neighbouring villages in the Scottish Borders. They might have fallen for her, but she did not fall for them. A world where the height of fame was an appearance for Scotland on the rugby pitch, the summit of ambition for the local young men, was not enough for her. There might have been thirty players on the field but Selina's heart did not miss a beat for any of them. Her father was a respectable solicitor and her mother had brought up Selina and her sisters. They were good people, her parents, pillars of the local community, devoted patrons of local charities for the poor and destitute. But Selina wanted a broader stage. She felt she needed wider horizons than the Rugby Club dances and the Mothers' Union. Glory and glitter and glamour were in her mind, evenings spent at fashionable soirées where the wealthy young men would fall for her beauty, weekends spent in unimaginable luxury at the country houses of England.

Selina had, in theory, come south to improve her mind at the great art galleries of London. She had already enlisted for an evening class in art appreciation at the Victoria and Albert Museum. Lady Lucy suspected that the real reason for her sojourn in the south was a young man called Sandy Temple she had met at an exhibition in Edinburgh. He worked for *The Times* in Parliament, Selina's young man, writing reports of the day's debates and occasional comment pieces on recent political developments. Selina dreamt that his proximity to the great world of politics and power would, in due course, reap a rich harvest of invitations.

Sandy was a son of the vicarage. His father, William Temple, had an adequate living in Chalfont St Giles, or rather it would have been adequate if he had not fathered so many children. Sandy had eleven sisters and one brother. Such money as could be saved with so many to feed and clothe had gone on his education at Winchester and Oxford. Mindful of his family responsibilities like a dutiful son, he sent regular subventions from his salary back to his mother in the country. Sandy was obsessed with politics. He always had been. His first lessons had come studying the debasement of Athenian democracy during the Peloponnesian War with Sparta, and the fights to the death that disfigured and destroyed the last days of the Roman Republic. When he said his prayers, which he usually managed a couple of times a week, he always remembered to thank God for giving him such a perfect job. For political obsessives, working in the Parliamentary and Political Department of *The Times* was to work in your very own corner of paradise. He didn't think Selina realized just how important his position was.

Sandy had been invited to tea twice in Markham Square, and on neither occasion had the hostess managed to be present in person. Family emergencies had detained Lady Lucy elsewhere. Now, as the Silver Ghost ate up the miles and her husband could not escape to his study or his club, Lady Lucy seized her moment.

'Francis,' she said, in that tone of voice that indicates an important topic is about to be broached.

'Yes, my love,' said Powerscourt, wondering what was coming.

'You know that young man Selina is friendly with, Sandy is he called, the one who works for *The Times*?'

'I do.'

'Well, I've been wondering, you see – I've only met him for a minute or two as I had to go out when he called. What did you think of him? You must have spent much more time with him than I have.'

Powerscourt could see it all now. This was in the nature of a scouting mission, a preliminary report to be posted to Selina's mother about the young man, later despatches to follow at regular intervals rather like the publication of the Court Circular in *The Times*.

'Well, Lucy,' he began, deciding that he wasn't going to make life too easy for her as he rather liked the young man, 'what do you want to know?'

'Come along, you know precisely what I want to know. What's he like, this Sandy? Can he handle himself in society? Does he know how to behave or he is one of these aesthetes with very strange clothes and even stranger manners you see sometimes these days?'

'You know what he looks like: six feet tall, light brown hair, blue eyes, dresses rather older than his years but that may be because he works in the Palace of Westminster. Manages to eat with knife and fork and spoon like the rest of us. Educated, I believe, at Winchester and Merton College, Oxford, where he claims to have spent more time on the river than in the library but still managed to collect a first class honours degree in Greats. Maybe it's all that time on the river, but it's hard to imagine him getting overexcited about anything. He seems languid, but I suspect he could move pretty fast if he had to.'

'You're talking as if you're writing his obituary, Francis. What's he really like?'

Powerscourt pulled out to overtake a couple of cyclists. He felt his defences were being worn down.

'He's fascinated by politics, my love, the way other people are by form on the turf or the football scores. Sandy can tell you who's up and who's down across the main political parties the way other people could report on the batsmen in form by reading the cricket reports. He's obsessed by Lloyd George's Budget at the moment. He's got some rather unusual views on the matter.'

'Is he some sort of revolutionary person? I don't think Selina's family would approve of that.'

'He's not a revolutionary man, Lucy. I'm not quite sure what his politics are, to be precise. You remember this Budget, Chancellor of the Exchequer Lloyd George proposing higher taxes on the rich to pay for more battleships and old age pensions for the poor? It's become a real bone of contention, with the rich in the House of Lords saying their way of life is being destroyed and that they'll fight to the death to stop the Budget becoming law. One day when Sandy was talking about it in Markham Square he began to quote great chunks from a speech Lloyd George had made months before in Limehouse in the East End, about the rights of the poor. Sandy said it was one of the finest speeches he'd ever heard.'

'Is he a supporter of Lloyd George, then? He's not exactly one of us, is he? Lloyd George, I mean.'

'No, he's not,' said Powerscourt, changing into top gear as a long straight section of road opened up in front of them, 'but I don't think Sandy is a supporter of any of them. He just likes watching the sport. I do know he thinks Lloyd George is the future, not necessarily Lloyd George in person, but people like him. He believes they'll have to go on widening the franchise until everybody adult has the vote so men of the people rather than aristocrats and people in the upper classes can become Prime Minister. Oh, and he thinks the landowning classes are finished, done for. It all comes down to Rhys the butler in the end.'

'Our Rhys the butler, Francis?'

'Our Rhys the butler.'

'What about Rhys the butler? This isn't some sort of parlour game, is it?'

'No, I'm deadly serious, Lucy. There is a question, mind you. Should Rhys the butler have the vote?'

'Well,' said Lady Lucy, 'I suppose I think he should have the vote. So should I, mind you.'

They both laughed.

'Another thing Sandy's very keen on is the decline of the landed interest. Possession of broad acres now in England brings very narrow returns financially or politically. The link between land – I think he's quite original on this point – and political power is gone and will never return. Or so Sandy says.'

'Do you think we're doomed, Francis?' said Lady Lucy with a smile. 'Bound to disappear under the rising proletarian tide and the onward march of the militant suffragettes?'

'I don't think we're doomed, Lucy. Not for a moment. There will always be one or two survivors left, clinging to the wreckage and complaining that things aren't what they used to be.'

Three days later, shortly before four o'clock in the afternoon, the vicar and the choir led the way out of the Church of St Nicholas in the Candlesby estate towards the bridge over the lake to the mausoleum where Arthur George Harold John Nathaniel Dymoke was to rest for evermore. At the very front of the little procession was the curate from the neighbouring parish, carrying a cross. Then came the vicar and the choir. Behind the choir came four black horses with black plumes pulling the coffin, then the family, then the friends and neighbours with the senior servants bringing up the rear. It was a family tradition that the body of a dead Earl was brought to the church for the funeral service from the Hall on a roundabout route that went through Candlesby village, past Candlesby school and on into St Nicholas. The tradition said that the shops would close, wreaths would line the route, and the villagers stand in respectful silence, caps or bonnets in hand, as the hearse passed by. The schoolchildren would congregate in a great block by their gates and watch the coffin on its journey. On this day the village seemed to be empty. No villagers were lining the streets, no wreaths were propped up on windows, no children were waiting to stare at the last Lord Candlesby who had controlled their family fortunes for so long. The servants were the only people walking behind the coffin on this part of the route and they resolved not to tell their new master that the coffin of the old one had passed through a deserted village. They dreaded to think what form of terrible revenge he might exact.

A fine rain began to fall as the procession made its way up the hill towards the mausoleum.

'Didn't think I'd come today,' one mourner said to his neighbour at the rear of the party. 'Still don't know why I'm here, to tell you the truth.'

'I know how you feel,' said his companion. 'I only came to make sure the old bastard was really dead. Got my tools in the back of the car ready to open the coffin up if it looks necessary, screwdrivers and things. Seems fairly certain he has left us, don't you think?'

'Pretty rum way to go,' said the first mourner. 'I wasn't here that morning but a chap who was at the hunt told me Candlesby's body was brought up to the house lying across his horse covered in blankets as if he was El Cid or some medieval warrior.'

His companion grunted. 'Hardly anybody saw the body, that's what I was told. Doubt if we've heard the end of it. So typical of the bloody man to go on causing trouble after he's dead, don't you think?'

'Were you here when he did that railway swindle?' The first mourner was in unforgiving mood. 'Not sure whether it was him or his father, now I come to think about it. They bribed the railway surveyor and the railway lawyer to send the bloody railway not through my land or your land where it was supposed to go, but through their land, Candlesby land. Must have made a fortune, the bastards.'

The procession was now halfway towards the mausoleum. Charles Candlesby was keeping an eye on his younger brother.

'How are you b-b-bearing up, James? Funerals can be quite b-b-beastly sometimes. Only if you care, mind you. Don't suppose anyone minds at all about Father.'

'I care,' said the youngest Candlesby, and began to cry.

'P-p-please don't do that, it'll start me off too. I care too, you know. The whole thing is too horrid for words.'

James took a series of deep breaths, as instructed by one of his doctors. The front of the procession was now filing into the great height of the mausoleum.

'Have you b-b-been in here b-b-before?' asked Charles.

James shook his head.

'It's quite special, really. If you ever wonder what the p-p-place the Delphic Oracle lived in was like, this is it. I always wonder if the architect had been to Greece and seen the real thing.'

The pallbearers were now lifting the coffin off the hearse and carrying it inside to be placed on a temporary stand while the vicar said a few prayers. Then it was carried down the stairs into the crypt where it was slid into one of the sixty-nine empty niches carved in the walls.

'We meekly beseech thee, O Father, to raise us from the death of sin unto the life of righteousness; we may rest in him, as our hope is this our brother doth: and that at the general Resurrection in the last day, we may be found acceptable in thy sight; and receive that blessing which thy well-beloved son shall then pronounce saying, Come, ye blessed children of my Father, receive the kingdom prepared for you from the beginning of the world.'

As the priest's last words echoed round the low walls of the crypt the pallbearers placed the coffin in its niche, closed the great iron door at the front of the vault and secured it with an enormous padlock. There was a brief moment of silence before they all filed out into the light of day and back down the hill. Richard, the new Earl of Candlesby, was wondering if he could choose which niche to occupy when his time came. Henry and Edward were wondering how soon they could get away to the inn on the outskirts of the village. James had decided to go to his apartment on the top floor where he lived with his medical attendant for a period of quiet. Charles had decided to talk to the neighbours who had come for the funeral. You could never tell, he said to himself, when a little bit of local gossip might not come in useful. The first mourner gave it as his opinion to his neighbour that the chances of the late Earl of Candlesby being received into the Kingdom of Heaven were so remote as to be inconceivable. He would rather, he went on, bet on the nag who pulled his milk churns winning the Grand National.

Five days later Powerscourt received a letter from Lincolnshire written in a rather shaky hand.

'Dear Lord Powerscourt,' he read, 'I wonder if I could ask a great favour of you. It concerns a recent action of mine as a doctor of medicine where I fear I have done the wrong thing. The matter is weighing very heavily on my mind. I do not wish to put the details in a letter, but I have to ask that you should come and call at the above address at your earliest convenience. I have recently contracted this terrible influenza and fear I may not be long for this world. I do so hope that you will be able to come before it is too late. Yours sincerely, Theodore Miller.'

'My word, Lucy,' he said, passing her the letter, 'I've heard of deathbed repentances from villains and murderers before, but never from a doctor. It must be some sort of record.'

'What are you going to do? Do you think this doctor is a mass murderer, wanting to tell you how many citizens of Lincolnshire he has done away with?'

'We met the chap after the *Messiah*, at the hotel. Very old character with wispy white hair, if you remember. He seemed perfectly law-abiding to me. God knows what he's been up to. He was very keen to take my address now I come to think about it. I'd better send him a telegram to say I'm coming and catch a train.'

By the middle of the afternoon Powerscourt was knocking on the door of the doctor's Georgian villa on the outskirts of Candlesby. The house was large with an enormous garden and a tennis court at the back. The doctor was poorly today, the housekeeper Mrs Baines told him, worse than yesterday and worse than the day before. But, she went on, he had repeatedly asked if Lord Powerscourt was coming and that seemed to bring him some relief. She brought him up to a room with great windows on the first floor where an elderly gentleman sitting up in bed in a red silk dressing gown and bright blue pyjamas was waiting to talk to him.

'My dear Lord Powerscourt, how very kind of you to come all this way. Did my letter arrive today?'

'It did.'

'Then you have made admirable speed. Can you tell me one thing and then we can get down to business?'

Mrs Baines tucked the doctor firmly into his bedclothes and left the room, promising to bring tea in about half an hour. The doctor was deathly pale and a film of perspiration covered his forehead only minutes after the housekeeper had wiped it.

'I have been making inquiries about you, Lord Powerscourt, and I discover that you have a most remarkable record. But tell me this. I learnt about some of your cases. The last one I came across was the Blickling wedding murder which ended up in the Old Bailey a couple of years back with one brother tried for the murder of another. Is there a more recent case which I have not heard about?'

He paused and panted, as if this speech had taken him close to the limits of endurance. He coughed for a moment or two and lay back on his pillows.

Powerscourt wondered briefly if the old man thought detectives resting between engagements were rather like doctors having a long gap between patients, that it meant their clients no longer trusted them.

'There have been a couple of cases since then, doctor,' said Powerscourt with a smile, ' but I'm afraid I can't talk about them. They were secret work, work for the government.'

'I see,' said the doctor, 'secret work. That sounds very special.'

Powerscourt had no wish to linger in the shadows of government employment. It had been unpleasant enough while it lasted. 'Perhaps you could tell me your problem, doctor, the one that brought me here.'

'Yes, yes,' said the doctor, wrestling briefly with one of his pillows. 'Do you know, I've thought about this moment such a lot, and now I'm not sure how to begin.'

The doctor paused. Powerscourt waited.

'It has to do with Lord Candlesby,' the old man said finally, and another coughing fit struck him, longer than the last.

'Which one?' asked Powerscourt as gently as he could.

'Sorry, my mind isn't what it was. It has to do with the one who died while you were here the last time. For the *Messiah*.'

The doctor looked hopelessly at Powerscourt as if his will could pass on all the information he wanted. Still Powerscourt said nothing.

'It has to do with the death certificate, you see.' Powerscourt thought that had taken a great effort. He suddenly thought the matter might be speeded up if he started asking questions rather than imitating the Sphinx.

'Perhaps you could just tell me, Dr Miller, how you first became involved?'

'I was called to the stable block at Candlesby Hall round about nine thirty maybe ten o'clock in the morning. I didn't see what had happened before, but apparently the members of the hunt were all gathered in front of the house. Candlesby himself was dead when I got there, carried up his drive on the back of his horse and covered with blankets.' The doctor rested once more, his eyes closing for a moment as if to shut out the painful truth.

'So you didn't have to treat him in any way? There was nothing to be done?'

'That's right,' said the doctor, looking slightly more cheerful now his story was properly under way. 'He was dead all right, very dead.'

Powerscourt racked his brains to think what sins the doctor must have committed if he hadn't had to treat Candlesby at all. Medical negligence seemed out of the question. But something very serious must have happened to bring him all the way from London.

'The problem . . . the problem has to do with the death certificate.'

'What did you put on the death certificate, doctor?'

Temporary relief for Dr Miller was provided by the arrival of tea. Mrs Baines looked sternly at Powerscourt as she poured two cups. 'I don't think you should be tiring the doctor out too much, Lord Powerscourt. I'll be back in half an hour and then you must let him rest for a while. You can always come back later on or first thing in the morning.'

The doctor refused a scone and a slice of Mrs Baines' home-made chocolate cake. Powerscourt succumbed.

'They were all on at me about the death certificate,' the doctor said as the housekeeper sped out of the room, closing the door firmly behind her.

'Sorry, who were they?' said Powerscourt indistinctly through a mouthful of chocolate cake.

'Sorry,' said the doctor. 'The three eldest brothers were on at me.'

'You've lost me,' said Powerscourt. 'Could we just go back to where we were before tea? What did you put on the death certificate, Dr Miller?'

There was that beseeching look again. Powerscourt noticed that the doctor's body was shaking beneath the bedclothes in irregular spasms. He suddenly stared at a print of Venice on his wall, boats swirling round the basin of St Mark, the Doge's Palace and the Church of San Giorgio Maggiore keeping watch over the waterway. He was whispering now.

'They made me say – oh, how I wish I'd never agreed to it – they made me say the Earl had died of natural causes.' Another coughing fit, a fit of remorse maybe, consumed him. Powerscourt thought suddenly that it wasn't youth, but age, that grows pale and spectre thin and dies.

'And he hadn't? Died of natural causes, I mean? Is that right?' Powerscourt thought he could see the whole thing now. It's my damned profession, he said to himself. If I weren't a bloody investigator I wouldn't be rushing to conclusions so fast.

The doctor nodded miserably.

'So Lord Candlesby died of unnatural causes then. Was he murdered? Had somebody killed him? And was that why the sons were so keen for you to put natural causes as the cause of death?'

The doctor nodded again. The Venetians in their gondolas and their sailing boats seemed to be bringing little comfort now.

4

'How was he killed, doctor? You must have had a good look at him.'

'I can't tell you that, Lord Powerscourt. They made me swear to keep that secret.'

'This isn't a case of a sprained wrist or ingrowing toenails, Dr Miller. We're talking about the most serious crime on the statute books of England.'

'I know, I know, but I can't tell you that. They made me swear.'

Dr Miller coughed violently, spasms shaking his body. Powerscourt took a hasty look at his watch. There were only minutes left before the dragon of a housekeeper was to return.

'Let me recap if I may, doctor. The hunt was meeting at Candlesby Hall. Before they could start – am I right? – the body was brought up, laid across a horse and covered in blankets.' The doctor nodded. 'The corpse is then diverted into the stables away from prying eyes. You are summoned. I presume you inspect the dead man. Then the brothers force you to say he died of natural causes before there is any possibility of a post-mortem and a scandal that will fill the national press for days. Is that right?'

The doctor nodded once more.

'So who brought the body up to the house? And how many people knew about the real cause of Candlesby's death?'

Suddenly a light seemed to go out in the doctor's system. He sank back on his pillows, eyes closed. Powerscourt pulled a black notebook from his pocket and began writing as fast as he could. If he was to make any sense of this strange affair he needed something more concrete than the ramblings of a dying doctor.

'I, Dr Theodore Miller,' the words sped from Powerscourt's pen, 'do hereby declare that on October the eighth, 1909, I signed a false death certificate. I said that the Earl of Candlesby had died of natural causes. He had not. He was murdered by a person or persons unknown.'

The housekeeper swept back into the room. Dr Miller woke up from his reverie. He smiled at Powerscourt.

'Please forgive me, Mrs Baines, I beg you to grant us a little more time. Lord Powerscourt and I have nearly finished discussing our business. This business is the most important thing I have to settle before I die. Don't make that face, please, I know I haven't long to go. I am a doctor after all.'

'Very well,' said Mrs Baines, 'but not too long now, or you'll be sorry.' And with a menacing look at Powerscourt she left the room once more.

'You know, Lord Powerscourt, it's a pleasure to talk with an educated and cultivated man like yourself. Most of my friends are dead now, and not many people come to see me these days.'

Powerscourt leant forward towards the bed with his notebook.

'I'll sign that for you in a moment, whatever it is,' the doctor went on. 'When you get to my age,' he continued, 'the past comes in on you like the tide. It just washes away what happened recently, last month, the day before yesterday. I can feel my memory going, you know. Trying to recall what happened a week ago is like trying to pull up a bucket from a well with no bottom to it. Sometimes I think I'm going right back to the beginning. I thought I remembered sitting up in my pram in my parents' garden the other night.

Maybe at the very end we just go right back to where we came in.'

'That's very interesting,' Powerscourt began, but the doctor interrupted him. The beads of sweat were back on his forehead, glistening like dew, and another coughing fit seized him.

'I know, I know,' the doctor said at last, 'you want me to sign this piece of paper.'

He fished about in his bedclothes and put on a pair of very thick spectacles. His face had turned paler yet.

'This seems satisfactory,' he said at last and signed it. 'You must do what you have to do with this document.' He stopped suddenly as if a great thought had come to him close to the end.

'Lord Powerscourt,' he said, 'will you look into this matter for me? Will you investigate the Candlesby death on my behalf? Think of this as a last commission from a dying man. I shall remember your efforts in my will. It would please me greatly if I could think that my sins are being sorted out. I would not die with such a heavy burden on my shoulders.'

Powerscourt smiled. 'I should be delighted to accept your commission, doctor. Now, I feel it is time to rest. I fear Mrs Baines will be upon us again at any moment.'

The doctor sank back on his pillows once more. Inside a couple of minutes he was asleep. The sweat was still there on his forehead, his colour was still deathly pale, but a slight smile played about his face as if he were happier now. Powerscourt tiptoed slowly from the room, wondering if the doctor was back in his pram once more, or playing in his parents' garden in the sunshine.

Powerscourt took himself for a long walk on his journey from the doctor's house to Mr Drake's hotel where he was to spend the night. This must be one of the most unusual cases he had ever undertaken, commissioned to solve a murder by a doctor who had lied on the death certificate. He was passing the back entrance to Candlesby Hall now, a pair of gate lodges with smoke rising from the chimneys, a prospect of farmland, and a herd of deer in the distance but no sight of the house itself. He was trying to work out what to do. As far as he could tell there were only two people, apart from the murderer, who had seen the dead Earl and must have some idea of what had killed him. But when he considered his own position he was not sure how to proceed. Officially, the death certificate said death by natural causes. If the two people who knew the truth refused to speak, sworn, presumably, to silence in the manner of the doctor, then all he had was a page in a notebook, handwritten, not even typed, which he suspected would have little purchase in the English legal system. If there was no agreement that there had been a murder at all, how could he investigate it? Anybody ill disposed to his efforts, the new Lord Candlesby for instance, could make life very difficult.

There was only one way forward. He would have to throw himself on the mercy of the Lincolnshire Constabulary. In his experience, if you told the police what you were doing at the beginning of an inquiry, they would as a rule bend over backwards to be helpful. Bring them in late and they would be surly and suspicious and occasionally obstructive. He asked George Drake the hotel manager that evening for the name of a sympathetic senior detective who operated in those parts. Detective Inspector William Blunden, he was told, based at Spalding, was his man. A message was sent saying that Powerscourt proposed to call on him at eleven o'clock the following morning. If George Drake had any curiosity about Powerscourt asking for guidance about senior detectives he didn't show it. He didn't mention it to anybody, not even to his wife. If Powerscourt was in trouble and had to confess his sins to a senior policeman, then he, George Drake, was not going to start any rumours.

Detective Inspector Blunden was a big man. A small child might have described him as a giant. He was over six feet three inches tall with powerful shoulders and massive hands. He looked, the Detective Inspector, as if he might have played rugby seriously, probably as a second row forward, and a couple of cups and a photograph on the side of his desk confirmed his sporting past. His eyes were not those of a leader of the pack, however; they were light brown and rather gentle. It was these soft eyes indeed that constituted his chief appeal for the girl who later became his wife.

'Good morning, Lord Powerscourt,' said the Detective Inspector, rising from his desk to shake Powerscourt by the hand. 'What a privilege to meet you!'

'Thank you so much for your time, Inspector. I'm sure you must be very busy.'

'Something tells me, my lord, that I may be even busier when I have heard what you have got to say.'

Blunden had been wondering before this meeting what a leading investigator from London could want from a provincial policeman in one of England's more obscure counties. The wall of silence constructed around the death of the Earl of Candlesby was so effective that it never crossed his mind that Candlesby Hall and its last master might be at the centre of Powerscourt's story.

Powerscourt told him everything: the breakdown of his car, his and Lady Lucy's emergency singing role at the *Messiah*, the meeting with Dr Miller, the summons to see him on his sickbed, the details of the day of the death. Or murder, he said, realizing he was now authorized to say that by the doctor's note.

'I'll give you the sequence of events on that morning in time order, if I may, Inspector. I got them in bits from the doctor yesterday and I don't have very much detail. The hunt was meeting in front of the house. They were getting ready to move off. Then they saw a horse with something that later transpired to be a corpse across it coming up that long drive that leads to the Hall. There must have been somebody leading the horse unless the animal knew its way home but I'm damned if I know who it was. The horse and the corpse are diverted into the stables away from prying eyes. The doctor is summoned; he doesn't live far away. He is bullied into agreeing to sign a death certificate saying the late Earl died from natural cases. Only he didn't. He was murdered, but that death certificate meant there was no question of a post-mortem or anything like that.' He handed over his notebook opened at the page with the doctor's statement.

'Well,' said Detective Inspector Blunden, 'this is a pretty kettle of fish and no mistake. One murdered Earl, but we don't know where he had gone to be murdered, if you see what I mean. Presumably one of the sons could have gone out and killed him and got back to the Hall before daybreak. And, if there was someone with the body, which seems most likely, how did they know where to find him? And the most difficult questions are something else again. The false death certificate. The lack of a post-mortem. How might we get round them?'

'I'm not sure', said Powerscourt, 'where the law would stand on this. There is one official death certificate, saying death by natural causes, signed by the good Dr Miller. There is a different account of events, also signed by the good Dr Miller, to say the first one was wrong and the poor man was murdered by person or persons unknown.'

'There is one thing that has just occurred to me, my lord,' said Inspector Blunden, twiddling a pencil in his enormous hands. 'Those injuries, to the dead man, I mean, they must have been pretty horrendous, don't you think? That might have accounted for the diversion into the stables.'

'It's possible,' Powerscourt replied, 'but it might just be the natural reluctance of the family to have all the members of the hunt come to peer at the corpse.'

'Unless we get a post-mortem we're not going to know how the Earl was killed. Unless we know how he was killed, my lord, we've precious little to go on to investigate a charge of murder. I've never had to ask for an exhumation before, but if the family want to keep the murder a secret I'm sure they could make life very difficult for us.'

'You can hear the lawyers now, Inspector,' said Powerscourt, a vision of his barrister friend Charles Augustus Pugh floating into his mind. '"Which should we believe, my lord, the official death certificate, properly signed by the doctor when he was still in good health, or this scribbled entry in a cheap notebook, the bulk of the testimony not even in the doctor's hand? The formal record of a man passing away, carried out according to custom and tradition, or the ramblings of a sick man close to his deathbed dictated to an investigator who hasn't investigated a case for nearly two years and was obviously desperate for a commission. I submit, my lord, that this appeal for an exhumation is vexatious and should be dismissed."'

'We've got another problem here,' said the Inspector with feeling. 'It's one unique to this county and it won't go away.'

'Really?' said Powerscourt, wondering what particular plague had struck the first-born of Lincolnshire.

'I shouldn't be saying this, my lord, but you are in the nature of an outsider here. The problem is our new Chief Constable. He's not been here long. He knows less about police work than my daughter and she's only three years old. He interferes. He asks for information about cases before anybody's been charged. It wouldn't matter if his interventions were sensible or even rational. They're not. One of my fellow Inspectors firmly believes that he takes cases home to his wife for her to decide what he should do. Only trouble is, she's even more stupid than he is. And because he's ex-army he's big on smart uniforms and polished boots and all that sort of thing.'

'What's his name, this new fellow?'

'Willoughby-Lewis, my lord, Bertram Willoughby-Lewis to be precise. Ex-Indian Army, ex-Major General. They say his brother's a top official in the Home Office. Maybe that's how he got the job.'

'Bertram? You did say Bertram, didn't you?' said Powerscourt, a smile spreading across his features. 'Thin cove, big moustache, very high-pitched voice not perfectly suited to delivering parade ground commands, yes?'

Detective Inspector Blunden looked confused. 'That's right, my lord, you've got him to a tee. Have you met him?'

'I think I have, as a matter of fact,' said Powerscourt. 'My friend Johnny Fitzgerald and I were stationed close by the man once during our time in India, but never under his command. Johnny could imitate the Willoughby-Lewis voice perfectly. He once managed to reroute an entire day's march for the Willoughby-Lewis troops by ringing their adjutants late in the day in his best Willoughby-Lewis accents and giving them new orders. There was the most magnificent confusion, especially when all the adjutants told the Major General that they had only followed the new orders because he had telephoned them in person. The only man who worked out what had happened was our commanding officer. God knows how he found out but he sent Johnny and me away on a trip for ten days to keep us out of the way.'

'I like that story very much,' said the Inspector. 'Now then, my lord, what do you think we should do?'

'Could we press right on and call on the new Earl this afternoon? We could say there are certain irregularities, something like that. I'm sure he should be our first port of call. Telephone? Telegraph?'

Blunden snorted. 'They've only just got running water up there,' he said. 'No telegraph, no telephone, no electricity, no motor cars; the place is still back in the Dark Ages. I could send a message saying we propose to call at eleven in the morning tomorrow. And that would give us an opportunity to make one or two inquiries ourselves, my lord. It seems to me that the key person to find is the man who escorted the horse and the body up that road. If he's a servant they'll have sworn him to silence. But there are one or two members of the hunt I know who will help us if I ask them. I don't think the family would be able to silence all of them. And I'll ask our people who know Candlesby village to make some discreet inquiries up there, not that they ever say much to officers of the law. That should give us a start.'

'Could I be very forward, Inspector, and make a suggestion entirely outside my province? Feel free to tell me to jump in the lake. But before you do anything I think you should talk to your Chief Constable. I know he's difficult but if you involve him right from the start then, in my long experience of wayward, unstable, unreliable or even insane commanding officers, he'll be easier to manage. That's all.'

Inspector Blunden looked closely at Powerscourt for a moment and then he laughed. 'You're absolutely right, my lord. There's nothing to lose.'

He rose from his chair and adjusted his uniform carefully. 'Could you bear to wait till I get back? Whole case may have been kicked into the long grass by then for all I know. Then you'd be on your own. But do you know, my lord, we haven't known each other for long, but I'd much rather we were working together.'

Richard, the new Earl of Candlesby, was in a bad mood even before he received the note from the Inspector proposing a visit at eleven o'clock the following morning. He had now spent the past day and a half working on the accounts with his steward and discovered that his debts were larger than he thought, his income smaller than he expected, and the threat of bankruptcy not yet very close but visible as a small dot on the far horizon, moving ever nearer fairly fast. The impending visit of some unknown private investigator and a Detective Inspector from Spalding left Richard worried. They could only be coming about his father's death. Richard didn't know what the penalty was for covering up your father's murder but he thought it might be pretty bad. As he rehearsed the questions he might be asked in his mind he suddenly realized how great his peril was. He had covered up the death. Therefore he had something to hide. He had insisted on the false death certificate. Yet more proof that he had something to hide. And that something, he said to himself bitterly, could only be, in the eyes of the law, that I covered things up because I killed my father. This was even worse than he had feared.

He told his brothers about the visitors due the next day and summoned them to a meeting early that evening in what was known as the breakfast room. There was what had once been a fine circular English oak table of about 1840 and some paintings of Naples on the walls where the grime had not yet obliterated the views.

Henry and Edward were the first to arrive, their cheeks still bright from a long walk around the estate, arguing over which treasures they should be allowed to take from the house. Charles came last, protesting that the subject of the meeting had nothing to do with him. He hadn't even been in the county at the time of the meeting of the hunt and the discovery of the body.

'Do keep quiet, Charles,' said Richard, writing something in a large red book on the table. 'This is very serious. If we make a false move tomorrow, we're done for. I've no idea who this Powerscourt person is, he's described as a private investigator, whatever that means, and the Blunden man is the local Inspector for these parts. Now then, Henry and Edward, I think they're going to concentrate on the arrival of the body. This is going to be like a parlour game but a

50

deadly serious one. I'm going to pretend to be the police Inspector, so be prepared to answer my questions.'

'Charades! Dressing up!' said Charles happily. 'How simply divine! I do think we should dress up p-p-properly though. There are p-p-policemen's uniforms in the b-box upstairs. Should I go and get them?'

'Will you shut up, Charles! If I have to tell you again you will just have to leave. Henry, Edward, can you tell me when you first realized that there was something unusual about the horse coming up the drive?'

Edward and Henry mumbled different answers that made very little sense. Richard took his brothers over the ground again, eventually writing down answers for them to learn before the policeman arrived the following morning. Charles's only other contribution met with little sympathy.

'If Father was wearing his scarlet coat,' he asked, 'why did p-p-people try to hide it under the b-b-blankets? It was very p-p-pretty, that coat. He looked very handsome in it.'

As Richard went to bed that night he realized that the chances of his brothers putting their feet in it were considerable and that he should keep Charles out of sight at all times. He had, after all, not been present at the vital hours. Most of all he wondered which of them hated him enough to betray him to the authorities.

Powerscourt spent the afternoon and early evening at the doctor's house. But the doctor was asleep, or in a coma, it was hard to say which, and he confined himself to long conversations with Mrs Baines. As housekeeper, nurse or companion she had served all over Lincolnshire but her particular expertise was with the county families, Candlesbys included. She collected them, male or female, young or old, in their last moments, he quickly realized, as other people might collect moths or butterflies. She told him that reclusiveness seemed to run in the Candlesby family every other

51

generation. One Earl communicated with his children and servants only by letter and another one once spent four and a half months without talking to a single soul. There was yet another who banished his daughter without a penny because she was smoking when he entered the room.

Most of all she told him about the one known to this day in the village as the Wicked Earl. Nobody remembered very much about him any more, or the manner of his wickedness, but Mrs Baines' grandmother had told her hair-raising stories when she was small.

'He went off to Italy, this Candlesby, Edward I think he was called, on that Grand Tour where the young men went to Italy and picked up a lot of unpleasant diseases in the big Italian cities. I'm trying to remember the painter he was interested in, Cara something, Carabaldi? No, he was a soldier who liked biscuits, wasn't he?' ,

'Caravaggio?' Powerscourt suggested in his mildest tones.

'That's the one,' said Mrs Baines triumphantly. 'Well, they say he wasn't as expensive as some of the other painters, so our Edward spent a long time in Rome and Naples and other places buying up as many pictures of his as he could. Most of the paintings ordered up were religious but that didn't bother the Cara man. Apparently he painted those female saints like they'd have their clothes off in half an hour if the price was right. And the other thing with the Cara man, apparently, he liked violence. Heads of John the Baptist or the dead Goliath, he could dash those off for you half a dozen at a time. Judith and Holofernes from the Bible, her with a great curved knife or sword and him with the blood pouring out of his neck, that went down well with our boy. Flagellations, whips and lashes on bare flesh were a speciality of the house.

'Eventually,' she went on, 'the wicked Edward brought them all home, all his treasures and all his Caras. He put the paintings in a great room at the back of the house on the top floor. He had it sealed up so that only he had a key. And then, this is what they say, Lord Powerscourt, he began to copy the paintings. Like the Cara man he could only paint from life, with real models. And so he tried to reproduce the works of the Cara man. As time passed the people in the house got used to these pretty young men coming in to be painted as Cupid or that David who killed Goliath. I've been told there were a lot of bloody crucifixion pictures brought back from Rome and Naples as well but nobody knows if Lord Edward ever went in for painting Our Lord on the cross with the nails and the vinegar and the thieves on either side.'

Mrs Baines paused at this point to ask if Powerscourt would like more tea or some of her special fruit cake. He declined.

'I must check on the doctor in a moment – I can't stay here all day gossiping to you – but there is one thing you must remember about Edward and his Cara man, whatever he was called. Isn't it awful, I've forgotten the painter's name already. The room's still there, the room with the paintings. In his will Edward stipulated that the room should remain locked for ever in his memory, Edward's that is, not the Cara man, and that he would leave no record of where he had put the key. One theory says it is handed down from one butler to another; we don't know. Everybody thinks he threw it in the lake but I'm not so sure. I'll be back in a moment, Lord Powerscourt, but if you have to get away don't wait for me to come down again.'

Powerscourt made his way back to the hotel, his mind reeling with images of bloodthirsty Caravaggios, the broken flesh, the bleeding neck, the crown of thorns being forced on to a bloodied head, being reproduced by a mad Earl in a vast palace in the wilds of Lincolnshire.

5

Richard, the new Earl, was up very early the next morning. A weak sun illuminated his inheritance. He checked the homework he had given his two brothers the night before. He stood at the great windows in the saloon, which had once been the main entrance to the house, and watched the deer trotting peacefully along by the lake. Where his right hand rested by the window he noticed that the paint had almost completely faded from the upper part of the shutters. What had once been a cream colour had now been reduced to a smudgy brown.

His brothers ate an enormous breakfast in the dining room. He, Richard, was too nervous to eat. If things went wrong today, there could be a great deal of trouble. He had taken the precaution the afternoon before of writing to his father's lawyers in London requesting a visit. 'Bunch of crooks really,' – he remembered his father's verdict on Hopkins Pettigrew & Green, HP & G for short – 'lawyers are meant to interpret law for the authorities; HP & G see their job as protecting the individual from the authorities and the law. No matter what crimes you commit – child snatching, robbery, fraud, embezzlement, the normal weaknesses of the aristocracy – they'll see it as their job to get you off. Probably do the same for murder, I shouldn't wonder.'

Between half past eight and half past nine Richard put Edward and Henry through their paces. He stopped well before the visit of the policeman and the investigator in case his pupils became so over-rehearsed that they sounded like automata. He arranged a space for the meeting in the saloon and opened a couple of windows so that anybody walking outside, or sitting on a bench, might just be able to hear what was being said on the floor above. If they cared to listen, of course.

Detective Inspector Blunden had secured a small carriage from the police pool to take himself and Powerscourt to Candlesby Hall.

'I have bad news, my lord,' were his first words after the morning pleasantries were over. Powerscourt raised an inquisitive eyebrow.

'You will remember we talked about a man, or the man, who brought the horse and the corpse up to the Hall on the day of the death?'

'I do, of course,' said Powerscourt.

'My contacts in the hunt told me yesterday that the man was called Jack Hayward, senior groom to the household, widely respected by all for his tact and his knowledge of horses.'

'And?' said Powerscourt.

'It's just this, my lord. Jack Hayward has vanished off the face of the earth. Nobody can remember seeing him after that day when he brought his dead master up to his house on the back of his horse.'

'What sort of age was the fellow?' asked Powerscourt, wondering suddenly if he had another murder on his hands. 'Did he have a wife, children, that sort of thing?'

'I was told he was about forty, my lord. His wife wasn't local, though they say she was one of the prettiest women in the village,' replied the Inspector, 'and there were or there are two children, a boy of eight and a girl of six. All gone.'

'Has anybody been inside the house?' Powerscourt was feeling seriously alarmed now. 'I mean, are things left so that it looks as if the Haywards are coming back? Or has everything been removed?'

'Nobody knows, my lord. The house is well locked up and nobody's thought to break down the door. What do you think happened?'

'Well,' said Powerscourt, cursing himself yet again for his ability to reduce any given problem into a series of numbered points, 'possibility number one is they have all been murdered. I would have thought it more likely, mind you, that the killer would only dispose of Mr Hayward and leave the wife and children alone. Possibility number two is that Hayward, aware of the tricky position he was in, finding or being sent for to collect the dead body of his master, bringing it up the road, observing, perhaps, the bullying of the doctor, decided for all their sakes to clear off and take his family with him. Maybe he wanted to keep out of trouble. Maybe they have fled to some of his relations or to some of hers. The third possibility, and perhaps the most likely one, is that somebody has bribed them or bullied them into going away until all this blows over. And I suspect there is only one candidate for that and we both know who it is.'

'The new Earl,' said the Inspector. 'Look, my lord, in a minute or two we should be able to see the house. I feel sure that we must be on the route Jack Hayward took with the horse the day of the murder. There's a fork in the road back there where one branch leads off towards the coast. The other one goes back to the main entrance a couple of miles behind us on the Spalding Road.'

As their carriage took them up the mild incline Powerscourt saw the house sliding into view. Chimneys and a flagpole first, then a top storey, a middle storey, then one slightly raised above ground level and presumably basement quarters for the servants and the staff below. Everywhere the stone was discoloured, cracked in places, the grass in the grounds around the side of the house unkempt and unmown. Roses that once trailed round two sides of the house had gone wild, looping over and round and under each other in a glorious chaos of disorder.

They could see the great circle of grass in front of the house now, the gates in the centre of the railings, the two pavilions connected to the main body of the house by walls with niches where the horses of the hunt had stood and pawed the ground such a short time ago.

'If you look over to the left, my lord,' the Inspector had not been here before but was recreating events from the information he had been given, 'that must be the stable block where Jack Hayward took the horse with the corpse. The point where he turned off must be very close to where we are now.'

'I'm sure you're right,' said Powerscourt, staring intently at the house where a face had just been withdrawn from a window on the first floor.

'Could I make one suggestion about these interviews?'

'Please do,' replied the Inspector.

'I propose we interview them one at a time, rather than all in a body. And I suggest that you take the lead in all the interviews and ask what you want. I'll just chip in when you've finished. I think that should make it more formal.'

'Just as you say, my lord. I'll be happy to go along with that.'

Detective Inspector Blunden jumped out of the carriage, closely followed by Powerscourt, and he pulled vigorously on the doorbell of Candlesby Hall.

Mrs Baines had scarcely left her post by the doctor's bedside all through the evening. One visitor had called to see him quite late but he had departed in rather a cross mood, saying that he couldn't get any sense out of the doctor at all and would come back the following afternoon. In vain did

57

Mrs Baines suggest that the morning was the best, if not the only time the doctor might be lucid. The visitor had other appointments in the morning.

The doctor drifted off to sleep, shortly after eleven o'clock. He might, in Mrs Baines' limited knowledge, be in a coma; she couldn't be sure. What she did know was that there was very little anybody could do for Theodore Miller in his present state. She could make him comfortable and keep him warm and clean until the end. And she didn't think the end was very far off now. She resolved to ring the other doctor, as the older citizens always referred to the upstart newcomer Dr Campbell, at seven o'clock in the morning.

She had lost count of the number of these vigils she had kept now, Bertha Baines, vigils with members of her own family, four of whom she had watched over into the next world, vigils with people who had employed her, she now realized, so they would not leave this world alone, terrible vigils with sick children whose parents had asked her to help out and found they were too busy with their other children or too exhausted to keep watch on their little ones as they slipped away, vigils with friends and neighbours who sent for Bertha because she was known to be good at that sort of thing.

She supposed watching over people as they died had become as much a part of her now as her other work as a nurse or a housekeeper. Just before midnight she went upstairs to sit with the doctor, fortified by an enormous pot of tea clad in three separate tea cosies, and a plate of biscuits. The doctor was always fond of a biscuit when he was well. Mrs Baines looked at him carefully as she began her vigil. She wiped the beads of sweat from his brow. He seemed comfortable with his blankets and his pillows. His breathing was regular but shallow. His hands wandered about over the bedclothes every now and then and Bertha seized one and held it in her own. The doctor looked content. How often had she looked in on these scenes. How often had she thought the patient was secure in their hold on life only for them to slip away a moment later. Truly, she had thought on many occasions with the terminally ill, it must be as hard to die sometimes as it is to stay alive.

Shortly before three o'clock in the morning, when her reservoir of tea was almost exhausted, she thought Dr Miller had stopped breathing, he seemed so still. Leaning forward she realized that his breath, though fainter than before, was still going. Just before dawn she plumped up his pillows once more, mopped his brow, tiptoed downstairs and came back with her *Book of Common Prayer.* She had checked years before with the vicar, who assured her it was perfectly all right to read the Lord's Prayer and the Catechism and the Collect of the Day aloud to her patients. 'Our Father, which art in Heaven, Hallowed be thy name . . . ' She held one of the doctor's hands as she spoke the prayer. There was a very slight rustling in the bed as if Dr Miller might be on the verge of waking up, but it came to nothing.

'Fulfil now, o Lord, the desires and petitions of thy servants as may be most expedient for them: granting us in this world knowledge of thy truth and in the world to come life everlasting.'

Looking at him, the deathly pallor, the deep wrinkles on his face and on the backs of his hands, Mrs Baines thought the doctor was much closer to life everlasting than he was to knowledge of God's truth.

At seven she tiptoed downstairs to telephone Dr Campbell. He said he would be over straight away. They always come quicker for their own, Mrs Baines said to herself crossly, remembering a nine-hour wait by the bedside of a dying child before the doctor appeared and then the child going before he had time to open his bag.

The doctor took Dr Miller's pulse and checked his breathing and all the other futile things doctors do by the bedsides of those they know are passing away. Their performance becomes a ritual to give comfort to the living rather than the dying.

'It could be any time, Mrs Baines,' he said finally, 'or he could linger on till tomorrow. I don't think he will wake again but I could be wrong. You have nothing to reproach yourself with – you have looked after him very well. Don't worry, Mrs Baines, I'll see myself out. Your place is here, I feel. Not long to go now.'

At half past ten the breathing became very shallow. Just after eleven Dr Miller breathed his last. Mrs Baines made sure he was gone and then she cried. She always cried when they left her. Then she went downstairs to send for all the people she had to involve now: the police and the undertakers and the solicitor. She made some more tea. She knew that Dr Miller had written a very short note to the lawyer early yesterday evening. She remembered suddenly the visitor from the evening before who wanted to call in the afternoon. Strange, Mrs Baines said to herself, he seemed a well-spoken man, the doctor's visitor, but he never left his name.

Detective Inspector Blunden firmly but politely rebuffed all Lord Candlesby's proposals after they had been escorted into the saloon on the first floor. The three eldest brothers were waiting there. On the way up Powerscourt's eye had fallen on a ceramic pig with only three legs and a stag on the walls whose left eye had fallen out. He was astonished at the general air of chaos the Candlesbys seemed to live in.

'Lord Powerscourt and I', Blunden said, 'are looking into possible irregularities concerning the death of the previous Earl.'

Very sorry, but no, it would not be convenient to interview all three brothers together even if that might be quicker. Afraid it would not suit to question the two younger brothers Henry and Edward at the same time. Very much regret, but it would not be possible to interview the new Lord Candlesby first, before his brothers.

'Dammit, Constable, or whatever you're called,' Richard was beginning to lose his temper, 'this is not satisfactory. This is my house and I make the rules round here.'

'That's as maybe,' replied Blunden firmly, 'but I represent the law. I ask the questions round here and I talk to people in the order I want.'

'And my colleague here', said Powerscourt in his most emollient voice, 'is a Detective Inspector, not a constable. Just thought we should get our facts straight.'

'Now then,' said Blunden, 'could we talk to Lord Henry first of all, if we could?'

The second brother shuffled over and draped himself across a chair by the window. The other two had disappeared.

'Thank you very much for agreeing to talk to us,' said Blunden pleasantly. 'Could I ask you to cast your mind back to the morning of the hunt? Friday October the eighth, I believe it was.'

'Of course,' said Henry.

'Can you recall', asked Blunden, observing with amazement that Powerscourt was busily writing notes of the interview in a large notebook, 'at what point or at what time you realized that a body on a horse was coming towards the house?'

'I don't know about the time,' said Henry doubtfully. 'I do know the stirrup cup was almost finished. Pity that, it was a cold morning.' He laughed nervously.

'Let me repeat the question. Can you remember when exactly you realized that a horse with something draped across it was coming up the road towards the house?'

'I think it must have been when Richard – my brother – went down to meet Jack Hayward. He is the chief groom and he had brought the horse with the body. Richard diverted the horse towards the stables. Everybody else went home. My brother Edward and I went back to the house. It was only later that Richard told us Papa was the dead man on the back of the horse.'

'So you never went to the stables at all?'

'Not that day, no. Richard wouldn't let anybody in there. Not till the next day.'

'I see,' said Inspector Blunden. 'Did you meet the doctor at all that day?'

'Which doctor?' asked Henry.

'Dr Miller.' Blunden was preparing to pull out soon. It was Powerscourt who had heard the evidence that disproved this theory.

'No, I didn't see Dr Miller at all that day. I didn't even know he'd been to the house.'

'Did you,' Inspector Blunden was on his last question, 'forgive me for asking this, did you take a last look at your father, a sort of farewell, if you like, before they took him away?'

'No, I didn't,' and for once Henry was telling the truth. 'I never saw him again and that's a fact.'

Now it was Powerscourt's turn to put the questions. A sneeze from the ground level outside carried in through one of the open windows. Powerscourt looked at the window carefully.

'Lord Henry,' he began, one aristocrat talking to another, 'have you or other members of the family seen Jack Hayward since the day of the hunt when he brought the horse up the hill?'

'No, why should we see him? He's only a servant. He doesn't come up here.'

'I see,' said Powerscourt. 'Were you aware that Inspector Blunden's people report that Jack Hayward has disappeared? Vanished off the face of the earth, or off the face of Candlesby at any rate.'

'No,' replied Henry, beginning to sound rather irritated at this level of interest in a mere servant.

62

'Fine. Do you by any chance know how Jack Hayward came to be leading a horse with your father's corpse on it? Do you know where he met them? Perhaps he told your eldest brother, who passed the news on to the rest of the family?'

'No,' was all the change Powerscourt got out of Henry on this one.

'One last question, Henry, and then you're free to go. Do you know what your father died of? It must have been something pretty unusual for him to be laid across his horse, with his face and upper body all covered up, don't you think?'

Henry had no trouble with that one. 'He died of natural causes,' he said. 'The doctor told us. It's on the death certificate. So it must be true.'

Powerscourt nodded to the Inspector, who thanked the young man and led him from the room. He was about to speak when Powerscourt put his finger to his lips and pointed to the open windows. Inspector Blunden grinned and nodded. He went into the next room to bring in Lord Edward Dymoke. As the interview progressed, Powerscourt realized that anybody reading his notebook might think he was in danger of losing his wits. He was writing the first interview all over again, almost word for word.

Edward used exactly the same phrase about Jack Hayward as his brother: 'only a servant'. And the same words about the death by natural causes: 'The doctor told us. It's on the death certificate. So it must be true.' Only somebody who thought other people might suspect or even know that the statement was false would say that it must be true. Powerscourt wished he had checked his watch as they came in and left the room. They should both have been there for exactly the same time, right down to the second.

'Richard now, and then we're nearly through,' said Inspector Blunden as Edward departed.

'Could I kick off this time?' asked Powerscourt. He

pointed to the open windows once more. 'I'm going to start somewhere different,' he whispered.

'Lord Candlesby,' he began once Richard was seated opposite him, 'I want to begin if I may with the moment you met Jack Hayward and the horse with your father on the back on the main drive in front of your house. What did Jack Hayward say to you?'

Lord Candlesby looked taken aback for a moment. 'What did he say to me?' he asked.

Powerscourt said nothing. The Inspector was writing in his notebook.

'I think he said something like my father was dead and we should take him to the stables. That's it. That's what he said. I remember now.'

'Did he give any reason for taking him to the stables?'

Richard paused again. 'I think he said we wouldn't want the whole hunt looking at my father as if he were a slaughtered bullock.'

'Did your father look like a slaughtered bullock once the blankets were removed?' asked Powerscourt, wondering if they had accidentally discovered exactly what the dead man looked like.

'No, no,' Candlesby replied, eager to move on, 'that was only a figure of speech.'

'Yours or Jack Hayward's? Figure of speech, I mean.'

'I – I don't know. I don't think it matters now, does it?'

'So here you were, you and Jack Hayward, just the two of you in the stables. Did he take the blankets off? Off your father's face, so you could see what had happened to him?'

'I asked him not to. I didn't want to look. I'm rather squeamish about that sort of thing, actually.'

'Did he tell you how he came to be walking the horse with the corpse? Did he say if he found it by accident, or did somebody come to his house in the night or send him a note?'

'He didn't tell me. Maybe he was being respectful of my feelings so he didn't want to say.'

Powerscourt thought this account of the meeting in the stables one of the more improbable accounts he had heard in a lifetime of listening to improbable accounts.

'So you didn't really have much of a conversation with Jack Hayward then? What happened next?'

'Hayward went off to bring the doctor and the undertaker's people. I was keen to get the formalities under way. After I'd seen them I went up to the house to tell the family.'

'Of course,' said Powerscourt, 'how very proper. Let me ask just one more question if I may. When you were in the stables, it was just you and Jack Hayward, nobody else?'

'That is correct.'

'Very good, my lord,' said Powerscourt. 'Now I think the Detective Inspector will want to ask you a few questions about the disappearance of Jack Hayward. Missing people are more in the police line than mine.'

'This won't take long, my lord.' Blunden was trying to be pleasant. 'Do you know when Jack Hayward disappeared?'

'I've no idea, I'm afraid. The first I heard of it was the day before yesterday. Damned nuisance – the man was a genius with horses.'

'And you've no idea where he is? He can't have just disappeared, surely.'

'As far as we're concerned, that's just what he has done – disappeared.'

'And you don't recall any previous occasion where he asked you about working in Wales, say, or your saying to him that he might like Yorkshire, that sort of thing?'

'I don't think anybody at Candlesby', said Richard, sounding for the very first time like the lord of the manor he now was, 'would ever have suggested he went anywhere else. He was needed and very much valued here.'

Powerscourt and the Inspector collected their belongings and prepared to leave, Powerscourt confirming before they left that a visit to the stables on their way out wouldn't pose any problems.

'Feel free to look around as much as you like,' said Richard affably. 'I don't think anybody needs to come with you.'

That was Richard's big mistake of the day. His coaching of his brothers, if a trifle excessive, had caused no problems. He felt his own performance had been convincing, though he wondered just how much Powerscourt knew about what went on in the stables. But there was one factor he had forgotten to control and this factor was now engaged in conversation with the Inspector and Powerscourt inside the stables.

'I'm Charles, the b-b-black sheep of the Candlesbys,' said Charles, introducing himself, 'cursed with being the fourth son and a stutterer. They keep trying to p-p-pack me off out of sight, my b-b-beastly b-b-brothers.'

'You don't live here, Lord Charles, do you? I don't recall seeing you about the place.'

'I escaped to Cambridge for three years,' said the young man, '*et in Arcadia ego*.'

'I was in Paradise too,' Inspector Blunden chipped in, keen to show off the remains of his Latin.

'My b-b-brothers tried to p-p-persuade me that I was too stupid to pass any exams. That would have meant no trip to the Senate House at the end to collect a degree. But I p-p-passed all my exams. I got my degree. Everybody dressed up for the occasion. Doctors wore scarlet.'

'And where do you live now, sir?' asked Powerscourt.

'I eke out a p-p-precarious living in London, teaching small boys at a p-p-prep school. The headmaster and his staff put on a great façade of caring for the p-pupils but it's more like Dotheboys Hall than anywhere else with the headmaster as Wackford Squeers.'

'What can you tell us about your father's death, sir?' said Inspector Blunden. 'Were you here when he was brought up on his horse or did that come later?'

'I was in London when it happened. Latin b-b-beginners class. *Amo amas amat*. Earnest little eight-year-olds in their

66

crisp white shirts. I took the train as soon as I heard. I arrived about seven.'

'And what impressions did you form about what had happened?' asked Powerscourt, suspecting that they might at last have found a more truthful witness than the ones encountered so far.

'Well,' said Charles, 'there was a great deal of anxiety. And I thought some story was being cooked up which wasn't true.'

'What do you mean?' Powerscourt, speaking very quietly, took a discreet look up at the Hall to check nobody was coming down to join the party.

Charles retreated a couple of paces into the shadows. 'I don't know what had happened to my father, but I thought he had p-p-probably been killed. And I think he must have looked frightful. Jack Hayward told me so the evening b-b-before he left. And whatever my b-b-brothers told you is p-probably a p-p-pack of lies. Richard's been rehearsing Edward and Henry in what they were to say to you.'

'Are you saying your father was murdered?' Inspector Blunden sounded incredulous.

'Yes,' said Charles. 'I mean, I don't know it as I wasn't here, but I think that's the most likely explanation. There was a lot of talk about the death certificate. I think they b-b-bullied Dr Miller into signing it saying death was by natural causes.'

'And Jack Hayward,' said Powerscourt, 'when did he tell you about your father looking frightful? And did he say he was leaving, going right away?'

'I saw him the evening of the death. I'd come down here to talk to the horses. I like horses. Jack was here. He loved horses too. He didn't tell me he was leaving though.'

There were faint noises of people coming towards the stables. Charles seized Powerscourt's arm. 'My father was a tyrant. Like some Central European despot who impales his enemies, thousands at a time, stake in at the bottom and out at the mouth. He'd have done that, my father. But I don't think he should have been killed. I haven't got much money, Lord P-powerscourt, b-b-but I want you to find his killer. I want you to investigate his death for me.'

With that he let go of Powerscourt's arm and drifted off. Powerscourt and Inspector Blunden made their way out to the drive to pick up their carriage. When Edward and Henry reached the stables the only noise to be heard was Charles, crooning quietly to the horses.

6

The drive and the gate lodges were well behind them when Powerscourt began to tell the Inspector the reason for his reticence with the inhabitants of Candlesby Hall.

'I think there were two reasons, Inspector, for not showing our full hand at this stage. The first has to do with Dr Miller. I wouldn't put it past them to send out another bullying expedition to make him change his mind. I wouldn't want to put him through that again. He was shaking, literally shaking, when he told me what had happened about the death certificate. And the second reason is more diffuse. Assuming the doctor was telling the truth, and Charles Dymoke confirms some of it, we now know that they are all lying about what went on after Richard met Jack Hayward and they turned off the road into the stables. They don't know that I have talked to Dr Miller and if I had divulged any of that information about the three of them bullying the doctor, they would know immediately where it came from. There was only one other person present, apart from them, after all. So we know they lied about who talked to the doctor; we know from Charles that they have been lying about the manner of the old man's death. We don't know who looked at the body. So, I think we have a slight advantage from withholding the fact that I talked to the doctor, though what we do with it for the moment I'm not altogether sure. I do wish we knew what killed the old man; it must have been something pretty unusual.'

A brief message was passed to Inspector Blunden when they arrived back at the police station. His face fell as he read it.

'This is sad news, indeed, my lord,' he told Powerscourt. 'Dr Miller passed away this morning. Peaceful, they say it was, whatever that means.'

'I'll call at the house this afternoon,' said Powerscourt. 'He was brave at the end to tell us what really happened up at the Hall.'

'I'm under instruction to report back to the Chief Constable on our return, my lord. Thank God he's not here full time. He spends most of his working life making things impossible for the people up at headquarters in Lincoln. What should I tell him about the exhumation order? Do we try for it now or do we hold our fire? I think we have to get a coroner on side first.'

'I'm going to have to read up about exhumations,' said Powerscourt. 'If my memory serves me, the family of the person to be exhumed have to give their agreement. That could be tricky. You could say, Inspector, that we're reviewing our position at this stage. That should impress the Chief Constable, reviewing our position. Military people like him usually get mental images of troops being inspected on parade grounds, line after line of redcoats stretching to the far reaches of the drill square; you know what I mean.'

The Inspector smiled. 'I'll plant that thought, my lord, and we'll see what answer comes back.'

Powerscourt resolved to contact Lady Lucy as soon as he could. He thought he might try an encircling movement on the Chief Constable. He was pensive as he walked over to Dr Miller's house. Originally, he thought, there were three people who had seen the dead man's face, three people who knew how he had died. Now one of them was dead. Another wouldn't tell him the truth. And the third

70

had disappeared off the face of the earth. Then he realized something else. He thought it possible, but not likely, that Richard, now the Earl of Candlesby, had killed his father. It just seemed an incredibly roundabout way of doing it – though that, of course, could have been planned to throw people off the scent. But if he hadn't, then there was another person or persons who must have seen his face and his injuries before he died. The murderer or murderers. And Powerscourt had no idea at all who they might be or why they had killed him.

He was still wondering about what had happened to Candlesby's face when he reached the doctor's house. Mrs Baines opened the door.

'Oh, it's you, Lord Powerscourt. I expect you've heard the news.'

'I have indeed, Mrs Baines. I've come to pay my respects.'

'There's only a son left of his family now, and he's in Montana or one of those places in Australia. Or is it America? Five children the doctor had at one point, but four of them died. Doesn't seem fair, does it, four of them being taken.'

'Montana's in America, Mrs Baines. Full of cowboys with big hats. Could I ask you a question about the doctor's last hours?'

'Of course.'

'Did he have any visitors in the period after I left him?'

'Funny you should say that, Lord Powerscourt; he did as a matter of fact. A gentleman called on him yesterday evening but the doctor wasn't able to say anything sensible. I told the gentleman to come back in the morning but he said he could only manage the afternoon as he had business to attend to first thing.'

'Did he leave his name, or a card or anything like that?'

'No, he didn't, but I'd know him anywhere. He had a great shock of red hair.'

When she looked back on it after Powerscourt had gone she felt sure from the look on his face that he had known perfectly well who the mysterious visitor was. But like the visitor himself, he hadn't chosen to tell her.

Shortly after eleven o'clock the next morning a cab from the station deposited a visitor at Candlesby Hall. The newcomer took a quick glance at the front of the building and whistled softly to himself as if he had just worked out how much it would cost to repair. He was shown into the saloon where the new Earl was waiting to meet him. Another quick glance round the room seemed to add even greater sums to those already required outside.

'Sowerby, my lord, Mark Sowerby, partner in Hopkins Pettigrew & Green, solicitors of Bedford Square, at your service.'

'Sit down, do, Mr Sowerby. How kind of you to come so promptly. My father did a lot of business with your firm, I believe.'

'That is indeed the case, my lord, and how fortunate we were to secure his custom.'

Mark Sowerby had that indefinable look about him that says people come from London. Maybe it was the sharpness of his clothes, on the fringes rather than at the centre of fashion. Maybe it was the eyes, forever darting from one place to the next as if greater business or greater beauty was just around the corner. Maybe it was the restlessness, the shifting about as though anxious to be aboard the next train back to the capital. He had small rather mean eyes and a sharp nose.

'I told you in my letter, Mr Sowerby, about my father's death and the fact that we have had a Detective Inspector round here with a private investigator in tow.'

'You did indeed, my lord. Would you have a name for the investigating gentleman?'

'Powerscourt, Mr Sowerby, Lord Francis Powerscourt.'

Sowerby let out another of his low whistles. 'He's got a

very fine reputation, my lord, that Powerscourt. I wonder if we could pay him to go away.'

'I'm not sure what you mean, Mr Sowerby. Pay him to go away?'

'Sometimes, my lord,' Sowerby was now leaning forward in his best man-of-the-world manner, 'we find that if they are paid by us more than they have been promised by the other party, they drop the case. After the payment has been made, of course.'

Richard stared sadly at one of the holes in his carpet. 'I'm not sure that would work,' he said. 'I'll think about it.' He didn't like to tell the lawyer from London that he would find it difficult to lay his hands on sums large enough to change an investigator's mind.

'We're getting ahead of ourselves, my lord,' Sowerby was rubbing his hands together now, 'as often happens when lawyer and client strike up an immediate rapport. Now then,' he pulled a dark blue notebook from his breast pocket, 'why don't you tell me exactly what happened at the time of your father's death. It helps if we can begin with the truth. Then you can tell me what you told the police. Don't worry if they're not the same, my lord. That's usually why people call us in.'

Richard told him the truth first of all. He realized that he had given so many different accounts of what happened that morning that he wasn't sure what the truth was any more. Sowerby wrote it all down. Then Richard filled him in on what he had said to the police and to Powerscourt. He didn't mention what had happened to his father's face. He did tell him that the groom Jack Hayward who had brought the body up the road to the Hall had disappeared.

Sowerby stopped writing with a flourish of his pen, which he returned ostentatiously to his pocket.

'Good! Excellent, I'd say! Couple of points, my lord. Did the police and the investigating man ask if you had killed your father?'

Richard shook his head.

'Right, my lord.' Sowerby sounded like a man on home ground now, one who had handled many similar cases in his time. 'One or two things occur to me. The first has to do with your brothers. Something in the way you told their story makes me think you don't trust them very much. So, keep them away from the police at all costs. The second has to do with the man Hayward. Did you have anything to do with his disappearance, my lord? Don't worry, I shan't be upset and I'm certainly not going to the police.'

Richard remained silent.

'I'll take that for a yes, my lord. Never fear. Let me just say that if he is coming back, I think it's probably best if the date of return is a long time away. And I think you should check with us before you bring Hayward back again. Then there's the death certificate, which you said was false. Do you know if that doctor – Miller, did you say his name was? – told anybody else about what he saw?'

'I don't think so.'

'You don't suppose that the Powerscourt person might have got to him in the meantime, my lord?'

'I don't think it's likely. Anyway, the doctor died yesterday morning. He was very old. He can't cause any more trouble where he's gone.'

'No, indeed, my lord. Thank goodness for that!'

Sowerby took a brief inspection of his tattered surroundings once more. He wondered if his client had killed the doctor as he believed he had killed his father.

'There's just one thing I should mention, my lord. It shouldn't happen, but it's as well to be prepared.'

'What's that?'

'If Hayward spills the beans, or if Dr Miller did speak to somebody before he died, there'll be calls for an inquest and probably an exhumation; that's when they dig up the body and get a pathologist to examine it.' He noted the horror on Richard's face and couldn't work out whether it was caused by the unpleasantness of the exhumation or what it might reveal.

'I don't think we want to dig up the body, my lord, do we?' Richard shook his head. 'We've got people back in the office in Bedford Square who have stopped more exhumations and post-mortems than I've had fish suppers. All members of the family are supposed to agree for a start. That should stop proceedings once and for all. But if you hear anything about a pending exhumation, let us know at once. At once, I say. It could be crucial.'

'One question, Mr Sowerby, if I may. Do I have to speak to the police when they come, or can I simply refuse to talk to them?'

'For the present, my lord, I think you should see them.' Sowerby thought his client was worried about incriminating himself. 'If they really come at you time after time, trying to find inconsistencies in your story, then you can accuse them of harassment. And, of course, don't forget that you can call on me or one of my colleagues to come and sit in on the interviews. Won't do the police any harm to have to wait until we get here.'

As Sowerby was driven away he was observed from the stables by Charles, who had overheard the introductions up at the Hall. 'B-b-bloody lawyer,' he said softly to the nearest horse. 'I'll have to tell Lord P-p-powerscourt all about him.'

'So how is the Palace of Westminster these days?' Lady Lucy was entertaining her cousin's daughter Selina and her young man Sandy, who worked for *The Times*, to tea in Markham Square.

'I think it manages to rub along all right, Lady Powerscourt,' said the young man, sipping politely at his Earl Grey. 'It's never completely quiet, mind you, or else there would be nothing for me and my colleagues to write about.'

'I took Sandy shopping this morning, Aunt Lucy,' said Selina. 'I advised him on a couple of shirts.'

Lady Lucy was not at all sure of the propriety in polite society about young ladies advising young gentlemen on the purchase of clothes. At least it had been shirts. It could have been worse, much worse. Indeed, Lady Lucy, so relaxed with her own children, found the whole business of being an aunt rather difficult. She felt that she asked far too many questions about where the girl had been and with whom she had been consorting, but some of the young men hanging around the great London art galleries thought that rules were there to be broken and that manners only existed to be flouted.

Sandy looked rather embarrassed about the shirt-buying expedition. Not for the first time Lady Lucy wondered if Selina wasn't too forward, too pushy. She thought Sandy seemed to be quite a shy young man and might prefer a quieter sort of girl. She had mentioned this thought to her husband, who told her not to be ridiculous, that Sandy was perfectly capable of looking after his own interests and wouldn't continue his liaison with Selina if he didn't want to.

'I tell you something that will interest your husband as well as yourself, Lady Powerscourt.' She rather approved the addition of 'as well as yourself' to the sentence. It showed Sandy thought pretty fast.

'And what might that be?' she said, smiling.

'You remember the Earl who died up there in Lincolnshire the other day? The one whose death is being investigated by your husband?'

'The Earl of Candlesby,' said Lady Lucy, 'and what a strange way to go. Do you have any special information you'd like to pass on to my husband?'

'I think it's more interesting to me than it will be to him,' said Sandy, 'but let me tell you about it anyway. The old Earl, the dead one, he never set foot in the House of Lords in his life. There are backwoodsmen and backwoodsmen in that place if you follow me. Sometimes the Whips can drag some of them kicking and screaming down to the Palace of Westminster to vote in an important division. But the real backwoodsmen won't even do that. It's a mark of shame to them ever to go to London to vote at all. So they sit in their remote castles and their leaking houses until they die. My information concerns the new Earl, whose name is Richard.'

'And what does this Richard propose to do?' asked Selina, feeling that she had been left out of the conversation for too long.

'He's going to take his seat in the House of Lords as soon as he is allowed. And then he's going to join the fight against Lloyd George and his Budget. I've bored everybody rigid with my stories about the battle between the government and the House of Lords about this Budget, but the Conservatives in the Lords are delighted to have a new recruit and one who isn't too old. Youth is always at a premium in the House of Lords. You know, people who can stand up unaided, walk without sticks, eat with their own teeth, that sort of thing.'

'How do you know this, Sandy?' asked Lady Lucy.

'It's quite simple really. People sometimes think reporters are far smarter than they really are. I wrote to him, and he wrote back. That's all. He sounded very excited about joining the House of Lords.'

'You make it sound as if he was joining the Garrick Club or the Carlton or one of those places,' said Selina.

'I'm not sure there's that much difference, really – institutional smell of cooking and carbolic and floor polish, awful school food all round,' said Sandy. 'The House of Lords is very similar to the Garrick or the Carlton. Lots of old boys asleep in the library after lunch. Terrible hunting prints all over the walls.'

Lady Lucy was about to reply when the conversation was interrupted by a slight coughing noise at the door. It was Rhys, the Powerscourt butler, recently promoted to chauffeur in the Silver Ghost. Rhys always coughed before entering a room.

'Telegram, my lady,' he said, in a voice that might have been announcing the death of the sovereign.

'Need your help,' she read. 'Not often I ask this. Maybe first time. Could be record.' Do get on with it, Francis, she said to herself with a smile. 'Do you have any relations in south Lincolnshire? Preferably grand ones who know Earls etc. When found, please come to Candlesby Arms. New cook. Better food. Bring Ghost. Bring JF. Bring Rhys. Love, Francis.'

Translating this, Lucy realized the main thing her husband wanted, apart from herself and the car and Johnny Fitzgerald, was a way into county society in the area round Candlesby. Her relations, and distant bells were already ringing in her mind about a second cousin married to a baronet who lived in a manor house near Great Steeping, would not have to provide entertainment or any of the delights of society. Wittingly or unwittingly, their job would be to provide Lucy and her husband with murder suspects.

Inspector Blunden reported to Powerscourt the following morning that there was still no decision from the Chief Constable about applying for an exhumation. 'This is so typical of the man, my lord,' the Inspector reported. 'He'll have been sidetracked by some other crime somewhere else. I've heard there was a great robbery at the Bishop's Palace up in Lincoln in the past few days. He's probably showing himself off up there, getting in the way of the investigating officers, poking his way around in the private rooms and throwing his weight around with the Dean and Chapter. What I don't understand, my lord, is how he ever managed to win a battle. He couldn't have kept his concentration for long enough. He'd have wanted to bring the cavalry back before they'd even reached the front.'

Powerscourt smiled. 'You will remember, I'm sure, Inspector, the story of Nelson raising the telescope to his blind eye at the battle of Copenhagen so he couldn't read the signal that told him to end the fighting. He went on, as you know, to win the engagement. Battles are mostly won in spite of, rather than because of, the orders of the commanders. I seem to recall that the Chief Constable only fought one battle and he only won that because the natives ran away before a shot was fired.'

'To listen to him,' said the Inspector sourly, 'you'd think he'd been successful at Blenheim and Talavera and Gettysburg and one or two more. Only a day or so to go before the King invites him to have a triumph through the streets of London.'

'Are you going to hold off making inquiries until there is some definite news about the exhumation?'

'Yes and no, my lord. I'm not going to make any inquiries into a possible murder. But I am going to make inquiries into the disappearing Jack Hayward and his family. If we could find that man and talk to him properly we'd be a long way to solving the mystery, if you ask me.'

'Good luck in your inquiries, Inspector,' said Powerscourt. 'I'm just going on a fishing expedition to Horncastle. To see the editor and chief reporter of the *Horncastle Standard*. Maybe they can provide us with a couple of murder suspects.'

Powerscourt's first impression of James Roper, the editor of the *Horncastle Standard*, was that he had one of the longest beards he had ever seen. It was black and very thick and seemed to be an even more massive structure than the one sported by the earlier Prime Minister, Lord Salisbury. He looked to be in his middle forties with bloodshot eyes and a right hand almost permanently wrapped round a tumbler full of a pale brown liquid which Powerscourt presumed to be brandy.

'Care to join me?' he boomed, shaking Powerscourt vigorously by the hand. 'Medicinal, you know. Doctor man recommends brandy in small but regular doses. Never asked me when I start, mind you. He might think' – Roper checked a large clock on the wall – 'that ten to twelve is a little soon into the gallops. Never mind. Let me introduce young Rufus here, our chief reporter, Rufus Kershaw.'

Rufus was certainly young. Powerscourt didn't think this slip of a lad could be more than twenty-five, his slim features, lack of a beard and clear brown eyes a mighty contrast to his superior.

'Please don't look at me like that, Lord Powerscourt,' the young man said with a smile. 'I am nearly twenty-six years old, you know. And I have been a reporter on this paper for the past nine years. That's a very long time, nine years. And it's amazing how much more people will tell me because they think they're only talking to a boy.'

'Now then, my lord,' Roper was refilling his glass with great care from an enormous decanter, 'may I ask what is the purpose of your visit here?'

'It is very simple,' said Powerscourt, 'but could I ask first of all that our conversation is off the record for now? It may be that the position will change over time – we shall see. Let me explain what brings me to Lincolnshire. I have been asked to look into the death of the last Lord Candlesby. Sorry to sound obstructive but are you gentlemen happy to be off the record for the present?'

There was a short glance and a quick nod between the newspapermen.

'We have a story about that affair ready to appear in our next edition tomorrow,' said Roper. 'Young Rufus here had better tell you about it; he wrote the story after all. And assume that we are all off the record.'

'I had heard you were here, my lord,' said Rufus. 'I

bumped into one of Inspector Blunden's men on the way to interview one of the hunt officials. I think they told me more than they told him, mind you, seeing I've talked to most of them a couple of times or more in the past few years.'

Powerscourt felt his card was being marked, very delicately, but marked all the same. He smiled at the young man.

'Did you draw any conclusions from your interviews, Mr Kershaw? Anything firm? Anything meaningful?'

'My very first boss, my lord, was forever asking if certain stories would make "a meaningful piece",' the young man said. 'It makes me smile to this day to think of the phrase.' He paused for a moment and whipped a notebook out of his pocket. 'I think it's all very clear, this story, up to a certain point. There's the hunt milling around the front of Candlesby Hall. There are the servants handing round the stirrup cup, little conversations full of hope for the new hunting season. The Master is late but the Master is often late. It is cold and the breath of horses and hunters is making vapour trails in the air.'

Powerscourt wondered if the last phrase would get past the sub-editor's pen.

'So far, so good. Then the picture grows dimmer. There is a horse, led by the chief groom, Jack Hayward, with a body across it. The body is covered with a couple of blankets. Quite soon, I don't yet know how soon, everybody gathers that the corpse is that of the Master of the Hunt and Earl of Candlesby. The death party turn off into the stables. Beyond that nothing is clear. The doctor is summoned. Jack Hayward and his family disappear the next day or the day after. Various outsiders begin to appear: yourself, my lord, the Chief Constable, a shady legal gentleman from a firm of solicitors in Bedford Square. The cabbie who drove him from the station to the Hall told me that, my lord. Man gave the cabbie his card in case he ever needed the best legal advice. Silly man! Most of the local cabbies go to Campbell

Moreton & Marsh in the High Street here. Cheaper than Bedford Square, I'm sure.'

'Does your article come to any conclusions, Mr Kershaw?' Powerscourt observed out of the corner of his eye that a giant's refill was being poured very carefully into the editor's glass.

'Please call me Rufus,' said the young man. 'I feel very old if you call me Mr Kershaw. No, I most certainly did not come to any conclusions for the simple reason that I didn't have any. I still don't have any. Do you, my lord? Have any conclusions, I mean?'

'No, I haven't,' said Powerscourt. 'May I ask you, were you aware that Dr Miller, the doctor in attendance on the dead man, is also dead? Mind you, he was very old.'

'Do you think there was anything suspicious about his demise?' So far the editor's brain seemed untouched by his brandy intake.

'I don't think so,' said Powerscourt, 'but let me try to move our conversation in a slightly different direction, if I may. I have been asked to investigate the death of the late Lord Candlesby. The person who asked me is certain it was murder. Therefore, I ask myself, is there anything in the man's past that could have led to his death? So I come to ask you gentlemen for your advice and counsel.'

Rufus Kershaw wrote something very suddenly in his book. The editor lifted his gaze from his decanter to Powerscourt's face.

'Now I see, Lord Powerscourt, now I see what you have come for. Well, I'm sure we can give you a few clues. Rufus, could you begin with the most recent story that might be relevant?'

'Yes, sir. I presume you are referring to the suicide of Lady Flavia Melville last summer. This, my lord, was a most frustrating story. You may think it is difficult to find out the truth about the body that joins the hunt. Well, it was even more difficult with this one. There is, I think, one

82

rule that used to hold but no longer does. Its day may have passed already, I don't know. Certainly I don't think it'll last another ten years. And this rule is that servants don't talk. They may talk to the police in confidence but they won't appear in court in case they lose their job or their house or their farm or all three together. In the Lady Melville case they must have said something but who it was or to whom it was said we still don't know. I have to tell you, my lord, that I am trying my hand at fictional short stories. I have had two published so far in *The Strand Magazine* and I hope for further success in the future. But I firmly believe that my account of the Lady Melville affair still owes more to fiction than to fact.'

'Bestir yourself with the bloody story, Rufus,' growled his editor. 'Some of us have to go to press later on.'

'Sorry, sir,' said the young man. He paused for a moment or two before he resumed. 'Not far from here, between Candlesby Hall and the coast at Skegness, lies the estate of Sir Arthur Melville, Baronet, with a fine Elizabethan manor house and many thousands of acres. Last summer he would have been fifty-seven years old. They say, how shall I put it, my lord, that he was never at the top of the class, Sir Arthur. He spent many years in the military before rising to the rank of captain, but beyond that, he never progressed. Anyway, back to this fairy story mansion of his. Last Easter he brought a bride home at last, a widow in her early thirties called Mrs Flavia von Humboldt, previously married to a German philosophy professor in Tübingen who dropped down dead in the university library next to the complete works of Aristotle. History does not recall what kind of existence she led in the confines of her German university – Kant and Nietzsche for lunch perhaps and Hobbes and Locke for supper – but it cannot have been proper preparation for life in Lincolnshire. She grew bored. Her eyes began to stray. Perhaps the fifty-seven-year-old was equally ill equipped for married life on England's east coast. After all, the hill station and the club and the punkah wallah do not translate happily to Lincolnshire. Anyway Flavia began a passionate affair with Lord Candlesby. They did not seem to care who knew. Discretion went out of the window along with common sense. The husband did not know. He thought they were riding together or inspecting horses when they were, in fact, engaged on other, rather more private recreations. All through the summer it went on, and into the autumn.

'They forgot one thing, the lovers, or they ignored it, and it probably did for them in the end. Because of her married name, von Humboldt, the locals thought she was German. Well might she tell all and sundry that she was christened Flavia Witherspoon in Margate, they didn't believe her. People on this side of the country, my lord, are even more hostile to the Germans than they would be in Cornwall or the south-west.'

'Why is that?' asked Powerscourt.

'Closer, that's why. I mean the Germans are closer. They could reach Skegness a damn sight quicker than they could invade Weston Super Mare. Anyway, the precise timetable gets a bit vague at this point but the sequence of events seems to go as follows. One day somebody sends Flavia copies of half the love letters she's ever written to John, Lord Candlesby. The next day they send him copies of half the letters he's sent to her. People say she was distraught and that Lord Candlesby told her to keep calm. Nothing happened in the letter-sending department on the third day. But on the fourth day the somebody, presumably the same somebody, probably a servant, sends all the love letters, all hers to him, all his to her, to Sir Arthur. They were timed to coincide with breakfast. It was said Sir Arthur swept a whole sideboard of dishes on to the floor in one single movement – kidneys, eggs, bacon, mushrooms, tomatoes, black pudding, fried bread, kedgeree, kippers, all felled by a baronet's fury. When she tried to apologize he told her that he was going to ruin her reputation by dragging her through the divorce courts. Even an Indian untouchable, he shouted at her, wouldn't go near her when he'd finished with her. Then he shouted some more insults after her – no better than a Whitechapel whore, Jack the Ripper too good for her, that sort of stuff. Sometime that afternoon she took an overdose of her husband's sleeping pills. She knew where they were. Then she walked into the sea. Her body was washed up weeks later near Hunstanton. Poor Sir Arthur! Married, cuckolded and widowed inside a year. People say that he blames Lord Candlesby for everything, leading his wife astray, disgracing her till she had to commit suicide. Sometimes, it is reported, but I have no means of knowing if it's true, he can be heard late at night in his cups, shouting from his balustrade that he'll kill that Candlesby one of these days, you see if he doesn't.'

'What a terrible story,' said Powerscourt. 'Is he still drinking a lot, poor man?'

'He is, I believe,' said James Roper, senior representative present of the drinking fraternity, 'but you can certainly see why Sir Arthur might want to kill the Earl. Now then, young Rufus, do you want to tell the duel story, or shall I?'

'Duels?' said Powerscourt. 'I thought they'd gone out years ago with Canning and Castlereagh in the 1820s.'

'Nothing ever goes out, as you put it, up here in Lincolnshire. This is the land time forgot. You know about la France Profonde, Lord Powerscourt? This is l'Angleterre Profonde, up here with the winds and the sand and the cold fury of the North Sea. Let me tell the duel story; it'll be a lot shorter than the first one.'

7

Lady Lucy Powerscourt was being driven north to the flatlands of Lincolnshire. Rhys, the Powerscourt butler and chauffeur, was driving as well as he always did, with no fuss but reaching quite remarkable speeds. Lady Lucy remembered him telling her recently that this car was just the latest form of transport he had driven. He had experienced every form of horse-drawn vehicle, from flies to broughams, known to man, camels in the deserts of Arabia, miserable animals in Rhys's view, an elephant in northern India, a paddle steamer on the Mississippi. None of them, he maintained, could hold a candle to the Silver Ghost, a car of such restrained power it was as if you had your very own four-in-hand waiting under the bonnet to sweep you on to ever greater speeds.

Lady Lucy had fulfilled the instructions in Powerscourt's telegram. With great difficulty, and the promise of two expensive lunches on her return to town, she had located an aunt, an aunt at a number of removes it had to be said, but an aunt nonetheless. This aunt, of unknown age, though Lady Lucy thought she must be well over seventy, lived at a place called Ashby Hall, in Ashby Puerorum not far from Candlesby in the Silver Ghost. Lady Lucy had already despatched a letter saying that she proposed to call, and to bring her consort with her. At least the aunt could look forward to inspecting Lady Lucy's husband, whom she had never met. Indeed, Lady Lucy had some difficulty working out if the elderly aunt had ever met her either.

When she thought of her husband now, she felt rather concerned about his future. For as long as she had known him, her Francis had been involved in solving murders and mysteries of every sort: frauds in the art market, blackmail in the royal family, murder in an Inn of Court. There had been danger, one occasion indeed when he had been knocking quite loudly at death's door and promised to stop investigating afterwards until Lucy agreed to absolve him from his promise. Then he had gone to St Petersburg, where she felt certain he had never told her how dangerous his adventures had been. Always, in all these cases, she knew but had never mentioned it, there was, for Francis, an element of a game, maybe a variant of the Great Game he had played out in India with the Russians. Solving the murder was like solving a puzzle or cracking a code. But it was no preparation for the secret work he had been asked to do in the past year or so by the government. This, Lady Lucy realized very quickly from watching her husband, was completely different. Murders, even when they crossed the path of the Tsar of Russia, usually involved one family or one extended family. Working for the authorities, as Francis always referred to his government employers, meant working for the whole country, millions and millions of people. Make a mistake in a murder inquiry and the wrong person might be convicted for the crime; make a mistake on government business and you could jeopardize the future security of your fellow countrymen. Francis said very little about his opponents, presumably investigators and policemen turned into spics by the other great powers, but Lady Lucy thought that on a number of occasions he had been as close to being frightened as she had ever seen him. These people take no prisoners, he had said to her once; they'd throw you over the side of the ship and leave you for the fishes without a second's thought. And somehow, though Lady Lucy didn't know how she knew it, they were going to come for him again, the authorities, and pressgang him into service once more for the good of his country. With all her heart she prayed the tocsin would not sound too soon.

James Roper topped up his glass and inspected his little audience.

'By the middle of the last century,' he began, 'duelling had more or less disappeared. I've often wondered if it didn't have to do with the decline in traditional values associated with owning land and the military and men of honour. It's hard to imagine a couple of cotton manufacturers in Lancashire fighting a duel if one fellow said the other's produce was a load of rubbish. They might try to put their opponent out of business, but it's almost impossible to think of them squaring up to each other by the waste ground at the back of the mill first thing in the morning. But here,' Roper waved his hands in the air for a moment, 'well, this is Lincolnshire. Old values may last longer here. Or perhaps the locals don't know any better.'

Rufus Kershaw restrained himself with difficulty from suggesting to his superior that he hurry on with the story. The message seemed to get through anyway.

'As far as we know, the last Lord Candlesby never served in the military. There was no tradition of it in the family. There was, however, a tradition of horse breeding and horse racing that went back a long way. I believe there are a couple of Stubbses from centuries past gathering dust on the walls of the big house in the usual way. For this incident, we must be talking thirty or forty years ago, maybe even more.'

Roper paused for a moment and stared deep into his brandy decanter as if some magical properties were contained within, or a djinn might be about to pop out of it. 'They say he always had a good eye for a horse, the late Earl. And he liked riding them himself, even though he might have done better with a professional jockey. One day, years ago, he was riding his own horse called Romulus in a race down at Fakenham. Odds of twelve to one. Candlesby wins all right but he has to give his horse a terrible whipping to get past a horse called WG who came second. This is where the trouble started.' Roper took a long draught of his medicine and carried on. 'WG's owner, not, alas, the great cricketer, but a respectable local farmer called Bell, told Candlesby in front of the crowd that he had broken all the moral rules of racing by whipping his horse like that. It was reported that blood was dripping from the animal's flanks in the winner's enclosure. It wasn't worthy of a gentleman, the farmer said. Now, of course, there's nothing more likely to arouse an Earl than to be told he's not a gentleman. There's not much else they can lay claim to these days after all. "Are you saying I'm not a gentleman?" asks Candlesby. "I most certainly am," says Farmer Bell. "Pistols or swords?" says Candlesby. "Pistols," says the farmer, who isn't quite sure what's going on. The next morning, very early, they meet by arrangement at a clearing by the river. The farmer fires wide on purpose. Candlesby shoots Bell through the heart and the farmer is pronounced dead within minutes.

'He had a son, the farmer, a little boy called Oliver,' James Roper was virtually whispering now, 'believed to be two or three years old at the time of the duel. His mother married again and the new family went out to Australia. Oliver joined the British Army and served for over twenty years.'

'Do we know where he is now, this Oliver?' Powerscourt thought something terrible was coming.

'Oliver Bell? He's back here now,' said Roper. 'He's taken a little house near Old Bolingbroke Castle not far from here.'

'And there's something else,' Roper went on. 'They say he trained as a marksman when he was with the military. They say he was one of the best shots in the British Army.'

'I see,' said Powerscourt, still unsure how Lord Candlesby died. Could it have been through multiple gunshot wounds?

He didn't think so but at this stage you couldn't rule it out. You couldn't rule anything out. 'I mustn't trouble you much longer, gentlemen. Do you have any more runners and riders in the Candlesby Murder Stakes?'

'This last one is my suggestion,' said Rufus Kershaw. 'I came across the details of it some time ago. I'll be brief, my lord. Many years ago the great contractors were bringing the railway through this county. If the line ran through your land you could become very rich. Not quite as rich as you would with high quality coal, but pretty good all the same. Rapallo or San Remo for your Riviera villa, maybe, rather than the more expensive Cannes or Monte Carlo. The estate next to Candlesby's was owned by a family called Lawrence who had lived in Lawrence House for hundreds of years. They were sure they had won the contract, these Lawrences. Surveyors and people with strange instruments had been wandering all over their land for weeks. Lawyers were discussing the finer points of the financial settlement and compensation for the disruption during construction, that sort of thing. Then at the very last moment, the Lawrences lost the contract. Candlesby got it instead, whether by bribery or blackmail or intimidation nobody knows. To this day the Lawrences have complained about it. For decades they've been telling anybody who would listen that they were robbed by Lord Candlesby. It's not fair, they say. He should never have been allowed to get away with it. There should be a law against this sort of thing. On and on they've gone for over thirty years about how they were cheated out of tens and tens of thousands of pounds.'

'I don't suppose you see our paper and the other local papers down there in London, my lord.' Roper tossed back the remains of his tumbler and waved his hand airily towards a glass-fronted bookcase which contained bound copies of his newspaper. 'If you had, you would have seen a series of advertisements over recent months. They were for the sale of the entire Lawrence estate, including the house and all its outbuildings.

'That auction was three weeks ago. The property was sold for just over half of what was asked for it. We have known for years in these parts of the extent and scale of the decline in our agriculture: falling rents, falling income from produce, falling prices for agriculture-related property. This is the worst we have seen since things began to go wrong.'

'They have a new tune now, of course, these Lawrences,' Rufus Kershaw went on. 'If they hadn't been cheated out of the railway money, they wouldn't have lost their estate and their house. Let's all feel sorry for the Lawrences! Death to the new Lord Candlesby!'

Powerscourt wondered if a great loss all those years ago could lead to murder now. 'There's just one last thing to do with this story,' said Rufus. 'The old boy, the old Mr Lawrence, the one who lost the railway deal, has not been well recently. When the price was so low at the auction he took to his bed and died two days later. He was over ninety years old, mind you. You won't be surprised to hear his descendants blame the Candlesbys for his death. If he hadn't been cheated out of the railway money, they claim, he wouldn't have had to sell up and deprive his descendants of what should have been their rightful inheritance.'

'I am very grateful to you gentlemen,' said Powerscourt, smiling at the two journalists. 'You have been most generous with your time. And what a splendid gallery of suspects!'

Rufus Kershaw smiled rather grimly back. 'As we said, my lord, as we said. This is Lincolnshire.'

Richard, the new Lord Candlesby, peered down the long corridor that led to the library in his great house. The corridor was empty. He closed the door. He locked it. Then he began to pace up and down. The Candlesby library had not escaped the general decay eating away at the fabric of the building. One bay where the books were stored had the wallpaper peeling off the walls. Damp had penetrated the bindings of some of the older leather-bound volumes and reached the pages where unauthorized water marks told of the steady advance of the rain that came in through the hole in the roof.

Richard stopped suddenly three-quarters of the way up the room. There was a scurrying noise as if a battalion of mice or rats were on the march in the wainscoting. He coughed. Then he took a deep breath. 'My lords,' he began in rather a hesitant fashion. That's no good, he said to himself, I sound as if I'm applying to clean the windows or perform some menial task. He tried again. 'My lords,' he said and paused again. Surely that was too loud. He hadn't come to shout at these people or to tell them off. A third time. Confident, but slightly reverential, he told himself. That should surely suffice.

The new Earl had hidden himself away in the library to practise his maiden speech in the House of Lords. Only that morning a letter had arrived suggesting he get in touch with some official or other to fix a date for his installation. Neither of his two younger brothers had ever seen him in the library. Indeed Edward wasn't exactly sure where it was. Richard made his way to a section labelled 'History' at the far end of the room, looking out across the overgrown vegetable garden. Some of these modern books, he remembered, must have come with a young tutor fresh down from Oxford who had been hired to improve their minds some years ago. Nobody paid any attention to his lessons. The three brothers talked all the way through at the top of their voices. If asked to do some homework, on the changes effected by Henry the Eighth for instance, they would write detailed queries about the various places and positions in which the King had enjoyed his wives and mistresses. If the tutor tried to have a peaceful walk through the woods on the estate, they would taunt him from their horses. If he went for a swim in the lake they would make off with his clothes. In the end, he cracked and fled to the sanctuary of a girls' school where he hoped – in vain as it happened – that the behaviour might be better and the quest for learning not totally extinguished.

Richard tried, and failed, to remember the tutor's name. He plucked out a book by a man called Edmund Burke. Dimly, he recalled the tutor prattling on about this fellow. He opened a page at random, looking for a quotation to embellish his first oration in the Palace of Westminster.

'All government, indeed every human benefit and enjoyment, every virtue and every prudent act, is founded on compromise and barter.'

That's all very well, the new Earl said to himself, but I'm not in favour of compromise and barter at this time. Total, uncompromising, unyielding opposition to Lloyd George's Budget, that was his policy. No room there for compromise and barter, no sir.

He moved along the shelf. Disraeli, he saw. He recalled his grandfather talking endlessly about Disraeli. Maybe he'd be better than that Burke chap. Then he noticed that Disraeli had written some novels. That put a black mark against him in Richard's book. Men should not write such things. If they had to be written, surely it was a job for a woman. Far better that they should not be written at all.

'His temper, naturally morose,' Richard read, 'has become licentiously peevish. Crossed in his Cabinet, he insults the House of Lords and plagues the most eminent of his colleagues with the crabbed malice of a maundering witch.' Richard wasn't altogether sure what maundering meant, but it was clear that this Disraeli was a good man for invective. The original target of his bile, apparently, was a Lord Aberdeen but Richard wondered if he couldn't use it against Lloyd George. He wrote Disraeli's words down in his book.

Gladstone, he spotted next. The grandfather who talked about Disraeli had also talked about Gladstone. Some ancient memory stirred in Richard's mind. Something told him Gladstone and Disraeli had not been the best of friends.

'It is upon those who say', he read, 'that it is necessary to exclude forty-nine fiftieths of the working classes from the vote to show cause, and I venture to say that every man who is not presumably incapacitated by some consideration of personal unfitness or of political danger, is morally entitled to come within the pale of the Constitution.'

Richard read it once. Then he read it again. Then he began to get angry. This was worse than bloody Lloyd George. This was like some demented person from the Labour Party who had recently arrived in Parliament. He remembered seeing a photograph in one of the magazines of a disagreeable-looking Socialist with a very vulgar moustache called Ramsay Madconald. This sounded like his sort of thinking. Hold on a minute, though, Richard said to himself. This Gladstone was a Liberal, not some bearded revolutionary from the trade union movement or the rougher parts of Scotland. He read the passage again. Within the pale of the Constitution. Votes for everybody, that's what the man was saying. Votes for the junior footmen. Votes for the laundrymaids. Votes for the under gardeners. Votes for the parlourmaids. It was monstrous. Richard leaned forward and tried to open a window. It was a long time since it had been opened. At last he succeeded. He seized the Gladstone book in his right hand and hurled it with all his force into the wilderness that had once been a vegetable garden. It landed next to the spot where the cabbages had formerly met the runner beans. Quite soon the greenery swallowed Gladstone up and he returned to the natural state he had left so long ago.

Richard was delighted with the demise of the former Prime Minister. He didn't think their lordships would approve if he were to hurl some volume of Lloyd George's speeches across the Chamber. But he began pacing up and down once more. After half an hour he reached the end of his first sentence. He felt rather pleased with himself. He'd got off to a good start.

Johnny Fitzgerald had a secret. He hadn't told anybody about it, not even his closest friend, Powerscourt. He felt rather embarrassed by the whole thing. The truth was, that unlike all members of the Powerscourt tribe who had travelled in the Silver Ghost, Johnny didn't like motor cars at all. They made him nervous. When they raced along a stretch of good road at considerable speed he was actually frightened. This, from a man who had fought with conspicuous bravery in all his many battles. When the Ghost whispered its way along the crowded streets of London, Johnny always thought they were going to crash or run over some innocent pedestrian. There was more. There was worse. The very motion of the Ghost made him feel sick. After half an hour of driving he would begin to feel uneasy, queasy, rather like, he thought, the sensation people described when they spoke of seasickness. Johnny had sailed thousands of miles back and forth from England to India and had never once been seasick.

So he had travelled to Lincolnshire by train. But now, as his cab carried him towards the Candlesby Arms, he knew that he would keep his secret as long as he could.

He found Powerscourt and Lady Lucy having an earnest discussion in the private sitting room Drake had prepared for them. They were discussing a visit to a place called Ashby Puerorum.

'Johnny!' said Powerscourt, rising to greet his friend. 'How very good to see you! How very good to have you on board for this case!'

'Always glad to be of service,' said Johnny, bowing low to his superior officer. 'What can I do for the cause?'

Powerscourt told him all the details of the case, the strange brothers, the rotting house, the mystery of the death of the previous Earl.

95

'Do you have no idea at all how he died, Francis? Forgive me for saying such a thing, Lady Lucy, but we have seen one or two dead bodies in our time.'

'No idea at all,' said Powerscourt sadly. 'But you will be pleased to hear, Johnny, that I have a special job I would like you to do.'

Johnny Fitzgerald groaned slightly. 'And what would that be, my friend?'

'This man Hayward,' Powerscourt began.

'The one who escorted the body back on the horse?'

'The very same, Johnny. Got it in one.'

Suddenly Johnny Fitzgerald knew what was coming. 'You want me to find him. Is that it?'

Powerscourt nodded. Johnny Fitzgerald rose and began pacing round the room. 'Why do I always get the really easy jobs, Francis? You know, drinking all night with the porters from the art galleries in Old Bond Street, rescuing Lady Lucy here from drowning in Compton Cathedral, travelling all the way to bloody Beaune in bloody Burgundy only to be sent straight back again on the next train? Life's too soft with you, Francis, I've always thought so.'

Powerscourt waited for the irony to subside. 'Have you managed to find out anything about the family?' asked Johnny. 'Where he came from originally? Where the wife came from?'

'I hate to heap more problems on your already overburdened shoulders, Johnny, but they're not exactly helpful in the village over there. They won't speak to me at all. I was hoping to ask Charles, the son who's on our side, to make some inquiries. Come to think of it, I have to go and see him about now. He sent me a note this morning.'

As Powerscourt set off for the Hall, Johnny turned to Lady Lucy. 'I need to do some serious thinking, Lady Lucy,' he said. 'Isn't it strange how suddenly thirst can strike a man. Maybe it's the flat countryside all around here and the tang of the salt from the sea that does it. Lead me to the bar and the brain can get lubricated into action.'

Charles was waiting for him at the stables where they had met before, talking earnestly to a dark brown horse with soulful eyes. Powerscourt noticed that his stammer virtually disappeared when he was talking to animals. Maybe it was only humans who interrupted his letters.

'Lord P-p-powerscourt, how kind of you to call,' he began. 'The others have all gone out, frightening what little wildlife there is in these p-p-parts on their horses. I much p-p-prefer the horses when they're in their stalls and you can have a decent conversation with them, don't you?'

'Is this one your favourite?' asked Powerscourt.

'This is Gladiator,' said Charles. 'Actually he's the sixth or seventh Gladiator we've had here. The first one won a lot of famous races over a hundred years ago, the Oaks, the St Leger, that sort of thing. There's a p-p-painting of him by that fellow Stubbs in the library. One of my ancestors almost b-b-bankrupted the estate dealing in horseflesh. But come, Lord P-powerscourt, I have things to tell you. And I can show you the house as my b-b-brothers are away.'

They set off up the path towards the great house. Charles pointed a long slim finger out across the lake. 'That's the death vault, the mausoleum thing over there,' he said. 'All the dead are locked up in there. Do you know, they've each got a sort of shelf to lie on in their coffin. It's like one of those very organized libraries, like the B-b-bodleian in Oxford. P-p-pull out a shelf and there's a load of b-b-books. P-p-pull out a shelf here and there's a corpse in its coffin.'

The young man looked wistful suddenly. Powerscourt wondered if he was thinking of his own parents lying in their allotted position in Hawksmoor's marble, waiting for the Last Trump.

'I thought of going into the Church once, you know, Lord P-p-powerscourt. I thought about it quite seriously. I always thought I'd have liked the Communion Service. Raising the host high above the altar. That sense of expectation you get at Communion. Loads of incense. Richly coloured vestments, p-p-purple if I ever got as far as b-b-bishop.'

'What made you change your mind?' asked Powerscourt.

'I was never quite sure I b-b-believed it enough, if you know what I mean. I used to have this dream of finishing a theology exam in Oxford one hot day in the summer term and a very old cleric with a vast b-b-beard collecting my p-p-papers and saying, "You don't really b-b-believe any of this nonsense, do you?" I always woke up b-b-before I could give an answer.'

They were now in the entrance to the Hall, a rather dark place in the basement lined with animal heads that had once grazed in the Candlesby grounds. 'There used to be a p-p-proper way in,' Charles told him, 'p-p-pillars, a hall with high ceilings, family p-p-portraits, usually on horses, lining the walls. This entrance looks as though it was designed for the coal merchant or the man who comes to clean the chimneys. It's too common for words.'

'Why was it changed?' asked Powerscourt.

'If your ancestors were as mad as mine,' said Charles sadly, 'anything was p-p-possible. They could have put the kitchen on the roof or turned the house into a zoo. Small stuffed animals, b-b-birds in glass boxes, antlers, the whole cornucopia of dead creatures has always had a great appeal to my family. They must all have b-b-been deer or red kites or tawny eagles in a p-p-previous existence.'

Charles led him round the house, pausing every now and again to point out some truly monumental piece of taxidermy or a picture where one of Gladiator's ancestors could just be glimpsed through the accumulated grime on the surface of the painting.

Powerscourt found himself in a strange world he would

never forget. In his youth he had seen houses in Ireland where decay was taking over as the family income grew less and less and was eaten up by mortgages and jointures. But he had never encountered anything as bad as this. Here the paint was flaking off the ceilings, long strips of wallpaper hung off the walls. There was dry rot in the floorboards. Sections of rotting plaster had dropped from ceiling to floor and disintegrated into yet more dust. Lady Lucy was to point out when he went back to the hotel that his hair was turning white in places. There were antlers on the walls whose heads were falling off, one-eyed owls, foxes with no tails. One of the previous Earls had collected animals of all descriptions and these were rotting away in glass cases that lay about in most of the downstairs rooms. And Charles told Powerscourt about the Wicked Earl, who had gone on the Grand Tour and collected some of the bloodier and more sadistic Caravaggios.

Time had stopped a long time before in Candlesby Hall. There was no electricity, no telephone, no motor car, no central heating, none of the conveniences associated with the modernity of 1909. If the Industrial Revolution had never touched great swathes of Lincolnshire, it had never even whispered its name in Candlesby Hall. Powerscourt thought the range in the kitchen might have been in use at the time of the French Revolution. The vicar in the next parish, an amateur historian of the medieval period, told him that the late Earl and his family were living in the seventeenth, or possibly the eighteenth century.

It was a week before Powerscourt realized one of the strangest things of all about this strange house. All the servants, with four exceptions, were male. And the only women on the staff were all over fifty.

PART TWO

THE SPECIAL TRAIN

An English peer of very old title is desirous of marrying at once a very wealthy lady ... If among your clients you know such a lady who is willing to purchase the rank of a peeress for £65,000 sterling, paid in cash to her future husband and who has sufficient wealth besides to keep up the rank of a peeress, I should be pleased if you would communicate with me.

Daily Telegraph, 1901.
Advert aimed at transatlantic market.

8

Johnny Fitzgerald stared at his full glass of beer for a long time. Lady Lucy had gone off to write to her children and would join him later. Johnny had spent a lot of time in his career with Powerscourt looking for people who had gone missing. Quite often they turned out to be dead. On at least two occasions they had turned out to be murderers. Only once, to the best of his knowledge, had he failed and he had always consoled himself with the thought that the individual concerned had gone missing on a ship and had probably fallen or been pushed over the side.

Still he did not try his beer. Reviewing the little he knew about the disappearance of Jack Hayward, Johnny tried to work out the circumstances of his departure. The reason was clear enough. Either the Candlesbys wanted him out of the way or he had decided to take himself out of trouble for a while. And he had decided not to leave his wife or his children behind as possible hostages. But which was it? Surely he would not have taken his wife and children into the unknown, some destination with no house for them to live in and no job for him to keep the family going. Would a man like Jack Hayward have contacts of his own he could mobilize to provide hearth and home at a moment's notice? Would his relations, not to put too fine a point on it, have the spare room or rooms to accommodate the Hayward ménage? And not just for a day, but for a week or a month or even longer? Johnny toyed with the idea of advertising for knowledge of Hayward's whereabouts in *The Field* or *Horse and Hound* or *Country Life*, maybe all three. He could pretend to be a solicitor looking for Hayward to hand over an inheritance, maybe even a bequest from the late Earl though Johnny wasn't sure the late Earl would have been in the business of leaving small bequests to his servants, however valuable they were.

What about the other option, that the new Earl had persuaded or bribed him to leave? How much would it cost to keep and to house a family of four for an indefinite period of time? Or had there been a job he could go to? Had some friend or relation said to the late Earl that if he ever wanted to get rid of that groom of his, he, the friend or relation, would happily give him a job? Maybe one of the late Earl's racing contacts would be happy to take in Hayward. Such people, Johnny said to himself, often have spare cottages at their disposal for extra stable staff or visiting jockeys. Or maybe it was a relation. Powerscourt hadn't said anything about relations, probably because he didn't know.

One thing was certain. Jack Hayward knew more about the murder than anybody else alive except the murderer. He knew, or he had been told, where to find the body. He might have even known the person who told him. He knew what the injuries were. He had probably heard some of the bullying as the doctor was persuaded to sign the false death certificate.

Johnny came back to where he had started. He could only think of two reasons for flight. One, that Jack was an honest man who did not wish to have to compromise his employer with the police. The other, that Richard Candlesby had bundled him off as fast as he could in case he told the truth. Had the son killed the father? Johnny didn't know. As he took the first sip of his beer he reflected bitterly that words like needle and haystack were totally inadequate. Grain of sand, Johnny thought, grain of sand in the bloody Sahara

Desert, all three and a half million square miles of it. He took another, larger draught.

Charles Dymoke drew two chairs up to the window in the dining room, looking out over the park to the lake and its island. Powerscourt could hear a burrowing, scratching sound inside the wall to his left. The mice or the rats were continuing their lifelong assault on the fabric of the house.

'I thought there was something you ought to know, Lord P-p-powerscourt,' said Charles, going slightly red in the face as he struggled with his stammer. 'A lawyer from London came to see Richard yesterday. Shifty sort of chap if you ask me. I caught his name as he came in. Mark Sowerby, of Hopkins P-p-pettigrew & Green, Solicitors of B-b-bedford Square.'

'He's not the normal family solicitor then?' said Powerscourt.

'No, no,' said Charles, 'they come from Lincoln and they're all about as old as the cathedral.'

'Did he come of his own accord? Or was he invited?'

'I think he was invited. Something was said about him working for my father. How can I p-put it? If your house was full of a terrible smell, Sowerby looked like the man who would come to fix it.'

'I see,' said Powerscourt, watching a herd of deer trotting peacefully towards the clump of trees beside the lake. 'I wonder what he came for.'

'There's something else I should tell you. I've been speaking to some of the servants. The night my father died, they say, somebody was heard coming back into the house about midnight, or a little earlier.'

'Were they indeed?' said Powerscourt. 'How interesting. I don't suppose anybody knows who it was?'

'Afraid not, my lord. Could have been anybody.'

'They didn't hear any other noises as well? Horses' hooves, that kind of thing?'

'Not as far as I know,' said Charles, wondering if he had discovered his true profession at last as a detective. Maybe Powerscourt could give him lessons. 'One last thing,' he went on, 'I nearly forgot. Jack Hayward, the groom who found the b-b-body, left in the dark when nobody could see him. A neighbour said hello to him about four in the afternoon; next morning the house was b-b-boarded up.'

'Well done, young man,' said Powerscourt. 'Do the village people speak to you then? They wouldn't speak to me at all.'

'Some of them do,' said Charles. 'Would you like me to see what I can find out down there?'

'Yes please,' said Powerscourt. 'That would be most helpful. I'm very grateful. And I tell you something else, Charles. I would like to talk to the servants here. Where would be the best place to do that? Would they feel most at ease talking to me in their own quarters here, or up at the hotel?'

'Here, I should think. I'll let you know when my b-b-brothers are away again, shall I?'

'Please do,' said Powerscourt. 'That could be very useful. And there's the steward, Mr Savage. Could he come to see me at the hotel in the morning? I wouldn't want him put in a compromising position by being seen talking to me up here.'

As Charles walked him back down towards the stables Powerscourt was delighted with one small success. He had his very own spy in the enemy ranks, a human equivalent of the wooden horse that might yet lead to the destruction of his opponents.

Lady Lucy stared in despair at the letter. It was covered with the smallest handwriting she had ever seen. She knew from the notepaper headed Church House, Ashby Puerorum, that it must have come from her aunt but for the present she had no idea what it said. A spider's hand would have been more legible. Eventually she borrowed a magnifying glass from the hotel staff and began, very slowly, to decipher the message. The first few lines seemed to be full of the conventional pleasantries welcoming her to Lincolnshire and hoping the family were well. In the third paragraph Lady Lucy came across a word that she thought was luncheon. Before the intervention of the full stop she discerned the word tomorrow. For a moment she was filled with panic. Then she read on. 'I hope you will not find the dietary requirements here too restrictive. A long period of experimentation has convinced me that conventional menus are wasteful and unhealthy, leading to distemper, bile and progressive decay of the body tissue.'

Francis is going to love this, said Lady Lucy to herself. He had always taken a perverse delight in eccentrics of every sort. She saw a word underlined several times. After multiple adjustments of the glass she discovered that the word was beetroot. God in heaven. 'I find that beetroot', Lady Lucy read on, 'is admirably suited to be the mainstay of any sensible eating regimen. My staff have successfully grown some of the little-known varieties, Bull's Blood, Boltardy and Cheltenham Green Top. I have given over most of my garden to beetroot cultivation. Out of season I have devised a system of storage in the ample cellars beneath my house. It can be soup or broth – beetroot and potato pie is very nourishing as is fried beetroot with hardboiled eggs. My own particular favourite is beetroot fritters served with toast and horseradish purée.'

Well, thought Lady Lucy, lunch is certainly going to be interesting. There was more. 'I am afraid I am also unconventional in the question of sweet courses. The usual offerings of today, heavy in sugar and flour and custard and lashings of unhealthy cream, will soon lead to the extinction of the nation's manhood and moral fibre, washed away in a sea of suet, and guarantee our defeat in the forthcoming war with Germany.' Maybe beetroot provides prophetic powers when taken in enormous quantities, Lady Lucy said to herself. Maybe it rots the brain. 'In earlier times,' the old lady continued, 'I fortified myself in the final course with berries, blackberries, bilberries, raspberries, blueberries, strawberries, redcurrants, all grown and preserved in my gardens and greenhouses. As the decades passed,' how long has all this been going on, Lady Lucy muttered to herself, 'I found the tastes of these fruits growing pale on my palate. I am sure they were healthy – indeed one of the teachers at the school next door claimed I could have survived a voyage to the South Seas on such a diet – but I had grown weary. Rhubarb, a food as delicious as beetroot, and with just as many culinary possibilities, has replaced them on my table. Again, I am self-sufficient in the supply of the produce.' Lady Lucy thought that the gardener or gardeners of Church House must have a pretty tedious existence.

There was one final blast in the penultimate paragraph. Lady Lucy was ready for anything now. 'Just one last admonition. I trust you will not be bringing any children or pets with you. You will, no doubt, be familiar with the old saying that children should be seen but not heard. My own view is that they should be neither seen nor heard in any properly run household. My own – how I regret ever having had them – were largely reared by the staff in the domestic outbuildings and only allowed in the main house for a spell of fifteen minutes a week on Sunday afternoons.' Perhaps the children had turned into monsters, locked away in the bedrooms above the stables, fed on a diet of rhubarb and beetroot, grown crabby and dyspeptic before their time. Perhaps they had run away. Or asked for more. Probably not that, she told herself.

The final paragraph was refreshingly conventional. 'I look forward to seeing you for luncheon tomorrow at twelve thirty. If you should desire drink – another fatal poison in Britain's bloodstream – I am told the vicar's wife makes a passable version of something known as dandelion wine. I have some in one of the outhouses. Yours etc., Leticia Hamilton.'

Lady Lucy screwed up her eyes and read it once more. She would ask Johnny Fitzgerald what wine he would recommend to have with the beetroot. Bull's Blood from Hungary or wherever it came from? Lacryma Christi?

Johnny Fitzgerald was fond of vicars and curates and gentlemen of the cloth but he did not share his friend's absolute fascination with the breed. Powerscourt had once said that he wished it were possible to preserve some of the more eccentric specimens and keep them in an attic, to be brought back to life at his pleasure. The curate of St Matthew and All Angels, Candlesby, the Reverend Tobias Flint, was a balding man in his middle thirties, clean shaven, with mournful eyes. He carried about with him an air of worry and general distraction as if he felt God was calling him to service in some other place but he wasn't, for the moment, quite sure where that other place was.

'Of course, of course, only too pleased to be of some use,' he had said in reply to Johnny's general request for help concerning the Candlesbys and Jack Hayward. 'How precisely can I help you?'

'To my way of thinking,' said Johnny, hoping his stay would not be too long in these uncomfortable chairs with the protruding springs that graced what the curate was pleased to call his study, 'the Earl may have sent the Hayward family away to some of his relations elsewhere in the county or the country. Mr Drake down at the hotel said you were a great man for their family history. Can you think of any place he might have sent them?'

'I see, I see,' said the curate, pointing suddenly to shelf after shelf of ancient books and files. 'It's my hobby, you know, the Candlesby family history. I'm never sure people in my position should have hobbies when we are meant to be doing God's work, but my wife always points out that lots of my colleagues ride to hounds or play politics in the

House of Lords. Anyway I've made a list somewhere of all the people they've married and where they came from. That should help. If only, if only, I could remember where I put it.'

The Reverend Flint peered helplessly at his shelves. Then some practical rather than divine inspiration seemed to strike him.

'How foolish of me,' he apologized to Johnny Fitzgerald. 'Wives, filed next to Wills in my system. Of course.' He pulled down a folder and began to read.

'I think the beginning of the last century would be a good place to start, don't you? The family got into a lot of trouble during the Civil War, you know – managed to fall out with both sides at the same time. Miracle they came' through, really. Let me see, let me see.' The curate sent his index finger skimming down the page. 'First marriage of that time, 1809, eleventh Earl, Thomas Dymoke, married a Herbert, Henrietta Jane, of Bag Enderby quite near here, June fifteenth. She was buried in the Mausoleum in 1862, distant relation of the Wilton Herberts, I believe. No indication of the two families remaining close. Something tells me that the girl's family didn't approve of the match. Next Earl, William Edward, 1845, married a Winifred Maria Horne of Louth, August ninth. I think this Winifred was an only child so unlikely to be many family connections left there.'

The curate ran a despairing hand over his balding head and turned a few more pages. 'This looks more promising: 1865, thirteenth Earl, Randal Henry Alexander Dymoke, married Margaret Alice Harrington of Silk Willoughby Hall, Silk Willoughby, on July twelfth. Now this bride was an only daughter with three brothers who must, therefore, have also been called Harrington.'

The Reverend Flint became animated, rubbing his hands together as though his life depended on it. 'Now then, Mr Fitzgerald, we need another couple of folders. Baptisms and Deaths, that's what we need. My predecessors always kept a record of the people from the big house and their friends and relations who came to funerals and baptisms, that sort of thing. Often they were godparents or pallbearers. We have two families of Harringtons making regular appearances up until two or three years ago. One of them still lives at Silk Willoughby Hall and the other is at The Limes, Wrangle Lowgate, very near the coast south of here. Does that help?'

'Indeed it does. I am most grateful to you,' said Johnny, anxious to escape ordeal by chair spring. He did wonder if this habit of recording the names and addresses of members of the gentry who came to family milestone services was a regular custom in the Church of England. He suspected it smacked of the behaviour of the oleaginous Mr Collins, rector of Rosings and humble and grateful recipient of the bounty of Lady Catherine de Bourgh in Jane Austen's *Pride and Prejudice*.

Walter Savage, steward of the Candlesby estate, was a solid-looking man of about sixty years of age with white hair and a very ruddy complexion that might, Powerscourt thought, be the result of years spent in the open air, or it might be the result of many years partaking of the solace of grape and grain. He had a very deep voice and a habit of wiping a hand on his trousers every now and then as if it needed cleaning.

'Well, Lord Powerscourt,' Walter Savage began, 'this is a pretty business and no mistake. I'd be pleased to help in any way I can. My father was steward here before me so you could say we're fairly well acquainted with the place by now. Perhaps you could tell me what you would like to know.'

Powerscourt had wondered before the steward came about whose side he would be on. Would he be a loyal supporter of the family, saying nothing that might do them harm? Or would he bear a grudge against them for some ill treatment in the past and pour out his venom in Mr Drake's finest sitting room with the prints of the Lake District on the walls?

'It would be very useful for me to know the general financial position here, Mr Savage. I don't want any figures or anything like that, of course, but it would be useful for background. Money in all its forms plays such an important part in all our lives these days, don't you think?'

Walter Savage grunted. 'Could I ask you a question before we go any further, Lord Powerscourt? Do you think the late Earl was murdered?'

Powerscourt stared for a moment into the dark eyes opposite. Better tell the truth, he said to himself. It had always been one of his mother's instructions to him and his sisters when they were growing up.

'I do, as a matter of fact, Mr Savage. But just at this moment I can't prove it and I'd be grateful if you'd keep that piece of information to yourself for the time being.'

'Of course, my lord, I shan't say a word. Now then, you asked me about the condition of the estate. I don't think it's an exaggeration to say I don't think it could be worse.'

'Really?' said Powerscourt.

'I'm sure an intelligent man like yourself knows the background to big landed estates like this one, my lord. They say things move in cycles, good after bad and bad after good. Well, the last good times round here were years and years ago. It's bad after bad after bad these days. Now rents are going down all the time. Foreign produce from abroad, even from as far away as Australia, is cheaper than what we can produce on our own land. Estates are worth less and less per acre. Fads keep coming along that suck the money out of big estates like this one. Twenty years ago drainage was all the rage. Get your land properly drained and the crops will improve, the value of your land will go up, everything will be rosy. People like the Earl here borrowed money

112

to carry out this drainage work. It may have made a bit of difference, I was never convinced myself, my lord, but the debts to the bank were real enough and they had to be repaid. We still haven't finished paying them off today, now I come to think about it.'

Walter Savage paused for a moment and shook his head. 'It's not as though there weren't enough debts already, my lord. Cast your mind back to the good times. Let's say you needed quite a lot of money to improve your house or look after your widowed mother or pay off your gambling debts or maybe, God help us, a mixture of all three. Your income is going up year after year and everybody thinks that will go on for ever. So you think that whatever you borrow now will seem a great deal less in ten years' time than it does today. But then the wheel turns or the bad fairy smiles on you or whatever happens when fortune changes. Your income does not rise. It falls. The loans do not seem smaller. They seem bigger, much bigger. What is a landowner to do?'

'More to the point, Mr Savage, what did this family do about it?'

'Well,' replied the steward, rubbing his hand along the side of his trousers once more, 'there were a number of things you could try. You could economize for a start. Cut out all unnecessary expenditure. No more grand balls. No more racehorses. No more expensive trips to Paris or Rome to spice up a jaundiced palate. Just quiet country living. They didn't do that here, of course. Or you could dispose of enough land to pay off your debts. No man likes to do that, selling your future to pay for your past. They didn't do that here either. They've got the worst of all possible worlds – enormous debts, tens and tens of thousands of pounds, and the debts are getting bigger, not smaller, as they can't always pay off all the interest. It's really sad sometimes, my lord. We had a record wheat harvest a couple of years back and the late Earl watched it all being packed up and taken away. "Do you know, Savage," he said to me, "that huge harvest won't even pay half the interest on our debts at the blasted bank." There are more exotic answers, of course. One very indebted landowner over at Barnby in the Willows down Newark way took himself off to the tables at Monte Carlo with money borrowed from his uncle. He told a few close friends it was, quite literally, do or die. Either he was going to make enough money to pay off the debts or he was going to shoot himself just as the casino closed.'

'And what happened?' asked Powerscourt, fascinated by the thought of rescue at the roulette table.

'The man was lucky. He won a fortune, far more than he needed, at baccarat and chemin de fer. Do you know, he's never gambled a penny since, not with his children or on the Derby or at the races or anywhere. He says, apparently, that he used up a lifetime's luck in two evenings at the tables.'

'He could have lost the lot, I suppose,' said Powerscourt. 'And then he'd have lost his brains as well. Are there any more conventional methods for easing the debt burden, Mr Savage?'

'I fear there are only the two proper ones I mentioned before, my lord. Spend less, or sell your way out of trouble. Or you could marry an heiress and her money would take care of everything. There have been those who've advertised in America for wives, you know. I remember someone sent us one of these from a newspaper in Kansas years ago, wherever Kansas is. I'll make you a lady, you pay off my debts, how about it, that sort of thing.'

'I've got a brother-in-law who knows all about money,' said Powerscourt. 'I think his firm owns a couple of banks actually. He always says that if you are going to borrow from a bank you should borrow an enormous amount.'

'Why is that, my lord? Doesn't seem to make sense.'

'Well,' said Powerscourt with a smile, 'his line, my brother-in-law's, that is, goes something like this. If you owe the bank a little bit of money, they sort of own you. They can sell off your land or your goods if you don't pay them back. But if you owe them an enormous amount, then you sort of own them. They'll go bankrupt if you don't pay back the money, you see, so they've got to keep you afloat.'

Walter Savage laughed. 'I reckon these Candlesbys must own the banks then,' he said.

'Can I ask you a question, Mr Savage?' Powerscourt had grown to like the steward, himself and his father toiling in vain in the service of their masters who refused to take advice.

'Of course, my lord.'

'Do you think the late Earl was murdered?'

That hand crept down to be wiped on the trouser leg once more. 'I do,' said Savage with scarcely a pause.

Powerscourt waited for him to say some more but he didn't. 'What makes you think that, Mr Savage?'

'What I'm going to say isn't very rational, my lord. I wasn't present at the meeting of the hunt or the arrival of the body on the horse and the diversion into the stables. But I've been around that house when people have died before. I know what the atmosphere is like. This time it was different. Those brothers weren't sad, they were anxious, they were worried, they weren't in mourning at all. And anyway, my lord, think about it. A body wrapped up so nobody can see it, brought back to the house by a faithful servant. How did he come to be dead? Why did nobody see the body apart from the eldest son and the doctor as I've been told? He was killed, I'm sure of it.'

'Let me ask you another question, as you've been so helpful answering my first one, Mr Savage. Who could have wanted him dead? Who could have hated him so much they decided to murder him?'

This time Walter Savage did pause. He looked at Powerscourt very carefully, as if he was thinking of buying him at auction like a horse.

'Well, my lord,' he said finally, 'he certainly wasn't killed for his money. Even in these changing times I've never heard of anybody being murdered for his debts.' Walter Savage paused, as if he wasn't sure where to go. 'I'm assuming, my lord,' he looked at Powerscourt once more, 'that what I am about to say will be treated in the strictest confidence.'

'You have my word on that,' said Powerscourt firmly.

'You see, my lord, it's like this, I'm not quite sure how to put it . . . He was a truly horrible man, the late Earl. There, I've said it now. But it's true. I think he was the worst human being I have ever met and I did spend a year or two before I was married visiting people in prison. The vicar said it might help their immortal souls if they talked to some normal citizens. Well, some of those people in Lincoln prison didn't seem to belong to the human race at all. The late Earl was horrible to his children, he was horrible to his tenants, he was horrible to his neighbours, he was horrible to any visitors who came his way. Anybody could have had a reason to kill him, anybody at all who came into contact with him.'

Powerscourt thought that the steward certainly wasn't narrowing the possible range of suspects.

'Did you know Jack Hayward well, Mr Savage?'

'I did, my lord. He came to see me the day he went away, about three in the afternoon that would have been.'

Once more Powerscourt waited for more information, but none came.

'Did he say anything about what had happened on the morning the body came back?'

'Not really, my lord. He just said it was terrible.'

'Did he say he was going away?'

'He did. That's why he came to see me. He came to say goodbye. We've known each other for nearly twenty years, you see.'

'Did he say where he was going? Did he say if he was coming back?'

'The answer to both these questions is no, my lord. I'll tell you what he did say, though. I don't think he'd mind.

He's the last person on this earth I would want to betray or let down, Jack Hayward. "This has all been absolutely too terrible for words," he said, staring into the fire in my little living room. "I can't tell you anything about it, Walter. One day, please God, I will tell you, but not now. Please don't ask me where I'm going. I can't tell you that either." With that he got up and left. When he reached the door, he stopped to say one last word. "Goodbye, Walter, and God bless you. Pray for us all. Pray for us every day as long as you live." And with that he was gone, my lord. I haven't seen him since.'

Powerscourt was lost for words. 'Thank you for telling me that,' he said finally. 'I am most grateful.' There seemed little left to say. The two men sat quietly for a while, lost in their own thoughts.

'Is there anything else I can tell you, my lord? I should be getting back soon.'

'Not for the present, I don't think,' said Powerscourt. 'Just one thing, though. Did the late Earl ever mention anybody who might want to kill him? Was there anyone he was frightened of?'

'Not that I remember, my lord. Mind you, there was one person he was always frightened of. You recall we were talking about banks earlier?'

'I do,' said Powerscourt, wondering if the bankers of Lincolnshire had taken to murdering their heavily indebted clients.

'When I was assistant steward to my father, it must have been nearly thirty years ago, the bank manager was a great brute of a man, six feet four if he was an inch and a fist the size of a blacksmith's. When he came over to meet the Earl, he would virtually lie down on the floor and grovel. Yes, my lord. How are the children, my lord? And your lady wife, my lord? This sort of thing could go on for five or ten minutes. The late Earl lapped it up, probably thought that was how everybody should address him. The bank manager today is a little tubby man with very strong glasses. Unlike most of them, he does actually look like a bank manager. I don't think he even got to his feet when the late Earl entered the room. "Well then, well then," he would say, waving a piece of paper from his bank – he always came with a piece of paper, maybe it was the same one – "things haven't got any better since I was last here, have they? They've got worse. What do you propose to do about it?" And he would look up at my late master as if he was some schoolboy who had just been caught cheating at exams. The Earl didn't like him. He didn't like him at all. He didn't like the message either. I think he was actually frightened of the tubby bank manager. "You know, Savage," he said to me once, "that ridiculous little man is the only person in the world who could take all this away – house, lands, horses, furniture, the lot. Can you believe it?'

Powerscourt felt he had just listened to a vital chapter in the social history of England called 'The Slow Death of Deference'. Things would never be the same again.

9

Sandy Temple, friend of Lady Lucy's sister's daughter Selina, was leafing his way through a number of old notebooks, filled with incomprehensible squiggles. Incomprehensible, that is, to people not inducted into the wonders of shorthand, an essential prerequisite for anybody who wanted to be a reporter for the parliamentary pages of *The Times*. Sandy was checking his old notes on proceedings since Lloyd George introduced his Budget in the House of Commons earlier that year. Since the furore over the Budget began Sandy had been keeping a diary. It covered every single day of the relevant proceedings in the Commons and in the country and would soon report on the Lords when the debate moved there. In the middle of the night, when everybody in his house was asleep, Sandy would dream of his diary being published when the battle was finished, a matter of public record rather like Daniel Defoe's *Journal of the Plague Year*. Every politician of substance would have to read it. He would be promoted. He would be famous. But for now, in the daylight, he pulled down a large notebook with a dark red cover and looked through the pages.

'Saturday October ninth, 1909,' he read, 'King's Cross station, nine o'clock express to Newcastle and Edinburgh. On my way to hear Lloyd George deliver a great speech in Newcastle. Sir Francis Weygand from the Treasury told me earlier in the week that it would be important. And Lloyd

George himself is on this train! The same train as me! I saw him a few minutes ago striding up the platform with his cane accompanied by a couple of officials from the Treasury and a scared-looking little man from the railway. Three or four porters gave a ragged cheer as the Chancellor of the Exchequer went by.

'I have been watching Lloyd George very carefully for months now. I feel I know him better than any other politician in the House. He has, I think, an immense talent for making himself unpopular, even hated by his enemies. David Lloyd George is, above all else, an outsider. He came to the Commons with no faction, no relations, no great estate, no cohorts of admirers stretching back to a shared past in the common rooms of Christ Church and Balliol and the dormitories of expensive prep schools in the Home Counties. He trades in a different currency, one of words and language. I think he is the most impressive orator in the country, less fluent than Asquith perhaps, but more natural, more passionate than Churchill. He knows how to talk to the working people of this country, a skill not learnt in the debating chamber of the Oxford Union.

'Some of the gossip I have heard circulated in the Commons about Lloyd George could only come from his enemies. Rumours have swept around the Welshman for years, many of them, I am sure, invented by the Conservatives. The Palace of Westminster has frequently been awash with stories of extramarital affairs. His wife refuses to come and live in London, preferring to stay close to her roots and her family in north Wales. The goat, as he is sometimes referred to, hunts alone. Even in adultery, if the stories are correct, Lloyd George remains true to his political affiliations. He only ever misbehaves with the wives of Liberal MPs, never with the wives of Conservatives.

'We are leaving Durham now, cathedral and castle standing proudly above the river. I wonder if Lloyd George has spent the journey preparing his speech. We should arrive in Newcastle in less than fifteen minutes. I am more excited than I can say.'

'Are you still engaged in that frightful profession of investigating?'

Lady Lucy's great aunt Leticia was a formidable old person. She was extremely slim, almost emaciated, possibly due to the eccentric diet, and her distinguishing feature was an enormous bun of silvery white hair which followed the movements of her head like a guardsman's bearskin. The first part of the conversation, before they sat down to the beetroot, had consisted of a microscopic investigation of Lady Lucy's past and the precise location in the family tree of all her mother's relations so that the exact degree of consanguinity could be established and pinned on an imaginary board, like a preserved butterfly. The relationship crossed over a number of cousins, some three or four times removed, and, thought Powerscourt, whose mind had been on other things, a great uncle who had emigrated to New Zealand but whose relations had come back to live in England, weary of sheep and Maoris. The vicar's wife's home-made wine, duly imported from the outhouses, had been rather a trial. Pressed to partake out of politeness, Powerscourt had managed to decant most of the ghastly beverage into a large pot full of herbs. He did not rate their survival chances very highly. Now the old battleaxe was moving in on him with her question about whether he was still investigating.

'I am as a matter of fact,' said Powerscourt, smiling politely at his new relation.

'How dreadful for you all. It's no profession for a gentleman, prying into people's lives and accusing them of murdering their wives or husbands.'

Powerscourt didn't reply. He could see Lady Lucy making some elaborate hand signs to him but he couldn't work out what they meant.

'Do you have a special celebration the day these miscreants are found guilty? Do you go out to celebrate at the Ritz?'

'Of course,' said Powerscourt. 'Champagne all round.'

There were more hand signs from Lady Lucy across the table.

'And what do you do', the old lady stared at Powerscourt as she spoke, the silver bun quivering slightly with suppressed emotion, 'on the day the criminals you have unmasked are hanged for their crimes and wickedness?'

'That depends', said Powerscourt gravely, 'on whereabouts the ceremony takes place. If it's out of London, in Lewes or Lincoln for instance, there's not a lot we can do apart from opening the champagne at the appointed hour. But if it's in town, Pentonville perhaps or Wormwood Scrubs, that sort of thing, we usually take a picnic basket and have a feast outside the prison. Lobster seems to go down very well on these occasions. If you listen very carefully at exactly eight o'clock in the morning you can sometimes hear the trapdoor opening and a scream or two as the chap is left dangling. That's always good fun. Quite a crowd sometimes, so you can't always hear the drop.'

The silver bun was rock steady now, the hair on special parade duty.

'What happens if you get the wrong person? Eh? Lord Powerscourt? Eh? What do you do then?' The old lady leant forward to press home her advantage and shook her finger at Powerscourt.

'Since you ask, I don't think I have got the wrong man or woman yet.' He began counting on his fingers. 'Twenty-two, twenty-three, twenty-four, all clear rounds so far. They usually own up in the end, you know; sometimes they tell you where you might have got something a tiny bit wrong. Can't always score a hundred out of hundred, after all.'

'Woman, did I hear you say? Do you send them off to meet their maker at the end of a length of rope too? How barbaric! And you dare to call yourself a gentleman!'

'If you were shot through the heart or strangled by expert hands, I don't think it would make much difference whether the perpetrator was male or female. You'd be dead just the same.'

'And I suppose you rejoice in equal measure if it's a woman or a man who's being hanged. Heartless, heartless man!'

'Of course,' said Powerscourt. 'There's always a time to rejoice over the sinner who repenteth and you can't do much more repenting than by being actually hanged by the neck till you are dead. I do have one new scheme up my sleeve but I think it will only work in London.'

Great Aunt Leticia shuddered. 'And what is that, pray?' Lady Lucy was making further signals, reminding her husband of a conductor trying to quieten his orchestra.

'It's like this,' said Powerscourt, leaning forward to establish better contact with the old lady. 'The Metropolitan Police have their own photographers now. They're expert in photographing dead people so everyone will know what their injuries looked like after the corpse has been lowered into the ground in its coffin. I've arranged that they're going to send me prints of all the best shots they take so I can hang them up on my walls.'

'What do you mean, the best shots?' asked the old lady suspiciously, peering at Powerscourt as if he came from another planet.

'Well, only the most gruesome ones, naturally, faces covered with blood, arms hanging off, bullet holes in the chest, noses blown away, that sort of thing. It'll be most amusing!'

'Francis, Francis, do give over,' said Lady Lucy. 'Can't you see, Great Aunt, he's making all this stuff up. He's been teasing you with his exaggerations for the past five minutes, maybe more. Not a word of this is true, not a word!'

'Is that so, young man?' The old lady peered at him closely once more. 'That none of what you have been saying is true?'

'It's all fiction,' said Powerscourt happily, 'every single word of it, though I did rather like the bit about the lobster. I'm sorry if it upset you.'

The old lady snorted. 'Well,' she said, and the faintest suspicion of a smile flickered across her emaciated features, 'it was all most convincing. Now then, we'd better move on to talk about the death of Lord Candlesby. I presume that's why you are here.'

'Your expertise and your local knowledge would be most welcome,' said Powerscourt.

'Most welcome indeed,' echoed Lady Lucy. The beetroot confection had been cleared away and a golden dish of rhubarb crumble was now being served.

'When you think about that horrible man's death, the remarkable thing about it is not that it happened but that it hadn't happened years before. I expect you've heard about the man he killed in a duel, and the woman he had an affair with who committed suicide?'

Powerscourt nodded. 'I believe', Great Aunt Leticia continued, 'that those were only the hors d'oeuvres of his crimes.' Powerscourt found himself wondering what sort of hors d'oeuvres you could provide based only on beetroot and realized he couldn't find an answer. 'There were other affairs, other members of the gentry whose wives he seduced. But I think we have to look elsewhere for his killer or killers.'

'And where do you think that might be?' Powerscourt asked.

'Why,' the old lady gave a toss of her head like a racehorse in the paddock before a race, 'in his own home, of course.' She looked round triumphantly at her little audience. 'Let me give you my reasons. Many of the domestic staff at Candlesby Hall don't stay very long. Some of them have scarcely time to unpack their trunks before they are thrown out or flee of their own accord. I have employed three footmen who walked out or were forced to depart in the past few years. There never seem to be many female staff in the place, for reasons I do not know. But these footmen told terrible stories about the man's cruelty. The servants were merely kicked or punched or knocked down. The children when younger were beaten, systematically, sadistically and far too often. Beatings never stopped until they were in tears or bleeding or both. Beatings would start for no reason at all: a door left open, a shirt button unfastened. If they had all misbehaved, windows broken by footballs, that sort of thing, they were beaten in relays, and when he had got to the end that dreadful man would go back to the first one in line and thrash them all over again. Some of those teachers in the great public schools claim that occasional beatings are good for a boy's character. I don't believe that for a moment. Beatings on the Candlesby scale must have a terrible effect on their natures. Is this a father's love, a parent's devotion, the cane whistling down on you over and over again?'

'You don't imagine', said an appalled Lady Lucy, 'that he was still doing it? They're all too old, those children, surely. The elder ones are all grown up; they could probably have knocked him out without too much trouble.'

'Oh, he stopped with the eldest ones,' she said. 'One of the footmen who left him five years ago told me that. He may have carried on with the little one, the one who's not quite right in the head. That's probably a good reason for a ferocious beating, if you're Candlesby, the fact that the poor boy's out of his wits.'

'I'm sure it's more than possible,' said Powerscourt, 'but don't you think the sons might have done something about it by now?'

'Good point, Lord Powerscourt, good point. I have thought about that,' said the great aunt. 'Maybe the beatings were like seed corn – they have taken time to grow. Something else may have come along, some later piece of cruelty, to light the fire.'

'If he beat the youngest one,' said Lady Lucy, 'that might have been enough to set them off.'

'You mustn't think those three eldest children are in any way virtuous or kind or well brought up. My footmen reported that they were wild, feral almost, savage, perfectly capable of murdering anybody. All except the fourth one and he's got such a terrible stutter people have left the room sometimes before he's finished a sentence, and the last one who's not right in the head.'

'I see,' said Powerscourt, wondering again how the late Earl had been killed, what the telltale marks on his body were. Had the three eldest brothers lured their father away to some remote spot and killed him in some spectacularly horrible way? Had they then left a note for Jack Hayward to find him? Powerscourt didn't think that explanation felt right.

'Great Aunt,' Lady Lucy was bringing the party to a close, 'we have to go now. Francis has a meeting with the police. But you must come and see us at our hotel. Why don't you come for tea a week today? We could bring you up to date with the latest news.'

'I tell you what I will do, my dear. Much better than tea. I'll organize a series of lunches for you to host at your hotel. You can meet the ladies of Lincolnshire and hear what gossip has to say about mysterious deaths at Candlesby Hall.'

Sandy was still engrossed in his own diary.

'Saturday October ninth, 1909, Palace Theatre, Newcastle. I am sitting in the press area to the left of the main stage. There must be about fifteen of us pressmen here crammed into a very small space. One of the ushers just told me that the place can hold over five thousand people and it is packed to the rafters this afternoon. Some of the local Liberal MPs are here – one of them was kind enough to wave at me just now – but these are the working men of Newcastle and Gateshead and Sunderland and South Shields, men who work in shipbuilding, in the docks, on the railways, down the mines, the men who man the sinews of industry in the North-East. These are the people who decide general elections. Suddenly the chatter in the theatre dies down, to be followed by a mighty roar, and the Chancellor of the Exchequer cames forward to the rostrum, hands held aloft in thanks for his welcome. How Lloyd George loves these occasions, the way he can play on the crowd, their affection for him, his sense of power over the multitude. I have always thought he is happier here with these vast crowds than he is in the House of Commons. I have long felt that his ideal site for one of these monster speeches would be a bare hillside somewhere in North Wales, with a wind blowing in from the sea and the rain not too far away.

'He begins by talking about the Budget, and how various industries are now doing better than they had been before he announced his financial measures in March. But he says there is a slump in dukes – because a fully equipped duke costs as much to keep as two dreadnoughts.

'There is a great deal of laughter and prolonged cheering at this point. The reporter from the *Daily Telegraph* on my left mutters disrespectfully about bloody Welshmen. Later on Lloyd George fires another broadside against the aristocracy which has the audience punching their fists in the air. Should five hundred men, he asks, ordinary men, chosen accidentally from among the unemployed, override the judgement of millions of people who are engaged in the industry which makes the wealth of the country?

'I am certain I have just heard one of the defining quotes of the battle between the Lords and the Commons, words likely to prolong the fight, to bring a sword rather than an olive branch to the Palace of Westminster. Maybe this is actually what Lloyd George wants to do, to enrage the members of the Upper House so much that they throw out his Budget and prepare for a final apocalyptic showdown over where power in Britain really lies, with the people or with the peers. *Alea jacta est*. The die is cast.'

'Have a look at this lot, my lord. Maybe you'll have some thoughts about what we should do next.' Detective Inspector William Blunden handed over a small pile of letters to Powerscourt. They were sitting in his office in the police station a couple of days later, hoping to plan their next moves.

'"Chief Constable to the Permanent Secretary at the Home Office, copy to the Archbishop's secretary, Bishop's Palace, Lincoln, copy to Lord Candlesby, Candlesby Hall,"' Powerscourt read aloud, '"You will have read, I am sure, of the recent death of the Earl of Candlesby, delivered to a meeting of his hunt wrapped in blankets on the back of his horse. We are not satisfied that the correct procedures were followed at the time of his death. We do not feel that the cause of that death has been properly established. We wish, therefore, to request your permission to exhume the body and to carry out a post-mortem so that the matter can be properly investigated. Yours etc., Chief Constable of Lincolnshire."

'"Dear Chief Constable, Thank you for your letter, etc. etc. etc. . . . I do not feel that you have given us sufficient information concerning the death of Lord Candlesby for us to grant permission for an exhumation in this case. I would remind you that you need special permission or a faculty from the Church of England if the aforementioned is interred in consecrated ground or in property pertaining to the Church. And I would also remind you of the need to acquire permission from all the members of the family before this request could be considered. Yours etc., Sir Bartleby Timson, Permanent Secretary, the Home Office, etc. etc. etc."

'"Dear Chief Constable, His Grace asks me to inform you that while he is normally sympathetic to all requests for exhumation, he feels moved to stay his response in this case. He feels that the reasons given might, in certain quarters, be considered inadequate. Perhaps you could get in touch with us here at the Palace when you have obtained the necessary permissions from the family and the necessary clearances from the Home Office. Yours etc. etc., Obadiah Forester, Secretary to His Grace the Bishop of Lincoln."

'"Dear Chief Constable, I would remind you that under the Burial Act 1857 permission is required from all living relatives before the authorities can even consider an exhumation order. I refuse you such permission. My brothers will be writing to you in the next few days to refuse you their permission too. Then I trust that this outrageous and unjustified request can be abandoned and the family left to grieve in peace, Yours etc. etc., Candlesby."

'"Dear Chief Constable, We act for the new Earl of Candlesby. It has come to our attention that a recent request has been submitted for an exhumation of the body of the late Lord Candlesby. Close inspection of the relevant legislation leads us to believe that this request is spurious and has no meaning in law. To the best of our knowledge none of the surviving children of the late Earl, all except one past the age of consent, will accede to this request. It is, therefore, going to be refused by the Home Office. We have written to the Permanent Secretary asking for copies of any further correspondence to be sent to us so we can monitor future proceedings. Yours etc. etc. etc. Mark Sowerby, Hopkins Pettigrew & Green, Bedford Square."

'My goodness me,' said Powerscourt with a smile, handing the correspondence back to the Inspector, 'these people could get through an awful lot of ink before they've finished. And I'd be fairly sure that those solicitors in Bedford Square would be the last to quit the field. I don't know how much they charge but it'll be a pretty penny.'

'If I might say so, my lord,' said Inspector Blunden, 'you don't sound very concerned about these letters.'

'Well, that's because I'm not,' said Powerscourt cheerfully, 'and neither will you be when you hear what I've got to say. You may remember I said last time we talked about this that I needed to find out more abut exhumations?'

The Inspector nodded.

'I tried a local library and that was no good. But I did ask them who the local coroner was. So I popped back into the car and set off to Spalding to find the good Dr Chapman, His Majesty's coroner for South Lincolnshire. I bought the fellow lunch, as a matter of fact. Very fond of fish, the coroner, fish and rather expensive hock. Never mind. The key thing he told me was this: in important police matters, like possible murder cases, where the suspects may include the relatives of the deceased, the coroner can take the decision on his own. No need to hang around waiting for faculties from the bishop and approval from Sir Bartleby at the Home Office; he can fire the starting pistol all on his own. We have to make sure that there's a chap from the undertakers there, and the coroner himself, and the man doing the post-mortem, and we have to do it in the dark when nobody can see. Quite what anybody would imagine was going on when they saw a body being dug up in the middle of the night doesn't bear thinking about. Still, the late Earl isn't going to be dug out of the ground, is he, just slid out of his shelf in that mausoleum. Much less alarming all round. And my coroner friend, over a large glass of brandy in the restaurant, recommended the best man in the country for the post-mortem. Fellow by the name of Carey, Nathaniel Carey at Bart's in London. Nobody's going to argue with his findings apparently. I've taken the liberty of dropping him a line.'

'Are you saying, my lord, that all we have to do is to write to this coroner and say we think the Earl was murdered?'

'Well, Inspector, I think we have to be a bit more specific than that about the very unusual circumstances of this case. Three members of the late Earl's family are suspects after all. There is the fact of the body being brought up across the horse with nobody able to see his face apart from three people, the doctor who is dead, the steward who has disappeared, and the new Lord Candlesby who is ambiguous, if you recall, on whether he actually looked at the body or not. There is the matter of the doctor, according to himself, being bullied to provide the verdict of death by natural causes, when he knew it wasn't true. Then, of course, removed from the pressure in the Candlesby stables, the doctor recants and says he believed the man was murdered. I think we need to stress that if any responsible person from the police force had seen the dead man they would have been able to form a view as to whether he was murdered or not. On balance, I would say we believe he was murdered by person or persons unknown. If not – and if the body is untouched, unmarked, inviolate – then we shall still be performing an act of public service by removing the rumours and gossip that are already swirling round the Earl's death.'

'That all sounds very persuasive to me,' said the Inspector.

'One other thought,' said Powerscourt. 'I leave it up to you and the Chief Constable whether to act upon it or not. I think I should say that we propose to bring in the new Earl, the red-headed chap, for questioning. If we do it at the right time, we could arrest him immediately after the post-mortem and the inquest.'

'Do you think he did it, my lord?'

'I'm not sure about that. It all seems rather elaborate, if you follow me, the hunt meeting, the despatch of Jack Hayward to collect the body, all that business in the stables which looks so suspicious you think he can't possibly have done it. Why not just push your father down some stone staircase when nobody's looking? "He must have tripped, Inspector, what a shame."'

'I shall go and talk to the Chief Constable now, my lord. This is one of the days when he's causing chaos with us rather than with the people in Lincoln.'

'I am going to pay a visit to the unfortunate Lawrences, who have had to sell their worldly goods. I wonder what they will have to say for themselves.'

Johnny Fitzgerald had called on one lot of Candlesby relations already. These Harringtons lived at The Limes, Lower Wrangle Lowgate, very near the coast. They had not heard, or pretended not to have heard, the news of the death of Lord Candlesby. Johnny supposed it was just about possible if they didn't read any newspapers and hadn't been out into town or into society since the death. He had found the reactions to the death unusual, to say the least.

'I say,' said Rupert Harrington, the paterfamilias, 'I know we're not supposed to put it like this, but this is the best news I've had for ages. Have you heard, Agnes,' he called out to his wife who was arranging flowers in the next room, 'that bastard Candlesby is dead!'

'Are you sure?' replied a rather feeble female voice.

Harrington looked at Johnny who nodded vigorously.

'No doubt at all,' he yelled through the wall. 'Definitely dead.'

'What marvellous news, darling,' the distant wife said. 'I'll ask Simmons to bring up some champagne straight away.'

So, over a glass or two of Dom Perignon, the Harringtons told Johnny their story. They had never gone willingly to any of the christenings or funerals where their presence had been recorded by the Reverend Tobias Flint. Mrs Harrington, she explained, had been brought up to regard the family as the centre of the world, its rituals sacrosanct, its requests for attendance at family events to be obeyed at all times.

'So, you see,' Mrs Harrington explained, 'I would have been letting the family down if I hadn't gone to those functions. Thank God, we won't have to go to any more now.

But, Mr Fitzgerald, I can't believe you came over here just to tell us the Earl is dead.'

'How right you are, Mrs Harrington. Let me explain.' Johnny told them about the corpse being brought up the drive to join the hunt by Jack Hayward, of the diversion of the body into the stables, of Jack Hayward's disappearance. Was he, perhaps, with them, helping out with horses maybe, being generally useful about the place? He was not, they told him. They only had two horses and they were old now, not fit recipients of the equine experience of a man such as Hayward. They wished Johnny good luck but had no suggestions for him.

The Harringtons of Silk Willoughby Hall had certainly heard of the death. Their reaction had been similar to that of their cousins near the sea. They had celebrated by going out to dinner in the most expensive hotel for miles around.

'I did go to the funeral, I admit that. Maybe it was hypocritical,' St John Harrington told Johnny, 'but I did want to see how the other mourners behaved. Mourners? I've seldom seen so many happy people in my life, rejoicing that the old bastard was dead and come to make sure he was put away in that chilly mausoleum for good. One fellow told me it was one of the finest days of his life. Rarely can death have brought so much joy to those remaining.'

These Harringtons had horses, plenty of horses. Johnny could see them trotting round one of the fields outside the windows. But they were not entertaining Jack Hayward and his family.

'I knew Jack Hayward quite well,' Daisy Harrington told Johnny. 'He used to come over sometimes and advise me about which horses to sell, that sort of thing. If you're trying to find him you're having to guess if he went where he was told by the Candlesbys, or where he decided to go himself, aren't you? Well, if you've come to us because you think Jack was sent here by the family, then you're wrong.'

Johnny wondered if he could enrol Daisy Harrington as a colleague in his quest.

'You see, he was very independent, Jack,' she continued. 'I don't think he'd have felt happy going somewhere he was told to go to; I don't think he'd have felt his family were safe and secure.'

'So where do you think I should be looking, Mrs Harrington?'

'I don't know. But I don't think you'll find him with any of the Candlesby relations.'

'Which means I shall have to try his wife's relations or his friends or places where he worked before.'

Daisy Harrington was frowning. 'I do know where he worked before he came here,' she said, 'but I can't remember the name of the trainer, I really can't. It was in Newmarket, that's all I can remember, you know, where lots of race-horses are bred and brought up. Jack used to tell me about those days sometimes.'

'Thank you very much,' said Johnny. 'I'm most grateful. I shall set off for Newmarket.'

As he made his way out of the house Daisy Harrington's voice followed him down the path. 'I say, Mr Fitzgerald, why all this interest in a groom who's disappeared? You don't think the Earl had a stroke or a heart attack or anything like that, do you?'

She waited in vain for Johnny Fitzgerald to answer. 'You think he was murdered, don't you?'

Her voice followed him down the drive and round the corner at the bottom. Daisy Harrington stood very still at her door for some time, staring at her empty drive and listening to the silence of the late afternoon.

10

There were sad signs of transience at the front of Lawrence House as Powerscourt arrived. A platoon of servants were carrying a selection of boxes, tea chests, portmanteaus, chairs, small tables and household bric-a-brac on to a couple of carts. Every now and then a plate or a glass or a bowl would escape from its container and smash to pieces on the ground, leading to fearful oaths and blood-curdling threats from the butler, who was conducting operations from the top of the steps wearing an enormous moustache and a magnificent red apron. A junior footman detached himself from his moving duties and brought Powerscourt to a drawing room at the back of the house, a splendid room with an elegant bay window looking out on a tennis court and a shrubbery. Even here the melancholy work of moving was proceeding. A rather nervous young housemaid was wrapping ornaments in newspaper and placing them carefully in a tea chest. Behind her two men were manoeuvring a long table out of the room. It seemed as though it could not fit through the opening but it was steered through with inches to spare on either side.

'Lord Powerscourt, I presume.' A tall white-haired man with a winning smile had come in and was shaking Powerscourt by the hand. 'Lawrence, Harold Lawrence at your service. We're moving, as you can see. We've got some men from Candlesby village in to help. It's amazing how clever they are with their hands.'

'How do you do, sir,' said Powerscourt, noting the man's very clear blue eyes and the lines across his forehead growing deeper with the passing years.

'Grace,' Lawrence turned to address the housemaid, 'you may go now, and thank you for your good work.'

The maid curtsied and departed. 'I have no idea if her work here was any good or not,' Lawrence told Powerscourt, 'but she looks so nervous all the time, poor girl; I've always thought it pays to be kind.'

'I'm sure you're right,' said Powerscourt politely.

'I see from your note that you are looking into the death of the late Lord Candlesby,' said Harold Lawrence. 'Would you permit me to ask a question or two before you question me, which I feel sure must be the purpose of your visit?'

'Of course,' Powerscourt replied, sensing that there might be steel here, lurking behind the good manners.

'As I understand it, the official record of the Earl's death said it was due to natural causes. Nobody has yet come forward to contradict that. And yet we have the local Detective Inspector, a man widely respected in these parts, still making inquiries among the hunt and the Candlesby villagers. And we have yourself, Lord Powerscourt. Inquiries have been made. You may have been discreet in your career, I'm sure you have been, but word gets out about your activities. Investigators like yourself do not stay in little places like this unless they are looking into cases of murder. I do feel we have a right to know. So which is it, Lord Powerscourt, murder or death by natural causes?'

'Let me give you a truthful answer, Mr Lawrence, and I would ask you to keep it as close as you can. I believe the Earl was murdered. Until I have found the means to prove that, I have to pay lip service to the natural causes theory, even though I don't think it's true. There, does that satisfy you?'

'Perfectly, Lord Powerscourt. Now I presume you want to ask me the usual questions about where we were on the day of the murder and so on. On the night in question the whole family, all of us, were in London. We went to see a play and we stayed a couple of nights in White's Hotel. I'm sure the people there will vouch for us if it should come to that.'

'Was the play good?' asked Powerscourt.

'Well, it was interesting, I suppose, if you like industrial disputes all over the West End stage. The wife is very taken by that fellow Galsworthy and his book *The Man of Property* about a bounder called Soames Forsyte that came out a couple of years ago. This play at the Savoy called *Strife* was also by Galsworthy but there weren't any Forsytes in it. I think the wife was disappointed. She had high hopes of Irene and Bosinney disgracing themselves behind a pillar.'

'I've heard a lot, Mr Lawrence, about the relations between your family and the late Lord Candlesby. Perhaps you could you tell me about it in your own words. Rumour and gossip, as you well know, have a habit of distorting or exaggerating the facts with these sort of events.'

'I don't think there's any exaggeration at all,' said Lawrence sadly. 'I really don't like talking about it very much. Our family were going to get the benefit of the railways running through our land all those years ago. Candlesby managed to make off with the contract instead. He grew rich, or he should have grown rich. We got poor. We're in no position to survive this agricultural depression in our present state, so we're cutting back. Smaller house, fewer acres, that sort of thing. It finished my father off, as you probably know, but I don't think he was long for this world anyway. He'd not been well for some time. There, is that what you need to know?'

Another loud crash from the front of the house indicated a falling down rather than a cutting back of the Lawrence property. There was a tremendous bellow from the butler in his red apron. 'What on earth are you doing? You stupid stupid man!'

'Tell me, Mr Lawrence, and I apologize in advance if

this is a difficult question to answer. Ignore it if you wish, I would fully understand. In some families, the dislike, maybe even the hatred for a man who has behaved like Candlesby abates over time, it grows less as the memory fades. But with others, the anger grows inside the family like a tumour. As the years pass it does not grow less, it grows greater so that the hatred for the perpetrator can be as strong, if not stronger, forty or fifty years on as it was at the start.'

Powerscourt looked closely at Harold Lawrence as he made his reply. 'I don't think anything of that sort has happened here,' he said. 'It was all a very long time ago. I don't think any of us think about it from one month to the next.'

'I'm very pleased to hear it. Tell me, this is one of those questions people in my profession are always asking. Can you think of anybody locally who might have wanted Lord Candlesby dead?'

'It's easier to answer that question the other way round, Lord Powerscourt. Far more people wanted the wretched man dead than wanted him to stay alive. You'll have heard about the duel and the adultery with the poor woman who walked into the sea and drowned herself. There are a number of other cuckolded husbands around but I wouldn't want to give you their names as I only heard about them in confidence. There's a farmer with land just north of Candlesby Hall who swears Candlesby poisoned his cattle. There's a retired general not far from here who claims that Candlesby raped his daughter and refused to make any provision when the girl became pregnant. You may find somebody with a good word to say about him. If you do, please let me know at once.'

Harold Lawrence pulled a watch rather ostentatiously from his waistcoat pocket. 'Now, if you'll excuse me, I must get on with the business of supervising this move. My wife has taken to her bed with nerves; it's all so upsetting. If there's any way I can help, please let me know.'

With that he shepherded Powerscourt to the front door. One of the carts, drawn by a fine pair of horses, was gathering speed down the drive en route to the Lawrences' new home. The last Powerscourt heard was another mighty bellow from the butler. 'See here, you useless footmen, all the dining-room chairs were meant to be out here by now, ready to go on the next cart. So where the bloody hell are they?'

Lady Lucy Powerscourt had finished the second of her lunch parties with the ladies of Lincolnshire. Another deputation was expected today at tea. During her time with Powerscourt she had volunteered on a number of occasions to eat for victory, to entertain various people whose only feature in common was that they might have something useful to add to her husband's investigation. Lady Lucy found these bizarre social occasions more testing with the passing of time but she did what she saw as her duty.

Mr Drake's hotel was not ideal for ladies who lunch with delicate palates and sophisticated tastes. Its clientele was largely male, used to large helpings of meat and potatoes with enormous trifles and apple pies for pudding. Often they had spent the morning out of doors, farmers, vets, surveyors, blacksmiths, and they had worked up a healthy appetite. Lady Lucy had conferred at length with Mr Drake and his chef, a young man from Boston with high ambitions in the catering trade. Mr Drake said he could see Lady Lucy's point, that the lunchtime offerings at the hotel were meant for healthy males with large appetites. But the ladies would eat it all, he assured her, and he said she might be surprised by the relish with which some of them disposed of the chef's famous trifles. The prospect of more and more of these heavy meals filled Lady Lucy with dismay. She decided on one last try for different offerings on the menu at a meeting with hotel staff.

'Fish?' she said in an interrogative tone that did not expect an answer in the affirmative.

'Fish?' said the young chef from Boston reverently, his mind suddenly filled perhaps with the crab and the plaice and the Dover sole and the scallops he had prepared in his previous establishment.

'Fish,' said Mr Drake speculatively, 'fish,' spoken by one wondering if his kitchen has all the right equipment to cook the things and if there are enough fish knives and forks in the canteens of cutlery.

'Fish,' said Lady Lucy again. 'Do you think we could get some fish on the menu?'

'I'd be more than happy to order it and to cook it,' said the chef, who secretly preferred cooking cod to roasting larger and larger cuts of the local beef. 'We could use the same suppliers we had in Boston. They weren't expensive.'

'Well,' said Mr Drake, 'so be it. As far as the ladies lunching with Lady Lucy are concerned, let them not eat cake, let them eat fish instead.'

After two days, Lady Lucy was to tell her husband later, there was already a pattern emerging. To begin with the ladies from Keys Toft and Toynton St Peter, Sausthorpe and Cumberthorpe would assume that they were not there to talk about the death of the Earl. Indeed not. Instead they would talk about the local weather or their children's progress or forthcoming attractions in the county, hunt balls or charity recitals. But once Lady Lucy had diverted their attention to the mysterious death of the Earl of Candlesby, it was as if the floodgates had been opened. Of course he had been murdered, said one. Don't be absurd, countered another, this is a modern country, people don't go round killing each other in 1909, for heaven's sake. A jealous husband, claimed a third, lured him to a lonely stretch of country and murdered him. When Lady Lucy inquired about who the jealous husband might be, the ladies laughed. There were, she was informed, so many to choose from.

'There's a whole list of possibilities,' said Mrs Devine from Keys Toft happily.

'I know this sounds unlikely,' Lady Folkingham entered the lists, 'but I think it was the vicar myself.'

'Which vicar?' chorused the ladies, as if all the vicars in Lincolnshire were known to be murderers.

'The one from Alford, of course.' Lady Folkingham stuck to her guns. 'Candlesby came to morning service there every Sunday for three months. I know as that's our local church. And he was always eyeing up the vicar's gorgeous wife – tall, willowy sort of a person with long blonde hair. Our butler swears he saw them once coming out of the most expensive hotel in Louth, looking as if they'd been up to something very naughty. And that vicar has a terrible temper. You should hear the way he shouts at the children in Sunday school.'

'You're not telling me, Bertha Folkingham, that the vicar went halfway across the county to kill the Earl,' said Mrs Stanhope from Toynton St Peter. 'Vicars don't do that sort of thing. Their superiors like the Dean and Chapter at the cathedral would have them drummed out of the Church.'

'But think what a perfect protection it would be, being a vicar.' Lady Folkingham wasn't going to retreat in the face of hostile fire. 'Nobody's going to suspect you for a moment. It's an ideal way to commit a murder, if you ask me.'

'I don't believe that vicar did it,' said the Honourable Mildred Grenfell from Cumberthorpe. 'I think that was all a blind, going to church in Alford, designed to put everybody off the scent. Don't you remember the wife of the vicar in Wainfleet All Saints, the one who went away last year very suddenly? Tall woman who looked as if she might have been a chorus girl in her younger days.'

Lady Lucy reflected that charity did not run very strongly through the veins of the ladies of Lincolnshire.

'I do remember her,' said Mrs Stanhope, 'flighty piece she was too; she attracted men like a water carrier in the

141

desert. They flocked to her, poor fools. But what does her disappearance – wasn't she called Hardy, Tabitha Hardy or something like that – what does that have to do with Candlesby's death?'

'I'll tell you what it has to do with Candlesby's death,' said a quiet woman called Mrs Morton from Skegness who hadn't spoken yet. 'I was told – in confidence, mind you, so I would ask you all to respect that – that she was carrying on with the Candlesby man. She was always going up to the Hall on the grounds that she liked looking at the deer. I don't think they were the only stag she encountered up there, if you follow me. The vicar finds out. There's a terrible scene with the wife. Candlesby refuses to have her living with him up at the Hall; maybe he did have some residual sense of the social proprieties, though I find that hard to believe. She goes away, nobody knows where. There is, for a while, a great murmuring in the parish of Wainfleet All Saints. No saintly behaviour is to be found except, maybe, from the vicar. Where is the vicar's wife? Is she dead? Nobody knew then about her links with Candlesby or it would be even worse. Is she coming back? Eventually somebody from the Church hierarchy, probably the Dean of Lincoln, he always likes telling people off, instructed the parishioners to keep quiet. But think of the vicar! Think how he must have been feeling!' The pinched, mouse-like features of Mrs Morton from Skegness grew especially animated at this point. 'His life is ruined. His career may never recover from the taint of being abandoned by his wife. Alone with his newly acquired housekeeper – who happens to be the worst cook in the east of England – he grows bitter. His betrayal, by the wife, and even more by Candlesby, gnaws away at him. He grows obsessive. And in the end,' Mrs Morton leaned back in her chair at this point with a flourish of her arms, 'his emotions and his obsessions take him over. He kills Candlesby in a fit of rage. It will be one of your husband's finest achievements, Lady Powerscourt, to bring this murdering vicar to book.'

There was a brief silence. The topic of murdering vicars seemed to have run its course. Lady Lucy made a mental note of the sections of the conversation she would report to her Francis. The ladies moved on to an abstract discussion of whether murder was more prevalent in the aristocracy than in the working classes. There was a surprising consensus that it was more common among the aristocracy.

James Candlesby, the youngest son who lived alone with his nurse at the top of the Hall, had not been well for some days. At first this took the form of wandering round the house on his own in the middle of the night, disturbing the mice and the rats and upsetting the bats in the basement. His nurse had sent word to the asylum outside Lincoln where the doctor who had been looking after him for some years was based. Dr Wilson, in spite of the entreaties of James's eldest brothers, had refused to admit him as a patient in the asylum. He would only grow worse there, he said. He believed, Dr Wilson, that James's eccentricities could be accommodated perfectly easily in the enormous house, especially if he was accompanied by a trained nurse.

This afternoon James's eyes were unusually bright and he was unable to settle anywhere, moving from chair to sofa to standing by the window for a few seconds and looking at the view. Something, in the nurse's view, was about to happen, and it did, in a way the nurse had never seen before. Lying on the floor and refusing to get up had once been the favourite. Then there had been days when James curled himself up into a ball and stayed under a table in the corner of the room. Sometimes there had been shouting – not any particular word, just a general shout that came across in the same inchoate fashion as the roar of a great crowd at a football match.

James went to a cupboard in the corridor outside his sitting room and pulled out a very large brush. He held it out in front of him as though it were a cross and he was the person carrying it in some religious procession.

'Onward Christian soldiers, marching as to war,' he sang, making his way slowly down the corridor,

> 'With the cross of Jesus going on before.
> Christ the Royal Master leads against the foe,
> Forward into battle see his banners go!'

He seemed to have forgotten the chorus. He was walking very deliberately, as if he was in a procession. He passed a glass case full of stuffed birds and started down the stairs.

> 'At the sign of triumph Satan's host doth flee,
> On then, Christian soldiers, on to victory!
> Hell's foundations quiver at the shout of praise,
> Brothers lift your voices, loud your anthems raise.'

He was on the second-floor landing now, where most of the bedrooms were situated. The nurse hurried down the stairs after him. James continued down towards the ground floor and the basement, passing a racehorse whose front features were still visible but whose hindquarters and rump had been overcome by the advance of the Candlesby grime.

> 'Like a mighty army moves the church of God;
> Brothers, we are treading where the saints have trod.
> We are not divided, all one body we,
> One in hope and doctrine, one in charity.'

As he reached the first floor, his elder brother Edward stuck his head out of the drawing room. 'For God's sake, you stupid lunatic,' he said, 'what on earth do you think you are doing? You're madder than usual today, even for you.'

James made no reply. His eyes appeared to be fixed on some distant goal. Perhaps he thought he was a crusader

144

from centuries past come to fight with the armies of Saladin in front of the walls of Jerusalem. Perhaps he was a recruit to Cromwell's New Model Army in the Civil War, dragged from field and barn to learn the arts of war before the battlefield at Naseby.

'Crowns and thrones may perish, kingdoms rise and
wane,
But the Church of Jesus constant will remain.
Gates of hell can never gainst that Church prevail;
We have Christ's own promise and that cannot fail.'

The mention of Christ's promise seemed to give James extra strength. He held the broomstick ever firmer as if he were escorting an archbishop to his stall in Canterbury Cathedral. He was down the stairs into the lower floor and out of the door into the outside world. There was no hesitation. He turned sharply to the left and began marching purposefully towards the lake. Henry and Edward both stuck their heads out of the saloon windows one floor up.

'Why don't you go and drown yourself, you mad person?'

'Put us all out of our misery, you stupid lunatic. Go straight into the water! Don't turn round! Don't bother coming back!'

With that the two brothers collapsed in hysterical laughter. James did not stop. He was quite close to the water's edge now. Charles had heard a noise where he was in the stables and began running as fast as he could towards the lake. James was on the edge of the water, marching straight on. The brothers were yelling out the chorus as an act of encouragement.

'Onward Christian soldiers, marching as to war,
With the cross of Jesus going on before.'

They sang it over and over, falling into helpless laughter

145

from time to time as they watched their brother advancing further into the water.

'Why can't you go in after him?' yelled Charles to the nurse.

'I can't swim,' replied the man.

Almost up to his neck now, James was still singing. Charles pulled off his jacket and charged into the lake. There seemed to be a struggle. Indeed it looked as if Charles might have knocked his brother out to make it easier to drag him away from the water. With the nurse arriving to help in shallower waters they managed to pull him ashore. The brush was still held firmly in his hands. They began to drag him across the grass towards the house in case he made another dash into the lake. When James came round a few minutes later he looked at them both very carefully. Then he burst into tears. From the first-floor window still came the chorus:

'Onward Christian soldiers marching as to war,
With the cross of Jesus going on before.'

'God help sailors on a night like this.' Detective Inspector Blunden was speaking to Powerscourt as the two men stood on the steps of the Candlesby mausoleum at ten to three in the morning. It had been raining hard since early evening and a wind had now got up, blowing in from the sea. Three of the Inspector's junior police constables were shielding their lamps against the storm. The clouds cleared over the moon every now and then to reveal the lake and the solid bulk of the house behind it like a great liner untroubled by the weather.

'Ten minutes to go,' said Powerscourt. The exhumation of the Earl of Candlesby was due to begin in precisely ten minutes. A small procession could be seen making its way up the hill towards the mausoleum.

'What about the key?' said Powerscourt suddenly, all too aware that if the new Earl had his way they would never get into the mausoleum at all.

'The coroner has that in hand,' said Blunden, pulling his cloak tighter around his shoulders. 'I think he gave out some pretty fierce warnings about disobeying an instrument of the law. The butler is to bring it at the appointed time.'

A tall man, wrapped in an enormous cloak, materialized out of the darkness.

'Carey,' he said, 'Nathaniel Carey, pathologist, at your service.'

As Powerscourt made the introductions another bedraggled figure joined them. The vicar who conducted the service of interment had come back to see the body removed. Later on he would have to inter the body once again. He nodded gravely to the other members of the melancholy party.

'Where are you going to conduct your examination, Dr Carey?' Powerscourt was whispering out of respect for the dead.

'They've made a room at the morgue in the hospital available for me. I hope to start first thing in the morning. Shouldn't take long. I mean, was the bloody man murdered or not? That shouldn't be too difficult to establish. Feel free to drop in around eleven. I should have something for you by then.'

Another group was advancing towards the mausoleum, led by the Candlesby butler carrying a powerful light. Behind him came the coroner, shrouded in a vast cloak, and the man from the undertakers who had supervised the burial, leading a cart drawn by two horses.

'Well,' said the coroner, 'all present and correct. I'm sure Thorpe can open up for us.'

Thorpe, the Candlesby butler, had on his belt one of the biggest bunches of keys Powerscourt had ever seen. Surely there were more keys on it than there were rooms in Candlesby Hall. The butler didn't hesitate for a moment. One quick glance down and a very large key, totally black, was inserted into the main door of the mausoleum. Within a minute the party were inside, the three policemen forming up around them with the lamps. The light shot across the great columns that reached up to the dome, flickering and fading as it went, dancing briefly across human faces. Their boots echoed off the marble floor. High up at the top of the building the bats were squeaking an ineffectual protest at this invasion under cover of darkness.

The coroner led the way downstairs to the vault. Some of the flagstones here were wet with damp. Powerscourt suddenly realized that in one sense they were fortunate. Sliding the coffin out of its niche down here would be much easier than digging it up from an ordinary grave in a cemetery on a night like this: the need to construct some sort of awning so nobody could see what was happening, the spades clogged with wet earth, the strain of pulling the coffin out of the ground, the constant rain and the howling of the wind.

Barnabas Thorpe whipped another ancient key from his ring and unlocked the iron grille that had enclosed Candlesby's coffin. The policemen pulled it out while Thorpe locked the gate once more. Then the undertaker supervised the transport out to the cart, the policemen and the undertaker himself acting as pallbearers.

Dr Carey looked at his prey with an appreciative eye, anxious to get on with his work. As the cart moved off the coroner came to say goodbye to Powerscourt and the Inspector. He shook them both by the hand.

'There, gentlemen, we have managed to secure what you wanted. I hope Carey's results will be to your liking. I am going to announce the day for the inquest when he has finished his investigations tomorrow. I don't like to call it beforehand in case any body parts have to be sent away for tests. A very good morning to you.'

Inspector Blunden led the way to the hospital morgue the following morning. He had, as he pointed out ruefully to

Powerscourt, been there far too many times before. There was the normal smell of hospital disinfectant. A couple of orderlies were cleaning the floor. They were taken to a small room to one side. A body was lying on a slab with a white sheet over its face but there was nobody else in the room. Dr Carey appeared after a moment or two, a large notebook in his left hand and an expensive-looking fountain pen in the other.

'Good morning, gentlemen,' he said cheerfully, placing notebook and pen on a small table in the corner. 'This one didn't take very long, hardly any time at all. Come, let me show you. You're not squeamish about dead bodies, are you? I have to warn you that this one is absolutely disgusting.'

Both men said they thought they would be able to cope. 'Here goes,' said Dr Carey, and pulled the sheet slowly back to about the level of the shoulder. It was one of the most revolting corpses Powerscourt had ever seen, and the battlefields of India and South Africa had been strewn with bodies hideously mutilated by the weapons of modern warfare. One side of Candlesby's face had not been touched at all. The other had been battered, hit, smashed, thumped, over and over and over and over again. The skin had been reduced to pulp. The bones had been beaten into strange and grotesque shapes. The nose had virtually disappeared. There was dried blood everywhere, caked in lumps on his shoulder, lining his body as far as they could see. There was a sickly smell of dried blood and death and the faint overlay of the hospital anaesthetic.

'You won't be surprised to hear that this poor man did not die of natural causes. I have to say I am at a loss to say exactly how he did die. I mean, after a fairly limited spell of this battering his heart gave up so the actual cause of death was heart failure. As for the time of death, it is difficult if not impossible to estimate so long after the event, but I would hazard sometime between ten in the evening and four

149

o'clock the following morning. So I can certainly answer the coroner's question, Was this death by natural causes? No, it was not. You gentlemen have lots of experience looking at dead bodies. Have you ever seen anything like this before? This brutal battering on one side of the face only?'

Neither man had seen anything like it. 'Would he have been upright perhaps?' Powerscout suggested. 'Lashed to a pillar so his assailant or assailants could attack him with a spade or something like that?'

'That's good, Powerscourt. He was tied up to something. His hands and ankles have marks on them as though he had indeed been secured on to pillar or post or some such.'

'You don't suppose our murderer has a rather bizarre way of killing people?' Inspector Blunden was rather hesitant. 'I mean, suppose he gets his man tied up so he can't move. Then he picks up his spade or his shovel or whatever it is. He gives one good whack to the man's face. If he's right-handed maybe it's easier to batter him on one side only rather than go round to the other side where the blows may not be so effective.'

'That's clever, Inspector. It may even be right.' Nathaniel Carey was nodding at Blunden. 'But there is something else I have to tell you. Whatever killed him might not have been a spade or a shovel or anything like that though I could be wrong. I have no idea what killed him.'

'Do you think you will be able to work it out – what killed him, I mean?'

Dr Carey looked at the corpse again. 'I'm not sure. I have preserved various sections of tissue which might tell us if certain other objects might have killed him. Beyond that, I can do nothing.'

'The way I look at it is this, Dr Carey, my lord,' Inspector Blunden said. 'We wanted to know if the man died of natural causes. We now know he didn't. He was murdered in a particularly horrible way. But now it's murder we can make progress in our investigation. We can question every single person in that house down to the mice in the skirting boards. We can search every room in the place. We can break into Jack Hayward's house if we have to and see if there are any clues in there as to where he's gone. I believe we have to wait until after the murder verdict is revealed at the inquest but that won't be long. We can begin our inquiries at last. The waiting's over.'

11

Johnny Fitzgerald didn't know much about The Turf. He could have told you that Charles the Second had a lot to do with establishing Newmarket as a centre for horse racing. He vaguely remembered somebody telling him about the great merits of Newmarket sausages. But when deciding on the best strategy for finding out if Jack Hayward and his family were here or not, he fell back on the tactics that had served him well in the past. He found the grandest public house and hotel in the place and inquired within for the name of a well-respected trainer.

'Do you have horses you want to place here, is that what you're about?' said the landlord in a quiet spell between orders.

'I'm looking for somebody, that's what I'm doing. Man who used to work here years ago. Now, if you could tell me the trainer who would most likely know about who's here and who's not, I would be most grateful.'

The landlord thought for a minute or two. 'Bamford,' he said, 'Dick Bamford. He knows most of what goes on round here. Apple Tree Farm is where you'll find him, on the Cambridge road.'

Just one string of horses passed Johnny on his way to the farm. They were picking their way along the road as if they were used to better surfaces and wider horizons.

Dick Bamford was slightly suspicious at first about

Johnny's mission. He had explained that he was working with one of England's leading investigators and the Lincolnshire police. But when Bamford learned that it involved a case of what looked like murder, and that Jack Hayward had disappeared very shortly after the discovery of the body, he grew more suspicious still.

'You're not suggesting that Jack killed this Candlesby person, that he ran away before he was arrested, are you?'

'No, I'm not, Mr Bamford,' said Johnny. 'I'm sorry I didn't explain about the dead man straight away. I promise you, nobody thinks Jack Hayward killed anybody. We just think he left in such a hurry because he knew too much. Maybe he knew enough to put the new Lord Candlesby in the dock. You see, only three people saw the body. Jack was one. The doctor was another. The son was the third. The doctor is dead and Jack has disappeared. There's only one person left around who has seen the corpse and knows what he died of and he says he never looked at the body at all. That's the new Earl, the eldest son. They may have taken the corpse out of its mausoleum by now and a pathologist may have answered some of these questions, I don't know. But can you see why we want to talk to Jack? It may be enough that we talk to him where he is at present so he won't have to go back to Candlesby if he doesn't want to. But unless I know where he is I can't even speak to him.'

'You give me your word', said Bamford, 'that you're not going to have him arrested the moment you find him?'

'I do.'

'Well then, I have no more idea than you do of where he is but I think my wife might be able to give you a steer. She was very close to Jack's wife when Jack worked for Laughton's, the big trainer down the road, very successful fellow. Bertha!'

He gave an enormous yell which duly produced Bertha from the kitchen, wearing a dark blue apron and with flour in her hair.

'You didn't have to shout so loud, Dick. The cat has gone into hiding again. Sorry, I didn't know we had company. Good afternoon.'

'Johnny Fitzgerald,' said Johnny, shaking a floury hand.

'Mr Fitzgerald is looking for Jack Hayward, dear. He was caught up in a mysterious death which may well turn out to be murder. He's left Candlesby Hall for the time being. And he departed in a hurry by all accounts, taking the wife and children with him. Mr Fitzgerald and his friends are keen to talk to him as he is one of the very few people to have seen the dead man.'

'That wouldn't be the old Earl of Candlesby, would it, the dead man, I mean, Mr Fitzgerald?'

'It would, I'm afraid,' said Johnny.

'Don't be afraid. Don't be afraid at all. Rejoice, rejoice. He was one of the worst men in England. Jack Hayward's wife has written to me many times with details of his crimes. She'll be so pleased.'

'I was hoping, Mrs Bamford,' said Johnny, keen to draw the conversation back to where he wanted it to go, 'that you might be able to help us in terms of where Jack Hayward would have taken his wife and family. I think it would have to be somewhere he could find work, and somewhere he could feel safe if anybody came looking for him. Do you have any ideas?'

Mrs Bamford looked doubtful. 'I don't remember having any conversations with Kathleen, that's the wife, about where they might go in an emergency.'

'What about her family? Where did she come from?'

'She was Irish, I'm sure of that. Now you're going to ask me which part, aren't you? Hold on a moment, let me think.'

Mrs Bamford went over to the window and stared at a corner of the stables. She went and looked at a small painting on the wall which showed a string of horses out for their morning gallop.

'Kathleen gave me this picture,' she said. 'Her people have something to do with horses, breeding them, training them, riding them, I can't remember. But there's a name on the picture somewhere. Here it is: O'Grady Stables, Cashel. Cashel's got a rock in it, I remember them telling us about it at school, though whether it's a sweet like Brighton rock or a great stone thing sticking up into the sky I don't know. Cashel, that's where she came from, Kathleen O'Grady as she was before she married Jack. Maybe that's where you should head for, Mr Fitzgerald.'

Johnny thought there was something biblical about the name. Rock of Cashel. Rock of Ages. Maybe the Haywards were hiding themselves in it.

Three days after the inquest with its verdict of unlawful killing, Powerscourt and Detective Inspector Blunden were on their way back to the Hall. The inquest had been regularly interrupted by Mark Sowerby, the late Earl of Candlesby's man of business from Hopkins Pettigrew & Green of Bedford Square. Sowerby had tried to establish that the exhumation from the Candlesby mausoleum had been unlawful because the family had not been consulted. The coroner informed him politely that he, as coroner, had full authority to order exhumations in cases of this kind. Sowerby's next assault had been to claim that as the exhumation had clearly been unlawful the inquest had no right to issue a verdict other than that of death by natural causes as signed off by Dr Miller at the time of death. Dr Carey, making notes in a large red notebook, was biding his time. When summoned to give his evidence he took care to give the most graphic description he could of the injuries delivered to the dead man's body. His description of the dried blood and crushed bone left one or two of the ladies in the court looking rather pale. Mark Sowerby made one last stand on behalf of his clients, still protesting that the inquest was unlawful and that therefore its verdict could not stand. By this stage the coroner's patience was exhausted.

'Mr Sowerby, you have tried my good temper long enough. Your ignorance of the law relating to inquests and exhumations is equalled only by your inability or your unwillingness to listen to the evidence. I do not see why this court should be troubled by your vexatious interruptions and your false disquisitions on the law. Gentlemen,' the coroner nodded to two policemen at the side of the court, 'take him away.'

Powerscourt and the Inspector had decided to divide their forces. The two principal powers among the Candlesby staff, they had decided, were likely to be the butler and the housekeeper. Powerscourt would take the butler and Blunden, who prided himself on his abilities with female witnesses, would interview the housekeeper. Blunden had also secured the consolation prize of the cook.

Nobody on the staff is young here, Powerscourt said to himself, as he was shown into the butler's room on the ground floor, next to where the silver was kept and across the way from the cellars. A couple of grandmothers, their arms piled high with clean sheets, passed him in the corridor like members of the chorus in some Greek tragedy. He remembered the steward and his melancholy account of his time here. Barnabas Thorpe the butler was well over seventy years old. He still had a fine head of hair, even if it had turned white, but his cheeks looked as though they had fallen in and his brown eyes looked sad all the time, as if they had seen enough.

'Very good of you to talk to me, Mr Thorpe,' Powerscourt began cheerfully. 'Tell me, how long have you been here now?'

The old man was counting on his fingers, working out the years of his servitude. 'Sixty-two years I've been here now, my lord. I came in 1847 when I was fourteen years old as a trainee footman.'

'So you're seventy-six now. That's about time to be thinking of retiring, surely.'

'I don't hold with this here retiring business, my lord. My father went on working till he was eighty-five, when he dropped down in his dairy, and my uncle went on till he was ninety-one. There's something about the Candlesby air, I reckon. It's the absence of all them modern things like motor cars and central heating and that electricity wiring, that's what keeps us going if you ask me.'

'Quite,' said Powerscourt, wondering how to proceed with this veteran of domestic service, a Methuselah in a frock coat. 'Perhaps you could tell us a little about the first two Lord Candlesbys you served before we move on to the one who's just died.'

'It's odd, my lord. People tell you when you're younger that you can remember things that happened a long time ago much better as you grow older, and you don't quite believe them. But it's true, the further back I go the clearer things seem in my mind. The old Earl, the one I served when I first came here, he was a good man. He was happily married, he cared about the estate, the whole agricultural business hadn't started to go wrong. Maybe it's because I was so young – I wasn't yet twenty when he died – but the sun seemed to be always shining. His youngest daughter got married in that time and the celebrations went on for days – dinners for all the tenants, dancing, presents for the girls. It was magic. He dropped down dead one afternoon, that Earl, and the place was never the same again.'

'Would you have said that he was eccentric, that he had some strange characteristics at all?'

'I know what you're getting at, my lord. There was plenty before him that were odd, like the one who went to Italy and came back with all those paintings that are still locked up in the top room by the back staircase. My first Earl, the old Earl, as I always call him, he was a Richard too, like the present one. The thing about him was that he wasn't eccentric. In this family, pardon me for saying so, my lord, he was odd because he wasn't odd, if you follow me. The next one, Edward he was, well, he started all right. It looked as though he would follow in his father's footsteps. Then some of the family failings began to click in. You could watch it happening: slightly eccentric at the beginning of the decade, very eccentric by the end of it, virtually off his head five years later.'

'What form did it take, this eccentricity, Mr Thorpe?'

'Well, there's a family failing for becoming recluses. Like those hermits who lived on top of pillars, my lord. They stop talking to people. They stop talking to each other. By the end the Edward one was communicating with the staff by letter. God knows how he communicated with the wife and children. And then there was the estate. In earlier times all the area round the house was given over to the deer, a lovely herd there used to be here, and lovely venison on the table too. They were banished. All the area where the deer had been was allowed to go back to nature so the wildlife could flourish. And why was the wildlife allowed to flourish? So it could be caught and stuffed, my lord. At one point we had a taxidermist from Lincoln come to live here for six months a year while he saw to the dead creatures from the estate. Then there were the catalogues from all the taxidermists within a hundred miles offering everything from stuffed llamas to wildebeest. You'll have seen all these glass cases clogging up the house; we had to throw out a whole lot more after that Edward died. His attention was so given over to all this nonsense that he didn't look after anything else.'

'I can see that this must have made life difficult for you all,' said Powerscourt. 'How did it affect your day-to-day routines?'

'Well, my lord, it was often very difficult when you had no contact with the man at all. And then, just before he turned fifty, there was something else. I think he'd read about some house down in Sussex having tunnels running underneath it which meant that the people in the big house would see even less of the servants – the footmen and the housemaids would be moving about underground. So we had to have tunnels too. There's one that goes from the kitchen area to the stables, and another that goes from the gardens to the area on the right of the house. No more under gardeners bringing flowers to the house across the lawn.'

'What did you all think of this new arrangement? Were you happy with it?'

Barnabas Thorpe smiled. 'Well, my lord, it works both ways, as one of the footmen put it. They might not be too pleased at seeing us moving around through the house, but we didn't like looking at them any more than they liked looking at us. So it was all square if you like.'

'What of your last employer, the Earl who's just died? How did he rate in the eccentricity scale?'

Barnabas Thorpe paused. 'I don't like to say too much about him, my lord. Loyalty to one's employers may be going out of fashion these days and I have no reason to keep quiet, none at all. But I still feel uncomfortable talking to you about him; I feel as though I'm letting him down even though he's not here any more. What can I say? He was cruel to his children, he would damage any friendships he might have had, he was terrible about money. I don't know how deeply he'd fallen into debt but in recent years we've had a parade of bank managers, insurance men, mortgage company men all trooping through the door.'

'Could I ask you, Mr Thorpe, where the bank managers came from? Was it Louth? Or Lincoln?'

'You could do a lot worse than talk to them, my lord. They're not north of here, they're south, in Boston. Lambert is the name of the manager person, Sebastian Lambert.'

'Could I just ask you one last question, Mr Thorpe? You've been most co-operative, and I'm very grateful to you. Can you think of any person who might want to kill your late master? Or any reason somebody might have for killing him?'

'The boys,' Barnabas Thorpe said sadly, 'the three eldest boys. The fourth one with the stutter isn't like any of the others and the last one, poor soul, he isn't right in the head.'

'Have you ever seen James be violent? Fall into a rage where he might do anything?' Powerscourt suddenly wondered if James had lost his temper completely and managed to beat his father around the face over and over again. Madmen, he remembered, sometimes discovered reserves of strength they didn't know they had. Perhaps James had killed his father and the others had covered up for him. Perhaps they had all killed him, taking it in turns to shatter the side of his face with whatever instrument of darkness they had used. Stop it, he said to himself, you're getting carried away.

'Well, I have seen him violent, as a matter of fact, but only once. And the violence was against himself, not against another person.'

'I am so grateful to you for your time, Mr Thorpe,' said Powerscourt. 'If anything else occurs to you, please get in touch. I shall be around the Hall quite a bit, I expect.'

Twenty minutes later he was reunited with the Inspector, who was carrying two medium-sized parcels. 'One of these is for you, my lord, and the other one is for me. Candlesby fruit cake, baked to an ancient recipe of 1763 from this house, composed of ingredients largely grown on the estate. Very good they are too. I was given a trial run of one of them along with a cup of tea. Did you discover anything of interest, my lord?'

'The butler was more forthcoming about the Earls of long ago than he was about the dead one from the other day. Traces of family loyalty still survive in spite of all the dreadful behaviour. He did say he thought the three eldest boys were the most likely to have done it.'

'Did he indeed? Well, the women, apart from detailed information about the meals the late Earl and his family ate, had very little to say. Maybe they had cut out all the gossip because of me. I've investigated two crimes in grand houses now, my lord, and the one thing you can guarantee, in my experience, is that the servants know absolutely everything that is going on. They know about illicit sexual behaviour because they make the beds. They know what the mistress of the house is thinking because she often tells them when they're brushing her hair. They know what's preoccupying the gentlemen because they're in attendance at the shoot as beaters or what have you and the grooms hear the tittle-tattle when the horses come back to the stables from the hunt or a ride. What the under footman knows at eleven o'clock, the parlourmaids know by lunchtime. What the butler knows by three o'clock is transmitted on at tea in the servants' hall. But here the networks seem to have broken down. The housekeeper and the cook haven't been here as long as the butler, my lord, and the one memorable thing they told me was about the menus. They've been the same since Victoria's first Jubilee, apparently. Never changed since.'

'And?' said Powerscourt, eager for more.

'Sorry, my lord, I don't even need to look at my notes. Candlesby beef on Sunday, Candlesby lamb on Monday, Candlesby chicken on Tuesday, pork from the butcher on Wednesday, Candlesby venison on Thursday, Candlesby duck on Friday and fish from the fishmonger on Saturday.'

'No pigs on the estate here?' said Powerscourt.

'No pigs, my lord.'

'Are we talking lunch or dinner here, Inspector?'

'This is dinner, my lord.'

'What happens at lunchtime? I presume the system is

so well set that it still goes on until somebody decides to change it.'

'Lunchtime was cold meat with vegetables, or pies. I believe most of the meat from the evening would be turned into its own pie: venison pie, chicken pie and so on. The late Earl was particularly partial to venison pie, apparently.'

'What a dreadful routine.'

'I don't think I'm going to recommend it to Mrs Blunden, my lord. She's a great believer in salads, the wife.'

'No sustenance in salads, that's what my father used to say. Never mind. Have you noticed something odd about the servants here, Inspector?'

'I wouldn't say I've had the time to do that yet, my lord. There's a lot to think about round here.'

'The curious thing about the servants at Candlesby Hall is that there aren't any. Not in the conventional sense anyway. No parlourmaids, no ladies' maids, no kitchen maids, no laundry maids, all of whom would be young and lively and frequent bait for resident younger sons, no young footmen, no young coachmen, no trainee gardeners. The minimum age of the staff here is about fifty years. I've never seen anything like it.'

Sandy Temple, friend of Lady Lucy's sister's daughter Selina, was sitting in the armchair by the side of the fire normally occupied by Lord Francis Powerscourt. He felt slightly guilty, Sandy, until he remembered Lady Lucy telling him and Selina that they were to treat the house as if it were their own and she hoped they would enjoy their brief spell together. Sandy usually came home in time for tea and went back to his own quarters after supper. But now was not a time for frivolity. Sandy had been asked for a political judgement by his immediate superior at *The Times* and he was determined to succeed.

On his lap was a large black book with ruled pages. On

the floor beside his chair were a series of smaller notebooks that might have fitted in a pocket. These were the shorthand books he kept of the debates in the House of Commons and the House of Lords. In the black book was the voting record of the Lords on all the bills that had been sent up to them from the Commons in the present Parliament. Sandy was making a list of all those peers who had opposed government bills. Those who had voted against the Asquith government twice got two stars against their name and so on. The number of rebels grew longer with the passage of time. Soon there were some peers with five stars against their name, joined by other new recruits with only one.

'Sandy, my love! How nice to see you! I've had such a tiresome afternoon at the V&A! I've ordered tea.'

'Bear with me a moment, Selina. I've got to finish this off today.'

'What is it?' asked Selina, keen to be involved in the great work of journalism.

There was a silence while Sandy added yet more names to his list. This is how it will be, Selina thought suddenly, when we're married, if we're married. Some husbands spend their time deep in the form book or the cricket scores. Mine will be ensconced in the parliamentary reports in the newspapers. Sandy knelt down and picked up one of his shorthand notebooks.

'I'm trying to work out, Selina, the likely size of the majority if the House of Lords throw out Lloyd George's Budget.'

Selina had listened to enough conversations on the subject of Lloyd's Budget to realize that this was very important. If pressed, she would have said that she thought this Budget had something to do with the poor and with big ships with a funny name but she wasn't quite sure; politics had never really interested her very much.

'I thought people said the Lords wouldn't dare throw it out,' she said, wondering how long this rather tiresome diversion was going to go on.

163

'Selina, please,' said Sandy, in an irritated voice, 'I've got to add up four columns of figures in a moment. Could I ask you to keep quiet until I've done that? Please?'

Selina felt tempted to ask how long this was going to take but thought better of it. She watched as Sandy's pen flew up and down the columns on his page. Even he was surprised by his figures. If you added together all those peers who had voted against one or more of the government's bills when they reached the House of Lords, you would have not just a majority, but a landslide.

'That's it, Selina. I was fairly sure before I started. They've got a huge majority against the Budget, if they want to use it, the Conservative leadership in the Lords. It'll be political dynamite. God knows who it might blow up, maybe the government, maybe the Lords. It could even backfire.'

Tea appeared at that moment and Selina busied herself with the role of hostess. 'What are you going to do with the figures, Sandy?' she asked.

'These figures here about the potential size of the majority? I have to take them to my boss at *The Times*. I don't know what he's going to do with them. I've just got time to drink this cup of tea.'

'I haven't told you, Sandy, we've been invited to stay in Norfolk for the weekend. In a rather grand house too. I think Lady Walpole's a friend of my mother's; that's where the invitation comes from.'

Selina was wishing she could lure Sandy over to sit beside her on the sofa. It would be much more cosy but she didn't want to be interrupted by someone coming back for the tea things.

'Will she be one of those hostesses who puts up lists of where everybody is sleeping?' said Sandy. 'A chap told me about all that the other day.'

'I don't think it would apply to us, anyway. You'll be in the bachelors' wing, I expect, and I may get a room on my own somewhere. We'll have to wait and see.'

Sandy brushed a crumb or two off his jacket and started out for Westminster. He was just on the far side of the door when Selina called to him.

'I've just thought of something, my love. She probably has a couple of peers who come for the weekend. Think about it. You'll be able to ask them in person how they're going to vote.'

12

It was going to be a great day at Candlesby Hall. Today was the day Richard, the new Earl, was to be installed and to take his seat in the House of Lords in London. His robes were ready for collection at a traditional tailor's tucked away in the side streets of Westminster. His two supporters, both diehard opponents of Lloyd George's Budget, were ready to welcome him in and see him through the ceremonial. He would be joining, one of the supporters had assured him, not just one of the most historic and most ancient chambers of its kind in the world, but the ranks of those who were not prepared to abandon their ancient freedoms to the whims of a tainted majority and who intended to oppose the dictatorship of the Liberal proletariat by voting against Lloyd George's Budget.

His brothers Henry and Edward were going to travel down with Richard and observe the ceremony from the gallery. And because this was such an important day Richard had decreed that they should travel in a special train, with accommodation reserved for them and for them alone. There was a dining car, a luxury lounge car and a private carriage for Richard, who wished to be left alone on this journey to contemplate his responsibilities and think about what he would say to his fellow peers. He had realized that he didn't have to give his maiden speech on the day he was introduced, but he thought he had better consider it anyway. This train had been booked a week or two earlier when the date of the ceremony became known. It was waiting for them at Boston station at ten to eleven in the morning, getting ready to depart at eleven o'clock sharp, as the horse-drawn carriage with the three brothers rode up to the station. Two guards in their uniform of dark jackets and the green cord waistcoats of the Great Northern Railway escorted the new Lord Candlesby to his special coach.

'Just to remind you all,' the new Lord Candlesby said at the top of his voice to all those within earshot, 'I am not to be disturbed. It is a very great responsibility for a man to take his seat in the House of Lords.'

As he watched his brother strut his way into the private carriage Edward Dymoke decided that he now sympathized with the more radical brethren who thought the House of Lords and the hereditary peers who made up its numbers should all be abolished.

The two brothers settled themselves in the luxury lounge with some of the newspapers and magazines provided. At exactly eleven o'clock the Great Northern Railway's fastest engine took them out of Boston and south towards Spalding and Peterborough before arriving in London.

Only when they reached King's Cross did anybody realize that something was wrong. Certainly the station staff back in Boston had been perfectly happy to let the train go. When they reached London and Richard did not appear, the brothers could not get into his carriage from the passageway along the train. The door appeared to have been locked or fixed in some way from the inside. The blinds on the platform side had been pulled down so it was impossible to see inside. It took two stout porters all their strength to gain entrance through the corridor, virtually breaking down the door. They saw that the new Earl had indeed made the journey south. But round his neck was a great red weal and his head had fallen on to one side. Lord Candlesby's Inauguration Day had been turned into his Death Day. He had been garrotted, and the killer and his deadly wire were nowhere to be seen.

The local police Inspector discovered quickly that this was a second murder, likely to be linked to the previous one up in Lincolnshire. He took it on himself to send the train back to Boston immediately with a couple of constables to guard the corpse on its journey home. He sent a wire immediately to Detective Inspector Blunden to alert the authorities and organize a post-mortem.

Half an hour after the train returned Powerscourt joined the Inspector at the station. The remaining Dymokes had been despatched to the Hall with a warning that the police would come to question them in the morning. The gruesome corpse, the second Lord Candlesby defiled in death, had gone to the local hospital to await the post-mortem.

'This is a terrible business, my lord,' Blunden said. 'I've sealed the station off, nobody is allowed in or out, though the killer must have been away hours ago.'

'He was garrotted, you said, Inspector – I presume there wasn't any room in the compartment to beat him over the head with some horrible instrument.'

'No, my lord. I'm sure you agree with me that the two murders must be linked in some way but I'm damned if I can see what it is. Ah, I think this must be the stationmaster come back to his post.'

'Masters, Geoffrey Masters,' the man said, shaking them both by the hand in turn. 'What a terrible thing this is, gentlemen. I've never heard of a murder in any station where I've worked, never. Please come to my office; we would be more comfortable there.

'As of this moment, my lord, Detective Inspector, you probably know more about what happened than I do. We have ordered every man who works here to be brought back to the station for questioning. I presume you would like to conduct as many interviews as you can tonight, if possible. My office here is at your service, and the waiting room has been cleared for more of your officers to conduct their interviews. I have reserved a temporary office for myself in the Railway Arms opposite.'

'That's very generous of you, Mr Masters,' said Inspector Blunden. 'What do you want to do, my lord? I'd be more than happy if you wanted to join me in these interviews.'

Powerscourt declined. He felt that the station staff might be more comfortable talking to one of their own rather than a man with a title and a Silver Ghost. He felt sure that many of Blunden's policemen would know some of the station staff from the local football club or the school or the church.

'I'm going to have a look at the carriage where the murder took place,' he said. 'Do you know, Mr Masters, if the special train stopped anywhere on the way? Something tells me it will have gone through Spalding and Peterborough, but I don't know if it actually came to a halt anywhere on en route.'

The stationmaster riffled through some papers on his desk and scratched his ear. 'It didn't stop, my lord, Inspector. It was booked to go straight through to King's Cross.' Masters began stuffing bundles of paper into his bag. 'And now, if you'll excuse me, I'll get out of your way. You know where to find me.'

The Detective Inspector had prepared a list of questions for the officials of the Great Northern Railway.

What time did you reach the station in the morning?

Did you see anything suspicious, or any suspicious person, when you arrived or later on in the morning?

Did you see how many guards escorted the party on to the train?

Did one person or two accompany Lord Candlesby to his special carriage?

Did you see anybody leave the train before it set off?

Could somebody have entered the train from the far side without being seen?

Were there any staff of the Great Northern you had not seen before, the crew of the special train perhaps?

How many guards were there on the train on its way south to King's Cross?

Powerscourt could hear the questions and answers like the distant responses of a church congregation at matins. He was making his way to the death train, as he had heard one of the young signalmen refer to it, down the main platform to the south, parked on a siding next to the main line. Two constables greeted him warmly. The very young one burst into speech.

'Please, Lord Powerscourt, sir, could I come with you, sir, and watch you as you work? I'm Police Constable Andrew Merrick, sir, from Skegness, sir. Detective Inspector Blunden knows I want to be a detective, sir.'

Powerscourt thought you could almost hear the words 'when I grow up' at the end of the sentence. The young man didn't look much more than sixteen though he couldn't be admitted into the Lincolnshire Constabulary until he was eighteen. The older representative of the law nodded benignly at his colleague.

'There's no harm in the boy, my lord,' he said, 'though he does get very excited about violent crime and murder and that's a fact.'

'Come along then,' said Powerscourt, with a smile. 'Let's make our way to the carriage where he was killed.'

There was a third policeman by the door into the compartment. He inspected Powerscourt briefly. 'I've seen you up at the Hall with the Detective Inspector, sir. You must be Lord Powerscourt. I presume you want to see the murder carriage, sir.' With that the policeman unlocked the door and turned on a light switch. The compartment was like a sitting room in a gentlemen's club in London. Great red armchairs were scattered about the carriage with two little writing tables. At the far end from the policeman were a couple of doors to let the passengers in and out. Powerscourt saw that one of the chairs was totally out of position, parked right up against the side of the carriage. There were faint marks at the top of the chair and footprints etched deep into the carpet.

'Was this where he was killed, my lord, sir?' Young Andrew Merrick was whispering, his face pale against the harsh electric light.

Powerscourt was down on the floor, looking ever so keenly at the various foot marks. 'Yes, I think it is,' he said. 'Now then, young Andrew, come down here and look at these footprints. How many feet would you say there were? Four? Six? What do you think?'

'Would I be right in thinking, my lord, that four would mean there were only two men here, the Earl and the murderer? But six would mean three men, the Earl, the murderer and his accomplice?'

'We'll make a Sherlock Holmes out of you before we're finished,' said Powerscourt. 'You're absolutely right. I think there were two killers here earlier today. You see, Andrew, it's very hard, but not impossible, for one man to garrotte another on his own. You try creeping up behind me with an imaginary piece of wire in your hand.'

There was a brief but conclusive struggle. Andrew was possibly over-anxious about killing such an eminent personage as Powerscourt. At any event he ended up on the floor.

'Think of it like this, young Andrew.' Powerscourt was brushing the dust off his suit. 'If there are two of you, one man has to hold the victim's arms still, probably behind his back. Then the other can proceed with the actual garrotting.'

He stepped back from the area around the chairs and inspected the floor once more. 'Don't suppose our murdering friends will have left their piece of wire or whatever it was behind them.' He moved away from the area where the struggle had taken place and stood looking at the door for a long time.

'Lord Powerscourt, sir,' young Andrew was back in the

hunt, 'do you think the killers stayed on the train all the way to London, sir? Wouldn't it be a bit strange to have to spend the journey with a man you'd just killed?'

'Well,' said Powerscourt, 'there are a number of possibilities. The door to the rest of the train was certainly locked. They could, as you say, have remained on the train all the way to King's Cross. Or they could have killed him before the train left. Or they could have jumped off the train some place where it had slowed down. Whichever way it was done, it would seem likely that the killers were wearing the uniform of the Great Northern Railway.'

Powerscourt put his hand to the door that led to the outside world. It opened easily. There were no clues as to whether somebody might have jumped out of it in the past twenty-four hours.

'See here,' said Powerscourt, whipping out a notebook and making drawings of the position of the chairs where the struggle had occurred, 'I want you to go back to the waiting room and the stationmaster's office where the interviews are taking place. I want you to bring back the man who drove this train to London and the senior guard on the special train. Quick now, as quick as you can.'

'Yes, sir, Lord Powerscourt, sir.'

Five minutes later young Andrew was back. 'Mr Jones, the driver, sir. Mr Smith, sir, the senior guard, sir.' Both were in their early thirties, Jones painfully thin, Smith more corpulent as if he partook liberally of the various meals on offer to his richer travellers. Both looked to Powerscourt as if they would be steady under fire.

'Thank you both very much for coming over,' Powerscourt began. 'This shouldn't take very long although I may want you to do something for us in the morning. Now then, Mr Smith, how many guards did you have on the special train this morning?'

'Two, sir, and myself. Even that was probably too many. There were only three passengers on the train.'

'And were your two men in this carriage at any time before and during the journey?'

'No, sir, they were not. We had strict instructions to leave the gentleman in here – Lord somebody or other, wasn't he? – on his own.'

'So not even at the beginning of the journey, before the train actually left, were there any people other than the dead man in here as far as you know?'

Smith looked puzzled. 'No, sir, there were not.'

'Let me tell you, gentlemen, and I would ask you to keep this under your hats for the present, there must have been two people in here, probably at the start. They may have been wearing GNR uniform so as not to attract attention. I suspect they entered the carriage by the door on the opposite side of the platform where the train would shield them from view. If there's a problem with how they got in there's an even bigger problem with how they got out. Mr Smith, you didn't see another two guards in uniform get off the train at King's Cross, did you?'

'No, sir.'

'Could they have slipped off the train without being seen?'

'It's possible, sir, just possible. We have to clear everything away as soon as the train has arrived – plates, glasses, cups and so on. That's why the guards are usually the last people to leave the train.'

'Excuse me, sir, Lord Powerscourt, sir,' – young Andrew was joining the grown-ups, – 'wouldn't they have killed the Earl near the start of the journey? Otherwise he could have called for assistance, or tried to escape into another carriage, sir.'

Mr Jones looked closely at the young policeman. He hadn't finished yet.

'As I said before, sir, would they have wanted to stay in the carriage all that time with a corpse, sir, Lord Powerscourt, sir?'

'I was just coming to that,' said Powerscourt. 'Mr Jones, you must know this line better than anybody. Are there any stretches where you have to slow down, so that a man could jump out without killing himself?'

'Before I answer that, my lord, can I ask why they didn't just tip the body out of the door once they had killed him?'

'My answer to that, Mr Jones, is that I don't know. Maybe they thought the body might be discovered before the train reached London and a hue and cry would begin sooner than they would have wanted. Though why they should refrain from throwing the dead man out of the carriage and then throw themselves out of it I have no idea. But come, Mr Jones, are there places where the jumping could have been done?'

Archibald Jones took a long time fiddling with his pipe and getting it to draw. 'I have been thinking about your requirements while we talked,' he began. 'The obvious place to jump would be as we draw close to King's Cross. There are always red signals there for no apparent reason. But you would have to work out the likelihood of meeting a train coming the other way. You could very easily get yourself killed. The other train might be on you before you knew it was there. There is another place you might jump, on the northern outskirts of Peterborough. The problem there is that the track runs along very close to rows of terraced houses. I don't think you would be in much danger of being killed by a train coming the other way, but the chances of being seen would be considerable. Two men in the uniform of the Great Northern Railway could cause quite a stir. So I don't think Peterborough would be the answer.'

Jones the driver drew hard on his pipe and blew a great cloud of smoke across the compartment. Just like one of his engines, Powerscourt thought. Maybe he's going to get under way in a minute.

'There is just one place where I think it might be possible,' Jones went on, 'and that's on the way into Spalding. Before the town, while you're still in open country, there's a cutting with thick grass and brambles and weeds and loads of blackberries in the autumn. You could throw yourself into that and hope the grass and general undergrowth would check your fall. There's a road into the town a hundred yards away.'

'And you wouldn't be overlooked?'

'No, sir.'

'What speed would the train be travelling at?' asked Powerscourt, suddenly remembering some hazardous leaps in the past with Johnny Fitzgerald.

'I should think about ten to twelve miles an hour, my lord.'

'Could you take me there in the morning? In this train with the same carriages?'

'I'm sure I could, my lord. I'll just have to clear it with the stationmaster in the morning.'

Powerscourt felt a tugging on his arm and a low but insistent cough.

Young Andrew was not to be denied. 'Lord Powerscourt, sir, Mr Jones, sir, what about the door? I was told it was closed when the train reached London. How did they close the door after they'd jumped out of it?'

Powerscourt strode over to the door. Before he reached it Jones gave him the answer.

'It opens outwards, my lord, the door, I mean.'

Powerscourt flung open the door and stared at the railway lines of the Great Northern Railway, a few stray carriages dotted about the tracks. A dull murmur could be heard coming from the stationmaster's office as the interviews went on. He thought about a trial jump but realized that it wouldn't tell him anything. Stationary leaps were just not the same.

Twenty minutes later he was conferring with Inspector Blunden.

'I'll get all these interviews typed up in the morning, my lord,' said Blunden. 'It would seem from what you learnt and what one or two people here said, that two people entered the Candlesby carriage at some point before the train left the station. Can't think how they persuaded him to let them stay. They may have had keys. Anyway, once the train left the station, I would say, they killed him.'

'We won't know about the jump until tomorrow,' said Powerscourt. 'But do you suppose they knew the line well enough to decide where to jump? And were they staff members of the Great North Railway? Or were they impostors? And if so, where did they get the uniforms? And, more important, how did they know where to jump off?'

'I'm going to ask the stationmaster to inquire about the uniforms tomorrow. And he said, my lord, that it's perfectly fine to take the train down the line tomorrow, but he can't let it go until half past two in the afternoon. He muttered something about signals.'

'Half past two would be fine,' said Powerscourt. 'May I take young Andrew with me? He might make a better fist of jumping into the undergrowth than me. Did anybody who noticed the two fake guards mention what age they might be? If they were over fifty I can't see them leaping out of trains.'

'There were two people', said the Inspector, checking his notebook, 'who noticed them, or thought they might have noticed them. But they made no comment at all on how old they might have been.'

Lady Lucy had been persisting loyally with her Lincolnshire ladies' lunches. They had, she felt, become rather a strain. There had been one where all the guests combined to claim a vicar as the murderer. Other candidates had been denounced, a Justice of the Peace, Lincolnshire's biggest landowner, a doctor who was widely suspected of murdering his patients. Her guest on this day had insisted on coming alone. Rachel Cameron was a tall good-looking woman of about forty years of age with dark brown hair and a bossy manner. She made interesting but inconsequential small talk until they had finished the fish. When the waiter had cleared the plates away she made her move. She leaned forward in her chair and fixed Lady Lucy with a conspiratorial stare.

'Lady Powerscourt, I'm sure you must have heard some pretty incredible stories about the murder of Lord Candlesby. The women in these parts don't have enough to do, so gossip and fantasy take the place of charity work or improving the lives of one's tenants.' She made it sound as if she, Rachel Cameron, lived on a higher plane than the ladies of Horncastle or Ingoldmells. 'I'm sure you will have heard of the terrible fate of Lady Flavia Melville last summer.'

'The poor woman who was having an affair with the Earl and committed suicide after their love letters were sent to her husband?'

Mrs Cameron nodded. 'I happen to know rather a lot about that affair. You see, I was very close to Flavia Melville, as she became after her marriage. I think I was probably her only friend in the county. It must have been so strange, living here surrounded by these philistines after a German university town. She used to say that the conversations were so different. She had replaced the pursuit of knowledge with the pursuit of the fox.'

Mrs Cameron paused for a moment. Lady Lucy said nothing. 'Her husband was perfectly polite, perfectly pleasant. But that was all there was. You know how you wonder with some people if the public persona is a facade, an invented personality? Flavia was deceived by the English customs. She once told me her husband's good manners were a facade hiding an abyss, that there was nothing behind them, nothing at all. It was, she said, like being married to a clothes horse that could speak a few stock phrases, nothing more. I think Sir Arthur began to irritate her intensely after about six months of marriage. I remember her coming to my house one day in the spring and walking up and down the garden saying, "What am I to do?" over and over again. I don't suppose many married women begin affairs out of exasperation with their husbands; perhaps they do. John was so very different from her husband. Decisive, arrogant, determined to take what he wanted without paying any bills, and I don't mean the bills you can settle with money. I don't think he treated her very well – he didn't know how. That might have been part of the appeal. For some people being beaten up, literally or metaphorically, can be very attractive.'

She paused again. 'You do understand what I'm saying, Lady Powerscourt? I'm not just talking to myself?'

'Not at all, certainly not,' said Lady Lucy. 'Please continue.' They waited for the waiter to refill their glasses with Mr Drake's finest Quincy.

'She changed so much during the months of their affair. She hadn't seemed particularly attractive before. People said Sir Arthur must have been pretty desperate to marry her. But now she glowed. She radiated a devil-may-care kind of happiness. I often thought Sir Arthur must realize something was going on but he didn't, or if he did he wasn't saying.'

She took a sip of her wine. 'Now we come to the end,' she said. 'I have never told anybody what I am about to tell you now, Lady Powerscourt. Most of it Flavia told me, some of it on a midnight trip to my house which lasted until the dawn and the little birds began chirping in the garden. Candlesby wanted her to go and live with him. He was desperate for her to do so. Flavia said she needed time. Candlesby was completely besotted. He refused to let the matter drop. This stalemate lasted a week. Then the letters started.

'One day somebody sends Flavia copies of half the love letters she's ever written to John, Lord Candlesby. The next day they send copies of half of the letters he's sent to her to John. There was a pause in the letters the third day. But on the fourth day the somebody, presumably the same somebody, sends all the love letters, all hers to him, all his to her, to Sir Arthur. It was terrible. People have always thought the servants can't have approved of her affair; people said that the servants knew where the letters were kept so they made copies and took a terrible revenge. But that was not the case. This is the secret at the heart of the tragedy that only a couple of people know. It's so terrible it's hard to believe.'

For a moment Mrs Cameron looked as though she might break down in the midst of her narrative but she steadied herself.

'Candlesby wouldn't take no for an answer. He was determined to bring her to Candlesby Hall as his mistress if she wouldn't divorce Sir Arthur and marry him. And this is the worst part. This is why she came to see me in the middle of the night after another row with her lover. She told me that it was John who sent the first two lots of love letters. This was before the whole lot were sent to Sir Arthur. He told her he would send them all to Sir Arthur if she didn't agree to leave him. You could see the twisted logic behind it all. If Sir Arthur found out about the affair through these letters then he might throw her out. Why not avoid the distress by leaving anyway? What she had always found upsetting was the difference in the letters. The ones he sent to her might have been to his estate manager or the butler, filled with details of arrangements and the dates of meetings. The ones she had written to him on the other hand were passionate outpourings about the happiness he had brought her and how she couldn't wait to see him again. Even Sir Arthur, she said, sitting on a bench by the lake in our garden at three o'clock in the morning, even he would realize that this was a woman he did not know, one who had never spoken to him in those terms or spun so many words of love.'

Rachel Cameron stopped once more. She looked worn out suddenly by the terrible events she was describing.

'You can stop for a while, if you'd like to,' said Lady Lucy. 'You could begin again when you are ready.'

Mrs Cameron smiled wanly. 'It's all right. We're nearly at the end now. I've often wondered if she had already decided what to do, as if she could only see one way out. She rushed into my house and found a copy of *Tess of the D'Urbervilles*. "I don't know," she said, "if I'm going to be like Tess or Sue Bridehead in *Jude the Obscure*. She kept repeating, "The President of the Immortals had finished his sport with Tess." She was still repeating it when she left my kitchen to creep back to her own house. That was the last time I saw her alive. The letters didn't come the next day. But they did come the day after that. And Flavia, consumed by now no doubt by love and guilt in equal measure, walks out into the sea and doesn't come back. Sir Arthur went out of his mind for some time. He only really recovered when a friend from his days in the army took him away on a walking tour of the Scottish Highlands. They were away for about a month.'

'Did he ever talk to you about Flavia?'

'This is the real point of my story, Lady Powerscourt. One of the things that helped to make Sir Arthur better was deciding to find out who had sent the letters. His friend from the army was very keen on it, apparently. Know your enemies, or some such rubbish, was what he used to say. And so he came to see me. He wrote beforehand, all very proper. He may have been drinking less than he had before but he still managed to down a third of a bottle of whisky in the hour he was with me. It took some time before he got round to what he wanted to say – maybe that was why the scotch was needed in such quantities. He started looking at the carpet rather than at me. Then he said that he had employed a private detective to find out about the letters.

'This is why I have come,' he managed to say. 'This detective person told me that he thought Candlesby sent the letters himself, in a desperate attempt to get Flavia to leave me. I couldn't believe it at first. Seems unlikely, what? But you knew Flavia. You were her closest friend. Did she ever talk to you about the letters?'

'Well, what was I to say? Would I be betraying my friend if I told him the truth? Would it send him back towards despair and larger doses of scotch if I told him? I think I must have delayed so long that he could have guessed what the answer was if he had been a sensitive man. But he wasn't. I tried to decide whether it would be better for him to know the truth, or be left in ignorance. In the end I told him the truth.'

'What did he say?'

'He didn't say anything at all, not for a while. He walked up and down the room for about ten minutes. Then he headed for the front door. As he was going he said, "The man's a bastard, a complete bastard. I'm going to kill him."'

PART THREE

CARAVAGGIO

The bulk of the great fortunes are now in a highly liquid state. They do not consist of huge landed estates, vast parks and castles and all the rest of it.

Arthur Balfour, 1909

13

Lord Francis Powerscourt was on his way to see the manager of Finch's Bank in Boston, where the Candlesby accounts were held. The manager was not at all what he had expected. Gone were the sober suits and white shirts of the popular stereotype of bank manager. Sebastian Lambert's suit looked as if it had come from Savile Row and the shirt and tie from one of Jermyn Street's finest tailors. He was a round sort of bank manager, a tubby man about five feet nine inches tall with long sideburns and a neatly trimmed moustache. Every now and again he would remove his glasses and rub the lenses energetically on the bottom of his tie. He ushered Powerscourt to a seat by a table in his office, whose walls were covered with pictures of the Derby and the other great classics of the turf.

'Never sure it's a good idea to have these pictures on the walls,' Lambert said. 'People might think the bank is encouraging them to go to the races and gamble their money away. Bad for the prudent customer, bad for the Nonconformist conscience. Still, enough of this. You said in your letter, Lord Powerscourt, that you wished to discuss the financial affairs of the Candlesby family, with particular reference to the old Earl who has just been murdered rather than his successor who has also just been murdered.'

'That is correct,' said Powerscourt. 'My concerns are with John, the previous Earl. I don't think money or the lack of it had a great deal to do with his death, but knowledge of the financial situation does enable a person like me to take a more comprehensive view of the victim. Naturally, Mr Lambert, whatever you tell me will be treated in confidence.'

'Thank you for saying that,' said Lambert, stretching out his legs. 'Where should I begin?' He seemed to derive inspiration from a very close finish in a classic horse race behind Powerscourt's head, where a grey horse was just beginning to pull ahead of a brown one.

'Let me begin with an observation about our aristocratic friends engaged in agriculture. They are not very intelligent. One man who got out of land completely and went on to make a fortune on the Stock Exchange put it something like this: "In Year One," my man said, "they're all growing wheat. In the end there's too much wheat on the market. So prices fall. The people who were into beef or dairy did well because there wasn't enough on the market so prices went up. Now then, in Year Two," my chap was well into his stride by now, "the farming fraternity all get out of wheat and into beef or dairy or whatever did well the year before. The same thing happens, of course. Too much beef or too much dairy means low prices. If they'd stuck to wheat they'd have made a killing, as most of their brethren had bailed out of it. Year Three, they all plunge back into wheat because of the high prices in Year Two and the same process kicks off all over again."'

'Did that happen to the Candlesbys? Were they numbered with the five wise virgins or the five foolish ones who brought no extra oil for their lamps?'

Sebastian Lambert laughed and rubbed his glasses vigorously on the end of his tie. 'I'm afraid that the estate managers fare no better than their masters when it comes to working out how to make money out of farming these days. You know as well as I do, Lord Powerscourt, that the decline in agriculture has been going on for a generation or more now. Hardly anybody escapes. Lower rents, lower value for the land, imported produce from all over the world putting more downward pressure on prices – it's a spiral that never stops. If the big farmers in these parts ask for my advice I often tell them to get out, sell up while they can, cash in their assets before they have to mortgage themselves to the hilt to pay the bills or pay the interest. The Candlesbys' – he waved an elegant arm in a circle in front of him – 'are in debt up to their eyeballs. The late Earl would not be told. He would insist on all the trimmings that prevailed in better times when his father was alive. Too many servants, too expensive a diet, too many fine clarets at the highest prices, too many racehorses at even higher prices in days gone by. There may be faster ways to lose money than owning racehorses, Lord Powerscourt, but I'm damned if I know what they are. There are two mortgages on the house worth over fifty thousand pounds. And remember that while the price you get for your corn may go down, the interest payments tend to remain the same. There are further loans and mortgages on various bits of the land for another forty-five thousand so the total is almost in six figures. The late Earl was thinking of taking out further mortgages to help him pay the interest on the existing ones. It's all pretty desperate. I can't see how they are going to get out of it, really. They might be able to sell the land and the house for more than the debts but I doubt it. There are so many families in similar situations at the present time.'

'Does this mean', said Powerscourt, 'that the new Earl, should I say the new new Earl – we're now on the second new Earl in no time at all – inherits nothing? Only mortgages and minuses on the family accounts?'

'Correct, my lord. If your parents haven't told you, it must come as a terrible shock when your father dies and you inherit a mountain of debts.'

Perhaps, Powerscourt thought to himself, the Candlesby financial position was such that you would want to keep the incumbent alive at all costs. Far better for them to be responsible for the debts.

'I am most grateful to you, Mr Lambert,' he said. 'I must go now. I have an appointment very soon to jump out of a train.'

'What interesting lives you investigators lead,' said Lambert with a smile, taking a final rub at his glasses. 'Let me wish you a safe jump.'

'Thank you,' said Powerscourt, 'thank you very much. Can I ask you a question?'

'Of course.'

'These racing pictures here,' Powerscourt waved his hand expansively round the walls, 'something tells me they don't all belong to the bank. I think most of them are yours. Would I be right?'

Sebastian Lambert gave a rueful grin. 'You are absolutely right, Lord Powerscourt. I don't think I want to know how you worked it out.'

'And do you go to the races yourself, Mr Lambert?'

The bank manager looked carefully at the glass panels on his door to make sure nobody could hear him. 'Well,' he whispered, 'I do, as a matter of fact. But I have to go quite a long way away from here. I don't think the bank and some of the customers would approve if the manager was seen placing a large wager on the two thirty at Lincoln. So I travel south to Epsom or Sandown Park. I once went as far as Exeter, God help me.'

'Disguise?' said Powerscourt hopefully. 'False beard, limp, strange clothes, that sort of thing?'

'Alas, no. I don't go round like Sherlock Holmes pretending to be a washerwoman or whoever it was. And could I remind you of one relevant fact, Lord Powerscourt? That last bit of information about the races, that's confidential, that is. Highly confidential.'

Powerscourt found Detective Inspector Blunden reading rather sadly through a pile of interview notes. 'There's a set of these for you over there, my lord. It's remarkable how little twenty or twenty-five people are able to tell you about the morning of a murder. Apart from the fact that two people thought they saw two men, height, hair colour, weight, age all unnoticed, going into the special train, that's about it. Hours and hours spent interviewing; we might as well have passed yesterday evening reading the railway timetables. God in heaven.'

'Has any information come out about GNR uniforms, Inspector? About where the people who work here get theirs, for instance?'

'That's not going to bring any joy to your heart, my lord. There are a lot of seasonal staff employed on the railway in the summer so the company keeps a good supply of the trousers and shirts and so on at one of the big clothes shops in the town. And nobody's been in there in the past month buying any uniforms. I went to see them myself while you were with the bank manager. It's all bad today.'

'I tell you what,' said Powerscourt, 'why don't you join us on a little expedition? Let's take a special train in the direction of Spalding. Let's pretend to murder an Earl in the early stages of the trip. Let's jump out of the door of the moving train when it is doing ten to twelve miles an hour at a cutting just outside the town. Remember, if you're the last man, to close the train door behind you when you go, or all our theories have turned to dust. And if it doesn't work the first time around we have to ask the good Mr Jones, the man who drove the train yesterday, to go into reverse and do it again. What do you say?'

The Inspector smiled. Powerscourt was always surprised how a spot of danger could cheer some men up. 'I'd be delighted, my lord. Much better than reading any more of this stuff.'

At a quarter past two there was an impromptu conference in the special train: Powerscourt, Inspector Blunden, Archibald Jones the driver and young Andrew Merrick, almost too overawed by his superior officer to speak.

'I've been giving this matter some thought, so I have, gentlemen,' said Jones the driver. 'We have one problem to do with how you know when to jump. I propose to give two short hoots when we are less than a minute from the cutting. When I reach it I'm going to give one continuous hoot, so just go at that stage. I'm not sure there'll be enough time for all three of you to jump. Somebody may have to be left behind.'

Andrew Merrick knew where his duty lay. He might be younger, he might be fitter, he might be nearer in years to the murderers than his superiors – none of that mattered.

'I'll come third,' he said. 'I'll jump, of course, if I can.'

'You remember what I said yesterday, my lord? A cutting, with long grass and brambles and general undergrowth. The hooter will tell you when to go.'

'Please, sir, Lord Powerscourt, sir, Inspector Blunden, sir, I have been conducting experiments around the station this morning.'

'And?' said the Inspector, who had come across young Andrew Merrick before.

'It's the door, sirs. I think it might be quite difficult to close it and jump at the same time.'

'Aha,' said Powerscourt. 'I may have the advantage of you all here. I have actually jumped off a moving train and closed the door. It was difficult but not impossible.'

'Whereabouts was this, my lord?' Jones was fascinated to meet a veteran jumper out of moving trains.

'It was in Northern India, in Kashmir actually. There were some other people on the train who didn't want me to leave it alive so it seemed a better bet to jump.'

'Right, gentlemen, I think it's time to go.' Driver Jones began moving off towards his cab. 'If all goes well I shall reverse back down the line to the cutting and pick you up. If all does not go well I can still pick you up and we can try once more. I think we have enough time on the lines for three jumps before the next train arrives.'

A few moments later they watched the tell-tale signs as

smoke began drifting past the window. Inspector Blunden began a series of stretching exercises he used to perform on the rugby fields of the Midlands. Andrew Merrick peered out of the window and tried to appear nonchalant. They were out of the town now, the train building up speed as it drove through the lush fields between Boston and Spalding.

Powerscourt felt nervous, almost frightened. It wasn't as if he hadn't jumped out of trains before. But he felt irritated now to be risking limb if not life on the case of two of the most unpleasant human beings he had ever come across. Murderers, in his experience, were not usually totally evil people. They all shared one fatal flaw, of course, depriving one or more of their fellow citizens of life, but they could also be clever or charming or witty. None of those adjectives could be used in conjunction with the Dymoke family.

Time to stop this introspection, Powerscourt said to himself and began touching his toes. The Inspector was leading the way to the carriage doors with Powerscourt behind him and the young man in third place, hopping anxiously from foot to foot. In the distance on their right they could just see the outskirts of Spalding. Above them a hovering bird was circling in the sky, looking for its prey. There were two short blasts on the train hooter. Inspector Blunden grasped the door handle firmly in his right hand.

'Good luck, my lord!'

Powerscourt smiled. One long continuous blast. They could feel the train slowing down. Inspector Blunden opened the door and jumped towards the cutting. Powerscourt had already decided that he would close the door behind him, thus ensuring that young Andrew would not have the chance to jump out of the train and break his legs. Powerscourt knew what he had to do. A few years before, he and Lady Lucy had gone to St Moritz to walk in the mountains and watch the skiing for the weekend. Bend your knees, he said to himself as he stepped on to the little rung just below the point where the door joined the carriage.

Bend your arms. Grab the door in your right hand. Jump as hard as you can. Swing the door closed behind you. Wait for the landing. Everything happens so fast. Now he was rolling forward along the cutting, the brambles cutting his face. But he was safe. He hadn't broken anything. Looking back, he just had time to see that the door was properly closed before the train turned a corner and vanished from view. Inspector Blunden was rubbing an ankle a few yards away.

'You seem to have made a better fist of it than me, my lord,' he said ruefully, continuing his massage programme.

'I only remembered just before I jumped', said Powerscourt, 'that it's better for some reason to jump upwards rather than straight out, if you see what I mean.'

'Well, I don't suppose I'll be doing it again for a while,' said Blunden, tottering slowly to his feet. 'We do know one thing now we didn't before. The two men, if there were two men who boarded the train at Boston, could have garrotted the Earl once they were out of the station and then jumped off the train just here. I don't suppose they'd have torn off their uniforms here and dumped them in the long grass. I'd better send a search party out once we get back to the station.'

'There is one thing we may have forgotten, though, Inspector.' Powerscourt was climbing to the top of the cutting, looking for their return train back to the station.

'What's that, my lord?'

'It's this,' said Powerscourt, waving happily at the sight of Jones leaning out of his driver's car. 'If the killers did murder the Earl and jump out here, either they were regular users of the line, or else they were employees of the railway who could easily have obtained access to the special train to garrotte Lord Candlesby. And they would certainly have known where to jump.'

Five days later another melancholy party made their way from the Hall up to the Candlesby mausoleum on its hill.

Richard was laid to rest in the next niche to his father. There were now sixty-seven empty niches left. Powerscourt calculated that if the death rate were maintained at the current level there would be standing room only in the death chamber in a couple of years' time. There were fewer mourners than there had been for the first funeral. Maybe Richard hadn't had as much time to collect enemies as his father. Certainly there were none of those mourners who had come to make sure the hated Earl was actually dead and buried.

Powerscourt was wondering if the two men had been killed because they were Candlesbys or because of some other more personal reason. He wondered if this was some long-forgotten curse or family skeleton risen from the rich land of Lincolnshire to harass the family. Two of the other brothers were there, Edward and Charles. The unfortunate James, last seen being rescued from the waters of the lake by his brother, had remained in his rooms ever since. The servants said that he sat or rather crouched by the fire wrapped in an enormous dressing gown and talked to himself.

'Isn't it odd, my lord,' Charles Candlesby was walking back down the hill with Powerscourt, 'how you can find you don't really like your relations? I never felt sad for my father though I thought I should. And I feel nothing at all for my brother. Am I a really b-bad p-p-person?'

Powerscourt smiled. 'I don't think so. You'd be surprised how many people feel the same way as you do about their relations. It's just that people don't really like to talk about it.'

'Is that so? The only one of my b-b-brothers I really love is James and he's still not very well.'

'Did Richard have any enemies, Charles? Anybody who might have disliked him enough to kill him?'

'Well,' said Charles, 'most of the servants disliked him. He was so rude to them. His p-p-problem was that he never went to school. He was b-b-brought up here. The tutors could never control him. So he got more and more arrogant. Candlesbys rule the world.'

Powerscourt doubted if a home education necessarily qualified you for death in a special train. He was haunted every day in this case by the memories of the two human heads, the first with one side of his face battered to pulp by some unknown instrument, the other with that dark purple weal round the neck and eyes that stared out of the head.

'Then there are the villagers,' Charles went on. 'They weren't fond of my b-brother at all. When he was b-b-bored Richard used to go down there and swagger round a bit. You remember, Lord P-p-powerscourt, I said I would ask around down there about the night my father was killed? Well, nobody would speak to me at all. They all clammed up. Do you think that's strange?'

'I do, as a matter of fact,' said Powerscourt. 'Look here, young Charles, I have a question for you. The room with the Caravaggios that your ancestor brought back from the Grand Tour, is it still there?'

'It is. I've always been too frightened to go in to see it, gory b-b-bodies and sweaty Neapolitan locals hanging Christ on the cross. Legend says the p-p-place is haunted. Ghosts are said to come out of the walls, day and night.'

'Well,' said Powerscourt, 'it's strange, possibly the strangest thing in this very strange house. Wasn't the man who collected the paintings and then locked them away known as the Wicked Earl?'

'He was,' said Charles. 'Somebody told me when I was small that he was the wickedest Earl of the lot. Just think how wicked he must have b-b-been!'

Selina Hamilton and Sandy Temple were taking a morning walk in the grounds of Woodlands, the house in Norfolk where they were spending the weekend. Sandy had discovered that love could be as exciting as politics and Selina was now a devotee of the country house practice of leaving lists of the sleeping arrangements pinned up on a noticeboard outside the dining room.

The company was diverse. There was an American financier called Wright whose main claim to fame was that he had just equipped a house in Surrey with thirty-two bedrooms, eleven bathrooms, a private theatre, three lakes and, most wondrous of all, an underwater billiard room enclosed in glass so you could actually watch the fish swimming in the lake as you prepared to make your stroke. The American financier never tired of telling whoever would listen about his house and his underwater room, the only aquatic site, he would say, pulling on an enormous cigar, apart from a transatlantic liner, where you could watch the waters as you potted your red.

There was a man who owned a chain of grocery shops who had been elevated to the House of Lords by the previous King. Sandy Temple felt sure money must have changed hands to lubricate this transaction, the King having too little of it and the shopkeeper too much.

There was a strange tall thin man called Burroughs who hardly ever spoke but who was believed to be the finest shot in England. There was Sir Arthur Cholmondley Smith, whose young and pretty wife was rumoured to have been first spotted by her current husband upon the music hall stage. There was Lord Winterton of Winterton Staithe, widely believed to be Norfolk's richest man, a proposition he did not argue with.

And there was a rich widow, Mrs Kennedy Miller, whose husband had made a large fortune manufacturing women's underclothing, a task he took so seriously that it killed him. His former wife was known to be in pursuit of a new husband with a more agreeable occupation and a milder temperament. Selina thought she was too obvious in expressing interest in the local unattached males her hostess might care to invite to dinner.

'Honestly, Sandy,' she had said, 'she may as well hang up a sign on her front saying "Available" like those boys with the sandwich boards you see in Oxford Street. I think it's just vulgar!'

Over in the woods to their left there was a sudden rattle of gunfire, as a shooting party from the house tried their luck with the local birds.

'You don't mind missing the shooting, Sandy, do you?'

'I loathe shooting, Selina, as you well know.'

'Have you had any luck yet with asking these lords how they are going to vote on the Budget?'

Sandy laughed. 'One down, one to go. I engaged our grocer lord in conversation yesterday evening.'

'Lord Hudder of Huddersfield?' asked Selina. 'That was quick work.'

'Well, I wouldn't say the conversation went all that well. Not to begin with, at any rate. Even now, after all his success, there's something about Lord Hudder that makes you think you're in a grocer's shop. It's as if he's wearing his apron all the time. He's imprinted the manner of the man behind the counter on his personality. You think he's going to ask if you want the bacon thickly sliced or the ham cut thin. Anyway, I asked Lord Hudder straight out how he was going to vote. He looked at me as if he thought I was insane. "What a ridiculous question," he said. "I always vote the same way. Approve the annual accounts and the other recommendations of the board. No need to say any more. Can't have the ordinary bloody shareholders saying anything, can we? Always complaining about the price of bananas in the shops or some ridiculous thing."'

'"No, sir, that wasn't what I meant at all," I carried on.' Another, longer, salvo rang out from deeper into the trees. A lone woodcock, possibly sole survivor of the carnage, flew overhead, aiming for a place of greater safety further south. "It's the Budget, Lord Hodder, the vote on the Budget."

'Our new noble Lord grew quite cross about now, Selina. "Don't be ridiculous, young man. Don't vote on the bloody Budget. Not in any of my companies. People will be asking for democracy next, for Christ's sake. Budget's a matter for the board, always has been." I'm terribly sorry, my lord, I said, I haven't made myself clear. I was interested in how you intend to vote in the House of Lords about approving Lloyd George's Budget or not.'

'"Lloyd George's Budget? House of Lords? Why didn't you say so? Tell you the truth," Lord Hudder poured himself another enormous glass of port at this point, Selina, "I'm not quite sure exactly where the House of Lords is. Is it inside Buckingham Palace? Bloody place is big enough, for God's sake. You see, I got a letter from somebody or other telling me I'd been made a peer of the realm and what did I want to be called. I wrote back and said I'd like to be called Lord Hudder of Huddersfield and the wife can be Lady Hudder – she does like a title, our Mildred. But since then, nothing. It's like somebody tells you you've been left a heap of shares in a relative's will and then forgets to invite you to the annual general meeting. Is this vote a bit like a company annual general meeting? Confirm the board of directors in place? Increase the dividend? That sort of thing?" At this point, Selina, I felt I should give up. But the noble lord wasn't giving up.'

'"I think I've got it," he says, downing the rest of his port. "Is this Budget thing the government's annual general meeting about the money, the taxes and all that sort of stuff?" I pointed out that there were various increases in taxation, taxes on development land, increases in death duties to pay for more dreadnoughts and welfare payments like old age pensions. "Sounds jolly good to me," Lord Hudder said cheerfully, the port beginning to take effect perhaps. "I like dreadnoughts. Kill lots of Germans. Death duties damned good thing too. No point in leaving your children lots of money. They'll only spend it, not earn it. Much better for them to have to make their own living. You just let me know when the vote is and where this House of Lords is and I'll go down there and support this Lloyd George fellow. Vote to keep him and the other directors in place. That'll be a good day's work."'

'The Conservatives won't be pleased if he does that,' said Selina. 'Why make a rich businessman a peer if he votes with the other side?'

'I just wonder if he'll do it,' said Sandy, staring upwards at another clump of refugee birds fleeing the scene, 'vote with Asquith and Lloyd George. He won't be a popular boy, that's for sure.'

'Sandy,' said Selina, grabbing him by the hand, 'I'm sure they will all have gone out for the shooting and the servants will have finished cleaning the rooms by now. Why don't we just take a little trip back to the house?'

14

The slaughter in the woods came to an end shortly after four o'clock in the afternoon. The American financier called Wright had failed to hit a single bird, morning or afternoon. His fellow guns felt he was more of a danger to them than he was to the wildlife. But he kept his good humour throughout the debacle, reminding whoever would listen that he was never allowed near the baseball field in his native country as he couldn't hit the ball. The tall thin man called Burroughs, however, shot an unbelievable number of birds. He never missed. He never spoke either. Of the two the shooting party preferred the man who shot none to the man who shot so many.

Shortly after tea Sandy Temple found himself seated next to the other peer of the realm at the house party. Lord Winterton of Winterton Staithe was as different from Lord Hudder as it was possible to be. Lord Hudder was recently ennobled. Lord Winterton's title had been in his family for five hundred years. Lord Hudder made his money from his chain of grocery shops. Lord Winterton had many thousands of acres in Norfolk and extensive property in Norwich and in London's West End. Lord Hudder had yet to speak in the House of Lords. Winterton had made his maiden speech nearly twenty years before on the early death of his father.

He looked about forty years old. Sandy thought you could see him, with that blond hair and the deep blue eyes and the arrogance of aristocracy, immortalized in uniforms of scarlet and black on the walls of the long galleries of the great houses of England, painted full-length by Lawrence or Reynolds, surrounded on all sides by his ancestors.

Sandy Temple decided to take the plunge. After a conversation with Winterton he could refer to 'peers I have spoken to recently' in his articles for *The Times* if he so wished. 'Excuse me, Lord Winterton, would you mind if I asked you a question?'

'Not at all,' said the peer, scarcely moving from his newspaper. 'Fire ahead.'

'My question is this,' said Sandy, 'how do you intend to vote when Lloyd George's Budget comes up in the Lords?'

'Do you have a personal interest in the matter, young man?'

'My name is Sandy Temple, sir. I work for *The Times*, in the parliamentary and political department, covering the work of both houses.'

'Delighted to meet you, Mr Temple. I do believe I may have read some of your stuff in the past couple of years. How nice to have somebody to talk politics with in this place. The rest of them are all obsessed with killing as many birds as possible.'

'And the Budget, Lord Winterton?'

'Ah, the Budget! This is one of the most difficult decisions I have had to take since first sitting on those red benches. I think I shall have to vote against my principles, not something I care to do very often. Perhaps I'd better explain, young man. I am a Conservative. I like to think of myself as a proper Conservative. I don't like change. I don't like reform unless it is absolutely necessary. I believe very strongly in preserving the great institutions of this country, the monarchy, the ancient constitution, the Church of England, the aristocracy, the armed forces and so on. I am more than wary when Conservative politicians start talking about the condition of England question or Tory democracy.

Those are not Conservative movements. Conservative politicians should aim to do less, not more. The condition of England is a question for the people of England rather than the politicians. Tory democracy is a contradiction in terms. Lord Salisbury, may God rest his soul, was the only politician in my lifetime to believe that his job in politics and as Prime Minister was to conserve, to keep things as they were, to steer clear of change.' Lord Winterton stopped suddenly. 'I say,' he said, looking closely at Sandy, 'I'm not running away with myself, am I? You can follow what I'm saying?'

'Perfectly,' said Sandy. 'Please carry on.'

'I have long thought that some day there would be a battle between the Lords and Commons. Power is slowly seeping away from the Lords; power is growing ever stronger in the Commons. Who's more important? If you look back at the Prime Ministers we have had over the past couple of hundred years more of them have come from the Lords than the Commons. But I think the sweep of history is with the Commons, not the Lords. I think they are probably tomorrow, if you follow me. I and people like me are yesterday. Sooner or later women will probably have the vote and all adult males will be enfranchised. The long slow tide that began sweeping through the constitution with the Great Reform Bill hasn't finished yet. That's why I'm going to support the government over the Budget.'

'I don't understand, Lord Winterton. Forgive me. You say you are a Conservative and you obviously are. But you're also going to support a bill that increases taxes and death duties. It'll probably cost you a great deal of money. I don't see how it adds up.'

'I can't have made myself clear, Mr Temple. My plan is, in a way, a delaying action. If you think that you are going to lose in the end, you want to end up holding on to as much power as you can. You don't want your opponents taking it away from you. If we behave ourselves, as it were, and let the Budget go through, there won't be a battle. Not this

201

time. It'll come later. But all our powers will remain intact. If we throw the Budget out, there'll be an almighty row which we shall probably lose in the end. Then we have to take our punishment, which would certainly involve a lessening or even a removal of many of the powers traditionally vested in the House of Lords. Better live to fight another day than end up with heaps of dead lying all over the battlefield. Do you follow me, Mr Temple?'

'Perfectly, Lord Winterton, but I should be most interested to know how many of your colleagues agree with you.'

Winterton laughed. 'That's a good question, young man. You will recall that the Conservative Party has been called many things, including the stupid party. I have been a great disappointment to my own family on this score. I let the side down by taking a double first in history from Christ Church when an undistinguished third was what was expected. Conservatives are suspicious of clever people. I have tried to explain my views to a number of my colleagues. It was hopeless. I might as well have been talking about Schopenhauer and German metaphysics. They simply didn't understand; their eyes glazed over. It was a total waste of time.'

'So which way do you think the vote will go? Will they let it through or throw it out?'

'Let me ask you a question this time, Mr Temple. What do you think will happen? You have been observing the Lords for some time, after all.'

'I would love to be able to answer your question, sir, but I cannot. *The Times* always emphasizes that we are not to have or to publish opinions of our own, only to report those of others.'

'I suppose I have to respect that,' said Lord Winterton. 'I am fairly certain about what they will do, myself. You will remember, I'm sure, that one of the characters in Thomas Hardy's *Far from the Madding Crowd* loses all his sheep when they fall over a cliff. If you think of my colleagues in the

Upper House as being those sheep, you will not go far wrong. Already they are egging each other on to throw the Budget out. They are massing in the field by the cliff and making sheeplike noises. When the vote finally comes they will run at full speed to the edge of the cliff and fall over. Not for nothing did that fellow call them the stupid party!'

Lord Francis Powerscourt was conferring with Inspector Blunden in his office. A great heap of unsorted papers lay sprawled across his desk. The policeman looked as if he was fighting a losing battle.

'Nothing, absolutely nothing, my lord,' he said. 'All those interviews over the past few days with all those people who were at the railway station and all we have, as I said before, are two witnesses who thought they saw two people in GNR uniform crossing the bridge to the far side of the special train, where they may or may not have garrotted the Earl. We know somebody must have got into that compartment but we can't be sure it was those two. That's all. No other witnesses to the mysterious pair. None of the staff on board the train noticed anything. They've all been questioned three times now. Nobody else reporting anything suspicious. No sight of the uniforms. Just this paper.' He waved at the pile in front of him. 'I've never known anything like it. It's as if the entire population have gone dumb.'

'Are the people who work on the railway all from round here? Or are there some who come up and down the line from Boston and so on to work here?'

'I think most of them are local. There's always been a tradition in Candlesby village of local men working on the railway but nobody there has seen anything at all – or else they weren't at work on the day in question. I had people over there yesterday afternoon.'

'So much of this investigation hinges round information we haven't got. How was the first Earl killed? Why was he killed? If we knew the answer to that question we might also know who killed his son. Do not despair, Inspector, we'll get there in the end.'

'Do you think there will be more murders, my lord? A third or even a fourth? Should we put a guard round Candlesby Hall in case sons three and four might be the next victims?'

'Do you know, Inspector, I don't think we should do that just yet. But I do think you should warn them, even the youngest, not to go out unless they have to and then to be vigilant at all times.'

Inspector Blunden began to cheer up at the thought of action. 'I'll go over there straight away and put them on their guard. At least then I shall feel I've done something useful today.'

Powerscourt wasn't sure whether keeping the third Candlesby son alive would add greatly to the general happiness but he kept his reservations to himself.

'Excellent, my friend,' he said. 'I am going to interview one of the chief suspects, well, one of the chief suspects according to the ladies of Lady Lucy's lunches. The man whose wife was having an affair with the old Lord Candlesby and ended up walking into the sea, Sir Arthur Melville. And before that I'm going to take Lady Lucy to the seaside for a walk along the beach.'

Lady Lucy Powerscourt was staring at a letter that had just arrived. The notepaper looked as though it had been torn from a child's school exercise book. There was no envelope. The missive had been folded in two with her name, slightly misspelt, on one side. Inquiries at the hotel's main desk could not reveal how it had come, whether by a person on foot or a person on a bike or a person in a motor car. It seemed to have arrived at the Candlesby Arms under its own steam.

'Dear Lady Powwerscurt,' she read it again, 'you are all barking up the rong tree about who killed Richard, Lord Candlesby. It was not one of these outside peeple. It was his own fambly. Believe Me. From One Who Knows.'

Lady Lucy was not sure if the letter came from a crank or a madman or someone who really knew what was going on. Long experience of her husband's affairs had taught her that the most unlikely explanation was often the correct one.

'What do you think, Francis?' she said to her husband as he joined her after his time with the Inspector. Lady Lucy thought Francis looked preoccupied. But then he often looked preoccupied in the middle of an investigation.

'She could be right, you know,' he said after a quick perusal of the letter.

'How do you know it's from a woman, Francis?'

'Well, I don't know that for a fact. It just seems more likely that it comes from a woman. Look at the handwriting for a start. I can't see a man signing himself off as One Who Knows. The thing may be disguised to look as if it comes from somebody who's not very well educated when in fact they can read and write as well as we can.' He turned and stared out of the window as if his mind was elsewhere. 'Come, Lucy, it's time for our walk by the sea.'

Ten minutes later they were in the Silver Ghost and heading for Skegness. Powerscourt was driving. Rhys had been left behind for the day. Overhead the sky was a brilliant blue. The seagulls circled ceaselessly overhead squawking their unintelligible messages to each other. About a mile from Skegness Powerscourt parked the car. A small track ran down to the beach. Lady Lucy watched her husband patting anxiously at his jacket pocket as if checking something was still there. She felt certain it was bad news.

There was a strong wind blowing straight into their faces as they set off along the beach that led to Mablethorpe. A couple of ships were beating their way southward towards Norfolk. Mr Drake at the hotel had told Lady Lucy that boats ran in high summer from Skegness to Hunstanton and back, with the passengers often going to inspect the royal residence at Sandringham on the other side of the water. Lady Lucy suddenly remembered that it was during his investigation into a scandal in the royal family at Sandringham that she had first met Francis all those years before. He had proposed to her, she recalled with a smile, during a performance of Beethoven's Ninth Symphony at the Royal Albert Hall, the actual proposal inscribed on newspaper in the middle of an advertisement for Colman's mustard. Lady Lucy thought she still had that newspaper filed away somewhere at home. When the investigation finished they had been married at the Powerscourt church in Northamptonshire with a wounded Johnny Fitzgerald as best man. She felt intensely happy for a moment. Then she looked at her husband's face. He was handing her a rather different letter from the one she had been reading earlier. Her heart sank as she saw that it came from the War Office. 'His Majesty's Secretary of State requests the pleasure of Lord Powerscourt's company as soon as his present investigation is over, Yours sincerely, Sir Arthur Jensen, Permanent Under Secretary.'

'Oh, Francis,' she said and tucked her arm into his.

'It's the devil, Lucy, the very devil.'

With that Powerscourt began walking away from Skegness. He stared out into the North Sea, moderate breakers pounding on to the beach. In his mind's eye he could see the great dockyards of Britain from Portsmouth to Glasgow filled with thousands and thousands of men building dreadnoughts, the new super battleships that rendered almost all previous warships redundant. Across the North Sea from where he was standing, in Kiel and Hamburg, in Danzig and Bremen, their German counterparts also had their giant cranes and the enormous guns that made up the German dreadnought fleet. Sometime soon they must meet in the dark waters of the North Sea in an engagement that could decide the course of the war in a single afternoon. He thought of the terrible photographs of the dead and the wounded after the critical battles of the American Civil War like Antietam and Gettysburg, long lines of men with one leg shuffling around the inadequate hospitals. Across the plains of Europe Powerscourt saw whole armies rising out of the earth like dragon's teeth, men clad for battle in grey and khaki and dark blue carrying rifles, Germans and French, English and Dutch, Russians and Italians. Rumbling behind them he could hear the thunder of the artillery and the crash of the exploding shells, the screams of the wounded and the dying, the rumble of innumerable trolleys along the corridors of innumerable hospitals that tended the innumerable victims.

He turned to face his wife. There were tears in his eyes. 'Sorry, Lucy,' he said, 'my mind was just taken over by a vision of war. I think it was worse than any of those horrific visions of hell in Hieronymus Bosch with the tortures and the torments.'

'Don't worry, my love.' Lady Lucy was keen to change her husband's mood as quickly as she could. 'It may be nothing. The War Office people, the authorities, as you refer to them, may only want to clear up some details from work you did before. There could be nothing in it.'

'If that was the case,' said her husband, a terrible land battle still pounding away in his brain, 'they'd have asked for the details in the letter.'

'Well, it can't be urgent,' Lady Lucy pressed on, 'or they'd have ordered you to come straight away.'

'I don't think that's necessarily true either,' said Powerscourt. 'They wouldn't want to draw attention to themselves by pulling me off this case.'

'Francis,' said Lucy sternly, sounding as if she was talking to a naughty twin back in Markham Square, 'I don't like it when you go all negative like this. It isn't good for you. I know you aren't looking forward to going back, as it were, but you've got to finish this case first. And you aren't going to do that by moping about on the beach thinking about battleships or whatever it was you were thinking about just now. Let's be practical. I think we should go and see this Melville man right now. It won't matter if we're a bit early. One of my ladies said he is drunk all the time anyway. And you're not to make yourself depressed thinking about things you don't know anything about like this latest message from the War Office.'

Lady Lucy stared at her husband, hoping she hadn't overdone the criticism. But he was smiling at her.

'You're quite right, of course, Lucy; you usually are. How fortunate I am to be married to such a sensible person. I shall concentrate on the matter in hand.' He kissed her gently on the top of her head. But when she looked at him surreptitiously a few moments later, she could see that he was still staring out to sea, looking, she thought, like some shipwrecked mariner scanning the horizon for the sails of rescue.

Sir Arthur Melville's Elizabethan house had been there for so long now that it looked as if it had been folded into the landscape. There was a small ornamental fountain at the front with a couple of peacocks on parade. Sir Arthur, the butler announced, would receive them in the library. Powerscourt expected some grand linenfold room with ancient bookshelves groaning with leatherbound volumes from centuries past. In fact the shelves looked as if they had only been put up the week before and they were filled with the great novels from the previous century: Dickens and Trollope and George Eliot and Conrad from Britain, Stendhal and Balzac and Flaubert from France, Dostoevsky and Tolstoy from Russia.

'Sold the other library, don't you know,' Sir Arthur said after the introductions. 'Old one, full of old books. Unhappy memories, you see. Late wife used to like reading and writing her letters in there next to some damned history of the Roman Revolution.'

Powerscourt and Lady Lucy nodded as if selling old libraries was an everyday practice.

'Got a damned good price for them, mind you. Some American fellow bought the lot. Think they're somewhere in New York by now, Manhattan I think he said.'

One of the peacocks had drawn up very close to the window as if it wanted to join in the conversation, inspecting them in a most superior fashion.

'Look here, I know why you've come. You said so in your letter.' Sir Arthur scrabbled about among the papers on his desk but failed to find the relevant correspondence. 'Never mind. I say, you do know what happened here, don't you, Flavia killing herself and so on? I don't have to tell you about that all over again, do I?'

Powerscourt noticed that at the mention of his late wife's name he looked like a man being whipped in the face.

'Certainly not,' said Powerscourt. 'There's no need to drag all that up again. We're more interested in how you've been coping since.'

'It must have been terrible for you, Sir Arthur,' put in Lady Lucy with a sympathetic smile.

'Well, I don't know. You see, I've never been very bright, I'll be perfectly honest with you. All those sums and translating bits of Greek at school, I couldn't cope with any of that. Once you realize you can't do it, that it's not for you, there's no point worrying about it. So I joined the army. I wouldn't be the first person to tell you that you don't have to be very bright to follow the colours. But I quite enjoyed army life. My first commanding officer warned me that I wouldn't rise up very far there either, never make Major, let alone Colonel, that sort of thing. He said they wouldn't trust me in command of a flock of sheep – those were his very words.'

Sir Arthur laughed. 'I told the fellow I didn't mind. So I had years and years in the army. When I saw how difficult it was to command troops in battle, my goodness, what a strain, I felt quite happy where I was.'

'Did you expect to get married after you left the army, Sir Arthur?'

'Well, that's the rum thing, if you follow me. There was I, not very bright as I say, getting on in years, set in my ways, not much of a clue what to do with women, then along comes Flavia, previously married to some university chappie, bursting with brains, Flavia, I mean, and she marries me. Well, I mean to say. I don't think I understood very much about women before we were married. I understand even less now. What did she see in that Candlesby person? Did she like him because he was such a cad? I just don't understand.'

'I don't think we will gain very much by going down that road, Sir Arthur,' said Powerscourt. 'Tell me, when it was all over, how did you feel about Candlesby? You could have been excused for feeling bitter towards him, if not more.'

'I suppose you mean did I hate him enough to kill him? I did hate him enough to kill him. But I rather fell into the bottle, if you'll forgive me for saying such a thing. I hit the bloody bottle in rather a big way, actually, starting after breakfast and continuing until lights out. There is one problem with all that. If you've got through a bottle and a half of claret before lunchtime, you're not going to be in a very fit state to go off and kill people. You'd fall off your horse for a start. I think I may have sat by the edge of the fountain and told the world how I was going to be avenged on him. I do have one thing to report though. I always managed to get upstairs last thing at night. No servants ever had to help me to bed. Army code was very strict about that sort of thing. Bad form for an officer to get too tight to walk. Bad for discipline; the men would lose all respect.'

Lady Lucy waved a hand in the general direction of the

desk. 'Forgive me, Sir Arthur, but are you laying off the drink today because we're here?'

'Not so, Lady Powerscourt, not so! I haven't had a drink now for thirty-three days and fourteen hours precisely.' Sir Arthur checked his watch as if it had been designed to show the length of his sobriety.

'That's very impressive,' said Powerscourt. 'But it does lead me to one important difference between drunk and sober. You said before you were not well enough to ride a horse in your drinking days. Now in the time of sobriety you would be perfectly capable of riding over to Candlesby Hall in the middle of the night and killing the Earl. Is that not so?'

Sir Arthur laughed. 'Good try, Powerscourt. But I didn't ride over there. I didn't kill the Earl. You see, I have almost stopped thinking about the Earl, especially now he's dead. He doesn't matter any more. In any case I hope to be away from here fairly soon.'

'Are you planning to leave your beautiful house, Sir Arthur?' said Lady Lucy.

'I am, I am.' Sir Arthur suddenly sounded like a small child with a birthday present. He pulled a large box file from a drawer and began pulling out piles of newspaper cuttings, hotel brochures, travel books, pages pulled out of newspapers. 'Look at this lot! The American who bought my library offered to buy the house as well. He said he planned to transport it brick by brick and chimney by chimney to some place called West Egg on Long Island Sound, wherever that is. Offered me heaps and heaps of money. Maybe I should have said yes, but I thought the house should stay here. I've thought about Paris, I've thought about the Riviera, I've thought about Sicily. Must be bloody hot in Sicily in the summer, I should think. Always been fond of the heat. But in the end I decided against all of them.'

'Why?' said the Powerscourts, almost in unison.

'Comes back to what I was saying before, you see. The only subject worse than sums for me at school was foreign languages. French, Latin, Greek, that sort of thing. Completely foreign to me, they were, what? My papa sent me to Paris for a month when I was eighteen to learn the bloody language. I might as well have been turned deaf and dumb. Couldn't even order a beer in a café at the end of it. Just about managed to secure the services of a porter at the station to help with my luggage when I went home. Even then, I had to use sign language. So I thought I'd better stay here.'

'Have you decided where you want to go, Sir Arthur?' asked Lady Lucy.

'I think so,' he replied. 'Cornwall. A house close to the water. Gulls squawking. Walks on the cliff. Royal Navy sailing past every now and then. Reassuring fellows in those circumstances, the navy. Friendly natives who speak English. I'm going down in ten days' time to have a look, as a matter of fact.'

'We wish you the best of luck,' said Lady Lucy.

'And thank you so much for your time,' said her husband.

Sir Arthur must have had some invisible means of communicating with his staff because the butler appeared at the door to show them out. They left him pulling on a pair of spectacles and opening a large envelope which said 'Polperro' in very large letters on the front.

'Well, Francis,' said Lady Lucy as the Silver Ghost whispered its way back to the Candlesby Arms, 'what do you think? Was Sir Arthur telling the truth?'

'I think he probably was,' said Powerscourt, 'but you have to be very careful with these people who claim to have no brains.'

'What do you mean, my love?'

'Well,' said her husband, 'I knew lots of people like him at school. The teachers told them they were stupid, they told themselves they were stupid and forgot all about it.

Plenty of sport for them, dead fish, dead stags, dead grouse, dead woodcock – you didn't need a great deal in the way of brains to do all that. Fifteen years later you discover that these people have all made fortunes in the City of London, rich as Croesus some of them. Must take a different kind of brain to do that. Zero marks for French and nought in mathematics doesn't seem to matter.'

'So do you think Sir Arthur could have done it?'

Powerscourt paused to hoot at a carriage in front which was perched right in the middle of the road and travelling at about five miles an hour. The driver waved happily as they passed.

'I don't think Sir Arthur could have done it, Lucy. And I'll tell you why. One of the many mysteries we can't answer about this case is just how the old Earl was killed. Blow after blow with some blunt instrument to one side of the face requires a certain amount of imagination. I don't think Sir Arthur would be capable of it.'

'Who would?'

'That, my love, is what we have yet to find out.'

15

Clueless in Cashel. Chaos in Cashel. Cashiered in Cashel. Johnny Fitzgerald was angry with himself for his failure to find Jack Hayward and his family. He had good reasons for thinking they might have come here to Cashel as it was where Mrs Hayward was born and her family, the O'Gradys, were still here at the stables that bore their name. Johnny cursed himself for being so obvious about seeking precise directions to their establishment. He had asked in the main pub in the town centre and again in the first farmhouse he came to on the Ballydoyle road. When he finally reached the O'Grady stables and farmhouse, it was as if they had been expecting him. The woman, who he presumed was Kathleen Hayward's mother, was extremely polite. No, the Haywards were not here. Whatever could have given him that idea? It was years since they had been here and they certainly weren't here now. Hadn't he heard they were in England now? Was she protesting too much? Johnny could see that the farmhouse was large, three storeys tall, and that there were various outhouses and cottages dotted along the drive. If you wanted to hide a family of four, this was where you could do it.

'Never mind, Mrs O'Grady,' he said. 'I'll be getting out of your way now.'

'So who was it that told you they were here? You couldn't

have come all this way without somebody telling you they were here, could you?'

These were dangerous waters. 'I should have told you at the beginning, Mrs O'Grady, I'm down here looking at some land between here and Kilkenny. I met a man in the pub there who said he'd heard that Jack Hayward, a man thought to be a genius with horses, was over staying with his in-laws. That's why I came looking for him. I wanted to ask if some land I'm thinking of buying would be good for training horses.'

'Well, I don't know if he's a genius or not,' said Mrs O'Grady. 'All I do know is that he's definitely not here.'

Johnny Fitzgerald suddenly wondered if women were better liars than men. He decided that they probably were, but he couldn't hang around to inspect all the stables and the farmhouse. It was time to go.

'Thank you very much for your time, Mrs O'Grady. I'm sorry to have been such a nuisance.'

She watched him go, Mrs O'Grady, arms folded across her ample bosom, a look of defiance on her face. Johnny could almost feel her gaze boring into his back. He turned and waved at the bottom of the drive. Mrs O'Grady didn't wave back.

As he walked down the road, he decided that he would have to withdraw his forces. Retreat had never appealed very much to Johnny when he was in the army but he felt he had little choice here. He needed to lose himself in some larger place than Kilkenny or Cashel. He would write to his old commanding officer and ask for his advice.

Two days later Powerscourt was walking by the sea again. He was feeling more and more frustrated at his lack of progress. There were, he had decided long ago, two places that were crucial to his inquiry. The first was the servants' hall in the house itself. He felt sure that they all knew more than they were telling him, that a terrible secret was hidden away somewhere behind their eyes. At least they talked to him. In Candlesby village it was as if the entire population had taken the Mafia oath of *omertà*. They had all retired behind walls of silence. The hotel manager, Mr Drake, had told him that there was some terrible influenza sweeping through the village and that the first victims had already been buried.

Behind him and behind the beach there stood a lone windmill, an elegant building, the six great sails inactive this afternoon. Far away on the sand a small black dot was advancing quite fast towards him. Powerscourt thought it was probably a bicycle. He was trying to think of a device that would bring Jack Hayward home to Candlesby. Always at the back of his mind now was the thought of the War Office and the authorities. What on earth did they want him to do this time? On the last occasion there had been information leaking out of one of the dreadnought shipyards. They were so secretive, these secret policemen, that they were reluctant to divulge the name of the yard. And when they did, all they gave him was a name, no information on who the suspects might be. Nearly three thousand people were involved in building the giant battleship. Just as Powerscourt thought he had identified the man responsible he himself was captured by German agents and held prisoner for over a week in a disused coal mine.

When he looked behind him, he saw that the bicycle had almost closed the gap. Furthermore he could now see who was riding it. He stopped and waited for the young man to arrive.

'Lord Powerscourt, sir!' Andrew Merrick panted, scarcely able to speak. Powerscourt thought he looked like a fish that had just been landed, panting its life away on the river bank. 'It's the jackets, my lord, they've been found, my lord, sir.'

'Jackets? What jackets?'

'The jackets of the two men who killed the Earl in the train, my lord.'

'Hold on a moment, Andrew. Let's take one thing at a time. How do you know that they are the jackets of the people on the train?'

'Well, we don't, not really, my lord. But the Inspector says you are to come at once, my lord, sir. Inspector Blunden wants some advice, so he does, sir.'

Half an hour later Powerscourt was back at the police station. Two GNR jackets were draped across a couple of chairs on one side of Blunden's office. Andrew Merrick stared at Powerscourt with a sort of 'I told you so' expression.

'Where did you find them, Inspector?'

'It wasn't our people that found them, my lord. It was the local doctor, visiting the house of Sir Arthur Melville. He saw the side of one of them poking out from around the ornamental fountain. It would appear the unfortunate baronet may have reverted to the bottle, my lord. The doctor thought Sir Arthur might have been taking his clothes off in a fit of inebriation.'

'Did this happen today, Inspector?'

'No, my lord, it was early yesterday evening. The doctor dropped the jackets in on his way home.'

'Did he see Sir Arthur? In person, I mean. Did he speak to him?'

'No, my lord. He only spoke to the butler. There was nobody else about as far as he could see. The butler reported that the clothes must have been dumped in the middle of the previous night. Nobody saw or heard anything unusual.'

'They never do,' said Powerscourt, looking at his watch. It was nearly ten past five. Most drunks, in his experience, began their innings around lunchtime and carried on till close of play. Sir Arthur might still be just about *compos mentis*, even though he had talked of beginning to drink after breakfast.

'One thing, my lord.' Inspector Blunden looked at

Powerscourt with a pleading air. 'I'm sure you've thought about this. Is there any test or anything you know of that might establish whether these are the actual clothes the murderers wore, or are they just two uniforms that happened to have found their way to Sir Arthur Melville's fountain?'

'I have thought about it, Inspector, and the answer is no. Of course they might be the clothes we are looking for, but they might not be. I presume there isn't any message in the pockets or anything saying "We are the killers' jackets", or anything like that?'

'I rather thought that's what you would say, my lord,' said the Inspector sadly. 'No, there is not.'

Sir Arthur Melville reminded Powerscourt of a previous commanding officer who had fallen into the bottle for a week or so after failing to win promotion. After seven days he returned to normal as if nothing had happened. Only here it was the other way round.

'Afternoon, maybe good evening by now,' he said, as Powerscourt was shown into the same library looking out over the garden that he had been in before, but this time Sir Arthur had a half-full glass of neat scotch by his right hand.

'Met you before, haven't I? Powerscourt, Powerscroft, that what your name is? Powerscribe?'

'Powerscourt, court, that's me.'

'Didn't you have a wife with you before, pretty wife, nice eyes?'

'I did,' said Powerscourt. 'I do.'

'Well, you're a lucky man, with a nice wife. Very lucky.'

Powerscourt thought the man was more drunk than he seemed. The eyes were red. The hands were steady but they always shook the day after, not on the evening of the whisky bottle.

Sir Arthur stopped suddenly. Something had put him off his stroke but Powerscourt had no idea what it was. A tear formed in his left eye and rolled slowly down his cheek.

'Wife,' he said sadly, 'wife, pretty wife. Used to have one of those. Not any more.'

Powerscourt thought he spoke about the pretty wife as he might have talked about a favourite hunter.

Now the drink seemed to be taking over. 'Anniver,' he began. He seemed to be having trouble with the words. 'Anniverse, anniversey, anniversary. Wife. Today, a year ago.' The tears were rolling down his cheeks now. 'This day last year she took some of my pills and walked out into the sea. Never came back.'

He paused again and looked imploringly at Powerscourt as if he might have the power to bring her back to life. Powerscourt wondered if Sir Authur had got the date of the anniversary right. He looked incapable of remembering anything in his present state.

'Hstaton, no, that's not right.' He paused to search what was still working in his brain. 'Hunstanton.' The tears were turning into a flood now. 'That's where they found her. Found what was left of her, I mean. Bloody fish. Bloody salt water. Bloody engine on the coastguard's boat cutting half her leg off.' Sir Arthur stopped to take a Goliath-sized gulp of his scotch. Powerscourt saw with astonishment that the glass was no longer half full. There was nothing left. 'It's no better, you know. Year later. Whole damned year later. No better, no better at all.' He paused and concentrated hard on refilling his glass, almost to the top this time. 'Time the great healer, people tell you; what a load of rubbish. Wounds will heal – I remember some bloody padre telling me that after the funeral. Wounds don't heal. They get worse. They suppurate. They rot your insides away. Do you know that, Powerscliff?'

Powerscourt was feeling desperately sorry for the man. He popped out to alert the butler that he was going now and to invite Sir Arthur to lunch at the Candlesby Arms the following day if he was well enough. As he passed the library with the ornamental fountain outside, he heard a plaintive cry like Polyphemus in his cave after he lost his eye.

'Where are you, Powers, Powerscribe, Powerscart? Dammit, man, I seem to have forgotten your name.'

Everything seemed normal as Powerscourt made his way up to his rooms in the hotel. Their suite was three-quarters of the way up a long corridor on the first floor. As he turned into it, he noticed that there was a package of sorts lying on the ground as if it had just been dropped on to the carpet. As he drew closer and took his key out his pocket, he saw that there were two pairs of dark trousers and a couple of jackets. They both carried the legend 'Great Northern Railway'.

Powerscourt picked them up and carried them in. Lady Lucy was sitting by the window.

'Francis!' She rose and gave him a kiss. 'How very nice to see you. What are these clothes doing here, my love? Do they need washing?'

'Well may you ask, Lucy. They were dumped right outside our door when I came up just now.'

Lady Lucy held one of the jackets up at arm's length as if it might be an unexploded bomb. 'These aren't the ones those men were wearing on the special train, are they?'

'Your guess is as good as mine, my love. We'd better have a look in the pockets.'

The only item of interest they found was a ticket from Spalding to London King's Cross whose date seemed to have been blacked out.

'That might have been for the day of the murder, Lucy. I don't know if you need tickets for special trains or not. I'm sure the Inspector will know.'

'Do you think the murderers wore these clothes, Francis?'

'No, I don't,' said Powerscourt firmly. 'I think somebody is playing games with us, that's all. There was another pair of identical jackets dumped outside Sir Arthur Melville's fountain last night. Sir Arthur was so drunk he would not have recognized the intruder even if he had been the Prime Minister himself. Come to think of it, Lucy, I'm not sure I like the fact that the jacket people know which one is our room. Maybe I should talk to Mr Drake about it all. Nobody will have seen anything, nobody will have heard anything. All will be perfectly normal.'

'Francis, I want to ask you a favour.'

'Please do, my love.'

'I'm sure you'll have heard about this terrible influenza down in the village. Some of the servants have stopped coming to work in case they infect everybody up here as well. The poor mothers are terribly over-stretched. They've got husbands to look after and their other children as well as the ones who are sick. Sometimes the husbands are taken ill too and there's scarcely any money coming in. I was going to go down, if you approve, and see what I could do to help. Buy them food or medicines in the Ghost, help with the nursing, do whatever I can.'

She paused and took her husband's hand. 'I wouldn't want to do anything that might undermine your investigation, of course.'

'I hardly think it's likely that some poor children from Candlesby village have been going round the county killing people, Lucy, especially if they're confined to bed with this dreadful influenza. You must do what think is best. Do you have enough money for now?'

'I'll be fine,' said Lady Lucy. 'I'm just going to talk to Mr Drake about sheets and things. I'm sure those poor children will recover better in clean linen.'

'I'll come with you to speak to George Drake, my love. I want to ask him about these jackets and the strange letter. I have a feeling he may know something about it all.'

Powerscourt was walking over to Candlesby Hall. He

wanted to have a talk with Charles and he wanted to ask him a favour. The question had been troubling him for days now. He didn't know if it had anything to do with his investigation. If he was honest with himself he suspected it might not, it had all happened so long ago. He wondered, yet again, about his summons to see the authorities and what it might bring. Maybe, he said crossly to himself, I won't even have the time to take Lucy away for a holiday when the case was over. He tried to think of somewhere warm on this November afternoon. He wondered what the weather would be like in Sicily. He had always wanted to see Palermo, much more beautiful than Naples, his next-door neighbour in Markham Square had told him, rotting Baroque churches falling down all over the city. Sanctified and consecrated Candlesby Halls, he said to himself, staring across at the crumbling facade and the one-armed statuary on the roof. The great house managed to look even more bedraggled in the damp and the wet than it had in the late autumn sunshine.

He heard voices over in the stable block, or rather, he thought, a single voice.

'Lord P-p-powerscourt,' said the unmistakable voice, 'how very good to see you. I've got important news for you.'

'Please tell me, Charles. Good to see you too.'

The young man drew him deeper into the stables where not even the horses could have heard them.

'On the night of the first murder, one of the servants says he saw lights on over in the village.'

'How many lights, Charles? When was this? Twelve? Two, three o'clock in the morning? And who was the person who told you?'

'More than one, light I mean, not p-p-person. And some-where between twelve and one, my informant thought. B-b-but I p-p-romised not to tell who told me.'

'Very well,' said Powerscourt. 'Do you believe them?'

'I do, my lord. I'm quite sure of it.'

'Why would the villagers be putting lights on in the middle of the night? What on earth was going on? Could your informant hear any voices?'

'I wasn't here that night. I was still in London, my lord. B-b-but everybody says there was a terrible storm. Maybe their roofs were leaking.'

'Well, that's interesting, most interesting,' said Powerscourt. Another fifty or sixty suspects had just arrived. 'Now then, Charles, I want to ask you a favour.'

'I'm sure we can help,' said Charles. 'What is it?'

Powerscourt felt ever so slightly embarrassed as he told him. 'I want to see the room with the Caravaggios.'

Charles Candlesby whistled to himself. 'I don't think anybody's b-b-been in there since Earl Edward died. They say he used to haunt the upper floors at night in the winter, wearing his nightclothes and carrying Goliath's head in his hand like in one of the p-p-paintings he b-b-brought b-back to the Caravaggio room.'

'Good God!' said Powerscourt. He knew he would never say so in polite society but part of him did actually believe in ghosts, even ones carrying giants' heads under their arms. 'Is he still at large, this chap? Perhaps he is David, not a Dymoke at all, though how King David of the Israelites could end up in England, I don't quite know.'

'Nobody has seen him since Mary the p-parlourmaid,' said Charles, 'and that was round about the time of the Chartist riots, my lord, a long time ago. There are terrible stories about those times, Lord P-p-powerscourt. P-p-people coming home from here covered in blood. Marks on their necks sometimes. Or left hanging upside down.'

'God bless my soul,' said Powerscourt. 'Now then, do you know who has the keys?'

Charles Candlesby thought for a moment. 'Well,' he said, finally, 'the p-p-person who should have them is Thorpe the b-b-butler. I've never seen inside that room, my lord and I'm not sure I want to do so now either.'

'Well,' said Powerscourt diplomatically, 'why don't you come with me and you can decide when we get there.'

'Of course.'

They found Barnabas Thorpe polishing a beautiful pair of Georgian candlesticks. 'Don't suppose we'll see these on the table again in my lifetime,' he said sadly by way of introduction. 'Keys, my lord, which keys would those be?'

Powerscourt wondered if deafness was going to be added to the many and varied difficulties of life in Candlesby Hall, but he merely repeated his wish to see the Caravaggio room.

Barnabas Thorpe shuddered slightly. He stared at Powerscourt for some time. 'Nobody's been in that room for well over a hundred years, my lord. Earl Edward, he was a right cruel man, they say, he brought those pictures back here in the 1760s or the 1770s and he died the week before Trafalgar. When the nation was celebrating that victory with feasts and bonfires, the people here were thanking God for deliverance from Earl Edward. They weren't too bothered about Bonaparte, apparently. One man said a French invasion would be a blessing in disguise – at least the people of Candlesby would get rid of their Earl, the Earl from hell some of them called him.'

Thorpe shuffled off into private quarters of his own behind a curtain and could be heard muttering to himself for some considerable time.

'Here we are,' he announced finally, and put a large black ring with three huge keys on it on his table. 'I assume, my lord, that if I don't agree to open up the room – I've no intention of asking this one who calls himself Earl now for any sort of permission – then you will be off to the police station and back inside the hour with a search warrant?'

'I'm afraid you might be right there, Mr Thorpe.'

'Very well, on your own head be it, my lord. I am not responsible for your going to this place. I will take you there. I will open the door for you. But I will not go in. When you are finished, you may call for me and I shall lock the room up again.'

With that Barnabas Thorpe led the way very slowly up the back stairs. The banisters were loose and the few windows into the inner courtyard of the Hall were thick with dust. Looking at the back in front of him, Powerscourt thought suddenly of the other aged retainer close to the heart of Candlesby Hall, the steward Walter Savage, with his tales of financial disaster. He remembered Savage's words about Jack Hayward.

'This has all been absolutely too terrible for words,' Jack Hayward had said. 'I can't tell you anything about it. One day, please God, I will tell you, but not now.' And then he had left, with one last word: 'Goodbye, Walter, and God bless you. Pray for us all. Pray for us every day as long as you live.'

That was it. Surely that was sufficient bait to lure Jack Hayward back across the Irish Sea. All he had to do was to arrest the steward, or rather have the Inspector arrest the steward, and tell Johnny Fitzgerald to do his worst. It might be underhand but Powerscourt thought the subterfuge would be justified if it enabled them to solve the mystery. If Hayward thought he had information that could save his old friend of twenty years or more from jail or even the gallows, he would come back. Surely he would come back. He remembered Johnny Fitzgerald's last telegram which had arrived that morning. 'Am now in very expensive hotel near Limerick. Will await instructions. Hotel filled with fish and fishermen. Cellar filled with Château d'Yquem. Rather sweet but needs must. Johnny.'

Powerscourt wondered if he should not abandon his crazy mission and reach the Inspector at once. Behind him Charles Candlesby was whistling 'I do like to be beside the seaside, I do like to be beside the sea'. Powerscourt wondered what strange memories had put that song in his mind. But Powerscourt felt, tramping up the final flight of steps, a grimy mirror reflecting a grimy investigator as he passed, that he had raised so much dust already that it would be folly to go into reverse now.

There was a dull clanking of keys. Barnabas Thorpe selected the largest one he could find and fitted it in the lock. When he tried to turn it, nothing happened. It was as if there was a vice on the other side refusing to let it move.

'Damn!' said Thorpe. 'I'm sure they told me it was that one.'

Powerscourt wondered how long ago the handover of keys had taken place. And who handed them over? Surely not Earl Edward in person. He wondered again what terrible things must have gone on in this room, or what terrible rumours had flown from it that they could still cause tremors nearly a hundred and fifty years later.

Charles Candlesby had stopped whistling now. The seaside seemed very far away. The old butler was breathing heavily. There was no other sound to be heard up here at the top of Candlesby Hall.

'How about you, then?' Thorpe was holding conversations with the keys now, as if they might tell him which one would open the door. Powerscourt had a distant memory of nursery rhymes, or was it children's stories involving locked doors and unsolved mysteries or imprisoned princesses on the other side. In went the other key. It too refused to move.

'If this next one don't serve, my lord, we'll have to beat the retreat for now.' He put the third one into the lock and turned it. There was a faint sign of movement. 'Maybe you should try, my lord.'

Powerscourt turned the key with all his strength. Very slowly, with a rasping, creaking sound, the key moved in the lock. Powerscourt looked at the door. To his right Charles Candlesby had turned very pale and was beginning to inch away.

'If you'll excuse me, my lord.' Barnabas Thorpe was feeling some strain. The sweat was pouring down his face and

Powerscourt didn't think it came from the effort of turning the key. It was fear, or something worse. 'I think I'll leave you now. I have things to do. If you'll excuse me, my lord.'

The clattering of boot on board told him that both his companions had fled the field. Powerscourt pushed the door hard with his shoulder and he was in. In with the paintings of Michelangelo Merisi, more commonly known by the name of the village where he was born. Caravaggio.

16

Powerscourt felt like some underground explorer deep below the earth's crust who rolls away a vast boulder to find himself in an enormous chamber, the walls adorned with cave paintings of strange creatures who no longer roam the earth. The air was filled with dust and a horrid smell, a compound of heaven knew how many dead insects and rotting objects and the passing of time itself. The dust was so thick that when his foot touched what was left of the dingy carpet small clouds billowed out over his shoe.

Powerscourt coughed harshly and tried to find some fresh air. The room was on the top corner of the house with a pair of windows looking out over the garden towards the lake and another pair on the adjacent wall looking out over a dark courtyard. Powerscourt pulled out his penknife and inserted it between the edge of the surround and the wood holding the glass of the window. His blade got stuck every now and then but it did eventually manage to run up and down the sash. He spent a few minutes heaving and shoving at the catch in the middle of the window and pulled as hard as he could. For a moment his coughing grew worse. Then the window shot upwards and fresh air flowed into the room. Powerscourt turned his attention to the other windows. After a quarter of an hour he managed to open two of them. You could, he decided, almost feel the bad air rushing past. A couple of rooks, who could never have seen the windows open in their lifetime, flew past twice as if to make sure their eyes were not deceiving them.

The room was very large. To the right of the door were a couple of tall cupboards. Another two were on the left of the door, with a bed in the corner, the pillows limp and flaccid to the touch, the bedcover, which might once have been a bright yellow, now a dingy brown. In front of the long windows looking over the garden stood a couple of easels, one considerably higher than the other, both festooned in dust and cobwebs. A large mirror was wedged between them. In the corner, still standing to attention, stood a grandfather clock whose face announced the time as twenty minutes past three. Time had not moved in here for over a century. There was an alcove to one side of the bed with the remains of a curtain drawn across the space.

But where, Powerscourt said to himself, were the Caravaggios? They certainly weren't on the walls. This earlier Candlesby had collected the paintings all over Italy and brought them back to his old house and stored them up here on the top floor. The people who lived here now were so frightened of the paintings or what had been done with the paintings that they were too scared to come in. He looked at the cupboards suspiciously. When he opened one of them he found on the top shelf a strange collection of clothes, what looked like a loincloth, a dark cloak, a sort of chemise with no collar that could have been worn by male or female, a strange circular headdress, various lengths and dimensions of scarlet and blue cloth that could have been used for anything. On the second shelf he found a skull, the vast open jawbone still yawning horribly at those who came to see it, a selection of twigs, a limp bamboo cane with split ends and a couple of berets, one in dark blue and one in pale green. There was a filthy candlestick and a mirror that had seen better days. Quite what these objects were doing there, Powerscourt had, for the moment, no idea.

He tried to remember the little he knew about Caravaggio. Born in the north of Italy and brought up in Milan. Moved south to Rome where he was employed by a courtier at the Vatican, then to Naples and various other cities round the Mediterranean. There had, Powerscourt's contact at the National Gallery once told him on the telephone, been rumours of fighting and drunkenness. He was believed to have fled Rome after killing a man. He had died young after a turbulent life. The National Gallery, Powerscourt's man told him, had three or four of his paintings stored in the basement, that final resting place for unfashionable artists. He had fallen from popularity, Caravaggio, very soon after he died. Few galleries, if any, had his paintings on display, except for a rather obscure one in Naples. Maybe the artistic world was anxious to forget such a controversial figure. One day, Powerscourt's curator contact had prophesied, Caravaggio would return to fame and glory once again. It happened all the time, he said. Just as some obscure share or bond which seems to do nothing for decades will suddenly spring into life when fresh seams of gold or silver are discovered, his works would come back into fashion. The swagger and the display and the mastery of light and drama that had entranced his contemporaries in his lifetime would be on display again in the great galleries of Europe. How odd, Powerscourt thought, if the fortunes of the Candlesbys and their estates could be restored by the paintings that had been left to rot up here since the time of the loss of the American colonies.

He had a violent coughing fit. The dust seemed to be making its way down to his lungs. He tiptoed over to the alcove with the curtain. Very gently he pulled it to one side. On the right-hand side was a great pile of paintings, about a dozen, he thought, maybe more. Another heap was against the opposite wall. The dust was lying in layers on the frames. Spiders had created gossamer Old Master drawings against the back wall. Powerscourt picked the right-hand paintings up one by one and carried them back to the bed. He leant them against the sides with a few on top of the covers. The dust twirled and swirled and whirled around his face until he had to go and put his head out of the window. He wondered suddenly if the Edward Candlesby who had purchased these pictures had leant out of this window and stared at his English estates stretching out to the lake and beyond into the Lincolnshire countryside, remembering the days he bought his Caravaggios amid the heat and the different dust of Naples and Rome. He wondered about the purchases on the Grand Tour. Had Candlesby fallen victim to the usual honey trap? You went to an art dealer, usually in Rome, some of whom sold only to British visitors. The dealer would inquire politely in reasonable English which of the Old Masters appealed to you the most. Raphael, you might hazard, or Titian perhaps. What a pity you have come today, the dealer would say. I have some very fine Raphaels and some wonderful Titians, but they are at my house in the country. I like them so much, signor, that I keep them at home for my own enjoyment. But for you, I will bring them back here to the Via Veneto. If you come back in three days' time, they will be here, waiting for you. What could be better! Maybe the dealer already has some fake Titians and Raphaels in store somewhere. If not, his forger goes to work and the fakes are ready for inspection on the third day. Some excuse about the need for final glazing would be made to give the works time to dry out properly. Perhaps milord would care to look at some other paintings in the meantime? Powerscourt suspected that Caravaggio might not fit into that particular mould. He was relatively unknown. High-class forgers might not take the time and trouble to learn how to reproduce him. The dealer might not keep any in stock in case he could never shift them. Maybe these were originals after all.

Two things struck Powerscourt as he looked through the paintings. The first was the artist's total mastery of light, spectacular even after a century and a half of dust and damp. It was as if he had a whole battery of searchlights of different power. Some of the faces and some of the bodies would have the most powerful light shone on them. The skin would gleam and glisten as if the subject were sweating slightly. Other, less important, characters received much less power. The contrast between the brilliance of the light shining on the body of St Jerome, for example, and the skull, half in shadow on his work table, gave the picture a power and intensity that held the viewer in its spell. Mastery of light heightened the drama. Even through the dust and the grime the light shone through. The other thing to strike Powerscourt was the faces. These were not the faces of aristocrats or warriors or great kings or ancient philosophers from the distant past. They were not the idealized beauties that graced the canvases of Botticelli or Bellini. Caravaggio was an unlikely foot soldier in the Counter Reformation launched at the Council of Trent towards the end of the sixteenth century, the Catholic Church's fight back against the Protestants. The heretics of Geneva or Wittenberg might ban paintings from the walls of their churches. The true believers in the Pope and the Mass were given large paintings on the walls and in the little chapels of the churches of Rome that were morality stories, but morality stories of a power and force that could not but impress. The faces in Caravaggio's pictures were taken from the streets, lifted from tavern or alleyway or choir to grace an artist's vision. This, Powerscourt remembered his man at the National Gallery telling him, was what gave them their contemporary feel. This was what enabled the poor and the destitute to identify with Caravaggio's characters. Titian's kings and doges inhabited a world far from the ordinary citizens. Caravaggio's people were real boys and real men and women, spotted by the painter perhaps and paid a pittance to pose for his brushes.

There were one or two charming paintings, probably

executed for some prince of the Church, of Bacchus with leaves in his hair, of cardsharps plying their trade, a boy with a basket of fruit. Caravaggio was drawn to drama as the dust was drawn to this high room that served as a sepulchre for his art. Here was the calling of St Matthew, here was the raising of Lazarus, the death of the Virgin. A number of the works, Powerscourt thought, verged on the sado-masochistic, or seemed to come from the pornography of religious violence. Death, blood and beheading were commonplace, painted with appalling realism. Judith with the head of Holofernes, for example, showed the progress of the knife against the warrior's throat. The beheading of John the Baptist showed the saint lying on the floor with the executioner poised above him in a well of light, knife at the ready. Christ was tied to a tree, flayed, scourged, and had the crown of thorns put on his head. Saints were crucified upside down or right way up, their agony and their faith earning a place in heaven.

Even through the dust and the grime the power of the artist illuminated this room at the top of Candlesby Hall. For the poor and the peasants of early seventeenth-century Italy, they must have seemed more wondrous than the modern cinema pictures. These were in colour rather than black and white with an intensity the camera did not possess.

But what of the other pictures, the ones on the opposite side of the alcove? Powerscourt moved some of the real Caravaggios to rest against the wall behind the easel. Out they came, the others, two or three at a time. When he inspected them, he was amazed. This, he thought, was the most unusual thing he had seen since the start of his investigation. These paintings were as grimy as the others. Dust and dark lines defaced the surface of the pictures as it did the ones by the window. But the subject matter was the same. These were copies, very imperfect copies, of the Caravaggios behind the easels. Here again was the boy with the basket of fruit, Bacchus with a crown on his head, the flayings, the decapitations, the crucifixions, the whole bloody agony from Gethsemane to Golgotha. But they were copies with a difference. This boy with a fruit basket did not come from the streets of Naples. He looked as though he might have come from the farms of Candlesby. There was something terribly English about his face.

As he rattled through the paintings, Powerscourt saw a host of people who must have been locals, summoned to this room to pose for their master. Rubbing lightly with his handkerchief and blowing at the corner of one painting, Powerscourt found a sort of signature. 'Candlesby', the writing said in the bottom right-hand corner, 'after Caravaggio'.

Inspector Blunden was not a happy man. He was on his way to interview Oliver Bell near Old Bolingbroke Castle west of Candlesby. Bell's father had been shot in a duel by the late Lord Candlesby many years before, and Bell had served in the British Army as an expert marksman. He was, the Inspector thought, far too obvious a suspect but his Chief Constable had been making suggestions so here he was.

Blunden had always had a feeling about murder inquiries. Some of them, he felt, you just knew were going to turn out well. It was only a question of waiting for the key facts to fall into place or a witness to come forward with the vital piece of evidence. The Candlesby murders were not like that. There was his interfering Chief Constable for a start. Then there were those posh people up at Candlesby Hall. Blunden would never have admitted it but he felt uncomfortable with these aristocrats. Part of him really believed that they were superior to him and his like. Another part of him told him that this was nonsense. Nevertheless, he found interviewing them difficult. With most of the population of Lincolnshire Blunden could have told you who was lying and who was telling the truth and been right almost all the time. This detection compass deserted him completely in Candlesby Hall.

Then there was Powerscourt. Inspector Blunden was very fond of Powerscourt and was glad he was on board. But he did find him difficult on occasion. Blunden's brain ticked over like on old grandfather clock. Steady. Reliable. Unchanging. The time on its face was always right. Powerscourt's brain on the other hand, the Inspector felt, was not like that at all. It was mercurial, it darted about, it jumped around. Inspector Blunden doubted if a Powerscourt clock would ever tell the right time. It would look very pretty as some clocks did, but as a timekeeper it would be all over the place. In some ways Powerscourt reminded him of a boy he had known at school. He was no good at the steady subjects, Albert Parker, but he was entranced by history and the romance of old buildings and battles and glory long ago. 'Show him a castle,' the history master had once said, 'and there'll be a princess locked up in the tower and a sword stuck in a rock that only the once and future King can pull out. Overdeveloped historical imagination, that's what it is.' Inspector Blunden knew in his bones that Powerscourt would have one brilliant flash of intuition – the Inspector preferred to call it guesswork – and the case would be over.

There was only one consoling thought in the Inspector's heart that morning and she was called Emily and she was three years old, Emily Blunden. She would sit in her father's lap and demand his total attention before serenading him with 'Baa Baa Black Sheep', over and over again. The Inspector had impressed upon his wife the need to widen the repertoire, but, so far, 'Baa Baa Black Sheep' was all they were going to get.

The little garden outside Oliver Bell's cottage was very tidy. Oliver Bell opened the door in a pair of dark blue trousers and an enormous sweater as if he was about to embark on a long sea voyage. He had a neat black beard and curly hair turning silver at the sides. He looked, Blunden thought, like a self-contained sort of person, one who does not need all that much of the company of his fellow men.

'Good morning, Inspector,' said Bell. 'I've been expecting you for some time now.'

The Inspector wondered if he had been derelict in the performance of his duty and would be sacked on his return to the police station.

'I'm sure you can understand my position, Mr Bell.' The Inspector had squeezed into a chair that was much too small for him. 'Your father killed in a duel when you were small, your coming back here a year or so ago, revenge always a very clear motive for murder and you a military man too.'

'I can fully see why you might regard me as a suspect, Inspector. In your job I would have done exactly the same. But I have to tell you that I have changed. I am no longer a soldier. I am a pacifist now, a Christian of sorts, a believer in the late writings of Leo Tolstoy and politicians like Keir Hardie and Ramsay MacDonald. I am going to London to work for the Salvation Army when you are finished with me. I did not care to leave until I had spoken with you in case you thought I was guilty and was running away.'

'Can you tell me where you were on the night of the great storm when Lord Candlesby was murdered, Mr Bell?'

'I can indeed, Inspector. I was here apart from an hour spent with my nearest neighbour, a retired clergyman who thought his roof was about to collapse. I was with him for fifty or sixty minutes. I'm sure he would confirm that.'

'Very well, Mr Bell, once I have confirmed that you will be free to leave. Just one other thing. Could I ask you couple of questions if I may?'

'That's what you people do,' Bell replied, with a smile.

'What made you change your mind? About the military, I mean. You had a very distinguished career in the army after all.'

Oliver Bell stared blankly at the Inspector as if he had travelled to some faraway veldt or a distant hill station in Rajasthan.

'I killed too many people,' he said finally. 'Sorry if that sounds gruesome. I must have killed hundreds and hundreds of people in my time in the army. Most of the time you never see them, your victims I mean. Near the end I did see three people I'd shot that very morning. One had been shot in the chest and his blood was everywhere. One had been shot in the belly and his guts were hanging out over his stomach like something in a butcher's shop. The third had been hit in the forehead and his brains were all over the others. Flies and other insects were all buzzing around for the feast. Man reduced to a treat for the smallest and least significant of God's creatures. I only killed two people after that. Most of the time I aimed too high or too wide.'

'I think you are a very brave man,' said the Inspector. 'My final question is this. Did you see or hear of anything round about the time of these murders that might help us find the killer?'

Oliver Bell thought for a moment. 'Just one thing, Inspector, and it could be nothing. Early in the afternoon on the day of the great storm I'd come back from Lincoln on the train. I'd been to the cathedral to hear a talk about the cloisters. It always refreshes me, Lincoln Cathedral. Every time I go there I think we don't deserve to be exposed to such beauty. Carlton Lawrence, the middle one of that family who had to sell up recently, he was coming out of the railway station. He looked rather nervous, as if he had just done something wrong or was about to do something he shouldn't. He kept looking around him as if he didn't want to be recognized. As I say, it could be nothing, Inspector.'

Oliver Bell watched the policeman go. I didn't think that would be so easy, he said to himself. Much easier than I thought. He went inside and began to pack his bags.

Edward Nathaniel, Earl of Candlesby, referred to by his detractors as the Wicked Earl, had been restored to the room

237

he created at the end of the eighteenth century. Powerscourt and the butler had brought him up two flights of stairs from his place on the dining-room wall next to the second Earl. Only Powerscourt had actually carried the portrait into the room. He was now ensconced on one of the two easels by the window. Powerscourt checked the various copies he had discovered and found that there were two pictures where Candlesby had painted himself as a copy of the Caravaggio original. One was of a saint often depicted in religious paintings. St Jerome is old and losing his hair. He is engaged in copying out the Vulgate, wearing a deep red robe as far as his waist. A skull and a candlestick and a mirror remind us that death is never far away, the very items that Powerscourt had discovered in the cupboard. Powerscourt suspected that Candlesby put the original painting on one easel and his own canvas on the other. When he had copied all the background, he had removed the original and aligned the large mirror on the easel in such a way that he could paint his own reflection on to the canvas. He was wearing the red robe Powerscourt had found in the cupboard, and the skull was nearby as it had been in the Caravaggio version. Unlike the real Caravaggio, there was little life and no energy in it. It was, Powerscourt thought, a poor thing.

But the others, what of the others? Did Candlesby know that Caravaggio used contemporary models from the street or the tavern or the house next door? Would they have told him that in those art galleries in Rome?

He rearranged the Caravaggio canvases once more and discovered that there was a clear sequence of paintings about Christ's last days, the flagellation of Christ, Ecce Homo or Here is the Man, the crowning with thorns, all concerned with Jesus being scourged and shown to the multitude by Pontius Pilate.

Powerscourt found three copies by the former owner of the house. He stared at them for a long time. None of these men was Candlesby himself. The models being flogged or crowned with thorns were all different people. Were they locals? Had Candlesby simply selected them from his labourers or his servants to act as models for his grisly hobby? Had he ordered them up here, beaten them or flogged them to the required degree and made them sit or stand or be twisted round a pillar, their wounds still bleeding so the paint would look fresh on the canvas? Christ in heaven.

Powerscourt staggered back from the Candlesby paintings and found himself in a dark corner with an enormous cupboard he had not seen before. He pulled very carefully at the door. It seemed to have been locked. Powerscourt vented his rage on the lower panels and kicked the door down. There were two smaller groups of paintings on opposite sides of the door panel. Leaning across the back of the cupboard was a tall piece of wood, eight or nine feet tall. He pulled it into the light. There was another shorter piece of wood joined to it about two-thirds of the way up. This shape had been used in the ancient states of Persia and Greece and Macedonia. It was employed widely in ancient Rome. Six thousand of Spartacus's slaves were hung on them along the Appian Way after the end of the revolt. Jesus Christ ended his life on one of them. The object in the cupboard on the top floor of Candlesby Hall was a cross, the holiest, the best known, the most powerful symbol of the Christian faith on earth.

Two old people and one four-year-old child had already died from the influenza in the village of Candlesby when Lady Lucy Powerscourt went to help. She was careful at the beginning not to make any suggestions and not to put herself forward. She told the women of the village that she was happy to be useful in any way she could, whatever would be most helpful to them. The women with the sick families were short of time. When their parents and their children were sick at the same time they were stretched to breaking point. So Lady Lucy found herself dividing her time between the very young and the very old. She read to the children, old stories from her childhood, stories she had told to her own children when they were the same age as the Candlesby ones. More stories were ordered, to be sent express from Hatchard's in London. When the children were too hot, or delirious, she would stroke their faces and hold their hands and whisper softly to them. Sometimes when she thought they were on the verge of death she found it very hard not to break down.

The Rolls-Royce Silver Ghost was seen a lot in the village, carrying supplies, fetching medicines, ferrying the doctor to and fro. Lady Lucy had ordered provisions to be despatched from Mr Drake's hotel, soup and fresh bread and roast chickens and fruit. Children who were only mildly afflicted by the influenza would be carried out to the great car with its gleaming silver bonnet, heavily wrapped up, and allowed to sit beside Rhys and inspect the controls for a couple of minutes. None of them had ever seen a motor car before. Every child in the village was promised a proper ride in the Ghost when they were better.

The social life had broken down most severely for the old, most of them female. In normal times their daughters would come to call, or their grandchildren, or their nephews or nieces. They would eat with the rest of the family in the house of one of their children. Now the mothers who cooked had their hands full with sick children, the grandchildren were laid low by the influenza and the neighbours were either confined to bed themselves or on nursing duty elsewhere. Lady Lucy would call on as many as she could find time for, making endless cups of tea, bringing bowls of soup or fresh chicken sandwiches. They were shy of her at first, the old ladies of Candlesby, but they soon realized that, though the externals of their lives were so very different, the central core was the same: children, husbands, family, home.

240

After a couple of days Lady Lucy would ask them about the men they had loved, the men they had married, the men they wished they had married, the men they wished they had never seen. The stronger of them would smile and ask her the same questions back. Some of the old ladies were rambling at the height of the influenza, their minds wandering, their speech virtually unintelligible. Lady Lucy stroked their hands just the same and made more tea. It was only later that she realized some of the things she was hearing might not just be the ramblings of the very sick. Was the key to the mystery of Candlesby Hall being revealed to her in small and unconnected batches as the diseased and the dying referred unwittingly in their ravings to things they would never have mentioned when they were well?

Powerscourt was now very angry indeed. He had pulled out the cross and found various marks in various places he did not like at all. In both lots of paintings, Caravaggios and Candlesbys, there was one disciple crucified upright and one crucified upside down. There was Christ being laid in the tomb, a dead Saviour who looked very dead indeed. Had Candlesby waited for a corpse to paint that particular scene? Surely he couldn't have killed the man just to have a model for the painting. Had he stolen the corpse from the undertakers? There were various severed heads he didn't care for either, quite apart from Judith with the head of Holofernes. There was Salome with the head of John the Baptist, David with the head of Goliath, both particularly bloody and realistic, blood dripping artistically from the severed necks, eyes staring in astonishment that death dared take them out of the frames of their lives.

Powerscourt's brain was reeling now. He didn't know what to believe. At best, you could assume that the old Earl had rented various locals to model for his imitations of the Caravaggios he had bought on the Grand Tour. But there were other, darker possibilities. The models might have been abused or beaten up or scourged or had their heads cut off. People of all sorts had told him that the Candlesbys were eccentric, that they beat their children, that they refused to speak to their sons and daughters and communicated only by letter, that children could be thrown out for not standing up when their father came into the room. This older Candlesby was undoubtedly of that tradition. Powerscourt suddenly remembered the butler and indeed Charles Candlesby himself refusing to come into the Caravaggio chamber. What did these Candlesbys think their fellow men were for? They were to be exploited, robbed, used, whatever the masters wanted. For the masters owned the servants and the tenants and the farm labourers as they might own a cart or a horse or a field or a house. They were just one more possession to be used at will.

God knows what rumours had circulated in times gone by. Maybe a William had gone up to the house to model for a holy painting and never returned. An Albert came back with the most terrible weals on his back, so weak and in so much pain he could hardly speak. A Peter said he had been hung upside down on a cross and left for hours. As he bundled the pictures and the props back into the cupboards a terrible thought struck Powerscourt. Maybe these weren't stories or myths of the Candlesby past. Maybe they were all true.

17

Powerscourt's brain was reeling as he rushed down the three flights of stairs from the top floor of Candlesby Hall. Some flying creature, possibly a bat, brushed his face as he sped past. Other demons rattled through his brain as he tried to make sense of the awful sights up there, looking out over the lake and the Candlesby fields. He managed to leave the house without having to speak to a single living soul and walked at top speed round the edges of the park. The deer watched him from afar, their lives largely peaceful, their great trusting eyes untroubled by the ghosts of flagellation and martyrdom from long ago. When he reached the hotel he found Lady Lucy sitting by the window in their room, staring sadly out at the bare trees and the flat landscape.

'Oh, Francis!' She rushed into his arms. 'Thank God you've come. It's very sad down there in the village. I don't know if they're going to come through.'

'Are all of them ill?' asked Powerscourt. He had already resolved not to tell Lady Lucy about the terrible things in the Caravaggio room.

'Well, not all of them. I should say about a quarter of the able-bodied men, slightly less for the women, thank God. It's the children and the old people who are worst affected. I feel for them all, you know, Francis. Not that I'd ever say anything, there's too much to do with the watching by the bedsides and stroking their foreheads or wiping their faces and trying to speak comforting things to them. You'd think you wouldn't feel so bad with the old ladies. They've had their time in a way, they've got married and brought up their children and done whatever women do in a village like that. Some of them seem ready to go, you know. But others are fighting for life. Even when they're tossing and turning in their rickety beds you can still catch a look that says, I'm not going to go yet, not if I can help it.

'The worst thing with the children is that they don't know what's happening to them. Oh, they'll listen to the stories we tell them and manage a little smile from time to time. But for a lot of the day they just look hurt and confused. They've never been ill in their lives so far, not seriously ill I mean, and it's terrible for them. Why can't they get out of bed and cause trouble as they usually do? Why can't they go out and run about in the fields? Why are they stuck in these beds, the sweat pouring off their bodies and the coughs racking their little chests? Nobody told them these were the rules.'

'I'm sure you are a great comfort to them, Lucy. I must leave you for a few minutes. I have a naughty plan to bring Jack Hayward back. I must bring Blunden on board and then we can send a telegram.'

Lady Lucy watched him go. She knew that she would continue with her nursing in Candlesby village until the influenza had passed. She didn't tell her husband about the ravings of the elderly ladies.

Powerscourt found Inspector Blunden in cheerful mood, making copperplate doodles at his desk.

'I'm feeling more cheerful about the case, my lord. God knows why. There's no reason for it, but I just feel we're going to win through.'

'Let me try to enlist your support in a stratagem that

would bring Jack Hayward back. I don't think you'll like it one little bit, but think of the prize, the man who brought the corpse back, the man who saw the battered face, the man who left the scene at record speed.'

'Tell me the plan then,' said the Inspector.

'You will remember me telling you how close Jack Hayward was to Walter Savage. They were close for twenty years. Hayward asked Savage to pray for him when he was leaving.'

Suddenly the Inspector rose from his chair and paced up and down the room. His face broke out into a rather wicked grin. 'I think I've got it, my lord! It's certainly devious, extremely devious, but I'm sure it would work. We arrest Savage and lock him up on some trumped-up charge. Then we send a telegram to your friend Johnny Fitzgerald announcing that Savage is in prison. Hayward hurries home to save his friend. How's that?'

'Spot on, Inspector, spot on.'

'Right,' said Blunden. 'I'm on my way to Candlesby Hall to pick up Savage. He should be locked up within the hour. You can send the telegram now if you like, my lord.'

Johnny Fitzgerald was growing weary of the bars and public houses of Limerick. He had spent many hours in their smoke-filled snugs, listening to the stories of the old men and the complaints of the farmers, all of them blessed with an unquenchable thirst for Guinness and the more powerful draughts of John Jameson.

So it was a relief early one evening when the hotel manager gave Johnny a telegram. He handed it over with the air of one who is certain that it contains bad news for the recipient, imminent arrest perhaps, or instant deportation to the colonies. Johnny read it in his room. Powerscourt, he saw, had not spared himself in the words department. Not for him the normal compression, the minimum of letters employed in the expensive business of the despatch of telegrams. Johnny remembered a military bookkeeper in India, the Skinflint of Darjeeling as he was known, telling Powerscourt that he didn't have to send out messages as if he were writing the principal leading article in *The Times*.

'Candlesby, twenty-sixth of November,' he read. 'Dear Johnny.' God in heaven, Fitzgerald said to himself, who the hell ever put the date and Dear Johnny in a telegram? 'I bring news from the front. Inspector Blunden has arrested the steward of Candlesby, Walter Savage, in connection with the murder of the two Earls. He is at present in Spalding jail. Savage has repeatedly expressed the wish that Jack Hayward was there to help him in his hour of need. You will know what to do. Lucy sends her love. Hope to see you soon in these wretched flatlands by the sea. Francis.'

As he sped off towards Cashel Johnny wondered if Savage really had been arrested or if this was some ploy to drag an unwilling Hayward back across the Irish Sea. He suspected, from his knowledge of Powerscourt, that it was a ploy, but that the steward Savage really was locked up in Spalding jail along with the drunks and the poachers and the cattle thieves.

A couple of hours later he was knocking once again on the front door of the house where he had been thrown out less than a week before.

'It's you again,' said the farmer's wife. 'The devil finds work for idle hands, so he does now. What in God's name do you want this time? I told you, Jack Hatward, or whatever he's called, isn't here.'

'We are faced with a grave situation now, madam,' said Johnny, trying to sound as serious as his old headmaster at school. 'I will not beat about the bush. Time is short. You tell Jack Hayward that one of his greatest friends over the water in Candlesby has been arrested for murder. His name is Savage, Walter Savage. Have you got that? He is at present locked up in Spalding jail with the other lawbreakers of Lincolnshire. He is asking for Jack to come to his assistance. He seems to think Jack could secure his release. I cannot foretell the future, madam, but if Jack does not come this unfortunate man Savage could end up being taken from the court where he has been found guilty and hanged by the neck until he is dead. You tell Jack Hayward that. I shall come back in half an hour. Good day to you.'

With that he strode off and found solace in the Kilkenny Arms two hundred yards away. Here, he thanked God, none of the natives spoke to him at all. He had long suspected that he would be accosted some day in one of these Irish pubs by people claiming to have survived the famine and demanding compensation in liquid form.

The woman's attitude was very different when he came back. 'You'd better come in,' she said, closing the door quickly. She showed him into a small sitting room adorned with ghoulish paintings of the Stations of the Cross. Johnny could hear a lot of talking in the passageway outside but he couldn't catch the words. In the distance, upstairs perhaps, he could hear a child crying.

'Who the hell are you?' The man was of normal height, clean shaven with curly black hair and an air of authority about him. Johnny wondered if he had the same influence on humans as he did on horses.

Johnny rose and shook him by the hand. 'Jack Hayward?' he said. The man nodded. 'My name is Fitzgerald, Johnny Fitzgerald. I work with a private investigator called Powerscourt, Lord Francis Powerscourt. We are investigating the murders of the past two Earls of Candlesby with the Lincolnshire police.'

'Murders?' said Jack Hayward. 'Has there been another one?'

'I'm afraid there has. Richard the heir was on his way to take his place in the House of Lords when he was garrotted on his train.'

'Great God. I didn't know. They don't put much Lincolnshire news in the papers round here.'

'It's Walter Savage we're concerned about here, Mr Hayward. He thinks you can help secure his release from prison.'

'I once visited a man in Spalding jail,' said Jack Hayward thoughtfully. 'They thought he had been stealing horses but he hadn't. But tell me this, how do I know you're telling the truth? This could be some terrible trick.'

Johnny had realized on his journey that he could show Hayward Powerscourt's telegram. Probably his friend had written it with that in mind. He handed it over. 'Inspector Blunden is the chief investigating officer. Lady Lucy is Powerscourt's wife.'

Jack Hayward read it very quickly. He stared at Johnny for a moment. 'All right. Dammit, I'll come. I don't want to come but I don't think that I have much choice. I can't let Walter down. If this is a trick, you'll have to pay for it. I'm not going to bring the wife or the children with me. They'll be safer here. I gather there is an outbreak of influenza in Candlesby village.' He stared at the Stations of the Cross for a moment. 'I'll just go and tell the wife and gather a few things. I should be ready to go in fifteen minutes.'

Forty-five minutes later Johnny was waiting with Jack Hayward for the express to Dublin. He had just despatched a telegram to Powerscourt. He had made it as short as possible. 'Hayward Redux', it said. Jack Hayward was coming home.

Back in Candlesby Hall the normal routines of life that had held for the past twenty or thirty years were breaking down. For Henry and Edward there was a great gap left by the absence of their tyrannical father, killed in a manner as yet unknown, and their eldest brother, garrotted in his special train on his special day. Henry was now the Earl of Candlesby, and his younger brother Edward was seized with jealousy at the caprices of birth. Why should he lose out just because he had been born a couple of years later? He might not have been bastard like Edmund in *King Lear*, but he felt the unfairness just as deeply. They made desultory plans for what they would do when the murders were cleared up. They would sell the house and the estate, a happy dream, until the steward told Henry the full facts of the financial situation. They dreamt on, their fantasies fuelled by drink. They would go and live in London – a life of glittering prizes where they would be welcomed as heirs to one of the great titles of the kingdom. They would go to Paris and sink into the voluptuous luxury of the most sophisticated city in Europe. They would go to California and start a new life in the new world.

Then catastrophe struck. They had both noticed – they had believed from their earliest years in the quantity rather quality school of wine consumption – that the bottles Barnabas Thorpe the butler brought up each morning were tasting worse and worse. They set forth on an expedition to the cellar, a great dark underground chamber in the basement near the kitchen surrounded by a rabbit warren of store rooms and pantries and the tunnel that led to the stable block. Neither brother had ever seen the kitchen or the wine cellar before. Each had a candle in his hand. They stared in disbelief at row after row of empty wine racks labelled Claret and Burgundy and Hock and Chablis and Port. Only in the far corner where the shadows and the dust were deepest was there a small section with bottles still in their place. There was no label, no indication of any kind as to where this stuff came from. This underground cave, as the French called their cellars, which had once held thousands of bottles to quench the thirst of Candlesbys past, was virtually empty. And when they spoke to Thorpe the butler about ordering fresh supplies from the family wine merchants, his reply distressed them as much if not more than the deaths of their father and brother.

'I'm afraid that will not be possible at present, my lord,' he had said in his most mournful voice.

'Why not?' said Henry, trying to sound like an Earl.

'I tried to replenish our supplies very recently, my lord. The wine merchants said that would not be possible. The wine here has been bought on credit for the past ten years. The firm are not prepared to extend any more until things settle down.'

'Bastards,' said Henry and Edward in unison. 'Things settle down? What does that mean?' Henry carried on.

'It means, my lord, that we shall not be able to order anything at all until one of two things happens, or possibly both.'

Henry raised an eyebrow. 'Like what?'

'The first is that the recent difficulties here' – a well-trained butler's finest euphemism for murder – 'are cleared up.'

'And the second?'

'The second is simpler. No more wine will be sent until somebody pays the bill.'

On the top floor, on the opposite side of the house to the Caravaggio room, things were not much better in the apartment where James lived with his attendant. James had not been seen much since the day when he marched into the lake and was only saved by the intervention of his brother Charles. The youngest of the Candlesbys, the one his elder brothers referred to as 'not right in the head' in their charitable moments and 'stark staring mad' in their normal moments, seemed to be deteriorating. He ran a high fever much of the time and had to be confined to bed, complaining of the cold in spite of a great fire roaring in the grate. When he got up James would sit huddled in an arm-chair wrapped in blankets and stare endlessly at the flames. When he spoke he did not make much sense, talking of storms and lightning and the wrath of God. Charles was his constant companion. His younger brother had an insatiable appetite for information about the murders. Which horse, he would ask, for like Charles he was a great lover of horses, had carried his father back from his death? What colour was the special train? How many niches were left in the mausoleum? Charles answered all his questions as best he could. He had no idea of the shape of the disease that was destroying his brother and even less idea of what form it might take in the future. But if love could have cured, James Candlesby would have taken up his bed and walked. Unlike the rest of his family Charles loved his brother very deeply and prayed against hope for his recovery.

James liked being read to, rather like the sick children in the village being cared for by Lady Lucy Powerscourt. He preferred poems to prose. He liked some of the more blood-thirsty passages in the *Iliad* when Hector's body is dragged around the walls of Troy. Shelley's 'I weep for Adonais – he is dead' was a great favourite. So was Milton's *Lycidas* and Tennyson's *In Memoriam* and John Donne's sonnet about the conquest of Death:

> One short sleep past, we wake eternally,
> And Death shall be no more: Death, thou shalt die!

James would clap his hands together on the bedspread and cheer at Byron's lines about the night before Waterloo:

> . . . the unreturning brave, – alas!
> Ere evening to be trodden like the grass
> Which now beneath them, but above shall grow
> In its next verdure, when this fiery mass
> Of living valour, rolling on the foe
> And burning with high hope, shall moulder cold and low.

It was the poetry about King Arthur and the Knights of the Round Table and the Lady of the Lake that entranced him most of all. He preferred Sir Thomas Malory's *Morte*

D'Arthur to the more effusive outpourings of Tennyson. The sword in the stone, the sword being thrown in the lake by Sir Bedevere were like a tonic to him.

Searching for a modern Merlin, Charles sent for the doctor. The medical man pronounced himself defeated by James' illness. He promised to return with a wiser colleague. When he did, there was then a very long examination of James and a whole host of questions about his mental state. The doctors retired to an empty schoolroom with faded maps on the wall and upturned desks lying about the floor, surrounded by the broken globes of a broken world. Eventually they sent for Charles and talked to him for half an hour. They were going back to speak with James in a moment, they said. They had just one question. Should James be told the truth about his condition?

Charles looked round the room, filled with memories of irregular Latin verbs and the details of the Wars of the Roses where early Dymokes had backed the wrong side just as they had in the Civil Wars. His eyes filled with tears.

'Tell him,' he said. 'Yes, I think that would be for the best. Tell him the truth.'

Inspector Blunden was seated at his desk in the police station at nine o'clock in the morning. He was doodling again on a clean page of a large police notebook. A series of Ls rolled out across the page. Along with thirty-seven other little boys and girls the Inspector had been taught to read and write in the village school by Mrs Rickards, a formidable woman with unorthodox but highly effective means of imparting knowledge to her charges. The ornate Blunden copperplate was one result of her endeavours. Then he left a space and added a row of Cs a few lines further down he added a number of JHs with a question mark at the end. The Inspector was preparing a rather unusual list of the tasks he had to perform that day. L was for Lawrence and the odd story from Oliver Bell that he had been seen behaving strangely at the railway station the day of the first murder. The C was for the clergyman who could establish Bell's alibi. The JH referred to Jack Hayward and the question of whether he had been found.

Constable Andrew Merrick reported for duty, his uniform cleaned and pressed by his mother, the shirt still a little too big in the collar, the trouser legs turned up but only recognizably by those who knew abut such matters.

'Sir!' said Merrick, looking, Blunden thought, like a puppy waiting for some kind soul to throw it a bone.

'Now then, young Merrick, I have a job for you this morning.'

'Sir!'

'We need to ensure that Oliver Bell's alibi for the night of the first murder is watertight. You know that cottage where he lived near Old Bolingbroke Castle?'

'Sir!'

Inspector Blunden wished the young man would stop saying Sir like that but discipline should not be slighted.

'According to Bell, he went to help a retired clergyman living in a nearby cottage. The man was old and thought his cottage was being damaged in the storm.'

'Sir!'

'Find this clergyman and take a statement confirming the story. Or take a different story if Bell's version is not true.'

'Sir!'

'Please stop saying sir like that, Merrick; you're beginning to sound like one of those machines at the funfairs which speak when you put your money in.'

'Sir! Sorry, sir. What happens if he's not there, the clergyman, I mean, sir?'

'Well, you go looking for him, don't you? The local church, maybe he's gone to say his prayers. The local shop, maybe he's gone to buy some groceries. You know the form, Merrick. You've been in the force nearly three months now.'

'Yes, Inspector Blunden.'

The young man turned to go. The Inspector placed a tick beside the letter C in his notebook. He was a kindly man, the Inspector, in spite of an occasionally gruff exterior, and he believed very strongly that he had a duty to bring on the young constables in his charge.

'And here's something for you to think about on your way, young man. You remember I told you the crucial bit of Bell's evidence about the middle Lawrence, Carlton Lawrence, not the old chap, at the railway station? How do we find out that he wasn't in London or at the theatre in London like his father said? And what was he doing back here?'

Andrew Merrick succeeded with great difficulty in not saying Sir. He managed 'Yes, Inspector Blunden,' and fled to the comfort of his official bicycle.

A cheerful 'Good morning, Constable Merrick' announced to the policeman that Powerscourt was on his way. A moment later he showed himself in and announced his purpose straight away.

'My dear Inspector Blunden,' he began, 'you find me in good spirits. Banish dull care, let a man's fancy roam free, that's what I say. The Ghost awaits without, ready to ferry us to the Candlesby Arms where a vital witness awaits us, Jack Hayward, freshly returned from the land of my fathers.'

'My lord, this is tremendous news. When did he get here, Jack Hayward, I mean?'

'Late last night,' said Powerscourt. 'I was going to call you but I thought Mrs Blunden and Miss Blunden might not care for a visitation at such an hour. Forgive me, I took it upon myself to put him up in the hotel, Inspector. His own quarters in the village are still locked up and somehow I did not want him to be seen there just yet.'

'The knowledge of his return might alarm the murderer, you mean,' said the Inspector, collecting a couple of pens and his smaller notebook.

'Indeed,' said Powerscourt, fastening on his driving gloves before the short journey to the hotel. 'I don't think you've had the pleasure of a ride in my splendid motor car,' he went on, opening the door for the Inspector. 'Please be my guest.'

Jack Hayward had been placed in one of the outlying wings of the hotel, away from the main concourse where anybody from the locality might have noticed him. Johnny Fitzgerald, in the unusual role of warder, acted as custodian of Hayward's health from the next-door room.

Inspector Blunden took charge of the situation. Jack Hayward's room was large with a window looking out over the garden. There was a little table with four chairs where the three of them sat. Hayward was wearing dark blue trousers, a crisp white shirt and a smart jacket, looking, Powerscourt thought, as if he were going to bid for a couple of horses at the Newmarket sales.

'Now then, Mr Hayward, I think it's better if we talk to you here, if you don't mind. It's a bit more public down at the police station, or in the more open parts of this hotel. I haven't told Walter Savage you're here yet, but I hope you'll be able to see him this afternoon if things go well. So, if you're comfortable, let us begin.'

If there was one thing Lady Lucy Powerscourt thought they needed in Candlesby village, it was soap in various forms. Soap to clean their front doors, soap to clean their kitchens properly, soap to clean the bedrooms and the bathrooms. Not that she would, for a moment, have accused the women of the village of being slatternly. She knew only too well now how hard they worked, how little spare time there was, if any, how the welfare of their husbands and the children and their own parents was always uppermost in their minds. But a little more cleanliness, she felt, would have been like another moat, another defensive rampart against the slow siege of the disease.

Some of the children were slightly better this morning. Some were worse. One little boy called Will was thought to be at death's door. Lady Lucy sat by his bedside and watched as he tossed and turned, his forehead burning, a deep frown on his emaciated face. She mopped his brow and held his hand. It was very hot to the touch. His mother flitted in and said she had to see her own mother across the street. 'A generation above me, and a generation below me,' she wailed, 'both about to go on the same day!'

She added that Will had always been fascinated by the Hall and was very fond of cats before she left for another sickbed.

Lady Lucy looked around the room. There were four other beds in it but none of those children were present. Will had been left alone with the strange lady the children called Liddy Lucy as if Liddy were another Christian name. There were no books in the room, so there could be no favourite stories about cats. She thought for a moment and began a long and complicated tale about a cat who visited Candlesby Hall. The sick boy was only awake part of the time but he would still remember bits of it when he told stories to children of his own.

Eventually one of the waitresses from the Candlesby Arms appeared with fresh vegetable soup for everybody. The little boy managed a few mouthfuls before he fell asleep, whispering to Lady Lucy before he went, 'Can we have some more story later?'

That afternoon, while Will dozed, she was back with the old ladies. The three she spent time with, in adjacent houses, were all very ill, rambling and muttering as they tossed on their beds. There was no demand for tea. Lady Lucy held their hands and stroked their foreheads and did what she could to make them comfortable. But it was on this occasion that she began to note down, on a clean page in her diary, the words that came up over and over again. 'That girl', 'all that money', 'deserved it, all of it', 'never seen so much money', 'storm'. Lady Lucy had no idea what the words meant but she thought it might be important. When she had collected more evidence, she said to herself, she would talk to her husband about it.

PART FOUR

THE TUNNELS OF CANDLESBY HALL

The impression left on me by my extensive wanderings is that English agriculture seems to be fighting against the mills of God . . . The possession of land is becoming, or has already become, a luxury for rich men, for whom it is a costly joy or a means of indulging a taste for sport. I am sure that one of the worst fates that could befall England is that her land should become either a plaything or a waste.

H. Rider Haggard 1902

18

'Now then, Mr Hayward, perhaps you could tell us in your own words everything that happened on the day of the old Earl's murder.' The Inspector spoke kindly, as if he were talking to a rugby player who had committed a foul by accident.

Jack Hayward looked at the Inspector and at Powerscourt. 'Of course,' he began. 'I have to warn you gentlemen that I have been over and over all this so many times in my mind that I sometimes wonder if I am making parts of it up. Anyway, it started with a knock at my door, a loud knock, very early in the morning.'

'Would you know what time it was? Just for the record, you understand.' Inspector Blunden had brought a brand-new pencil with him to take notes.

'I don't know, I don't have a watch and we don't have a clock that works in the house. I would guess that it must have been between five and half past five in the morning. There was a cheap-looking envelope lying by my front door. I say cheap because I've seen the expensive ones Walter Savage uses when he sends important letters out from the Hall.

'It was addressed to me and there was a message inside scribbled on the back of a page torn from a child's notebook. Here it is, gentlemen.'

Jack Hayward reached onto a pocket and produced his

letter. He looked at his two interrogators, who were mesmerized, hearing the best account of the first murder they had heard so far.

'"Go to the bottom of the main drive," he read out, "and turn left for four hundred yards or so. Take a horse with you. You will find something you know."'

'May I keep that piece of paper for now?' said the Inspector.

'Of course, it's no use to me any more.'

'Please go on,' said Powerscourt. 'Your account is very clear.'

'You will remember that this was the night of the terrible storm,' Jack Hayward carried on. 'It was beginning to die down now, but the wind was still very strong. I did wonder at one point if I should wait until the weather had improved but I thought not. If it was important for somebody to ride over to my house at five in the morning, then surely I could bestir myself. I went to the stables and took the master's horse, Marlborough he's called. I'm sure you will ask me why. I have to tell you I have no idea why I did that. Marlborough was a horse I knew very well. He knew me. He was a very sensible animal, quick and strong. If there was going to be trouble, there could be no better companion. I did wonder if was a horse or a deer or a cow or some other animal that might be in difficulties.'

'Forgive me for interrupting,' said Powerscourt, 'but were you expecting trouble? When you reached your appointed destination, I mean?'

'I have asked myself that question so many times, Lord Powerscourt. I think some part of my brain must have thought there might be trouble ahead. That's all I can say.'

'So,' said Powerscourt, 'you set off. Did you see anything on the way?'

'I did not, my lord; it was hard to see anything at all. It

was tricky work, keeping control of the horse in that wind. Anyway, I reached the bottom of the drive and turned left. After a quarter of a mile or so I saw what I had been sent to find.'

Jack Hayward paused. Neither the Inspector nor Powerscourt spoke. There was a distant smell of roasting chicken seeping out of the hotel kitchens.

'Lord Candlesby was lying on the ground. His body had been wrapped in a couple of blankets. It was hard to see the face but I had a torch with me and I took a quick look at it. Have either of you gentlemen seen that face? The late Earl's face?'

'We both have,' said Inspector Blunden. 'We had the body brought out from the family mausoleum. One of England's most distinguished pathologists is not sure to this day precisely how he was killed.'

'That was very smart of you,' said Hayward. 'Well, what more is there to say? I looked around, I listened very carefully for a couple of minutes but there was nothing or nobody I could see or hear at this point. It was growing lighter by the minute. Any sensible murderer would have been back home tucked up in bed by now.'

'You were sure even then it was murder?' asked Powerscourt.

'Well,' said Jack Hayward, 'there couldn't be any other explanation, could there? Not with wounds like that and one side of his face smashed in like a child's doll.'

'So you took him home,' said the Inspector.

'Well, this was the most difficult part of it for me. I had the devil of a job to lift the body up on to the back of the horse for a start. The Earl's horse didn't like it, you see. They don't like the smell of human blood, horses. Maybe Marlborough knew it was his master's blood but I think that is fanciful. Twice I got the body up on the horse's back only for Marlborough to buck and rear and throw his master to the ground. At one point I thought I might be there for hours.'

'What did you do?' The Inspector had filled many pages by now.

'I took a break. I changed the arrangement of the blankets so that one covered his face. I thought the smell might not be so bad that way, if you were a horse, if you see what I mean. I rubbed some earth over the whole of the body, or rather the blankets that covered it. I took the horse for a walk and talked him through what I wanted him to do. I told him three times. Then I tried to put the body over his back again and this time it worked. I walked Marlborough round and round in a circle for about twenty minutes with the Earl across his back, talking to him all the time, and he was fine. Then we set off for Candlesby Hall. I was up close by Marlborough's head all the way, whispering to him. I was terrified, you see, that the horse might bolt right away across the county and then where would we be?'

Jack Hayward paused again.

'I don't know how long it took me to walk the horse and the old Earl up to the house from the bottom of the drive. Half an hour? Forty-five minutes? I just know it was very slow work.' He was nearing the end of his tale now, Inspector Blunden and Powerscourt as attentive at the end as they had been at the start.

'I'd forgotten about the hunt that morning. That was why the master was wearing his scarlet coat, of course. Once I saw them all I grew really alarmed. The horses, not as well trained as my Marlborough, might smell something they didn't like and head off across the countryside. The ladies might scream if they caught sight of the dead man's face. So when the Hall was just in sight but still some distance away, I stopped again and tried to rearrange those blankets once more to make sure nothing could be seen. I didn't know who would take charge of the proceedings. I knew they would all be expecting a live Lord Candlesby to appear at any moment and take charge.'

Jack Hayward stopped and stared at the carpet as if checking his memories.

'No doubt you will know that we headed for the stables as soon as we could. I managed to have a word with Richard, the new Earl and he agreed to the diversion. It was just as well because Marlborough was growing very tense indeed. It was as if he knew something was wrong. Once we reached the stables I got the body off the horse as quick as I could and on to a table. I found another blanket to put over it. I told a stable boy to take Marlborough away and feed him. I expected the younger Candlesbys to ask where I had found their father but that took some time. All they wanted to do was to cover up the fact that he had been murdered. For some reason, that had to be concealed at all costs. They didn't care about how he was killed or who might have killed him. They didn't even seem very sorry. They all talked at once, each one swearing at the others until Richard established some sort of order.'

'Would you describe them as rational or maybe hysterical?' asked Powerscourt. 'Sorry to sound like a doctor, but I'm sure you know what I mean.'

'I know exactly what you mean, my lord,' Jack Hayward replied. 'I think Richard was tending towards the rational, and the other two, Henry and Edward, were very close to being hysterical.'

'Could I ask just one question at this point?' The Inspector was chewing hard on the end of his pencil. 'Were they surprised by their father's death? You'd have expected them to be in shock, not shouting at each other, surely.'

'Maybe shock can take a number of forms, I don't know. You're really asking me if any of them knew this was coming, aren't you? I have thought about that for a long long time but I can't give you an answer. I just don't know.'

'So the body is on a table. Richard is taking control. Have they decided to send for Dr Miller yet?' Powerscourt said, looking past Jack Hayward to the wood behind the garden.

'Yes, they had. And that was when they got rid of me. I think they had forgotten I was there but they were already discussing how to persuade the doctor to say it was death by natural causes when I was told to go and fetch the doctor and notify the undertakers. But Richard made a point of saying he wished to see me at the stables in an hour's time.'

This was new information. The Inspector whistled softly to himself. Powerscourt ran his hands through his hair.

Jack Hayward was sounding tired by now. He was speaking more slowly than he had at the beginning. 'That meeting was very short. He said he wanted me to go away at once, that very afternoon if possible. He gave me five hundred pounds, that's over two years' wages for me. He said he didn't want to know where I had gone. After three months, he said, I was to send him an address and he would tell me if I could come back or not.'

'Did he say anything about your wife and your children?' asked the Inspector.

'They were to come too. You know the rest. I'm sorry, my mind is spinning after going over all this stuff again. Do you think we could stop now or take a break? I'd really like a cup of tea.'

'Of course,' said the Inspector. 'Why don't you take some time off and come back in an hour? Sorry we kept you at it for so long.'

'I'd like you to think about what I should do for the best, gentlemen. Should I go back to Ireland for the time being? Or should I go back to my house in Candlesby village?'

Powerscourt and Inspector Blunden were checking their notes when there was a knock on the door.

'Come in,' said the Inspector.

A very out-of-breath Constable Merrick greeted them. 'Sorry to interrupt, sir, my lord,' he panted, 'but they told me at the station that you'd be here.'

'So?' The Inspector was sounding rather cross.

'Sir,' the young man was almost completely out of breath now, 'it's important. I wouldn't have come and interrupted you if it wasn't important, sir, my lord.'

'What is it then?' asked the Inspector, recalling that Merrick might be very young but that he was far from stupid.

'Two things, sir.' The young man took two deep breaths suddenly like they had told him to do in his training when imparting information to superior officers under difficult circumstances. 'You asked me to check out Oliver Bell's alibi – the retired clergyman in a nearby cottage who was worried about the storm. There is no clergyman, sir, my lord. There is no cottage either. I checked everywhere, in the village, at the school, with the farm worker who does live in a nearby cottage. And I found the present vicar who happened to be in the village. He'd never heard of any retired vicar or whatever he was in his parish.'

'Good God!' said the Inspector. 'So Oliver Bell has no alibi at all for the entire evening of the storm and the murder! I wonder why he bothered to tell me such a pack of lies. Maybe he thought we wouldn't check his story.'

'And what was the second thing, Andrew?' Powerscourt thought he already knew the answer.

'This is the other thing, my lord, sir. Oliver Bell, sir. He's disappeared. The cottage is locked up. Nobody knows where he's gone.'

'Forgive me, my lord.' Blunden was collecting his pencil and his notebook. 'I've got to get back to the station to organize a lookout for Bell. Use your judgement about Jack Hayward, my lord – I want to keep him here but I don't think he should go back to the village just yet. Bell may have got clean away by now. Just when you think you are making progress, some other damned thing comes along and knocks you down. Come along, young Merrick, you have done well.'

Powerscourt took Jack Hayward for a walk in the woods. He thought the senior groom might feel happier out of doors.

'Forgive me if I ask you a rather personal question, Mr Hayward,' Powerscourt began. 'You don't have to answer it if you don't want to. Who do you think killed the old Lord Candlesby?'

'I'm happy to answer that question, my lord. My first thought was that it was the eldest son, Richard. But now he's gone too. So that can't be right. I have to say I don't know any more. And you, my lord, do you know?'

Powerscourt shook his head. 'I wish I did,' he said, 'then I could get back to London and see my children.'

'Have you decided what you and the Inspector would like me to do, my lord?'

'Yes, we have. It's not that simple, I'm afraid. The Inspector doesn't want you to leave Candlesby. He doesn't want you to go back to Ireland or go anywhere else just yet either. Quite soon he's going to want to take a statement from you, a more formal version of what we talked about just now. So I think you should stay on here in the hotel for the moment. You won't have to pay. We would ask you to be quiet in case the murderer hears you are back and decides to kill you or kill somebody else to protect his identity. You're going to be a key witness if this thing ever comes to trial, you see. Are you happy with that, Mr Hayward?'

'Please call me Jack, everybody else does. Yes, I'm happy with that.'

'Is there anything else you've forgotten to tell us? Any advice?'

Jack Hayward paused and kicked a large branch off the

path into the undergrowth. 'There's just one thing, my lord. It only came to me this morning. I was thinking about the actual murder and those terrible wounds to one side of the face. Everybody thinks in these cases of there being only one murderer. But suppose there were two, or more likely, three or four. Two men hold him and the other two take turns to bash the side of his face with a spade or something like that. Then they change over and repeat the performance.' He paused again. 'It's only a thought, Lord Powerscourt; it could be total rubbish.'

'It's clever,' said Powerscourt. 'I have thought of it before now. Mind you, the pathologist said the wounds might not have been caused by a spade, but he wasn't sure. Maybe the reason I haven't done anything about it so far is the thought that finding four or five murderers would be four or five times as difficult as finding one.'

'One last thing, Lord Powerscourt. I came back here because of Walter Savage. Is he still locked up in the jail? Can I go and see him? And what was he locked up for anyway? He's perfectly harmless.'

'It was the Inspector who locked up Walter Savage,' said Powerscourt disloyally. 'He thought he was withholding evidence about the night of the murder. Inspector Blunden felt a day or two in the cells might help his memory. But I think it's all been cleared up now. Walter should be out of jail later today.'

'Really?' said Jack Hayward, staring hard at Powerscourt. 'How very interesting. How convenient for Walter to come out today.'

Powerscourt said nothing.

Political London, Tory London, Conservative London, Anti-Lloyd George London was in ferment. The peers in the House of Lords had defied the will of the Liberal majority in the House of Commons, elected by millions of British citizens, and thrown out the Liberal Budget by a huge margin. Everybody knew there was a natural Conservative superiority in numbers in the Lords, but this majority was huge, over two hundred and fifty. It was a landslide. It was a triumph for the anti-Lloyd George faction in the Upper House, who had brought down to the vote peers who had never been there before, peers who hadn't attended since the time of the Boer War, peers who spent their time in peaceful enjoyment of what remained of their estates, peers who hated London and who hated politics but had been persuaded for a final turn-out to save their inheritance and enable their class to save the nation from itself.

The celebrations were being held in Wigmore House, situated between Grosvenor Square and Park Lane, the home of one of the leading rebels, Lord Wigmore, known to his friends as Wiggers, or, more simply, Wigs. It was a couple of days after the vote and a lot of thought had gone into the festivities.

Sandy Temple and his Selina had been given an invitation by Lord Winterton of Winterton Staithe, the man Sandy had talked politics with at the weekend house party in Norfolk. The two had met by chance in the lobby of the House of Lords and Winterton had whipped an invitation out of his pocket.

'You'd better come to this,' he told Sandy. 'Celebratory party. May be closer to an orgy. Wiggers is always keen to lower the tone. Probably ought to be a wake.'

Now they were standing outside the front door at a quarter past eleven at night, Sandy in full evening dress, Selina in her most fashionable evening gown. Both felt rather nervous. A wall of sound, cheers, shouting, bands playing, champagne corks popping, poured out of the great house. They were greeted by a huge butler who must have been well over six foot six. Floating round, champagne bottles in hand, were more very tall servants, footmen in livery of black and green, all over six feet. The entrance hall was high with a black and white marble floor, the walls adorned with Wigmores past, sitting proudly on enormous horses outside enormous houses. Sandy was to learn later that when Lord Wigmore left the army he took the largest sergeant majors, sergeants and privates he could find with him to man the barricades in different uniform in the various Wigmore properties across Britain. Taking a glass of champagne each, Selina and Sandy advanced into a huge central saloon, feeling and looking rather like the babes in the wood. A fountain in the centre of the vast room was sending bubbly liquid high into the air. Various young ladies who seemed to be drunk already were lying on the side of the fountain lapping up its contents.

'So clever of Wiggers to get his champagne fountain working,' one young fop observed to his friend. 'They say it hasn't worked since the party the family threw at the time of the Great Exhibition.'

'Means you don't have to worry about refills,' said his friend, plunging his glass in the fountain and refilling it with champagne. 'Such a bore having to look for those waiters with a bottle, don't you think?'

'The stuff in the bottles is meant to be better, Pol Roger or something like that. Can't remember the name of this fountain stuff but a cousin told me it's what they serve in the Lyons Corner House.'

The two young men drifted off, arm in arm. Sandy, who was as interested in the architecture as he was in the guests, observed that there was a series of huge rooms opening off this central atrium, dining room, drawing room, study, Old Masters room. They were hailed by Lord Winterton.

'Good to see you both,' he said. 'I don't think I've been to a party like this one in my life. It's victory but I think underneath most people know it's a hollow victory, maybe even a Pyrrhic victory when you think you've won but you've actually lost. It won't last. At some point the Commons will come looking for revenge. But for now, eat, drink and be merry, for tomorrow we die.'

An enormous cheer went up from what might have been the drawing room. 'Some damn fool lord in there', said Winterton, 'stands on a table every now and then and calls on the company to drink Lloyd George's health. Never fails to get them going. Chap just moves round from room to room.'

On the top floor a detachment of Parisian whores were plying their trade energetically in the servants' bedrooms. They had been imported specially from Paris for the occasion and reckoned they would make more money in this one night than they had in the previous two years. The queue stretched down the stairs. Cheers would ring out every time a young man, usually fastening the buttons on his military uniform, made his way down the stairs and cleared a path for the next candidate.

Lord Winterton led Sandy and Selina down to the bottom end of the great saloon. A huge marquee turned into a ballroom had been erected running from the end of the house down into the garden with artificial grass replacing the wet lawns en route to the high wall at the end. Winterton pointed out the shooting range way over to the left. 'Wigmore's changed the look of the targets for this evening. No more of those boring circles in different colours tonight. Now you can shoot at the face of Lloyd George on the left and Asquith on the right. Our host has had to replace them twice already they tell me, the targets shot to pieces.'

They had reached the lake now. Two imitation Venetian gondolas with closed compartments amidships were drifting slowly across the water towards the island in the centre. The noises coming out of one of them showed that they were fulfilling the same function they did on the waters of the basin of St Mark.

Behind the island was an enormous bonfire. 'Two o'clock,' said Winterton, 'Wiggers is going to make a speech. I wonder if we should try the dancing in the meantime.' London's finest band was working its way through the waltzes of Strauss. Wigmore had apparently given orders that he wanted only waltzes on this night. The musicians were playing them faster and faster. A couple of handsome aristocrats took Selina off to the dance floor. Sandy thought the dancers were more abandoned than he had ever seen at a great party like this. Deep down, really deep down, perhaps they know, he thought. Tonight we dance. This morning we dance. At dawn we dance. Tomorrow our downfall begins.

Shortly before two a strange cart began to make its way towards the bonfire. There seemed to be some objects in the bottom but it was hard to make out what they were. The cart, Lord Winterton observed to nobody in particular, looked exactly like a tumbril, the conveyance used to transport the French aristocrats to the guillotine in the days of the Revolution and the Terror.

The band played on. The people inside the gondolas showed no sign of coming out. The traffic up in the servants' quarters showed no sign of abating. But everybody else began to assemble round the bonfire, some holding bottles of champagne. To the left and right of the revellers the other great houses of Grosvenor Square and Park Lane stood dark and silent in the night. To the front, Hyde Park stretched out across a sleeping London towards Kensington and Notting Hill. The tumbril, pulled by two tall footmen, came to a stop at the side of the bonfire. In front of it two more footmen carried a large table and a set of steps. The crowd back at the dance floor began to open out like the waters of the Red Sea. A dark-haired aristocrat, dressed in the robes of a hereditary peer of the House of Lords, was making his way towards the bonfire.

'Go for it, Wiggers!'

'You tell them, Wigs!'

'Hurrah for Wigmore!'

Lord Richard Peregrine Octavius Wigmore, one of the principal architects of the defeat of the Budget, was moving down his grounds to address his people. Sandy was right in front of the bonfire, standing close to Winterton. Selina was still being whirled round the dance floor by a handsome hussar with a scar on his left cheek, oblivious to bonfires and high politics. One of the footmen held the stairs steady while Wigmore climbed on to his table. You could never tell what a lot of champagne might do to a man, even if he was a lord. Wigmore tottered uncertainly towards the very front of the table. The two footmen appeared by his side as if by magic. Good servants will support their masters at all times and in all places. He banged his foot on the table. Gradually the crowd fell silent.

Wigmore raised his hands to the crowd. 'Ladies and gentlemen,' he began, 'before I say a few words, I think we should give thanks to those who made this evening possible. I hope you will agree with me that our manner of giving thanks fits perfectly with their contributions to this occasion. Let us give thanks for the Welsh wizard's greatest friend in politics, President of the Board of Trade, Winston Churchill!'

Two of the enormous footmen pulled a guy, like those seen on Bonfire Night, out of the tumbril. The face of Churchill, at once babyish and devious, glowered from the top. The footmen held it aloft for a second or two to be inspected by the crowd. Then they hurled it into the bonfire where it flared up immediately. Sandy thought it must have been treated with petrol.

'Our esteemed Prime Minister, Herbert Henry Asquith!' In went the incumbent of Number Ten Downing Street, the flames catching hold of the hairs on his head. Once again there were huge cheers from the crowd.

'Finally, the man we have to thank for this evening and

this celebration, our revered Chancellor, David Lloyd George!'

The loudest shouts so far shot up into the night sky of London where the stars were clear and bright. 'Lloyd George! Burn him, burn him!' the crowd shouted, waving their fists in the air. This went on for some time. Indeed Sandy thought it could have gone on for ever if Wigmore hadn't called it off.

'My friends,' he went on, 'I have been reading my history books to find a precedent for what has just happened in our great capital. It took me a long time. Marlborough's triumphs, Wellington's many victories over the French, even Nelson at Trafalgar did not seem appropriate to what the Lords did two days ago. I think we have to go back further than that and I think we have to take our greatest playwright with us.' He paused. Sandy Temple, who had heard him often in the House of Lords, thought he was more eloquent in his own back garden than he had ever been speaking from the red benches.

He spoke very quietly when he resumed.

'"This day is called the Feast of Crispian."' Silence had fallen over the great crowd. Even the revellers in the gondolas held their peace. 'At Agincourt a small, dispirited English force defeated a larger, better equipped army of Frenchmen. The underdog triumphed as it did today. The people who bore the brunt of the fighting would never forget it.

> 'And Crispin Crispian shall ne'er go by,
> From this day to the ending of the world,
> But we in it shall be remember'd;
> We few, we happy few, we band of brothers;
> For he today that sheds his blood with me
> Shall be my brother; be he ne'er so vile,
> This day shall gentle his condition.'

All across the grass, from one end of the garden to the

other, the revellers linked arms and swayed slowly in the night air. Wigmore was still speaking softly, resisting the temptations of the battlefield shout.

> 'And gentlemen in England now a-bed
> Shall think themselves accursed they were not here,
> And hold their manhoods cheap whiles any speaks
> That fought with us upon St Crispin's day.'

Lord Wigmore looked round his audience, still swaying like flowers in a spring breeze.

'The band will cease playing at six o'clock. But I propose that we round off our evening in a fitting manner. Love of country, love of England underpinned everything we did today. Let us therefore all sing the National Anthem.'

For some reason the huge crowd took it fairly fast, unlike the funereal pace it was normally sung at. Sandy Temple thought they made it sound like the 'Battle Hymn of the Republic'. As the crowd began to drift home he found that Selina was still dancing, her head resting on the shoulder of another young officer. Suddenly Sandy made an important discovery. This, he realized, was the world Selina wanted to live in, the world of London high society, of powerful men and powerful women, of salons and luncheon parties and extravagant dinners where politicians rubbed shoulders with great financiers and newspaper magnates and the new class of millionaires. She wanted to be a chatelaine in these high-flying gatherings. But for him? Sandy knew they were not for him, these evenings. At best he would be a sardonic observer. He would never belong. There could be no point in marrying Selina. They would only make each other unhappy. He took a last look at her waltzing in ecstasy round the floor and walked on through the atrium and out of the front door into the pale light of dawn filling the Mayfair morning. He would write to her this evening. Like

Theseus, he had abandoned his Ariadne on the island, dancing the dances of the transported with the god Dionysus himself. All Sandy had to do now was to remember to change the sails.

19

Inspector Blunden was back behind his desk. Powerscourt and Constable Merrick were seated on either side of the round table in the centre of the room.

'I've put out a general alert for Bell,' said the policeman, 'ports, railway stations, and such hotels as we can reach. I often wonder how anybody was apprehended before the invention of the telegraph.'

Constable Andrew Merrick, emboldened perhaps by his previous success with Oliver Bell and his non-existent alibi, was holding his hand up as if he was back at school.

'Well, Constable Merrick, what do you have to say for yourself now?' Blunden felt he couldn't be too harsh with the lad after his good work.

'Sir, my lord, you asked me to think about how we might find out more about the movements of the middle Mr Lawrence, sir, Carlton Lawrence, the one reportedly seen at the railway station, sir.'

'What of it?' said Blunden. 'I'm not sure how much credence we can attach to that evidence now. Maybe Bell was trying to throw mud in our eyes.'

'Well, sir, my lord, we could ask at the station. Ask if anybody else saw Mr Lawrence, I mean.'

'Very good, young man. We'll make a detective of you yet. But that wasn't what you were going to say before, was it?'

'No, sir, my lord. That was about Mr Lawrence. I was going to suggest the photographer's shop, sir, my lord.'

'The photographer's shop?'

'Yes, sir, my lord. You see, there was a big wedding last year.'

'Wedding? Photographer's shop? What is going on here?' Constable Merrick had turned a deep shade of red. Even the two deep breaths taken very slowly failed him on this occasion.

Powerscourt coughed what he hoped was a diplomatic cough. He had no idea how much his comment was about to infuriate the Inspector.

'If I could make a suggestion, Inspector. What I think our friend is trying to say is this. There was a big wedding in the Lawrence family last year. Maybe it was a member of our Mr Lawrence's family, his son or daughter perhaps, more likely a grandchild. There will probably be photographs of the occasion taken by the local man. With luck we will be able to find a photo of Mr Lawrence from the photographers or the newspapers to aid in his identification in London and elsewhere. Would that be right, Constable?'

'Yes, sir, my lord.' Merrick was nodding like a puppet. 'It was a daughter, sir. Mr Lawrence's granddaughter.'

How typical of Powerscourt, the Inspector said to himself. Put two and two together and make five. How very irritating. He consoled himself with the thought that Powerscourt wouldn't be any use in the second row of a rugby scrum.

'Well then,' the Inspector said, 'you'd better get off to the photographer's and the railway station. Let's hope you have good luck.'

'Sir, my lord.' Constable Merrick had his hand up again. Powerscourt felt, looking at him with affection, that the young man had spent far more time at school than he had in the police service. Putting his hand up must still seem the natural thing to do.

'It's about going to London, sir. I've never been to London, sir.'

279

'If you think, Constable Merrick, that I am sending you to London you are out of your mind.' Blunden's brain filled with possible disasters: Constable Merrick lost in the capital, unable to find his way home, Constable Merrick taken and sold into slavery, Constable Merrick seized and put to work in some terrible factory, Constable Merrick incarcerated for ever in the Marshalsea.

'I wasn't thinking of that, sir, my lord, I was only wondering if I could go with whoever does make the journey, my lord, sir. To be of assistance, sir.'

'You get off to the photographer's and the railway station now, there's a good boy.'

Merrick trotted off. Powerscourt, unaware how annoyed his last intervention had made the Inspector, tried again.

'I have a suggestion to make about London, Inspector. My companion in arms Johnny Fitzgerald is here now. He went to Ireland to bring Jack Hayward back, you will recall. He's not doing anything in particular at the moment. He would be the perfect person to go to London and make inquiries. Maybe he could take Constable Merrick with him. I'm sure they'd make a formidable pair.'

The Inspector laughed. 'Excellent plan, Lord Powerscourt. Let's do it.' He couldn't get the rugby question out of his mind. 'Tell me, Lord Powerscourt, did you ever play rugby in your younger days?'

Powerscourt remembered that the Inspector had been a mighty power in the world of the scrum and the line-out and the rolling maul.

'I did, as a matter of fact.'

'And where did you play?'

'Why,' said Powerscourt, 'I played in the centre.'

Bloody typical, the Inspector said to himself. I should have guessed. Centre, a bloody centre, one of those irritating people who could see a gap in the opponents' defence and be through it before anyone knew they had gone. Centres could pass through the eye of the proverbial needle. Clever players, centres. Tries under the posts. Glory boys. The darlings of the women.

Lady Lucy was walking back to the hotel that evening after another day of nursing. Will, the little boy she had entertained with the cat story, was on the mend. He would try to sit up in bed now and give her a hug when she came in to see him. One of the rambling old ladies had gone to meet her maker. The other two remained, still talking nonsense in their delirium, but letting slip every now and then just one word which Lady Lucy thought might be significant for her husband's inquiry. She had added another that very evening, another small brick, perhaps, for her husband to build a wall of evidence that might solve the mystery. 'Sail'. What 'sail' meant Lady Lucy had no idea but she added it to her list. She would have to tell Francis about it soon.

'Good evening to you, Lady P-p-powerscourt. I trust I see you well?'

Charles Dymoke was wearing a long cloak that reached down to his feet and a dark grey Russian hat. He looked like a Cossack on patrol out in the steppes.

'Charles!' said Lady Lucy. 'How very nice to see you. What takes you to the village late at night?'

'I have heard about your nursing activities, Lady P-p-powerscourt. They are going to make you a saint soon. I was delivering a b-b-basket of vegetables, and arranging for some wood to be brought over tomorrow.'

'Noblesse still obliges then, Charles? That's very good of you.'

'The vicar, who does not go to Candlesby village in case he gets ill and leaves the village without a p-p-priest, says I am the first one of my family in five hundred years to care for the p-p-poor. He tells me my p-p-predecessor was called Charles the Fair. He was hanged at B-b-boston Assizes

281

eventually, though not for helping the p-p-poor. But tell me, how is it with your husband?'

Charles did not like to mention Lady Lucy's husband's sojourn in the Caravaggio room. He suspected she had not been told about it.

'Francis?' said Lady Lucy with a smile. 'He is well. He is anxious to find the answers in the case, of course.'

'Can you tell him I have some news for him? I went to see Walter Savage the steward when he came out of prison today. Something very odd about that arrest. I must p-p-pass on what he said to Lord P-p-powerscourt.'

'Why don't you come for breakfast tomorrow and tell him then?'

'Do they have p-p-porridge? My old nanny always s-s-said I had to have p-p-porridge.'

'They do, Charles. And ham and eggs and kidneys and tomatoes and things.'

'I hate kidneys,' said the young man from Candlesby Hall, 'but I'll come for the p-p-porridge.'

Andrew Merrick received confirmation from three different sources that Carlton Lawrence had indeed been seen at the railway station at the time specified by Oliver Bell. Now he was off on his travels.

Johnny Fitzgerald tried to tell the young man all he knew about London on the train down to the capital. He told him that the great majority of the people who lived in the city were very poor, that the better off and the rich were scattered across the city in clusters, in Mayfair and Belgravia and Chelsea in the West End, in Hampstead and Highgate in the north, in Blackheath and Dulwich in the south-east, in Richmond and Wimbledon in the south-west. The prospect of visiting the Tower of London or Buckingham Palace or the Houses of Parliament left Constable Merrick cold. There was only one place he felt he had to see this time, he told Johnny. And where was that? Scotland Yard, Andrew replied, if there was time. If the police force was to be his profession then he had to see the headquarters. Surely, he pointed out, a devout Catholic would go to St Peter's if he was in Rome.

'Just put on your best policeman's brain, Andrew, and tell me what you think of this. Ever since Francis' – Andrew Merrick had worked out long ago that Francis was Powerscourt, though he was amazed the man had a Christian name at all, since he, Andrew had always thought of him as Lord Powerscourt as if Lord was his first name – 'told me what the old man Harold Lawrence said about the trip to London, I've always thought there was something odd about it. So does Francis. Most of the family, certainly all the ones from Lincolnshire, were on this expedition. Old boy Lawrence told Francis about it very deliberately, as if it was something he'd been told to say. And then he mentioned both the hotel, White's, where they stayed, and the theatre, the Savoy, where they saw the play. Harold did not mention that his son Carlton peeled off somewhere in the middle and went back to Candlesby. But why? And why did the old boy not mention it to Francis?'

'Maybe the old boy forgot about Carlton, sir. Maybe he didn't even know he'd gone.'

'It's possible. But think about it. If he had mentioned a hotel but with no name and a theatre with no name we could never have checked anything at all. London has too many hotels and too many theatres.'

'Maybe they had worked out that we would come and ask for the names of the hotel and the theatre. Maybe that was the whole point of the trip to London, to give themselves an alibi.'

'I don't like it,' said Johnny Fitzgerald darkly. 'I don't like it one little bit.'

Twenty minutes later they were inside White's Hotel,

one of the newest and grandest in the capital. A short walk across an enormous entrance hall and halfway down a long corridor lined with hunting prints led them to a door labelled General Manager, James Thomas. The bearer of the title was remarkably young, scarcely over thirty, Johnny thought. He heard their request for information very seriously and without interruption, making a few notes with a gold pen in a small black notebook.

'A murder case,' he said quietly, 'and the key events all some time ago. I do hope none of our guests were involved. Now then, I am going to send for the people most likely to have had dealings with these Lawrences.' He rang a small bell and a very young man with ginger hair appeared, dressed in the regulation white shirt and dark red uniform. Johnny thought he might be even younger than Constable Merrick, if such a thing were possible.

'Tom,' said the hotel manager, 'can you bring the following people here to my office: the reservations manager with his ledgers for the last couple of months, the head waiter who was on duty on the evening of Wednesday the sixth and Thursday the seventh of October together with the waiter who served the Lawrences those two evenings, the same for the waiter at breakfast the following morning, the chambermaid who made up their rooms and the head porter who was on duty the evenings they were here. He may remember ordering a cab.'

Tom duly departed. 'Can he remember all that, your young man Tom?' asked Johnny incredulously. 'Without taking a note?'

'He can remember a lot more than that,' the hotel manager smiled. 'He has what they call a photographic memory and great ability in mathematics. He's more than helpful with the accounts. Tom came to us from Hoxton, where his father is a successful bookmaker. Maybe that has something to do with it. I have just engaged a tutor to see how great his potential is. If he is as promising as we think, I hope to persuade the directors to pay for him to be educated up to the point where he can go to university.'

Constable Merrick was having one of the best days of his life. He was to give his parents a limited account of the hotel personnel: the bent old man with a tiny white beard and a twinkle in his eye who divulged the facts about the Lawrence reservations; the waiters, one French with a moustache, one Italian with a beard, at dinner and at breakfast who reported them as a perfectly normal family; the chambermaid who had made up their beds and reported that all the beds the Lawrences were meant to be in had been slept in on both nights; the head porter who had indeed booked them a cab. All had recognized the Lawrences from the wedding photograph. All, except the head porter, recognized the middle Mr Lawrence as being present on all occasions, though the head porter who had ordered the cab couldn't be sure as it was dark. The one curious thing was the booking. That had originally been made for the Wednesday night only. The rooms were booked some six days before. Then the second night was added the day the party arrived. Constable Merrick wrote it all down, wishing he had young Tom's powers of recall.

James Thomas brought them to a quiet corner of the reception area when the evidence had been presented and ordered them some coffee. 'You may wish to think about what the staff just told you. With most people this kind of detail can take a while to sink in. And you may well think of one or two other people you wish to talk to or a question you wish to ask. Just come back and knock on my door if you do.'

The porters performed their arabesques across the carpet, with trays and cake holders and glasses. The clientele wandered in and looked as if they owned the place. Dotted about the huge room, usually in corners, were enormous potted plants with flowers of green and red.

'Let's pretend, young Andrew, that the purpose of this trip was to provide an alibi for somebody, almost certainly

Carlton Lawrence, the middle one. Why did they add an extra day to their stay in the hotel? What made them change their mind? Something in London? Something in Lincolnshire? And what was Carlton Lawrence doing back in Boston station on the Thursday? How do we find out if our man could have got back to London in time to sleep in his hotel bed?'

'I've thought of that one, sir. Somebody else could have slept in their bed for half the night and Carlton could have slept there for the other half. But I've got the train times. I took them down in the station while we were waiting for the express earlier today.'

Constable Merrick consulted his notes and appeared to be carrying out some powerful calculations in his head. 'How about this, sir? There's a train from London to Boston that arrives at three ten. There's a train from Lincoln to Boston that comes in at three fifteen – Oliver Bell could have seen Carlton Lawrence at the station while one got on and the other got off. There's a train back to London, leaving Boston at four fifteen, arriving at eight thirty. That's pretty slow – it must have stopped everywhere. So he could have done it, gone up and down to London, I mean, our man Carlton Lawrence. But why would he want to go back to Boston or Candlesby for an hour or so? And another thing, sir. We don't have any definite proof that Carlton Lawrence came back to White's at all. Various witnesses, including Oliver Bell, report seeing him at the station. Nobody reports him leaving Boston on a London train.'

Johnny had a different thought. It was a question for hotel manager James Thomas. Had the Lawrences received any telegrams while they were staying at the Ritz? Yes, they had, came the answer: just one, at five fifteen on the first evening, despatched from Boston, Lincolnshire.

Their last request at White's Hotel was for a further word with the head porter about the Thursday evening. Johnny showed the Lawrence photographs once more. 'I know it's a long time ago,' he began, 'but do you remember Mr Carlton Lawrence, this gentleman here, coming into the hotel on his own during the evening?'

There was a pause while the head porter scanned through his memory. Johnny Fitzgerald and Constable Merrick waited patiently. An ordinary porter walked past them with a small briefcase in his hand.

'That's it!' said the head porter. 'He was carrying a briefcase, rather larger than the one that's just gone by. Your gentleman, Carlton Lawrence I think you said he was called, came into the hotel about a quarter to nine in the evening in question, the Thursday, I'm sure of it. He went out again about five minutes later without the briefcase. He must have dropped it off in his room.'

John Galsworthy's *Strife* was still playing at the Savoy Theatre. The staff, accustomed perhaps to watching detective plays on the stage, were quick to grasp the nature of their inquiries.

One usher reported that she had taken the Lawrences into the theatre and directed them to their box on the first floor. Another remembered bringing them the programmes and making sure they were comfortable.

She was able to recognize about half the party from the photographs. She said her memory for people wasn't as good as some of the girls who could recall faces they had shown to their seats the year before, but she thought there had been one empty seat in the box at the start of the play. She couldn't be sure, but she thought all the seats were full at the end. That was all. Carlton Lawrence, when pointed out in the photograph, could have been there or he could not. She couldn't be sure. That was all she had to say.

Forty minutes later Johnny and Constable Merrick were ensconced in the Powerscourt drawing room in Markham Square. Powerscourt had insisted they use his house as a base during their time in London.

287

'I have no idea what I think after today, young Andrew.' Johnny had found a bottle of Beaune hiding in a Powerscourt cupboard. 'Tell me when you reckon it's wide of the mark.'

Johnny took an unusually small sip, for him, and began. 'Let's assume the whole thing's an alibi. The only person it can be an alibi for is Carlton Lawrence, son of old man Lawrence whose estate was sold recently. Originally it must have been for the Wednesday, the first day of their stay in London. Then it has to be put back a day. Maybe Carlton would have gone back to Boston station on the Wednesday if the date hadn't been changed. Quite what it is or was an alibi for we don't know. Most likely it's the murder. But he couldn't have murdered Lord Candlesby because he was back in London by then on the Thursday. You can look at his appearance at Boston station on the Thursday in one of two ways. Either he was very unlucky to be seen, or, and this is the more devious option, he went in order to be seen. Maybe he was hanging about the place for quite a while in order that somebody would recognize him and tell the police later.'

'But if he wanted an alibi, sir, surely it would have been for something happening in Lincolnshire rather than in London. Otherwise why go to London at all? On the other hand why go back to Boston station if it's in that area that you want to establish an alibi? It doesn't make sense, sir.'

'Why do you think Carlton Lawrence went back to Boston?' Johnny Fitzgerald thought he could hear noises coming from the upper floors.

'Could it have been a woman, sir? Maybe Mr Lawrence had promised to bring a mistress some enormous great jewel like a diamond?'

'In that case why didn't he bring the woman with him? Or make a separate trip? We don't even know if he was married.'

'He must have been married, sir; it was his daughter's wedding in the photographs. Maybe we're looking at it the wrong way round, sir.' Constable Andrew Merrick was feeling extraordinarily grown up, conducting conversations involving mistresses and extravagant jewellery in one of Chelsea's most fashionable squares. 'He could have been bringing something from London to Candlesby, or he could have been bringing something from Candlesby to London, sir, some legal documents perhaps, that they had forgotten to bring with them. They might have had legal business in London about the sale of their estate.'

'What was in the briefcase, do you think, young Andrew?' Johnny Fitzgerald was swirling his wine round in his glass like an expert sommelier.

'Legal documents, as I said, sir? Money? Maybe he owed some people a lot of money over the forthcoming sale of the estate.'

'My head's beginning to hurt,' said Johnny, 'and it's not this wine.'

Screams could be heard dimly from above, followed by a lot of shouting.

'What's going on, sir?' asked Andrew. 'It sounds as if somebody is being tortured on the upper floors.'

'Quite right,' said Johnny. 'Two people are being tortured. They're five years old and they're being put in the bath. That's what all the fuss is about. I'm their godfather, God help them. I'd better go and say hello in a minute.'

Andrew Merrick thought of Powerscourt and Lady Lucy having children as another astonishing event, like Powerscourt having a Christian name. Surely, he had thought, such exalted beings didn't go round having children like everyone else, even if they were twins.

'How about this,' said Johnny, now about a third of the way down the bottle. 'Alibi literally means being somewhere else. Or that's what I think it means. When would you need an alibi for the first murder in this case? As far as we know, you would need it for sometime in the small hours of the morning or even later. On the first day our man is definitely in White's Hotel, miles away from the murder scene. On the second day, the day of the storm and the murder, he is probably back in White's, still miles away from the murder scene. Why did they go to such trouble to establish an alibi?'

Constable Merrick had only had one tiny sip of his wine. He thought it was delicious. I'm going to turn into an alcoholic, he said to himself, just like my granny said.

'I'm not convinced about the second day,' said Constable Merrick. 'Maybe Carlton has a twin, or a brother who looks like him. Maybe he was introduced into the party the second day. Remember, the person who served them all breakfast in the morning wasn't the same person who served their dinner the night before. The staff would assume that the breakfast one was the same as the dinner one when it could be a completely different person altogether. It seems possible to me that Carlton Lawrence was just unlucky. He arranged for the substitute to take his place. He shoots off to Lincolnshire. He kills old Candlesby. Then he hides up until the party come home.'

There was a hesitant sort of knock at the door.

'Ah, Mary Muriel – she looks after the children, Andrew – how nice to see you. Do come in. May I introduce Constable Andrew Merrick, from Lincolnshire? How are the little ones?'

Mary Muriel smiled. 'They're much the same,' she said, 'only older. I won't come in, sir. The fact is that they are asking for you to come and tell them a story now they're in bed. I don't know how they found out you were here, sir, but they certainly know it now.'

'They have their own sources of information, those twins,' said Johnny darkly, 'floorboards, banisters, walls.'

He found Christopher and Juliet in bed, well tucked up, but not losing the power of speech just yet.

'Johnny!' they shouted in unison.

'Story! Story! Toad! Toad! Poop-poop! Poop-poop!'

For what seemed like an eternity Johnny Fitzgerald had been reading the twins *The Wind in the Willows*. He was now, he thought, on the third reading and the twins showed no signs of tiring. He sometimes wondered what the record was for completed readings of the entire book and hoped that the winners received autographed first editions. The arrival of *The Wind in the Willows* had coincided with the arrival of the Powerscourt motor car and various extracts could be heard being shouted from the back seat by the twins when they were travelling in the rear. A respectable middle-aged lady, walking quietly along the King's Road in Chelsea, Johnny had been told, had looked most put out when pursued by yells of 'Washerwoman! A washerwoman!' coming from the back of a Rolls-Royce Silver Ghost. Johnny remembered there had been trouble the previous time he had read this particular passage. The twins had become overexcited. It was impossible to calm them down. Powerscourt had had to come upstairs and read them some spectacularly boring bits of the Authorized Version of the Bible with list after list of who begat whom and with no fighting at all.

The twins loved everything about *The Wind in the Willows*, but they especially liked the last battle between Toad and his friends, the Rat, the Mole and the Badger, and the forces of darkness, the stoats and the weasels and the ferrets who had taken over Toad's ancestral home, Toad Hall. Johnny, on his last reading, had left it at the point where the Toad party, led by Badger, has advanced into the Hall by means of a secret tunnel.

'Settle down, settle down,' said Johnny, suddenly realizing that he might possess a secret weapon in the calming-down department one floor below in the drawing room. He sat on the corner of Christopher's bed and eyed them gravely.

'Let us begin,' he said. Johnny always started like that:

> 'The Badger drew himself up, took a firm grip of
> his stick with both paws, glanced round at his
> comrades, and cried –
> "The hour is come! Follow me!"
> And flung the door open wide.
> My!
> What a squealing and a squeaking and a screech-
> ing filled the air!'

'Aaah! Help! Yaroo! Look out! Whoops!'

In full voice, Johnny reckoned, Christopher and Juliet would have a good chance of bringing down the walls of Jericho.

After three more pages, with the twins now in uproar, he tiptoed out of the door and shot down the stairs.

'Constable Merrick,' he said, panting slightly, 'duty calls. There is a danger of a serious breach of public order one floor up. You are to proceed upstairs at once and sort it out. I recommend most strongly that you wear your helmet!'

'Sir!' Constable Merrick had performed this sort of duty at home before now. He had younger brothers and sisters himself. By now the impact of his uniform had dissolved completely. He was not the master but a figure of fun in his own house.

Here in Markham Square, however, he felt, things might be different. He climbed the stairs as noisily as he could, fixing his helmet to his head as he went. Outside the twins' door he paused and coughed. As he went in he took out a pencil and a notebook and inspected the twins with great severity.

'Now then,' he began.

He did not have to say more. Unknown to him, and unknown to Johnny, an enormous policeman with a huge helmet had told the twins off one day in the park recently for digging up the flowers. His helmet had made an indelible impression. Now the twins were underneath the bedclothes, pulling blankets and sheets over themselves as fast as possible before he could make a single note. He stood by the door for a moment, humming to himself. The peace of sleep seemed to be stealing over Christopher and Juliet.

For weeks afterwards Constable Merrick's ghost haunted the house. Nurse Mary Muriel would warn her charges that she thought she heard the policeman's footsteps on the stairs. They would fall into bed immediately. Powerscourt was to say afterwards that Constable Merrick had been able to do what few could perform in their lifetime. He could keep the twins quiet. He had achieved a sort of eternal life up there with the schoolroom and the boxes of dressing-up clothes and the broken toys on the nursery floor of Markham Square.

20

Barnabas Thorpe, butler of Candlesby Hall, was a worried man. The general uncertainty about the future, with two members of the family involved in unsolved murders, concerned him. The behaviour of the two eldest surviving brothers, Henry and Edward, concerned him even more. They had discovered another wine merchant who would extend them a line of credit. That very morning carters had been unloading case after case of claret and burgundy, port and Madeira into the cellars. Only Barnabas Thorpe had read the fine print of the agreement, left lying around on a broken table in the saloon. It stipulated an enormous rate of interest if the bill was not paid in full within thirty days. After that wealth beckoned for the wine merchants. Thorpe thought it unlikely that the bill would be paid on time.

Then there was the poor strange boy, as Thorpe had always referred to James, on the top floor. The boy's illness was not Thorpe's province, but reports of his deterioration filtered down through the floors of Candlesby Hall. A medical doctor, expert in the strange ways of the semi-insane, was in attendance now, as well as the nurse. The boy was delirious part of the time, rather like the old ladies of Candlesby, talking of King Arthur and the Lady of Shalott and apparently able to quote lines from Tennyson's poem at will. Barnabas Thorpe had always regarded any interest in poetry as conclusive proof of the softening of the brain, if not actual insanity itself. Only Charles Candlesby knew the true position about his brother's health. It was he who had sanctioned the extra expense of hiring the doctor. Only he knew how long the engagement might last.

Charles Candlesby, indeed, was the only positive person in Barnabas Thorpe's book at this time. Helping the poor, looking after his brother, he was at once the most unlikely Candlesby, but at the same time the most likeable member of the family. This morning he was polishing off an enormous bowl of porridge at the Powerscourt breakfast table in Mr Drake's hotel. He was becoming a regular visitor.

'Would you like some more porridge, Charles?' said Lady Lucy, who always treated him as a favourite son.

'No, no thanks,' said Charles, 'I'll just tuck into a couple of eggs and a few rashers and maybe a tomato. Nothing much.'

'Charles,' said Powerscourt, finishing off some toast, 'do you mind if we talk business for a moment?'

His mouth full of bacon and tomato, Charles managed a vigorous nod of the head by way of reply.

'It's this,' said Powerscourt. 'I don't know why I didn't think of it before. You know the habits of your family up at the Hall. Why was your father wearing his scarlet coat on the night he died? We have no idea why he put it on. The pathologist thought he died sometime between the hours of ten in the evening and four the following morning. Now, suppose you go out, intending to meet somebody at the earlier time of ten – he must have been going to meet somebody surely, unless he wanted to wander round in the storm which seems unlikely – wouldn't you expect to come home again after you met them? And you'd have plenty of time to put on your scarlet coat the next morning in time for the hunt. You didn't have to put it on for the early rendezvous the evening before. Your father was hardly going to meet a fox at that time of day, was he?'

'I'm not sure', said Charles sadly, pulling a piece of bacon out from between his teeth, 'that I like where this is going to go. B-but p-p-please continue.'

'Let us look at it from the later date given by the pathologist, four o'clock in the morning. Suppose he left home at three for his rendezvous. Again he is wearing the scarlet coat. Why? He must think he is not coming home before the hunt – that he needs to go out dressed in his hunting gear because he has to be wearing it in the morning. So what was he intending to do all that time? Between, say, ten or eleven the night before and eight o'clock in the morning when he would have to set out back to the Hall?'

Powerscourt left his question hanging in the air.

'Boat?' said Lady Lucy. 'Would he have gone somewhere in a boat?'

'Not in that weather,' said Powerscourt. 'Every boat in the county will have been tied up at her mooring that night.'

Charles looked at them sadly. 'Surely,' he said, 'there's only one conclusion. My father was going to meet somebody. He intended to spend the night with them and go b-b-back for the hunt in the morning. That's why he was wearing the coat. And', he looked embarrassed now, 'the somebody was p-p-probably a woman.'

'We don't need to dwell on this,' said Powerscourt, 'but where on earth, in all that empty space, would you meet a woman? Where would you find one? There isn't a house for miles.'

'Maybe', said Lady Lucy, 'he did ride for miles, but inland, to the next village. There's nothing to say he went straight to where he was collected by Jack Hayward. He needn't have gone near the sea at all. He could have gone in the opposite direction. His murderers could have brought him back and dumped him where he was found.'

Powerscourt put his head in his hands and groaned slightly. 'Here's another thing. The horse. Jack Hayward went to collect him with a horse, Marlborough, your father's horse. But your father must have set off on a different horse.

What happened to that one? The one Lord Candlesby left his house on?'

'B-b-bolted? Stolen by his killers? Sold by his killers?' Charles was looking more cheerful all of a sudden.

'The one person who would have known for sure if a horse had disappeared from those stables was Jack Hayward,' said Powerscourt, spinning a marmalade jar round faster and faster on the tablecloth. 'And he was shuffled off the scene before he had a chance to check anything at all.'

'You said, Francis,' Lady Lucy chipped in, 'that Jack Hayward took the Earl's horse Marlborough to go to collect the body. Why didn't the Earl take his own horse out when he went to meet whoever it was?'

'God only knows,' said Charles. 'I'm lost, I really am. But b-b-before I forget, Lord P-p-powerscourt, I must tell you what Walter Savage told me when he came out of p-p-prison.'

'Please do,' said Powerscourt, relieved to have moved off Charles's father's amorous activities on the night of his death.

'Walter Savage came to see me yesterday,' said Charles, 'and he told me something he hasn't said before. You have to remember that Walter is old. His b-b-bladder isn't what it was. He has to get up several times a night. On the night of the murder, he opened the window to see how the storm was doing. He heard a noise coming from Candlesby village. This was about one or two in the morning, but it might have been earlier. He said it sounded like cheering. He went back to bed and thought no more of it.'

'Cheering?' said Powerscourt. 'Cheering?'

'That's what he said. He wasn't certain, b-b-but it sounded like cheering.'

Inspector Blunden felt that the people of Lincolnshire were plotting against him, conspiring to leave the county and deprive him of suspects. First Oliver Bell had fled, misleading the constabulary about his alibi on the night of the murder before he left. Now the Lawrences had disappeared. First they had gone to London in great numbers, pursued afterwards by Johnny Fitzgerald and Constable Merrick. Now they had vanished, leaving no information at all at their various houses about where they had gone. And worse was to come. A messenger arrived with a summons. He and Powerscourt were to meet the Chief Constable. Constable Merrick was sent for and ordered to the Candlesby Arms on his bicycle at full speed. He was to bring Powerscourt to the police station with all possible despatch. Inspector Blunden hoped Powerscourt would come in his Silver Ghost.

He did. Fifteen minutes later, before the constable had reappeared, Powerscourt was conferring with the Inspector in his office. Inspector Blunden was in happier mood this morning. His wife had managed to introduce another nursery rhyme into his daughter's repertoire. Last night after supper Emily Blunden had sat on her father's lap and recited 'Jack and Jill went up the hill', with the emphasis on 'hill' for some reason, to her father's great delight.

'What's up with the Chief Constable?' said Powerscourt. 'Homework not delivered on time? Changing rooms left in a sorry state?'

'God knows,' said the Inspector. 'This is all we need at this point to have him sticking his nose in where it isn't wanted. He once changed the entire direction of a case because his wife thought she knew who the murderer was.'

'Did she?'

'Certainly not. She'd just overheard some people talking in the butcher's shop.'

'Maybe she's been to the greengrocer's this time,' said Powerscourt happily. 'I've always been suspicious of greengrocers myself. All those enormous vegetables looking as though they might rise up out of their baskets and commit a crime.'

'We'd better go, my lord,' said Blunden. 'One thing he can't stand is people being late.'

'Late on parade,' said Powerscourt as they made their way up the corridor, 'one of the most serious offences in the military rule book. Probably more serious than murder, now I come to think about it.'

The Chief Constable was waiting behind an enormous desk, looking, Powerscourt thought, rather like a wild animal about to spring upon its prey. Two huge watercolours of Simla, summer capital of the British Raj, hung behind his head, one, to Powerscourt's great delight, showing an enormous number of troops manoeuvring on a vast parade ground.

'Thank you for coming. Good to see you both,' he said in a tone that hinted he was less than pleased to meet them again. 'Now then. This murder. These murders.' He looked down at his papers as if to check that there had indeed been two murders. 'Bumped into the Home Secretary at my club yesterday. Fellow wanted to know what was going on. One or two backbenchers been making noises, apparently. Questions likely in the House.' The Chief Constable looked pleased at his apparent mastery of parliamentary procedure. Powerscourt wondered which London club might contain the improbable pairing of the Home Secretary and the Chief Constable.

'He wasn't complaining, the Home Secretary. Understood these things could take time. He did mention a very recent case in Hampshire where the murderer was arrested and charged within forty-eight hours of the crime.'

Inspector Blunden was looking resigned, like a hospital patient who knows he is about to receive mouthfuls of a particularly disagreeable medicine. Powerscourt was feeling rather angry.

'So bring me up to date, would you, Blunden. Are you any nearer to finding the murderer?'

Blunden decided to say as little as possible. 'I believe we

are making progress, Chief Constable. There are a number of leads we are following up. Our most important witness has just been brought back from Ireland. We are still digesting his evidence.'

'Digesting?' snorted the Chief Constable, 'This isn't a gourmet restaurant in Paris, man, it's a murder case. From what you've said so far, Blunden, you have no more idea who committed these murders than the Home Secretary, have you, Blunden?'

'I don't think that is true, and I don't think it is fair either,' said Powerscourt, perfectly willing to meet the Chief Constable at a place of his choosing, weapons to be decided later. 'This is one of the more difficult cases I have ever been involved in. I believe it will be solved soon because of a line of investigation so secret that I would not tell you about it under any circumstances.' Lady Lucy had told him late the previous evening about the cryptic clues muttered by the old ladies in their delirium. 'Indeed, I have not yet told my colleague here about it.' Powerscourt nodded genially to Inspector Blunden. 'So you see, Chief Constable, I don't think the position is as bad as you paint it. Maybe you will have news for the Home Secretary in the near future.'

'What is it?' barked the Chief Constable, waving his monocle at Powerscourt as if it were a weapon. 'This secret source? I demand to be told. I am the Chief Constable round here! I have the right to know!'

Powerscourt thought for a moment. He had no intention of telling the Chief Constable anything. Nor did he necessarily want a fight. Nor did he want to embarrass Inspector Blunden.

'Chief Constable,' he began, 'I would like to make use of a military analogy, if I may. I served for a number of years as chief intelligence officer to the forces under the control of General Richardson on the North-West Frontier.'

The Chief Constable seemed to cheer up slightly at the mention of the military.

'Chukka Richardson?' he said. 'Damn fine polo player, Chukka, damn fine.'

'The same,' replied Powerscourt. 'On a number of occasions we would be summoned to his quarters, my colleague and I. Either we would propose a scheme to the general, or he would propose a venture to us. Always he would make it very clear what he wanted done. But he never issued a direct order. Nothing was ever put down on paper.'

Powerscourt looked closely at the Chief Constable to see if any light of understanding, even a glimmer, was visible. He saw nothing that pleased him. Bertram Willoughby-Lewis' face was as blank as a sheet of fresh notepaper. 'The general used to say that some damned fool in Whitehall might start asking questions if things were written down. He had a very low opinion of the damn fools in Whitehall, General Richardson. So we would carry out his orders. We never told him any of the details of the operations. He made it clear he never wanted to know. We went about our business. He stayed in his tent. The natives were confounded. Everybody was happy. The gentlemen of Whitehall would not have been happy but they were not there.'

'That's all very interesting, Powerscourt,' said the Chief Constable, 'always fond of a good story myself, but I don't see what the North-West Frontier has to do with dead Candlesbys here in Lincolnshire. I say again, tell me about your secret source. There's no time to waste, man. We need to press on.'

God in heaven, thought Powerscourt. The Chief Constable was remarkably stupid, even for a military man.

'The reason, my dear Chief Constable, why our military operations in India were so successful is that nobody knew about them. Nobody could get in the way.' Meaning, people like you, he muttered to himself. 'This secret source is so delicate that anybody interfering with it could destroy it completely. It must be left to work at its own pace and in its own way. I believe it will help us solve the mystery, but not if it is interfered with. It is like a watch that will function perfectly as long as nobody tinkers with the mechanism.'

'Damn it, man, you are insubordinate. I demand to know.'

'And I', said Powerscourt with a smile, 'refuse to tell you.'

'I could have you arrested, damn it,' spluttered the Chief Constable.

'I don't think you would find that very helpful,' said Powerscourt. 'You'd lose all access to the secret source that may solve the mystery.'

A temporary pause in the confrontation came when a messenger hurried in to remind the Chief Constable that he had to return to Lincoln at once for a grand dinner with the dean and chapter of the cathedral. He picked up his papers and his cane and shuffled to the door.

'Mark my words, Powerscourt, you haven't heard the end of this.'

Powerscourt was so incensed with the ridiculous man's behaviour that he fired straight back. 'Neither have you!'

Blunden and Powerscourt did not speak until they were back in the Inspector's office. 'My God, my lord, I shouldn't think anybody's spoken to him like that in years. And thank you for taking the heat off me, my lord. I am most grateful.'

'Think nothing of it, my friend. I am perfectly serious about this secret source. I wouldn't have mentioned it except for the fact that anybody with half a brain would have left us to get on with it rather than strutting about demanding to know what it is. Stupid man!'

'I've been thinking about this source, my lord,' said Blunden. 'I was thinking about it in there. I don't want to know anything about it. I don't want any names; I don't want any information at all. That way I can tell the Chief

Constable that I don't know anything about it with a clear conscience.'

'I think that's sensible for the time being, actually, very sensible, if you don't mind my saying so. No offence. I don't think I'd tell the Chief Constable the time of day, if he asked me, after that display. Very well, Inspector, but there are a number of things I think you could have ready to go when I give you the word.'

Powerscourt spoke for a couple of minutes. After he had finished, Blunden whistled softly and began making elaborate notes in his book in his finest copperplate.

Lady Lucy hoped to speak to her husband before she set off for another session with the sick of Candlesby. She knew that he had been thinking of something he wanted her to do, but he had said he wanted more time to think about it. She was a couple of paces outside the hotel with an enormous basket on her arm, looking, she felt, rather like Little Red Riding Hood, when the Silver Ghost whispered into view.

'Hop in,' said a familiar voice, 'and I'll take you down. I've just had a set-to with that stupid Chief Constable. Bloody fool threatened to have me arrested.'

'That would have been a first,' said Lady Lucy, 'first time you'd have been arrested, I mean, rather than you arresting the murderer. It might have been rather interesting, Francis, the inside of a cell, that sort of thing, prison food, those fashionable prison clothes.'

Powerscourt laughed. 'I'll tell you about it later, my love. If the men in uniform should come to take me away, Lucy, send word to Charles Augustus Pugh to get here as fast as he can and have me sprung from the jail. And send word to Rosebery as well. Former Prime Ministers are always good to have on board in a crisis. I think the Chief Constable might not be happy in a very short time. Anyway, I've always wondered what prison food is like. Seriously, Lucy,

303

this is what I want to suggest with your old ladies. We have just a small collection of words or phrases from their ramblings so far that might be relevant. I cannot emphasize enough that you must exercise your own judgement about what I'm suggesting. If you hear one of those words again or a different word that you think might be relevant, try asking a question. Where did the money come from? Why is the sail important, that sort of thing. I simply don't know enough to imagine what their response might be. You must feel your way, Lucy. If you think it's not working, just back off.'

A crowd of Candlesby children had gathered round the Silver Ghost as it purred into the village. They gave a ragged cheer when Lady Lucy got out. She was already a heroine to them. Powerscourt opened up the bonnet and showed the children the engine. One small boy wanted to know how it worked. Powerscourt had to confess that he didn't know. He said he didn't know how a horse worked either. But he promised to send Rhys, the butler cum chauffeur, the next time. Rhys knew how the Silver Ghost worked. He knew how horses worked too. Rhys had piles of motoring magazines by his bed at home. He rather missed them up here in Lincolnshire.

Lady Lucy was taken in hand by the two ladies who organized the nursing in Candlesby village. They were known to her as Maggie and Mary and didn't appear to have any surnames. The young ones were nearly all recovered, they told her; only one little girl was left on the danger list. But three new old ladies had been taken sick, and one of them was already very ill indeed. Lady Lucy was taken first to see Will, the little boy she had entertained with the cat story. He gave her a big hug when she came in and asked after Christopher and Juliet. Lady Lucy had told him about her twins, who were more or less the same age. Will told her the doctor had said he could get up for an hour the next day. Will was looking forward to that. Then she was taken to Bertha, the old lady who was very ill. Her bedroom was so small there was scarcely room for another grown-up. Lady Lucy perched on the edge of the bed and mopped the old lady's face. She was sweating profusely and muttering into her pillow. 'No shoes,' Lady Lucy heard two or three times. She had resolved to write everything down now in case Francis could find a meaning where she couldn't. Bertha dozed off for a minute or two, holding desperately on to Lady Lucy's hand. When she woke up she looked briefly at her visitor and sank back on the pillow. Lady Lucy had noticed that none of the old ladies ever had more than one pillow. Strange sounds came from Bertha now that might have been muffled screams. She tossed about as if her life depended upon it. 'Wind,' she said suddenly, 'great wind.' A pause and then she said, 'Poor Lucy, poor Lucy.' Lady Lucy thought it generous of the old lady to sympathize with her in her hours of nursing. 'Men,' Bertha said now, 'men.'

Lady Lucy thought that she might try a question.

'Which men, Bertha?' She spoke very softly and stroked the old lady's forehead once more. It was burning hot. 'Which men?' she tried again. The old lady began to speak. 'Men,' she said, 'men.' Lady Lucy kept quiet now. It didn't seem as if the questions were going to work. She would try again later. Bertha was now deeply asleep, snoring vigorously. Lady looked at the sheets that had seen better days, at the dirt ingrained on the floorboards and the accumulated grime on the walls and on the small window that looked out over the main street. Cleanliness is next to godliness, she remembered some grown-up telling her when she was small. Well, God should come down here and clean the whole village. He could probably do it in a minute or less if he set his mind to it, Lady Lucy thought. As the night fell the old lady began muttering again. 'Shoes,' she said, and 'Wind.' Only by leaning very close could Lady Lucy hear the other words, 'Pay the doctor, pay the doctor,' over and over again.

This time she met no Charles Candlesby on her way home. Powerscourt wrote all the words down in his own notebook.

George Drake, manager of the Candlesby Arms, was a very worried man. He had checked the barometer in his reception area five times that morning. The message was bad. There was going to be another storm. One of his porters, a man who had lived with Candlesby weather for over sixty years, man and boy, prophesied that it would be worse than the last one. So George Drake toured the breakfast tables in the dining room, warning his guests what was to come and asking them to make sure that all their windows were securely fastened. At one of his tables, the one by the window, he had different news to impart first.

'Lord Powerscourt, Lady Powerscourt, Johnny Fitzgerald, you will remember the strange message with the even stranger spelling delivered to you here some days ago? And the GNR jackets dumped in the corridor outside your room? That is all sorted out now. The practical joker has been told that if he ever tries anything like that in my hotel again he will be fired. Immediately. You can regard the matter as closed.'

'Very good, Mr Drake. Thank you for clearing that up. Now what of this weather? Is it going to be bad?'

George Drake nodded. 'Oh, yes, very bad.'

The news was greeted with great interest.

'Another storm then? A bad one?' said Johnny Fitzgerald, pausing briefly in the demolition of a kipper.

'Probably worse than the last one,' said George Drake, moving off to spread more bad news.

'How interesting, how very interesting,' said Powerscourt, in the middle of a poached egg.

'Do you think we should, Francis?' said Johnny.

'I'm sure of it, certain.'

'Should we go now, or wait till it's really got going?'

'Well,' said Powerscourt, 'I think we should finish our breakfast first. We can take the Ghost the first part of the way.'

'I'll bring my stuff,' said Johnny, referring to the strange collection of implements that enabled him to gain entrance to most of the locked doors in the kingdom. 'Just in case.'

Lady Lucy had often seen her husband and Johnny Fitzgerald finish each other's sentences but this display of telepathy was new. They seemed to be reading each other's minds. 'I'm terribly sorry,' she said, 'but do you mind telling me what you are thinking of doing? I'm rather in the dark here.'

Powerscourt smiled. 'Sorry, Lucy. I should have thought it was obvious. The first murder was committed in the middle of a great storm. We are going to retrace the last journey of the victim in the middle of this one. We should certainly be able to see more than he could.'

'Well,' said Lady Lucy, 'just make sure you don't get yourselves killed.'

21

Powerscourt and Johnny Fitzgerald set off shortly after nine o'clock. They were both wrapped up against the rain like Egyptian mummies with hats from Jermyn Street. Johnny Fitzgerald had a great stick to beat off any wild animals they might encounter. The left the Silver Ghost by the gate lodges and joined the road that Jack Hayward had taken early in the morning with Lord Candlesby dead on the back of his horse. They turned left, away from the stables and the house.

The wind was growing louder and angrier by the minute, howling and shrieking as it rushed around the landscape. Powerscourt had already lost his hat once; Johnny had a hand firmly wedged on top of his. The rain was lashing down, dripping from their faces on to the tops of their collars. The land was pasture here as far as the eye could see, grazing for Candlesby cows and Candlesby sheep. The sea was a mile or two to the right. Powerscourt remembered Charles telling him that from the bottom of the drive the land was theirs, as far as the eye could see in all directions. And still the family was burdened with a mountain of debt.

'My God, Francis, this is pretty hard pounding,' shouted Johnny Fitzgerald.

'Four hundred yards,' Powerscourt yelled at his friend, 'four hundred yards from the end of the drive to the place where Jack Hayward found the body.' He paused to negotiate a particularly vicious gust of wind.

'I'll count the yards, Johnny. You've always had trouble getting beyond sixty-five.'

'That's not fair, Francis and you know it,' said Johnny, shaking a fist at his friend. Powerscourt was counting his paces on his fingers now, trying not to lose the number. A couple of trees loomed up in front of them, like stragglers left behind by a retreating army. One hundred and sixty-seven. Pausing behind one of them Johnny announced that they were no bloody use as a shelter against the storm. They were making very slow progress, bent over against the force of the wind. Two hundred and fifteen.

'Francis?' shouted Johnny.

'Yes?' Powerscourt yelled back.

'Can you speak?'

'Three hundred and five. Hold on a minute,' roared Powerscourt, concentrating on his fingers and the steps of his boots. They were climbing very slowly up a little hill which seemed to go on for a long time. Lincolnshire is meant to be flat, Powerscourt said to himself, but it's only flat in parts. Four hundred. They weren't even at the top of the hill yet. They couldn't see very far in front of them, the rain was so thick. 'Somewhere round here it must have been', Powerscourt announced at the top of his voice, 'that the body was dumped.'

'They didn't exactly put up a memorial to the fellow,' bellowed Johnny, surveying the empty landscape. 'Not a sign to be seen.'

'What were you going to say back there, Johnny?' Powerscourt had turned to face his friend.

'What I was going to say was this,' Johnny bawled into the tempest. 'Suppose you are our aristocratic friend who's now the corpse. Here you are in the middle of this frightful storm. You're struggling through it in the dark. You may be on a horse, you probably are, but even so it's not exactly a bed of roses, is it? What keeps you going? What on earth, in these godforsaken parts, are you going to find that makes your journey worthwhile? Answer me that, Francis.'

'God knows,' cried Powerscourt, pausing to inspect the landscape from the top of the hill. There seemed to be a small bay off to their right, spray rising in great billows along the little pier. Powerscourt thought he could hear the noise of the sea, mingling with the louder noise of the storm. There was a slight tang in the air.

'Is that the sea over there?' yelled Johnny. 'You don't think somebody was waiting for him in a boat, do you?'

'I'm not sure, I don't think so.'

They both bent forward into the wind. Johnny announced that he had a bloody leak in one of his bloody boots and his bloody sock had turned into a bloody sponge. They were making their way up another little hill.

'Who was that bloke in Shakespeare who wandered round in a bloody great storm, Francis?'

'You're showing a distressing lack of respect, Johnny. I presume you're referring to King Lear.'

'That's the fellow. Lear. King Lear, they called him.' An enormous gust of wind stopped Johnny in his tracks. 'And didn't he have some other chap with him? Some sort of funny man?'

'I think', Powerscourt shouted into the gale, 'that your English teacher has a lot to answer for. Lear's companion was the Fool.'

'Told you he was a funny man,' yelled Johnny triumphantly. 'They were on a heath somewhere, weren't they? Hampstead Heath probably – that'd be a good place for a King. Something tells me, Francis, that your man Lear was mad. Left his wits in his daughter's house. Ranted on all over Hampstead Heath in the storm with the Fool telling jokes.'

'Something like that,' shouted Powerscourt, reluctant to be drawn into detailed exegesis of Shakespeare's tragedies in the midst of a typhoon. But Johnny's memories seemed to be flooding back.

'There was another daft old bugger, wasn't there, Francis, in that play? Not on Hampstead Heath with the mad King, I think. Worcester, Foster, Bicester he was called, something like that.'

'Gloucester,' shouted Powerscourt, 'Duke of Gloucester, Johnny.'

'Gloucester. That's my boy,' bellowed Johnny happily, bending over to empty the rain from the brim of his hat. 'He was really mad, I think. Didn't his enemies pull his eyes out?'

'Afraid so.'

'Just what I told you, Francis. What a pair they must have been, one old and mad and chuntering on about his lost kingdom; the other one blind as a bat and ranting on about whatever he ranted on about. It's a wonder they weren't both locked up in an asylum, it really is. Do you know what my English master used to say about that play, Francis?'

'No idea, Johnny, no idea at all.'

'He used to say that it was all topsy-turvy. The Fool was wise, Lear could only understand when he was mad, Gloucester could only see when he was blind. Something like that.'

Powerscourt was leaning forward now, listening. 'Listen, Johnny, can you hear another noise, not the wind, not the sea, something else, some kind of whirring noise?'

'Did the fellows in the play hear that too, I wonder, wandering round Hampstead Heath in the pouring rain?' Johnny too leant forward into the wind. 'I can hear something, Francis. It must be just over this little hill.'

They remained silent, bent again into the gale, the rain biting into their faces. The storm seemed reluctant to let them reach the peak of the hill. It howled and screeched around them with redoubled force. The rain was now coming straight at them, striking their faces with such force that it stung. Then they could see over the top. At first the landscape looked no different. Then Johnny saw it.

'My God, Francis, look at that. Some fool's forgotten to lock it up.' Three or four hundred yards in front and to their right was a windmill. The sails were free and were hurtling round and round at an incredible speed. Powerscourt felt slightly sick. He started to run. 'Come, Johnny, best foot forward. I think this is the end of the road.'

A few minutes later they were underneath the sails of the windmill. It was a pretty building with larger windows than usual. But it was the sails that fascinated Powerscourt and Fitzgerald. They made a racketing clacketing hacketing sort of noise as they hurtled round, almost as loud as the wind. They were about eight feet off the ground at their lowest point. Powerscourt thought of that battered face in the morgue, one side of it shattered into small bloody pieces. He thought of the pathologist Nathaniel Carey saying that the victim's heart would have given out after a certain amount of this punishment. For the first and only time in this investigation he felt sorry for Lord Candlesby. Whatever his failings, and God knew there were plenty of those, he did not deserve to die like this. He noticed that four out of the six sails were intact. On the other two the bar at the bottom was broken, the canvas of the sail escaping into a mad dance as if the rigging on a sailing boat had broken free of the mast.

'What in God's name happened to these two, Francis? Do you think this was how he was killed? Tied on to something to bring his face level with the sails? Left here to die and then carried off in the blankets?'

'I do think that, Johnny. I've thought it ever since we saw the windmill. The broken sails must have struck him on the forehead and split. Maybe the others struck him lower down the face, on the cheekbone perhaps.'

'Do you suppose the killer lured him here once the storm started? Or was the rendezvous fixed before

312

they knew there was going to be a bloody typhoon like this one?'

'I don't know,' said Powerscourt. 'I suspect the rendez-vous was always going to be the windmill. When the storm came the killer had the macabre thought to lash him on to something and let the sails kill him. Did you notice these sails, Johnny? They're held together with wooden spars as if they were on a ship. Imagine those crashing into you at this sort of speed. It would have been terrible.'

Another gust of wind sent the sails whirring round even faster, the canvas on the broken ones flapping around like sheets on the devil's washing line.

'I wonder how they secured him,' said Johnny Fitzgerald, getting down on his hands and knees to examine the ground. There was a shout after a few minutes. 'Look here, Francis, there are four holes in the ground here as if a table or something was put on the grass. Maybe they fixed my lord Candlesby on to a chair lashed to the table.'

'We need some mechanically minded person, Johnny. I'm sure Inspector Blunden will be able to get hold of the right man. God, what an awful way to die, pounded to death by the sails of a windmill in the storm.'

Johnny Fitzgerald continued to scrabble about on the ground. Powerscourt walked round the windmill twice. So beautiful an object, he said to himself, to be the instrument of such a terrible death. He peered in at the windows but could make little sense of what he saw.

'Johnny,' he called, 'could you get us inside?'

Johnny Fitzgerald marched up to the door. He pulled a large collection of keys from one of his pockets. 'Don't want to break the door down unless we have to,' he said cheerfully. Halfway into his collection of keys they were in. They were in a dark room full of machinery. The next floor was devoted to more machinery and a collection of strange wooden tools that looked like a cross between a spade and a fork. Powerscourt suspected that somewhere in there was the device that could stop the sails. The next floor, some way off the ground was domestic. There was a sofa, a couple of chairs and a table, all of good quality. The floor above contained a double bed with fresh pillows and sheets but no blankets. Powerscourt suspected the bed must have been made or assembled on site. He couldn't imagine how anybody could have got it up the narrow stairs. But up here, almost above the sails, you could see the sea – now glowering and grey far out, great crashing breakers further in – and imagine that you were in your own private world. Powerscourt shuddered and hurried downstairs.

'I was going to ask if you could stop the sails, Johnny, but I think we should leave them so the police can get the full horror.'

'Three or four of those sails have dark marks on them,' said Johnny, 'and two of the wooden struts are broken, as we know.'

'I wonder how long he was left tied up, his face being smashed by the sails. I don't suppose we'll ever know.'

Powerscourt took a last look at the inside of the windmill. 'I think we should be on our way. I must tell Inspector Blunden at once and one of us has to phone the pathologist. He said we were to ring if we thought we had found what killed him.'

Two hours later, dripping water all over the police station floor, he reported the news to Inspector Blunden, who led a small party off to the windmill.

'Sadie, she's called, that windmill,' the Inspector said to Powerscourt as he left. 'Who'd have thought a Sadie could do a thing like that.'

'Inspector,' Powerscourt said just before the police party departed, 'I nearly forgot. I think the time has come. You remember what we talked about the other day, the inquiries to be made? Can you set them all in train? All except the last one?'

'I certainly can, my lord. A lot of them I'll do myself when we get back. Maybe we can have the case all sewn up before the Chief Constable comes back in two days' time.'

Five minutes after that Powerscourt was in the bath and Johnny Fitzgerald became the first customer of the day in George Drake's hotel bar. 'Just something to keep the pneumonia at bay,' he said to the barman. 'You could get yourself killed in a bloody great storm like that.'

Lady Lucy was on nursing duty once more in Candlesby village. Johnny Fitzgerald was still ensconced in the hotel bar. Powerscourt lay back on his bed, swathed in three of the hotel's softest towels, and contemplated the next few days. Now, at last, he said to himself, we know how Lord Candlesby was killed. We know how but we don't know who. Well, maybe we do. Every time we think we make an advance, finding Jack Hayward and hearing his story, now discovering how Candlesby met his death, there's still another question over the next hill. Who killed him? Powerscourt thought he might know the answer but he couldn't prove it. He didn't think he would ever be able to prove it. There were other questions to settle. When and where and how should he and Inspector Blunden reveal their findings? He didn't want to talk of death and windmill sails and garrotting in the hotel and there wasn't a room that was suitable in Inspector Blunden's police station. He wondered suddenly where Sherlock Holmes would have announced his discoveries in this case to an astonished world. Then he had it. The truth of The Man with the One-Sided Face would be revealed in the saloon at Candlesby Hall with the paint peeling off the shutters and the deformed animals in their glass containers. Charles could organize it. Two days from now, he thought. Maybe three. He went off to arrange a meeting with the pathologist Dr Carey on a crackling line to Bart's Hospital.

Lady Lucy was back with the old ladies. None of them were any better. Mary and Maggie told Lady Lucy she was lucky so far. None of her patients had died while she was on watch. Today she had brought some drawing books and coloured pencils for the children. Her popularity with the youngest inhabitants of the village rose further yet.

It was hard to tell if the old lady she was with now was alive or dead. She lay on her side, perfectly still. Lady Lucy felt a great wave of sadness when she saw the holes in the old lady's nightdress. It would be bad enough to be stretched out in bed in a nightdress with holes, but to die in one would be too much. She wondered if she could contrive some means of smuggling new nightdresses into the village without being accused of charity or condescension. For the moment she couldn't see a way of doing it. Perhaps Francis would know.

The day after the discoveries at the windmill Lady Lucy's husband took himself to London. He had secured an appointment at pathologist Nat Carey's hospital. After he learnt the news, the doctor drew a series of doodles on his notepad. Powerscourt saw that they were windmills.

'Of course,' he said. 'That must be how he was killed. How stupid of us not to think of it, with windmills dotted about all over that coast. There's just one thing, though.'

'What is that, sir?'

'Well,' said the great pathologist, 'this is more your province than mine actually. It's miles away from my expertise. But suppose you really wanted to kill this man. Suppose you really hated him. Would it be enough to watch him being beaten up by the sails of a windmill?'

'I see what you mean,' said Powerscourt, thinking back to the terrible storm, the marks on the sails, the waves and the spray crashing on to the pier at the little bay. He thought too about the marks on the body in the morgue.

'There was a strange-looking instrument, like a spade or a fork, in the basement. Maybe the murderer had a bash at the face every now and then. In between the blows from the sails of the windmill.'

'Two possible means of death are usually very convincing for a jury,' said Nat Carey, preparing to shuffle off to his lecture room and his medical students. 'I've never been able to work out why.'

Powerscourt paid a brief visit to his home where the twins were cross with him for coming on the train. 'Why couldn't you come in the Ghost, Papa?' they kept saying. 'Then we could have taken Rupert for a ride.'

The twins had recently acquired a new friend, exactly their age, who lived on the opposite side of Markham Square and refused to believe that anybody owned a motor car called a Silver Ghost. He paid a brief visit to his old friend, former Prime Minister Rosebery, and asked for assistance in case things turned nasty in Lincolnshire. But the principal reason for his visit to the capital was lunch, lunch with his barrister friend Charles Augustus Pugh. Powerscourt wanted to check whether certain kinds of evidence were admissible in murder trials. He thought he knew the answer but he needed to be certain. Pugh, happily devouring an enormous plate of Escoffier's finest scallops washed down by a bottle of Rully Premier Cru at the Savoy Hotel, ascertained the facts in the case and left Powerscourt in no doubt at all about the matter.

The night before the meeting Powerscourt held a long conference in the Candlesby Arms with Inspector Blunden, who brought news of the various inquiries Powerscourt had requested. Blunden was resigned about the views of Charles Augustus Pugh.

'I thought that's what he would say, my lord,' he said, staring moodily at his beer. 'I thought that's what any defence lawyer would probably say. Doesn't seem fair, does it? By the way, my lord,' he changed course suddenly, 'I suppose you want the last part of the operation to start tomorrow?'

'Yes please,' said Powerscourt. 'Reveille at six o'clock. Knock on the doors at six thirty.'

Johnny Fitzgerald, who always knew all that his friend knew about any particular case, had decided to make the acquaintance of the gentlemen of the press who had advised Powerscourt earlier in his investigation. He met Rufus Kershaw, chief reporter of the *Horncastle Standard*, in the bar of the Admiral Rodney Hotel. Kershaw had some interesting gossip to report. There was a rumour circulating, believed to have originated at the golf club, that the Chief Constable was thinking of having Powerscourt removed from the case, if not actually arrested. Was there any truth in this asked young Rufus, over his second pint of Lincolnshire Poacher best bitter. Absolutely not, said Johnny. No truth in it whatsoever. Have another pint. However, if Rufus were to turn up at Candlesby Hall at about five o'clock on the following afternoon, there might be some developments to report. Kershaw did say that his editor, James Roper, thought the Chief Constable was not fit for his job and was more than happy to print anything that might show him in a bad light.

Of the three, it was Lady Lucy who made the greatest contribution to the cause in those fallow days before the meeting. She had continued her nursing duties. Two nights before the Candlesby assembly she was asked to sit with a younger woman she had not met before. Her new patient was asleep when Lady Lucy walked into the bedroom. She had nursed two of her children back to health and then seen her sister die from the influenza three nights before. When she woke up, Sarah Carter, who must have been very blonde and very beautiful in her youth, told Lady Lucy, in between bouts of delirium, that she was sure she was going to die. The disease had come for her, she said, God was calling her home to join her sister, though she doubted if the trumpets would sound for her on the other side. Nothing Lady Lucy said could persuade Sarah Carter otherwise. Shortly after nine o'clock she fell into a troubled sleep. Lady Lucy thought about the poor woman and all the other poor women in the village, their lives blighted by poverty and disease, their futures little more than a continuation of the present, their only hope that in the new world opening up outside their village their children who survived the squalor might be able to build a better life. Not that Candlesby village would equip them for very much, she reflected sadly. Shortly after half past ten Sarah Carter woke up, looking troubled. Lady Lucy wiped her face and held her hand.

'Can I tell you something?' Sarah Carter said suddenly. 'I'd like somebody sensible to know it before I go. She never did anything wrong, whatever people might think. I'd like you to hear about it.'

'If you think it would make you feel better, I'd be honoured to hear it.'

Sarah Carter paused for a moment and looked closely at Lady Lucy. She seemed reassured by what she saw and by Lady Lucy's steady gaze.

'It's about my daughter,' she said with a slight smile. 'She's called Lucy too, Lucy Carter.'

The Silver Ghost took them the short distance from the hotel to the house. The normal calling cards were in evidence as

Powerscourt, escorted by Lady Lucy and Johnny Fitzgerald, made his way into the saloon at Candlesby Hall, the multi-coloured pillars with the stains, the missing antlers, the great dark marks on the walls like the work of some malignant tumour, the stuffed animals in their glass cases. Somebody had put a table with two chairs at one end of the room with a couple of rows of other chairs arranged in random rather than uniform fashion in front of them. It was going to be like a lecture at university, Powerscourt decided, where the outgoing undergraduates hadn't bothered to put the seating back where they found it. Inspector Blunden was seated on the left-hand side of the table, a police notepad in front of him filling up with ornate copperplate squiggles. Powerscourt was pleased to see that he too had been hon-oured with a police notebook of the same type and a police pen. Maybe he could bring a couple home for the twins.

The rows in front of them were filling up. In the front, fiddling with his monocle, was the Chief Constable, flanked by a rather sinister-looking Chief Inspector who Blunden whispered was called Skeggs. Powerscourt wasn't sure how those two had got there. Beside them sat Henry, now Lord Candlesby, and his brother Edward. This was their house after all. Behind them sat Lady Lucy and Johnny Fitzgerald, with Constable Andrew Merrick beside them. Charles Dymoke, wearing an elegant grey suit, was loung-ing against the fireplace, looking like some aristocratic ancestor posing for his portrait.

The Inspector handed Powerscourt a letter.

'Arrived this morning, my lord,' he whispered. 'I think it might interest you.'

'Dear Inspector Blunden,' Powerscourt read. 'I gather you have been looking for me. On the evening of the murder I was with a lady in Lincoln who is not my wife. Her father had just died and left her a lot of money. I only went back to the cottage to collect my stuff. I was in such a state when you called I said the first thing that came into my head. I did not kill Lord Candlesby. I was miles away. Yours faithfully, Oliver Bell.'

'Gives a whole new meaning to feeling uplifted by the cathedral in Lincoln, Inspector,' said Powerscourt. 'The Salvation Army and the later works of Tolstoy seem to have lost out to the more profitable activities of Mammon.'

The Inspector smiled and took a wary look at the audience. Then he rose to his feet and stared hard at Constable Merrick, who was chattering away with Johnny Fitzgerald about football teams. 'My lords, Chief Constable, ladies and gentlemen,' he began as silence fell over the room, 'thank you for attending this rather unorthodox gathering. Thank you to the family also for allowing us to make use of this room.' Powerscourt's eye was drawn to a strip of wallpaper that had become detached from its place on the top of the wall and was now snaking about fifteen feet down in a dramatic bid to reach the ground. 'I think it would be fair to say,' Blunden went on, glancing at his companion on his left, 'that the bulk of the work in this case has been done by members of the Lincolnshire constabulary.' There was a vigorous nod from the Chief Constable and his villainous-looking Chief Inspector in the front row. 'The intellectual firepower in the case has come from our own force, of course, but especially from Lord Powerscourt and his companions.' Inspector Blunden had never entirely recovered from the news that Powerscourt had played rugby as a centre. 'So I think it is fitting', the Inspector concluded, 'that he should summarize the position as we see it today.'

Powerscourt rose slowly to his feet. He had some notes in his pocket but he decided to leave them where they were. He had been thinking about what he was going to say in the train up and down from London.

'Thank you, Inspector. And could I take this opportunity of thanking you and all your colleagues for being such valiant companions in arms in this difficult case.'

There was a loud 'Hear, hear' from the Chief Constable and a handclap or two from his sinister companion. 'I was originally asked to look into this case', Powerscourt went on, 'by the late Dr Miller on his deathbed, and by a member of the family here in this house. Our purpose today is in the nature of a report to the members of the Candlesby family so they can learn what happened to their father and their brother. Nothing can take away their grief, but something, some news, might stop the endless uncertainty and worry.'

There was a muffled grunt from Johnny Fitzgerald who thought his friend was laying it on a bit thick. Lady Lucy kicked him sharply on the ankle.

'I do not bring any certainty about what I am about to tell you today. I do not believe for a moment that my theories, shared and shaped as they are by the good Inspector on my right, would stand up to the more forensic examination of a courtroom. Let me begin with the day of the meeting of the hunt and the discovery of the body of the previous Earl. And let me apologize to those in the family if I appear to be speaking harshly of other family members. The truth may sometimes be unpalatable to our nearest and dearest.'

Powerscourt suddenly noticed Johnny Fitzgerald making a sign at him that dated back to their army days and meant 'Get on with it, troops becoming restless.'

'I don't think anybody will deny that the Candlesbys are a strange family. They are the ones who only communicated with their sons and daughters by letter, even though they lived in the same house. They are the ones who cut off their children and banished them for not standing up or for smoking when the father entered the room, never mind the one who collected Caravaggios on the Grand Tour and tried to reproduce them in an upstairs room in this house, using local people as models for some of the bloodiest scenes in the New Testament. I have been in that room. I do not think I would ever go in it again. It showed a total contempt by the then Lord Candlesby for his fellow men, whom he obviously treated as mere possessions to be used at will. I would draw your attention to the fact that there are virtually no women servants in this house and that those who are here, with no disrespect to them, are well over fifty years old.'

Charles Dymoke had produced a small cigar and was blowing smoke rings all round the fireplace. Constable Merrick was leaning forward to help his concentration.

'The key to the events of the night of the storm and the morning of the hunt meeting is a girl.' A ripple of astonishment ran round the room. Many of those present had never heard of a girl in the case until today.

'I am going to call her Helen for today, in memory of Helen of Troy with her intoxicating beauty. Our Helen lives in Candlesby village with her parents and her brothers and sisters. She is eighteen years old and extremely beautiful, more than beautiful enough for men to lust after her. I do not know if Lord Candlesby had ordered up young women from the village before, as if he were ordering extra loaves from the bakery. I think he probably had.' Lady Lucy was making a face at him now. 'I feel sure that he regarded the women of the village, married or single, young or middle-aged, as his property to be taken when he wanted. You can imagine how the request would have been put. If the victim did not agree, the parent would lose their position, the family would be thrown out of their home, their relations would be hounded. This behaviour explains why there were no women under the age of fifty working in this house. Nobody was prepared to take the risk.'

In view of the presence of the Chief Constable and his acolyte, Powerscourt had decided on the spot to conceal the name of Lucy Carter in case a posse of policemen was despatched to arrest her before he even sat down.

'Sometime before the murder, Candlesby will have sent his ultimatum. The girl was to meet him at the windmill near the sea late in the evening. She had no choice. Candlesby rides out in his scarlet coat, rather odd, you might think, for a seduction scene. But he intends to spend the night with Helen of Candlesby. Undoubtedly he intends to have his way with her again in the morning before he returns home to the hunt and the stirrup cup. So he has to be wearing the clothes he will need in the morning.'

'She's your secret source, isn't she, by God, Powerscourt!' The Chief Constable was slapping his thigh. 'She'll look very pretty in the witness box, I'm sure!'

Powerscourt ignored him. 'I do not know what roused the village that night. They must have endured similar maltreatment before. Maybe Helen's father was able to lead the resistance. For Helen did not go to the rendezvous alone. A group of her father's friends from the village went too, literally like a guard of honour. There may have been half a dozen, there may have been ten or more, I cannot be sure. But they were there. I am sure that they had decided to kill Candlesby before they set out. Maybe they hadn't given much thought to how they would do it.

'So, the Earl reaches the windmill. The girl is waiting on her own, I suspect, like live bait, an act of great bravery. The honour guard give Candlesby a minute or so in the little sitting room to become excited at the prospect ahead in the bed on the next floor. Then they rush in and take him. Maybe they beat him up a bit. All this time, remember, the storm is raging outside with tremendous force. Somebody suggests unlocking the sails and fixing him to a chair on a table which will mean that one side of his face is continually exposed to the blows of the sails as they shoot by, a truly terrible way to die. The old Mr Lawrence told me on the day his possessions were being packed up for his move that he had employed a number of men from Candlesby village to help. They were, he assured me, very good at loading things onto carts. They were very good with their hands. Part of the appeal for the villagers was that their victim would be able to see the other sails approaching even as the one in front of him crashed into his face. Maybe they took it in turns to beat the side of his face with a strangely shaped instrument like a spade found in the basement of the windmill, the villagers queuing up for revenge as the tempest raged and the sails sped by. I don't know if the girl stayed to watch. Probably not. One of the men took Candlesby's horse and brought Helen home, safe and sound, to her mother. As far as I know, they have kept the horse, or sold it.'

Edward Dymoke had fallen asleep, overcome by adulterated claret at lunchtime. He was snoring slightly until his brother prodded him awake.

'I think the villagers decided to leave the body as far away from the windmill as they could so people would not suspect how the dead man had been killed. One of them took a couple of blankets from the bed upstairs – there are only sheets on it now – and wrapped them round the corpse. They carried it to the place where Jack Hayward was told to find it some hours later. Walter Savage, the steward, thought he heard a sound like cheering in the village around one o'clock in the morning. That could have been the men returning from their night's work, and being applauded by the rest of the village who would have stayed up for news.'

The Chief Constable had slapped his monocle in his left eye and was inspecting a bundle of documents in his hand. Charles Dymoke was looking very serious by his fireplace. Lady Lucy was watching her husband.

'I turn now to the other murder,' Powerscourt went on, taking care never to look at the Chief Constable or his assistant. 'I have reason to believe that Helen was again involved. Maybe the son decided to avail himself of the pleasures denied to his father. I believe he too rode out from Candlesby

Hall on the night of the first murder. Maybe he was going to watch. Maybe he was going to avail himself of her too. But for some reason he turned back. Maybe the storm was too much for him, comfort winning out over lust. More likely his father told him to clear off. He, Candlesby, was going to enjoy the prize on his own. Charles Dymoke reported the servants hearing somebody coming back to the house around midnight. That must have been Richard with his red hair. Anyway, another invitation was issued to the girl to a meeting at the windmill the day after Richard was meant to be installed in the House of Lords. Members of the House of Lords of all people have rights they can enjoy. Richard would not have known his father was killed at the windmill. Many of the villagers work on the railway. Two of their number were selected, or perhaps they volunteered, for the next killing. When you'd killed one Candlesby, maybe it was easier to kill another, I don't know. Once in their uniform they could pass through the station more or less unnoticed. The GNR regalia rendered them virtually invisible. The two of them boarded the special train. Nobody suspected anything. They killed Richard. Then they jumped off the train and went home. I should point out that a large number of Inspector Blunden's men raided the village of Candlesby at six thirty this morning. Every single adult male in the place was questioned about their whereabouts on the night of the first murder. You will not be surprised to hear that they were all asleep in their beds, every last one of them. Their wives would vouch for them, their children too, if necessary, since many of them had only one room for the whole family to sleep in. They looked, in the words of Constable Andrew Merrick who was one of the police party, as innocent as newborn lambs.'

The Chief Constable jumped to his feet. 'That's it then. All the villagers were obviously lying this morning. Not questioned with sufficient vigour, I expect. The case is solved. All we have to do is to get from the girl the names of those who went with her to kill Lord Candlesby and then we've got it! The villains can receive a good dose of English justice!'

'I'm terribly sorry, I really am,' said Powerscourt. 'I'm afraid it's not as simple as that.'

22

The Chief Constable glowered at Powerscourt, screwing his monocle tighter and tighter into position. Inspector Blunden had the air of one who wishes most devoutly that the earth would swallow him up whole immediately. Johnny Fitzgerald was growing restive, as if he might go and knock the Chief Constable down. Charles Dymoke had a slight smile playing round the corner of his mouth as if he were keeping score.

'I'm sorry,' said Powerscourt again, looking at the Chief Constable steadily. 'I haven't finished yet.'

'What do you mean, you haven't finished yet? It's perfectly obvious what we have to do! Let's get on with it! Skeggs!'

The villainous-looking fellow sprang to attention. Nobody knew how things might have developed had there not been an intervention from a most unexpected quarter.

'For God's sake, Chief Constable, do sit down and do shut up.' Charles Dymoke's stutter seemed to have deserted him in this hour of need.

'I would remind you, sir, of two things. It was I who invited Lord Powerscourt to carry out his investigation. I and my brothers have a right to hear his full report. Second, this is our house. It is not a police station or a police examination room or a cell for the detention of the guilty. You are our guest here. As with all unwelcome guests, the hosts may ask you to leave.'

Charles sat down and blew a few more smoke rings. The Chief Constable turned red. Chief Inspector Skeggs glowered at the world in general. Johnny Fitzgerald laughed.

'As I was saying,' Powerscourt carried on as if nothing had happened, 'I think matters in this case are not as simple as they might appear. For a long time I thought it was a matter of the poor and the exploited against the big house, the droit de seigneur against the human rights of the villagers. I do not think that any more, but I find this even more difficult to prove. Consider, if you will, the family Lawrence. There is certainly motive there. They have a long-standing grudge against the old Lord Candlesby for cheating them out of a considerable and recurring amount of revenue from a railway concession. When I went to speak to old Mr Lawrence – this on the very day when they had been forced to move out of their ancestral home through lack of funds, funds they felt they would have possessed in abundance had it not been for the theft of the railway contract – he took great pains to tell me that the whole family had been in London at the time of the first murder.

'He gave me the name of the hotel they stayed in, White's, and the name of the theatre where they had been to see a play in the evening, the Savoy. Did he protest too much?

'I think it will be easier if I describe the Lawrence trip to London in chronological order. On Wednesday October the sixth the family sets off for the station. Before they leave Boston, Carlton Lawrence, the eldest son of the old Mr Lawrence I met when he was moving house, tries to withdraw a very large sum in cash from his bank. The manager informs him that they don't have that much money in Treasury notes in the safe, but promises to wire ahead to the London branch nearest to White's Hotel where the funds required will be ready for collection the following morning. The Lawrence party reach their hotel in the middle of the afternoon. At five fifteen a telegram arrives from Boston. I will speak about its contents a little later if I may.'

Johnny Fitzgerald was staring intently at a couple of stuffed foxes, perched in their case at the very edge of the billiard table and looking as if they might make a run for it at any moment. Chief Inspector Skeggs was inspecting a pair of handcuffs very closely, as if preparing a fitting for Powerscourt's wrists.

'The following morning, Thursday October the seventh, the day of the first murder, Carlton Lawrence goes to his bank and withdraws a very large sum in cash. He stows it in his briefcase and goes back to Boston. There's a train from London to Boston that arrives there at ten past three. A number of people report him hanging round the station for the next hour, never venturing very far away. Perhaps he was waiting to meet somebody. Carlton Lawrence then took the train back to London, leaving Boston at four fifteen, arriving at eight thirty. What was he doing up there in Lincolnshire? Whatever it was, he was back in London, not for the start of the play, but probably in time for the end of it. He went back to the hotel on his way from the station to the theatre where he was seen to have dropped off his briefcase – maybe he didn't want to be seen at the theatre carrying it. He was able to sleep in his bed in his London hotel and be seen at breakfast the following morning. Between the hours of ten in the evening on Thursday the seventh of October and four in the morning the next day the old Lord Candlesby was murdered. Carlton Lawrence was in London all that time.'

The Chief Constable was turning red in the face. Unbeknown to everybody else in the room, he played a regular round of golf with Carlton Lawrence on Saturday afternoons. His friend was being traduced in front of all these people.

'So, what was going on?' Powerscourt continued. 'We know that the Lawrence money came from the sale of their house and estate. We believe that all the bills outstanding from that transaction have been settled. We believe from reports in Candlesby village that the place is awash with money, more than the villagers have ever seen in all their days. For once in their lives the Lawrences had enough money to take their revenge on the man who had robbed them of the railway contract and all the monies they believed were due to them. I believe the original day set for the meeting between Helen and the Earl was the Wednesday. Then Carlton couldn't come up with the cash. Promissory notes, cheques, bills of exchange, none of these financial instruments have any currency in Candlesby village. The meeting was rescheduled for the Thursday. Maybe they said Helen was unwell or recovering from the influenza, so the date is switched to the following day, Thursday. Carlton collects the cash, meets a Candlesby intermediary at the station, and hurries back to London for the curtain calls at the Savoy. The whole purpose of the expedition was to create a near perfect alibi for the Lawrences in general and Carlton Lawrence in particular. He couldn't have been murdering the Earl by the windmill if could prove he was in London at the time.'

Constable Merrick was still writing busily. He was becoming more than ever determined to become a detective and solve great mysteries in front of an astonished audience.

'So, if my theory is right, the Lawrences paid the villagers to kill the earl. I would remind you again that when I went to see old Mr Lawrence he mentioned that he was employing a number of men from Candlesby village to organize his move. "They're marvellous at packing the carts," he told me, "very clever with their hands." Which of them, Lawrence or villagers, is guilty in law I am not qualified to say. It may be germane to note that the entire Lawrence family have gone away again, not to London this time, but to an unknown destination. The house they were moving to on the day I met old Mr Lawrence is let for the next six months with an option for renewal. We have to thank Inspector Blunden and his men for this information.'

The Chief Constable was recovering his composure now. He was exchanging a series of notes with Chief Inspector Skeggs, planning his next move. Johnny Fitzgerald was looking at them carefully, and checking his watch. Charles Dymoke had lit another cigar and was blowing smoke rings at the ceiling. Lady Lucy seemed to have disappeared.

'I have nearly finished, ladies and gentlemen.' Powerscourt was on the last lap. 'I do have one very important caveat at the end. Earlier this week I went to London and took the advice of one of London's leading defence lawyers. I laid the broad outlines of the case before him. His advice was clear and unambiguous. It would, he said, require a miracle more remarkable than the raising of Lazarus to secure a conviction in this case. The defence would instruct everybody in Candlesby village, male and female, to say nothing at all. The only other witness to the sad events of that night by the windmill is interred in the Candlesby mausoleum. The prosecution case would collapse for the lack of evidence. It is not for me, thank God, to decide whether or not to proceed with a prosecution. I doubt if the Candlesby family would care to have their father's peccadilloes and worse brought before a court of law and trumpeted abroad in the newspapers, but that is a matter for them.'

Powerscourt sat down. The Chief Constable rose to his feet. Johnny Fitzgerald groaned aloud.

'How right you are, Powerscourt, to tell us that it is not for you to decide whether to proceed with a prosecution in this case. You have failed miserably. You admit yourself that your discoveries would not stand up in a court of law. You can take your failure away with you and never return. We of the Lincolnshire constabulary shall not fail. It is for me, thank God, to decide whether to prosecute or not. I have no doubt that we shall be successful once we have collected enough witnesses. I repeat what I said before. Will you please give us the name of the girl you referred to as Helen? Come along now, you are not above the law.'

Powerscourt looked him in the eye. 'I will not,' he said firmly.

'Skeggs!' said the Chief Constable. 'Prepare to make an arrest! I repeat, Powerscourt, for the last time, will you give to us the name of the girl you called Helen?'

Events intervened before Powerscourt had time to reply. There was a noise of heavy boots on the floorboards outside. A boy of fifteen or so burst into the room. His eyes were bloodshot and seemed to be staring right out of their sockets. His hair was wild. Tiny flecks of foam hovered at the corners of his mouth. He had a gun in his hand and was waving it about as if to shoot somebody at any moment. James Dymoke had come to join his brothers in the family conclave.

'I've locked them both up, my guards, my jailers,' he announced to the company. Charles was advancing across the room towards his brother. Henry and Edward looked frightened. Powerscourt realized that something and somebody completely unpredictable had entered the room. The irrational, maybe even the mad was standing less than ten feet away from him with a gun in his hand.

'And I've got the keys of my room.' James giggled and patted his jacket pocket. 'I gather you've been discussing who killed my father and my brother,' he carried on, the flecks of foam growing larger as he spoke. 'Didn't think to ask me. Pity, that. You've got it wrong. All wrong.'

At this point he pointed the gun at his eldest living brother. 'You killed my father. You killed Richard too. You think I haven't heard you talking to yourself when you thought nobody was listening, about what you'd do when you were Earl? All the pretty ladies you were going to have? All the nice food you were going to eat every day? Well, you're not going to be able to have those thoughts any more. Not where you're going. Not now.' He fired at Henry. The bullet passed peacefully beyond Henry's left side and ended up safely embedded in a stuffed peacock on the far side of the fireplace. James ran out of the room and hurtled down the stairs towards the lower floors. Charles, closely followed by Powerscourt, Johnny Fitzgerald and Constable Merrick, raced off in pursuit. They could hear the footsteps clattering down into the basement.

'He's going to the tunnels!' shouted Charles. 'He always loved those as a child.'

Powerscourt put a hand on Constable Merrick's shoulder. The boy was just eighteen. This was no place for one so young, with a mother and father at home and a madman with a pistol up in front. 'Constable!' said Powerscourt. 'Can you please go back and report to Inspector Blunden. Suggest to him that he puts a guard on the exits from this and any other tunnels it might lead to. Tell him – and this is most important – that nobody is to fire at the young man or threaten him in any way! Go now!'

Constable Merrick shot off. They were in the tunnel now, a red-brick construction that twisted its way under the house, scarcely higher than a man and with room abreast for just a couple of people at a time. James' boots could be heard clearly further ahead. Drips of cold water fell from the ceiling. In the short corridors that opened off the main passage tens of tiny rats' eyes peered in amazement at their visitors. Johnny Fitzgerald had snatched a torch from a shelf in the ante-room. Enormous shadows of a monstrous Powerscourt and an elongated Charles Dymoke were etched on the walls until Johnny turned it down.

'Where does this go, Charles?' Powerscourt spoke as quietly as he could but his voice must have carried even so. The shot echoed down the tunnel and back again, bouncing off the walls and fading to an echo. Nobody knew where the bullet went. Powerscourt thought this was a very dangerous place to be. A bullet could ricochet off the walls for a long time, killing or wounding anybody who got in the way. Charles drew his hands into a fork and pointed further up the tunnel. To the right he pretended to be a horse, making hoof noises with his feet. The stables. To the left he whispered 'Garden' as quietly as he could. However hard they tried they were still making a lot of noise as they went, boots and shoes sounding loud as they hit the brick floor of the tunnel. An enormous ante-chamber appeared to the left. Charles took a long swig of an imaginary bottle. The cellars. Johnny Fitzgerald smiled. There was more water on the bottom now, a tiny rivulet flowing back towards the sculleries and the pantries beside the kitchen. James must have stopped to take a better shot. The bullet stuck this time in a gap between the bricks and did no damage. Three bullets gone. Powerscourt was counting, as he had counted the yards towards the spot where the old Earl's body had been dumped. Charles made the tunnel sign again. It sounded as though James was running now. The noise grew distant.

'He'll be going to the garden and the lake,' whispered Charles. 'He used to hide down here pretending to be a Christian in the catacombs hiding from the Romans until a few years ago.'

Powerscourt decided not to point out that the said Christian had almost certainly been caught and thrown to the lions in the Colosseum.

They were at the junction now, the passage to the stables going uphill, the one to the garden sloping slightly down, as if towards the lake. Charles led them to the left. 'Do you think he wants to kill us?' asked Powerscourt. 'Or is he just trying to get away from anyone coming after him?'

'I don't think he knows what he is doing,' said Charles. 'His mind's gone. Poor boy.'

As if in confirmation there was a loud shout from further along. 'Will you please go away?' The voice was almost sobbing. 'Please! Why can't you leave me alone?' A despairing fourth bullet was despatched down the tunnel but it got lost somewhere in the bends. This tunnel had slightly more water on the bottom. They were sloshing along now, water seeping over the sides of their shoes. On the walls bright green slime had taken over from the handsome red bricks nearer the house. Like the rest of the bloody place, Powerscourt thought, nobody's bothered to maintain it in living memory.

Charles was pressing on. There was a bad smell now, coming from further up. 'Way out's near the compost heap,' Charles whispered. 'Nobody's managed to move it since the tunnel was built.' Extreme stress, Powerscourt suddenly realized, must be the best cure for stammerers ever invented. Maybe they could organize courses for the sufferers down here in the Candlesby tunnels, the stutterers pursued by mad people with pistols. Charles could lead the way.

Johnny Fitzgerald was waving his torch forward in confident arcs. 'I think he's gone, Francis; I think he's out of the tunnel now.' He turned the torch behind him for a moment. Ahead there was a very small pinprick of light. The smell was growing worse. A couple of rats, refugees from the compost perhaps, shot past them back down the tunnel. In the far distance they heard another shot, muffled by the earth and the bricks. 'Damn and blast!' said Powerscourt. 'I hoped nobody was going to threaten him. It'll only make him more dangerous.' Five shots gone, Powerscourt said to himself. One left.

'Let's run,' said Charles suddenly. 'I'm sure he won't be waiting to pick us off as we come out of the tunnel.' Three pairs of pounding boots echoed back towards the stables and the cook's private cupboards. The tunnel was lower here. Johnny Fitzgerald swore violently as he failed to duck enough and scraped his head on the roof. Charles was muttering to himself as he ran. Powerscourt thought he was saying the Lord's Prayer over and over again. They shot out of the tunnel as if they had been fired from a cannon. No hostile bullets greeted them.

A group of people were lined up behind the tunnel entrance. The Chief Constable was in the front. 'My God,' muttered Johnny Fitzgerald, 'the old fool thinks he's back in command. God help us all.' Behind the Chief Constable stood Skeggs, looking, Powerscourt thought, like a faithful hound waiting to pick up the dead birds, with Inspector Blunden and Constable Merrick stationed behind them. The reserves, expecting fresh orders. The two brothers seemed to be still in the house, awaiting developments. Between them and the lake James Dymoke was walking slowly towards the water. He seemed to be reciting poetry at the top of his voice, not concerned about the group of men behind him, many with pistols. He stopped once to pick up a piece of wood about the size of a walking stick and twirled it in the air.

'Good to see you've arrived at last!' said the Chief Constable. 'No idea why it took you so long. Now then. We're going to charge. Skeggs and me and the three of you. Like the cavalry. I'm in command, of course. I'll give the orders. Take the madman from the rear. Take him off to the nearest asylum quick as we can. Now then, what are you waiting for? Fall in! Prepare to advance!'

Nobody moved. Johnny Fitzgerald whispered to Powerscourt that he was happy to knock the Chief Constable out. One blow should do it, he said. He'd been thinking of it all day. Powerscourt said it was Charles' call, his land, his county, his brother.

'Don't be ridiculous,' said Charles Dymoke. 'If you charge he'll turn and shoot. Somebody might get killed. Hold your peace. I'm going to talk to him.'

Charles set off towards his brother. James was now very close to the lake. A faint breeze was causing ripples on the surface. On an island in the middle a couple of herons watched the proceedings with care, their long necks turned towards the action. It began to rain.

'James?' Charles was only about ten feet behind his brother. James turned round. As he did so, the Chief Constable, having moved Blunden and Merrick into the front line, yelled, 'Charge!' and pointed his finger towards the lake as if he was back in India, attacking the natives. What James saw was a group of five men charging towards him, some waving their pistols in the air. He must, Powerscourt decided, have thought they were coming to kill him.

James raced towards the lake. He plunged into the water as he had done before. Chief Inspector Skeggs knocked Charles to the ground as he hurtled past. James took the stick in his right hand and whirled it round his head a few times. Then he shouted as loud as he could. His voice must have carried back to the house.

> 'Then with both hands I flung him, wheeling him;
> But when I looked again, behold an arm,
> Clothed in white samite, mystic, wonderful,
> That caught him by the hilt, and brandished him
> Three times, and drew him under in the mere.'

The wooden stick, Excalibur, the sword of Arthur in James' befuddled mind, floated away on the surface of the lake. 'Tennyson,' said Charles, scrambling to his feet, '*Idylls of the King*. I think he knows most of it by heart. He'll have turned into Sir Bedevere or somebody by now. Better if it was Merlin but I doubt it.'

The charging party stopped at the edge of the water. James was up to his neck. Charles had reached the edge. Powerscourt and Fitzgerald watched, some ten feet away.

'Stop!' said James. 'Stop! All of you! And you, Charles! This is it! This is the end!' With that he pulled the gun from his pocket, placed it in his mouth and pulled the trigger. The explosion echoed round the lake. After a minute where he seemed to totter very slowly from side to side, James Dymoke fell into the water. A small red ring formed round the place where his body had been. The ripples stretched back towards the shore and out to the island. Charles dived into the water but he had little hope.

'I'll have to get Jack Hayward to pull him out,' he said sadly as he returned to dry land. 'He always knows what to do in these situations.' Jack Hayward, Powerscourt thought, always at hand to retrieve the body of a dead Candlesby, young or old.

The military party had dissolved with James's death. Inspector Blunden and Constable Merrick were trudging slowly towards the house. The Chief Constable was addressing the faithful Skeggs.

'If only Powerscourt and his friends had done what they were told,' he said, 'everything would have been fine.'

'Everything would not be fine.' Charles Dymoke had a vicious tone in his voice now, water dripping down his shirt and his jacket. 'If you hadn't indulged your taste for petty heroics with that ludicrous charge, my brother wouldn't have felt threatened. He might still be alive. You stupid, stupid man. Get off our land now! Get out of our house! Go on, before I put the dogs on you!'

The Chief Constable slunk away, muttering something about the merits of military discipline no longer being taught properly in schools. Charles went to stand in front of Powerscourt. He looked extremely young.

'Nobody knew . . .' He began to cry, very quietly. 'Nobody knew about it but me. James didn't have more than a month or two to live. The disease had taken over. The worst thing is,' the tears were coming faster now, 'I said to the doctors that they should tell him. How long he had left, I mean. If I hadn't done that, he wouldn't have known he was dying. He wouldn't have killed himself.' Powerscourt gathered the young man into his arms and held him very tight for a very long time.

Lady Lucy was waiting for him when Powerscourt returned to the hotel an hour or two later. He told her about the death of James and the latest lunacies of the Chief Constable. 'I've got a confession to make, Francis,' she said. Powerscourt wondered what was coming. 'When the Chief Constable was going on and on about the secret source I suddenly thought it wouldn't take very long to identify Lucy, Lucy Carter, I mean. So I left the saloon and drove down to the village. I put her lying down on the back seat in case anybody saw us and brought her back to the hotel.'

'Where is she now?' said Powerscourt.

'Mr Drake has found her a room here nobody knows about. She's fast asleep up there now. I told her mother Lucy could act as my maid if she needs to stay away for a while.'

'Let me just recap a moment here, Lucy,' said Powerscourt with a smile. 'You went from the Hall to the village to the hotel in the Ghost? That's right, isn't it?'

Lady Lucy nodded. 'I did,' she said proudly. 'It's not all that difficult, driving, once you have got used to it.'

EPILOGUE

Powerscourt and Lady Lucy went back to London after the third funeral. The Chief Constable tried to bring a case against every male in Candlesby Village but failed at the committal hearing, where the judge threw the case out and criticized the prosecution for wasting the court's time with nonsensical claims. Charles Augustus Pugh, retained by Powerscourt for the defence, shared a bottle of champagne with him afterwards. The following week the Home Secretary announced that the Chief Constable had resigned, on health grounds. Johnny Fitzgerald announced that they had probably taken him off to the nearest asylum.

Henry, now Lord Candlesby, began a programme of serious retrenchment at the Hall. It was, he said, a nonsense to be living with that much debt and he set about reducing it in a sober and responsible fashion. People said he was a changed man.

Powerscourt always remembered the case of the murdered Earls as having to do with Charles, who was neither murdered nor the murderer, but now a frequent guest at the Powerscourt house in Markham Square. Charles had stood with Powerscourt on the strip of land between the lake and the mausoleum at Candlesby Hall after James' funeral shortly before Christmas and quoted Shakespeare. His stammer seemed to be gone for ever, banished by the terrible events at his home. 'Let us hope', he said, 'that "Our revels now are ended." Three corpses should be enough for anybody.

> 'Out, out, brief candle!
> Life's but a walking shadow, a poor player
> That struts and frets his hour upon the stage
> And then is heard no more: it is a tale
> Told by an idiot, full of sound and fury,
> Signifying nothing.'

'I think my father strutted and fretted his hour upon the stage, you know, Lord Powerscourt. The candles flickered for a little time. I always loved him so much, you know, even though he was such a terrible man. I have thought since his death that it was appropriate that he, of all people, was wearing those clothes the night he was killed. All his life he was a hunter, a hunter of women, a hunter of money, a hunter of fowl and foxes, a hunter after power and the gratification of his own desires. How right therefore that he should be dressed as Master of the Hunt and meet his death in a scarlet coat.'